Published in Great Britain 2014
by Mills & Boon, an imprint of Harlequin (UK) Limited,
Eton House, 18-24 Paradise Road, Richmond, Surrey, TW9 1SR

HOTBED OF SCANDAL © 2014 Harlequin Books S.A.

Mistress: At What Price?, *Red Wine and Her Sexy Ex* and *Bedded by Blackmail* were first published in Great Britain by Harlequin (UK) Limited.

Mistress: At What Price? © 2010 Anne Oliver
Red Wine and Her Sexy Ex © 2010 Pamela Brooks
Bedded by Blackmail © 2009 Robyn Grady

ISBN: 978-0-263-91191-6
eBook ISBN: 978-1-472-04486-0

05-0714

Harlequin (UK) Limited's policy is to use papers that are natural, renewable and recyclable products and made from wood grown in sustainable forests. The logging and manufacturing processes conform to the legal environmental regulations of the country of origin.

Printed and bound in Spain
by Blackprint CPI, Barcelona

MISTRESS:
AT WHAT PRICE?

BY
ANNE OLIVER

When not teaching or writing, **Anne Oliver** loves nothing more than escaping into a book. She keeps a box of tissues handy—her favourite stories are intense, passionate, against-all-odds romances. Eight years ago she began creating her own characters in paranormal and time travel adventures, before turning to contemporary romance. Other interests include quilting, astronomy, all things Scottish, and eating anything she doesn't have to cook. Sharing her characters' journeys with readers all over the world is a privilege…and a dream come true. Anne lives in Adelaide, South Australia, and has two adult children. Visit her website at www.anne-oliver.com. She loves to hear from readers. E-mail her at anne@anne-oliver.com.

With a big thank-you to my critique buddies,
Kathy, Sharon and Linda, for helping me bring
out the best in Mariel and Dane's story.

Thanks also to my editor Meg Lewis,
for her patience and advice during the revision process.

CHAPTER ONE

'REMIND me again why I dragged my jet-lagged body to a wedding with you when I could be sleeping it off in the comfort of my own bed?'

Mariel Davenport glanced at her sister Phoebe over the obligatory glass of champagne—except Mariel's glass sparkled with mineral water. After the stress of packing and avoiding the press, then the long-haul flight from Paris, the last thing she needed was alcohol.

She skimmed the elite crowd, dripping with diamonds and couture and French perfume. Some she knew; most were strangers. Ten years away was a long time.

Phoebe flashed a smile, brown eyes sparkling. 'Because you're my big sister and you love me, and we haven't seen each other since that Mediterranean cruise three years ago.'

Mariel arched a brow. 'Not because your boyfriend left you in the—?'

'*Ex*-boyfriend,' Phoebe snarled, all humour extinguished. She topped up her champagne flute from the bottle on the nearby table with a sharp chink of glass on crystal. 'Kyle's history.' She tossed back a mouthful of bubbly in disgust. 'Men. Who'd trust them?'

The words pierced the thin armour Mariel had struggled to wrap around herself since leaving Paris. 'Who indeed?'

Phoebe's eyes widened in obvious dismay. 'Oh, Mari, I'm sorry…'

'Don't be. I was a fool; it won't happen again.' She bit down on the inside of her lower lip. Hadn't she made that very same vow once before? Right here in her home town?

'That's the spirit.' Phoebe's firm nod had her blonde bangs bouncing. 'New Year's resolution: no men. Until the next full moon at least.' She grinned, then tucked her hand into the crook of Mariel's arm as the band struck up a popular party hit. 'Let's mingle.' The happy couple had left but the revelry lived on. 'Or we could dance,' she suggested. 'It'll take your mind off things.'

Mariel shook her head. 'You know I love nothing better than a good party, but not tonight.' What sane people would choose New Year's Day to get married anyway? She raised her glass and pointed it towards the crowd congregating on the makeshift dance floor beyond the open French doors of the luxurious old Adelaide Hills mansion. 'You go ahead. I'm fine. I'll just loiter here a while.'

'Are you sure?'

'Positive.' She fixed a smile on her lips and shooed Phoebe away. 'Go.'

Mariel watched her sister thread her way through the colourful crowd, her silk and diamonds shimmering beneath the heavy chandelier. Only then did she allow herself a much-needed sigh. Phoebe knew nothing of the mess Mariel had left behind in Paris except that it was over between her and French fashion photographer Luc Girard, her business partner of seven years and lover for the past five.

He was probably the reason she'd thrown up— twice—somewhere over China. She massaged the heel of her hand over the affected area. The organza of the latest and probably last addition to her after-five wardrobe shifted beneath her palm.

Turning her back to the room, she sipped water and studied the guests through the gilt-edged mirror over the mantelpiece.

The bride's parents, who'd spared no expense for their daughter's special day, were conversing with another wealthy Hills couple near the floor-to-ceiling ice sculpture, now dripping in Adelaide's January heat.

Was that little Johnny…? What was his last name? Mariel frowned at the blond guy, trying to remember. Not so little now, she thought with a twinge of nostalgia. And there was nothing she liked better than a guy in a well-tailored suit. As her gaze moved on, she realised several of the well-suited men were eyeing her up. And not-so-little Johnny What's-his-name was headed her way. Great. Just what she *didn't* need.

She knew she attracted men. With her face on the cover of Europe's top magazines, and becoming a familiar face in Australia, it was inevitable. But tonight she could have done without the attention. Especially tonight, since she'd just sworn off men for life. Another sigh slipped past her lips as she automatically checked her lipstick in the mirror, straightened her shoulders and turned, smile back in place.

Well, surprise, surprise. Daniel Huntington the Third, who refused to answer to anything but Dane, leaned a

shoulder against the doorway and watched Mariel
Davenport hold court, her little flock of male admirers
clustered around her, apparently hanging on every word
that spilled from those luscious coral lips.

She was the last person he'd expected to see here this
evening. Nor had he anticipated the quick punch to his
solar plexus as he cast a critical eye over the breezy
black halterneck number, with its plummeting neckline
and incy-wincy skirt. He was pretty sure if he stood
close enough and let his eyes skim casually down he'd
see her navel.

Not that he intended to stand that close. With his six-
foot-three advantage he could see her well enough from
here. He thought he might just be able to smell the
perfume she used to wear—that hint of black roses and
sweet sin seemed to waft across the few feet between
them. Alluring, seductive. It suited her, from the tips of
her raven-black hair, piled on top of her head, to the soles
of her perfectly pedicured feet and shiny stiletto sandals.

He couldn't see her feet, of course, or those mile-
long legs that had her topping out at nearly six foot, but
he knew her well enough. First class all the way.

She hadn't noticed him yet, but he lifted his beer in
mock salute, then poured a fortifying mouthful of the
cool bitter brew down his suddenly dry throat.

Was she with someone? he wondered. Her French
lover? Odd how his fingernails bit into his palms at the
thought. He'd been fine about that little detail until a
moment ago.

Until he'd seen her again in all that glorious flesh.

But, no, she must have come alone—because if
she'd had a partner Dane was pretty sure the man would
be attached to her side like some fashion accessory.

He flexed the fingers of his free hand, flicked them against his thigh, and watched her flash that cover-winning smile at her fans. The one thing Mariel loved was attention, be it personal or the camera. And from what he'd heard about her career over the past years, and seen in the latest beauty magazine that her sister had touted, the camera loved Mariel.

Fashion designer turned photographic model.

He considered speaking to her, but he wasn't about to become one of her fawning admirers. Good grief, a couple of those guys had been exploring Play Dough and finger paint when she'd been experimenting with make-up and mobile phones. Did they not realise? He expelled a harsh breath through his nostrils. He could wait.

'Ah, here's our very own newly announced *Babe* magazine's Bachelor of the Year.' Justin Talbot materialised beside him. 'I was wondering where you'd got to, my friend.'

'Looks like you found me.' Dane glanced his way, mentally shaking his head at the snazzy dove-grey waistcoat, matching tie and wing-tip collar Justin's new wife had obviously picked out. Dane didn't believe in conforming to dress code unless it was for a funeral.

'You've done us proud,' said Justin, clapping a hand on Dane's shoulder.

'Easy for you to say.' Dane scowled, his gaze unerringly finding Mariel again. 'You dobbed me in.'

As if he needed more women hounding him. Since he'd won the title he'd grown very weary of the relentless parade of would-be starlets clamouring for his attention.

'Think of it as doing your bit for charity,' Justin said.

'There are better ways to raise funds,' Dane muttered. 'And the press is having a field-day.'

'What did you expect? Millionaire businessman, founder of OzRemote *and* eligible bachelor. Hey…it's Mariel Davenport.'

Dane felt Justin's voice switch from jovial to slightly breathless like a prickle between his shoulderblades. He shrugged the feeling off. 'So it appears.'

'Jee-ee-z. Looking good, Mariel,' Justin murmured. 'Even better than that photo spread Phoebe showed us. She hasn't been back in…how long? What's she doing at Carl and Amy's wedding?'

'Ten years.' And five months. 'And your guess is as good as mine,' he muttered, frowning into his amber liquid.

'Wasn't she living with some French guy?'

'Yep.'

'You spoken to her yet?'

'Nope.' Sweat trickled down Dane's back, making his shirt stick. He tossed back the remainder of his beer and thought about stepping outside for some fresh air. The atmosphere was stifling in here, even with the air-con working overtime.

'Why not?' Justin queried. 'You two were pretty close. I remember—'

'That was a long time ago.'

A lifetime ago… The night before she'd left for overseas. In her bedroom, the full moon filtering through the open window, its silver light bathing her milk-white skin, her eyes black pools of wonder, gazing up at him…

Dane shifted his stance, cleared his throat as every hot-blooded cell south of his larynx mobilised. 'You right for a drink?'

'We're leaving in a moment, Cass has an early start

tomorrow. I'm going to say hi to Mariel before we go; want to join me?'

Dane shook his head. 'I'll catch up with her later.' He turned and pointed himself in the direction of the nearest drinks waiter.

But, damn, he couldn't let it go. His head swivelled in time to see Justin plant a kiss full on Mariel's smiling lips. He knew it meant nothing more than what it was— a welcome home—but a sudden tension locked Dane's jaw, making his teeth clench. His fingers tightened around his glass.

He watched his mate whisper something close to her ear and Mariel turned slowly to look Dane's way. So slowly—or maybe it was just that the moment seemed to crawl to a stop—that he had time to experience, in graphic detail, the full effect of that face, that attention, focused wholly on him.

The way the high cheekbones flushed with colour, the flutter of long black lashes as she blinked those emerald eyes at him, just once. The way her glossy lips parted slightly—in surprise or dismay?—then lifted infinitesimally at the corners, resembling something approaching warmth.

Whatever—it faded like a rose in winter, no doubt as she took in his rigid jaw and neutral stare. Because, frankly, he couldn't seem to drum up anything else. She lifted a hand, let it hover a moment before she smoothed a non-existent strand of hair behind her ear.

Her eyes were still locked with his. Until her gaze lifted to his hair. And, yeah, some might say it needed a trim. Her nostrils flared slightly as her gaze shifted to his open-necked shirt. His throat prickled; his Adam's apple bobbed. Hell. He was glad he didn't have a woman, particularly an ex-fashion designer, telling him how he should dress.

And thanks to Justin's intervention he had no alternative—manners dictated he at least speak to her. Forcibly unclenching his teeth and loosening his grip on the glass, he started forward.

Mariel watched Dane Huntington saunter towards her, his casual, almost arrogant manner all too familiar. Whatever Justin was saying—if he was saying anything at all—faded. Her stomach juddered once, as if she'd hit more of that air turbulence she'd experienced on the final approach into Adelaide.

Phoebe, where are you? Get me out of here, she pleaded silently. She should have known she'd bump into him sooner or later, but Dane was the last man she wanted to face right now, with her body clock out of sync and her digestive system doing nasty things to her insides.

She'd wanted to look her best when she saw him again. Show him what he'd missed out on all those years ago, when she'd been a naïve seventeen-year-old who'd thought the young Dane Huntington was her sun and moon and everything in between.

Well, she wasn't so naïve now, even if it had taken every one of those ten years. Seconds ticked by, but they felt like minutes. His cool grey gaze remained fused with hers, no hint of a smile on those beautiful lips. Lifting her chin, she sucked in her stomach and eyeballed him boldly as he drew nearer.

Dark hair with glints of auburn covered his ears and carelessly kissed the back of his neck. Some things hadn't changed, she thought with attempted disdain.

And he still scorned traditional dress code. He was tie-less. His black collarless shirt with white stitching along the seams was undone at the neck and revealed tanned skin and a smattering of dark hair.

The fashion designer inside her winced. Black jeans, to one of Adelaide's Society Weddings of the Year, for heaven's sake? But, to her chagrin, the wholly inappropriate image made her thighs melt and her pulse do a strange little blip.

She straightened, clutching her glass tighter to hide the fact that her fingers were trembling, and said, 'Hello, there,' before he opened his mouth. 'Happy New Year.'

She did *not* lean in for a kiss.

'Mariel. Happy New Year to you, too. How long have you been back?'

'I flew in yesterday morning.'

'Just in time for Carl and Amy's big day.'

His whisky-on-velvet voice flowed over her and he smiled—finally—and her pulse did another of those little blips. With her height she didn't often experience men looking down at her and it made her feel delicate. And feminine.

She stiffened. She didn't *want* to feel delicate and feminine with Dane Huntington. Ever again. But—and how crazy was this?—she wanted him to see her that way.

To remember... Did he remember?

How could he forget?

'Coincidentally Dane mentioned you just the other day,' Justin said, and Mariel saw the familiar little tic in Dane's jaw.

'Oh?' Dane had been talking about *her*? 'Why was that?'

'My wife, Cass, and I are thinking about going to Europe in October, and since you live in Paris he thought maybe you could give us the guided tour.'

'Did he?' She speared Dane with the pointy end of her gaze. 'He didn't try to look me up when he was there. When was it—five years ago, Dane? Mum mentioned it in an e-mail.'

'It was business, Mariel,' he said. 'There wasn't time for sightseeing. Or anything else. It was in and out. What brings you home?'

'Family. I needed a break.'

'One would think if you wanted to be with family you'd have come a week earlier and celebrated Christmas with them.'

Oh. 'I'm ashamed to say I left it too late and the airlines were fully booked.' She refused to look away beneath his close scrutiny. Look away and he'd know she was lying.

'That's too bad.'

'I'm here now.'

'So you are,' he said lazily, eyes still locked on hers.

Justin, obviously feeling the weird tension, switched topics. 'Our Dane won *Babe*'s Bachelor of the Year contest.'

'Is that so?' Mariel lifted her glass and took a sip to soothe her throat, noting the dark look Dane flashed at the other man.

'You remember the one,' Justin went on. '*Babe* magazine runs it every year.'

'Ah, yes, *that* magazine,' she drawled, infusing her tone with a large dollop of sarcasm, and was rewarded with a flare of colour on Dane's cheekbones.

And what do you know? Dane Huntington, master

of cool, actually looked hot. The hot-and-bothered kind of hot. Amused, she watched his head tilt as he stretched his neck, as if easing the tension there. The smile that touched her lips was more of a smirk.

'The side benefits: dates with ten different babes.' Justin grinned, with the devil's glint in his eyes.

Mariel's stomach clenched around the image Justin provoked, but she held on to that smirk for all she was worth.

'Uh-oh, my wife's giving me the eye,' Justin said. 'I'll leave you two to catch up. Great seeing you again, Mariel.'

'You, too.' Mariel smiled at an attractive brunette watching them as Justin threaded his way in her direction, then turned back to Dane. 'So…*Babe*'s Bachelor of the Year, huh? How does it work again?'

'Like Jus told you,' he clipped. 'A bit of fun. And it's for a good cause. Charity fund-raiser. I need a refill—how about you?' Jutting his chin, he motioned her away from several interested onlookers towards a punchbowl in the middle of a table.

He ladled orange liquid into two crystal cups, offered her one. 'Thank you,' she said, careful to avoid contact with his fingers.

'You mean these *babes*—' Mariel drew the word out with sarcastic relish '—wherever they come from, they rate the contestants and the highest score wins? What are they scoring you on, I wonder?' She couldn't help the wicked smile…but inside, somewhere deep and almost forgotten, something hurt. 'I can't wait to see you on the cover of the magazine.'

He shook his head. 'It's not as bad as you think.'

'How bad am I thinking?'

'The date ends at the front door.'

Biting back resentment that she thought she'd got over years ago, she said, 'That'll be a novelty for you, then. I've heard you're a regular Casanova these days.'

His lips stretched into an indolent grin that didn't reach his eyes. 'Don't believe everything you hear.'

The back of her throat tickled at the sound of that lazy tone. She glanced down, flicking her eyes to his again before they had time to indulge in the snug fit of his jeans and the way his exclusive hand-made *casual* shirt clung to his chest, even if the seam was too narrow for his broad shoulders. 'If you're going to look the part you'll really have to update your wardrobe, or acquire a new tailor.'

'Ah, ever the fashion designer. And looking a million bucks tonight,' he said, his gaze skimming her body, just a tad longer than might be considered polite in company. 'One of your designs?'

She met his eyes, paused, smiling inwardly, then sipped her drink. 'No.' *Hah.* He obviously knew nothing about her designs.

'That's right—you're a photographer's model these days. I saw your picture in a magazine here a couple of months back. Phoebe showed us. Very nice.'

His gaze swept over her once more. Was he comparing her to his girlfriends? According to Phoebe's regular newsy e-mails from home, Dane enjoyed more than his fair share.

It no longer bothered her. After all, she'd put Dane in her past where he belonged years ago. Hadn't she? Standing here, within his all-too-compelling aura, she wondered if she was as certain about that as she'd thought.

'Not any more.' She took another long gulp to wash the sudden bitter taste of Luc's betrayal from her mouth.

'Oh?'

'There you are, Mari,' Phoebe interrupted with breathless haste, clutching her mobile to her breasts and saving Mariel from having to discuss her ruined career.

'Hi, Dane.' She barely spared him a glance, and Mariel had the fleeting thought that life had gone on here as usual while she'd been away. Phoebe leaned in and murmured, 'Kyle just rang. He wants to meet me. Now.'

Mariel stared at her sister, incredulous. 'And you agreed? What happened to your New Year's resolution?'

Phoebe bit her lip. 'I know, I know, but…'

'Don't let him call the shots, Pheebes.'

'I won't. But I've got to meet him halfway, don't I?'

Mariel raised a brow at the gleam in Phoebe's overbright eyes. 'And where's that?'

'Um…a spot we like to go. Oh, and in case I don't see you, I won't be around when you get up. I'm on an early-morning flight to Melbourne. There's a music festival on. So I've asked Brad Johnston to drop you home. You remember Brad; he's keen to catch up with you again.'

'Ah…' Stomach sinking, she glanced over Phoebe's shoulder, saw the familiar fuzzy-haired guy weaving his way through the crowd. More than keen, if Mariel wasn't mistaken.

'You two came together?' Dane asked.

'Yeah, my wonderful sister came to keep me company…um…because Kyle couldn't make it. You don't mind, do you, Mari?'

'Of course not, but I think you should consider—'

'No need to bother Brad,' Dane cut in, his voice disturbingly deep, disturbingly close. 'It's all arranged, I'm taking Mariel home.'

CHAPTER TWO

'OH? OKAY…but…' Phoebe's eyes darted between the two of them.

'I'll let Brad know,' he told her.

'Okay. Thanks, Dane. See ya later, sis.' Phoebe pecked Mariel's cheek and was gone in a whirlwind of pink and perfume.

'Arranged?' Mariel muttered, glaring at him while every internal organ traded places.

'Wait here,' he ordered, and was gone before she could utter another word of protest.

Hardly. But she stood immobile, feet stapled to the floor, while she watched him dispatch Brad in less than five seconds. Why weren't her legs moving? Why wasn't she getting the heck away before it was too late?

Dane could tell Mariel was unsettled by the sudden turn of events as he made his way back. Her eyes glinted dangerously, that beautiful mouth a slash of coral in her pale face. But, he noted with satisfaction, she'd made no attempt to disappear amongst the guests.

'I was hoping to leave early,' she said the moment he reached her side. Setting her cup down, she unzipped the diamante bag that swung from her shoulder. 'About now, in fact. I wouldn't want to spoil the evening for you. You probably came with someone...' She pulled out her mobile. 'I'll call a cab.'

'I told you. I'm taking you home. And it's not a problem; I came alone.'

'Oh...' He saw her register that fact as her eyes clashed with his again.

Not a problem? Dane gave himself a mental slap on the forehead. They had unfinished business that went back ten years. To a night of youthful passion on a girly patterned quilt, the night-cooled fragrance wafting inside on the moonbeams.

Then a very ugly end outside his father's garage.

Not a matter that could be sorted out tonight, Dane knew, but he'd taken one look at Brad and some sort of proprietorial instinct had kicked in.

'But you'll want to stay, enjoy...' She waved a carefully manicured hand. 'Whatever...'

'I'm ready to leave when you are.'

'Very well,' she said with quiet formality, her spine rigid. 'Thank you. I'd like to leave now, if that's okay. My body clock's still on Greenwich Mean Time.'

'We'll say our goodbyes, then.' He placed a hand on the small of her back. He hadn't counted on the heat that rushed into his palm at that first electrifying contact. Beneath his palm the sensuous fabric of her designer dress shifted against her flesh, making him wonder how she would feel without the silk.

Just smooth, sleek skin.

She flinched as if burned. So she felt it, too, he mused as he steered her towards their hosts. Interesting. Had she and her French lover called it quits? She'd returned alone, and there'd been a definite chill in her reply when Paris had been mentioned.

The paparazzi, eager for their quota of celebrity guest snaps, were milling about the property's open gates. A security guard waved Dane through. Bulbs flashed and a blur of faces bumped up against the window.

'You'd be accustomed to this?' he asked, steering his way through the photographers. 'I should have asked if you were okay with it.'

'Yes and yes. But in this case they're not aimed at me.'

'That ain't necessarily so. You're somewhat of a celebrity yourself these days.'

'Not so much here. And it's not as if I'm your date or anything.'

He glanced her way before spinning the car onto the country road, leaving the press behind in a spray of dust. 'They don't know that.'

She didn't reply. In fact she looked serenely ahead, watching the moon-drenched paddocks and stands of gum trees flash by. Every so often a light glinted from a farmhouse behind the regular curtains of foliage.

She wasn't as calm as she let on, he noted. The grip on her bag was white-knuckled, and her thumbs massaged the strap in tiny jerky movements against her thighs.

Thighs that looked smooth and silky and…very naked.

Eyes on the road. Only on the road. Sweat broke out on his brow. He switched the air-conditioning to full blast. 'Too cold?' he asked a moment later, more to fill the silence than anything else. Silence that seemed to throb with the sound of the bass from the stereo speakers.

'No…no, it's…cool.'

She changed position, and he didn't have to look to know she'd stretched those long naked legs out in front of her. Within the Porsche's confines her roses-and-sin perfume wound around his senses like a long-forgotten dream. He thanked whatever lucky star was out tonight that it was only a short drive over the next ridge of hills.

Through childhood she'd always been his best mate, generous and loyal and stubborn. By seventeen she'd turned into a confident, ambitious young woman who wanted to take on the world. *And leave him behind.*

He shook off the edgy thought and glanced her way again. At twenty-seven… Well, right now she was all about lusciousness and impact. But how well did he know this grown-up version? 'You were saying you're not modelling now?' he prompted into the silence.

She hesitated. 'No. My business partner and I parted ways.'

'Luc?' She'd carefully avoided mentioning the fact that he'd also been her lover. 'Phoebe told me all about him.' Slight emphasis on 'all'.

'Yes. Luc. I don't want to talk about it. *Him.*' She waved a disconcerted hand. 'Any of it.'

'I'm sorry,' he said, and hoped he sounded sincere. And why wouldn't he be? He'd only ever wanted the best for Mariel.

'How's your father?' She spoke suddenly, as if she'd plucked something—anything—out of the ether to switch topics.

'He was okay when I spoke to him a couple of months ago.' And that was all Dane needed to know, all Mariel needed to know, and all he wanted to say about his old man.

'And your mother?'

'Still living in Queensland, last I heard.' With her man of the moment.

'So…by that I take it you don't live at home now?'

Home. Dane scowled at the white line dissecting the road as it curved over a rise. Had the generations-old homestead set amidst acres of rolling Adelaide hills ever been a home? 'Home' implied two parents who were committed to each other, their marriage and their offspring. At least it did in Dane's opinion; it seemed his parents thought differently.

'I moved out years ago. Soon after you left, in fact. I've got my own place in North Adelaide. It's close to work. Jus and I have an IT business there.'

'Then I'm taking you out of your way.'

'Not a problem. I like driving.' He glanced in the rear-vision mirror, frowned at the car which had been tailing them since they'd left the wedding, and with a sharp twist of the steering wheel pulled over to the edge of the road. 'Especially when you get a view like that.'

An almost full moon lifted out of the landscape, bleaching the fields and spilling inky shadows beneath the gums. From the corner of his eye Dane watched the car behind slow down, pass, then continue on.

'Oh…wow.' Mariel shimmied upright, her face animated in the soft glow. 'I've missed this. It must be the atmosphere here, but the Aussie moon looks so much bigger than the Parisian moon.' A quick grin danced over her features. 'And wouldn't they kill me back there for saying that?'

'They wouldn't if they were here,' Dane murmured, his thoughts tumbling back in time. As a kid, how many evenings had he spent watching possum shadows play amongst the trees against a star-studded sky? Gazing at the moon in all its phases?

Waiting until it felt safe enough to go inside?

He shook his head, edged back onto the empty road. Being with Mariel after all this time was tossing up old memories.

The last time he'd seen her she'd been careening down his father's driveway, grating gears and spraying gravel as she fishtailed onto the road.

He pressed his foot harder on the accelerator. The sooner he got her home, the better off he'd be.

The better off they'd both be.

A few moments later they approached her parents' home. Dane checked the road behind him again before turning into the driveway. Since Mariel didn't have a remote, he climbed out, punched in the code Mariel gave him on the panel set into the stone pillar and the tall gates swung open. They continued down a long drive, where blue agapanthus bordered a healthy lawn on one side, a row of old pines on the other. Ivy climbed the walls and iron lace framed a wide veranda. As they came to a stop three security lights winked on, but no light shone through the front door's stained glass.

He peered up at the blackened windows. 'Your parents out?'

'They left for a Pacific cruise yesterday. Thanks for the lift.' Her eyes flicked to his. He glimpsed nothing in those dark depths, as if she'd blanked all thought.

He didn't want her to go in yet. Not this way. Hell, not as this polite and distant stranger.

He reminded himself their childhood friendship had been years ago. She wasn't the young, innocent girl he remembered, with her fairytale dreams. She was a successful, mature and independent woman.

And what a woman she'd grown into. Those youthful curves had only grown lusher, and if it were possible her face more beautiful.

He switched off the ignition, sensed her instant panic. 'Mariel…'

'*No.*' She closed her eyes briefly. 'Not tonight.'

His hands tightened on the steering wheel momentarily. But tension showed in the lines around her mouth, the smudges beneath her eyes. 'I'll walk you to the door.'

'It's okay; this isn't the city,' she said, swinging the car door open.

'I'll walk you to the door,' he repeated, and pulled his key out of the ignition. Some things hadn't changed—still as stubborn as she'd always been.

And as fast—she was already halfway up the path before he'd climbed out. The aftermath of the day's heat still blanketed the earth, thick and smelling of dried eucalypt and pine.

Metal tinkled as she fumbled with house keys, holding them aloft and squinting at them under the porch light.

'Allow me.' Dane took the keys from her hands. The brush of skin against skin sent a tingle through every nerve-ending in his fingers, up his arm and straight to his groin.

The flash of awareness when their eyes met was a stark reminder that they could never go back to the easy camaraderie they'd once had.

He wasn't sure he even wanted that with her any more. Less than an hour in her company and his wants, his desires, were fanning to life inside him like a bushfire sweeping up from the valley floor.

She broke eye contact first, and a breathlessness caught at her throat when she said, 'Phoebe gave them to me, but I didn't ask her which one opened the front door…'

He fitted a key into the lock but the door opened without it. 'Not locked,' he said.

'Oh…that's probably my fault. I assumed the door automatically locked once closed.' Someone who didn't know her as well as he did wouldn't have noticed the slight sag in her posture.

Dane stepped past her and through the doorway, located the light switch. A warm glow from the antique foyer lights gleamed on polished wood and brass fittings, and brought a rich luxury to the burgundy carpet runner.

She glanced at the discreet panel on the wall as she followed him inside. 'Damn. I didn't even remember to set the alarm. Dad'll throw a fit if he finds out.'

'Only if you tell him.' Without looking at her, he started down the hall. 'I'll check the place before I leave.'

'That's not necessary,' she assured him quickly. A sudden nervous energy spiked her voice.

'Yes. It is. Anyone could have come in.'

'I look after myself these days.'

'I'm sure you do.'

A few moments later, ground floor covered, he started up the stairs, switching on lights as he checked the rooms. Mariel followed, muttering protests. He paused at the last door on the left.

Mariel's room.

So he left the light off. But as soon as he'd stepped inside he realised he'd made a mistake. Moonlight flooded the room, spilling over an open suitcase, a dressing table strewn with tubes and bottles. He breathed in the mix of feminine potions, powder and perfume like a man who'd gone too long without.

He'd never denied himself the pleasures to be found in a woman's bedroom, but at this moment he couldn't remember a single one that had ever compared to that one all-too-short time in Mariel's arms.

Dangerous thoughts. He dragged his attention back to the task he'd set himself. 'Everything seems to be okay, so—'

'Of course it is,' she snipped. 'I told you it was. But did you ever listen to me? No. Oh… Why did you have to come in and…? *Be you.*' She punctuated those final agonised words with a long slow breath.

The old guilt rolled nastily through his gut. In the pregnant silence that followed he heard the wind sigh through the trees, an echo of his own feelings. 'I thought that was what was so good about us,' he said, his eyes fixed on the moon but not seeing it. 'We could be ourselves.'

'Once upon a time, in a galaxy far, far away. Maybe.' Mariel switched on the light. He didn't know why, except that maybe the moonlit scene reminded her, too. He turned to face her. She'd folded her arms across her chest and was watching him with unnerving calm. Either that or she was a damn good actress.

'It's been a while, Queen Bee.'

He felt rather than saw her little hitch of breath at the use of her old nickname, then she pulled herself up straighter, lifted her chin. 'I'm not that inexperienced, trusting little girl any more.'

'Dane…' Mariel said, reaching for him with passion-drenched eyes that hinted at vulnerability.

The kiss.

Their first fully-fledged kiss.

A goodbye kiss, because she was leaving and for who knew how long?

He met her eyes squarely, ready to admit the pain he'd inflicted on her young pride an hour later. 'I was eighteen and an insensitive jerk.'

But that was then. This was now. And *now* was full of possibilities. She wasn't an innocent; she was an international sensation. A modern woman who'd no doubt had her share of men over the years—a thought he didn't particularly want to dwell on.

Her mouth twisted with grim humour. 'Has anything changed?'

A grin tugged at his mouth. 'Nope. Still that same insensitive jerk.' He couldn't help himself—he stepped closer, so their bodies almost touched, and brushed a finger down her cheek.

She shook her head. 'We're not those kids now. It's in the past. Leave it there.'

But Dane couldn't leave it there, whatever the hell *it* was, because his brain had ceased to compute anything so complicated as reason or words or sentence structure. All it recognised was the fragile face he suddenly found himself holding between his palms, emerald eyes swimmingly close, the seductive scent of her perfume, her hands against his chest and her indrawn breath as he leaned in to touch his lips to hers.

He tasted heat and sun-warmed honey, and he slid his hands through silky hair then down over smooth shoulders and chiffon to haul her closer, so he could absorb the fuller, richer flavour as her mouth opened for him.

He closed his eyes as her body grew pliant, melting against his. Fingertips scraping against his shirt. Soft throaty murmurs. Fast, warm breaths against his cheek—

Hard, flat palms pushing at his chest—

Heaving a breath, she reared back, eyes dark and wary. 'Why did you do that?' She touched the fingers of one hand to her lips then spun away.

Good question. Damn good question. He noticed the wisps of hair he'd dislodged from the clasp at the back of her head floating about her temples and around her neck. 'Perhaps I wanted to see if it was the same as I remember.'

She turned, eyes flashing with residual passion…or desire or anger—he couldn't tell through the sexual haze still blurring his vision. To give himself a moment he paced to the dressing table, picked up a bottle of perfume, set it down.

'And was it?' She closed her eyes, as if regretting the question, then shook her head. More silken hair tumbled over her shoulders. 'Don't answer that. I don't want to know.'

'Or maybe I just wanted to kiss you for old times' sake.'

He leaned nonchalantly against the dressing table as if his blood wasn't thudding through his body like a big bass drum. As if his jeans didn't feel as if they'd shrunk two sizes in the crotch. 'You kissed me back, Queen Bee.'

The shared knowledge singed the air between them, and she drew a shaky breath but didn't reply.

'And it felt good. You thought so, too.'

She let out a stream of air through her nostrils. 'Isn't that just a typically arrogant male response?'

'Am I not a typically arrogant male?'

She glared back, unsmiling, or was that a hint of humour at the corner of her mouth?

'Good,' he said, taking it as a yes and venturing a grin of sorts. 'Now we've got that sorted, I'll check outside.'

Mariel shot a hand up, palm out. Oh, no, she wasn't letting him off the hook that easily. 'Not sorted, Dane. Why don't we just get it out in the open now, then never speak of it again?'

His smile faded. 'Okay,' he said slowly. 'Why did you come to see me that night? We'd said our goodbyes at your place.'

'That kiss. It meant something to me. It meant *everything* to me.' Her heart twisted, remembering.

'It was a goodbye kiss,' he murmured.

'I thought—stupidly and naïvely, I realise now—that I was in love with you. And when you kissed me…like that…I thought…' She waved it away. 'Well, I went looking for you because I wanted to ask you…to tell you I was coming back…that we…'

That evening was still as clear as day in her mind. After *The Kiss*, she'd driven to his house. She'd seen his car lights on in the garage…

'I heard a noise,' she said. 'I was so pathetically dumb I thought you were in pain. Imagine my shock-horror when I saw Isobel on the bonnet of your car and you going at it like…well.'

She recalled that she must have made some sort of sound, because they'd both turned and seen her. Then bizarre fascination had held her in thrall for those few agonising seconds while her gaze swept the two of them and her heart shattered.

'*I hate you, Dane Huntington, I never want to see you again!*'

She didn't remember how she'd made it to the sanctuary of her car—it was the feminine giggle and the 'Poor Mariel' that stuck in her mind, and the sound of Dane's footsteps behind her, his calls for her to wait up. *Wait?*

Dane shook his head and she knew he, too, was remembering. 'Thing is, Mariel, as close as we were, as much as I cared for you, the one thing we never discussed was our sex lives.'

'Or lack of.' She held his gaze unapologetically.

'We should have. It would have saved any misunderstanding. I came by the next day to apologise, but you'd already left. So I'll apologise now. For hurting you.'

She nodded. 'Accepted. But you didn't have any reason to apologise. I realise that now. You didn't see me the way I saw you.'

Maybe not then. She read the message in his eyes and something fluttered inside her. Or perhaps it was something else that had stopped him.

'I tried contacting you several times,' he said. 'You wouldn't take my calls. You won't know I was in Paris a couple of years later. I dropped by to see you, but your landlady told me you were in London for the weekend with your boyfriend.'

'He wasn't my boyfriend; he was a fellow student.'

'Student, boyfriend—it makes no difference now.' He needed air. 'I'll go check the garden.'

It took a good ten minutes to scour the perimeter of the extensive grounds. Not that it was absolutely necessary. But it gave them both some time.

As he returned to the house light from the kitchen's stained glass windows flowed into the adjacent atrium, turning the abundant greenery within to the colours of amber and ripe plums.

From the other side of the glass he saw Mariel,

sitting on the edge of the raised pond beside a stone maiden pouring sparkling water from her jug. A moth, distracted by the light, fluttered above her head. Shards of crimson and gold light sliced through the fronds of a potted palm, danced on the water and reflected over the face he hadn't had the pleasure of looking at up close and personally in a long time.

She'd needed to chase her dreams overseas, he reflected. And she'd excelled. He'd been right in not taking their relationship to the next logical step. Thinking herself in love with him would have brought her nothing but grief. She might never have left, and he hadn't wanted to be responsible for that.

Marriage had never been on his agenda.

He focused on her once more. She'd braced her forearms on her thighs and held an open can of beer between her palms. Her posture drooped and he was hard pressed to remember any occasion when Mariel had allowed herself that indulgence since early high school. She probably hadn't noticed that her dress gaped at the front, revealing more creamy cleavage. Another tinny sat on the ledge beside her.

He took that as an invitation.

CHAPTER THREE

MARIEL tilted the can to her lips and rolled the familiar bitter Aussie brew around her tongue. So much for tonight's decision to avoid alcohol. The night seemed to call for it after all. She stiffened when she heard Dane's footfall on the marble tiles, then made a conscious effort to appear relaxed. Rolled her shoulders. Stretched her neck. Unclenched her fingers on the can. No way would she allow him to see the effect he'd had on her tonight.

'I didn't take you for a beer kind of girl,' he said, appearing from behind the foliage.

'When in Oz…' She tossed him the other can. 'Happy New Year, again.'

He caught it one-handed, popped the top, but remained standing a few steps away. It gave her another moment to take in the whole man. And what a man. He'd always had a well-toned body, but he was no longer the eighteen-year-old she remembered. He was twenty-eight and in his prime. His face had weathered somewhat under the harsh Australian sun, but it only increased his rugged appeal. Harsher jaw. Darker stubble. Eyes that saw more, knew more.

She forced away the shiver of disquiet that rippled

down her spine and looked further. Beneath his shirt he was all hard muscle. She knew because when she'd pushed him away earlier he'd been as unyielding as concrete.

Model looks? No, not smooth enough, not conventional enough, with that careless hair. Scowling, she tipped another mouthful of beer down her throat. He was more the dark heroic type.

Not hers.

'So what are your plans while you're here?' he asked, sitting beside her. He assumed the same sitting position as her on the edge of the circular pool, not quite touching her. But she could feel his body heat across the tiny space. Her skin prickled with the awareness that if either of them moved a millimetre she'd feel the hair on his arm brush against her skin.

She sat perfectly still and said, 'At the moment I'm not thinking beyond chilling out and surfing the sofa for a few days—*after* I've thoroughly reacquainted myself with my bed.'

And, yes, in the charged hiatus that followed she knew he'd caught the image she'd unthinkingly tossed out there. Damn.

He cleared his throat and said, 'You're staying a while, then?' into the charged stillness.

'Yes.' She had no choice. But she wasn't telling *him* that. He might still be Dane, but he was a man… The fiasco in Paris was still so raw and recent it brought a chill to her bones. Her shoulder muscles tensed and tightened.

'Mariel.'

She turned at his simple touch on her shoulder, ready to flee. Or fight. Or mash her mouth against his. *Sheesh.*

'I can feel the tension in your body from here.' He

set his beer aside and reached up, took a pin from her hair. 'For goodness' sake, woman, loosen up.'

She sucked in a breath. 'What are you doing?'

'When in Oz…' He took out another. 'I always liked your hair down,' he murmured. 'It'll relax you.'

'Relax…?' Her thoughts disintegrated. Mesmerised, she gazed at him, his eyes focused on the task as he concentrated on removing the clasp on top of her head.

'Yes…' Then his fingers were in her hair, and she was turning towards him while he loosened it, so that it tumbled down over her shoulders and released the pressure, massaging her scalp in slow circles on either side…

Oh, yeah… She forgot all about tension and tired muscles. She wanted to arch and purr and follow him to the ends of the earth. No one had hands like Dane. No one smelled quite like Dane. A hint of spicy soap and his own brand of musky, masculine scent.

And he felt right at home, with his body heat warming her all down her left side, while water trickled over the smooth stones beside them and the air was heavy with the scent of damp earth and vegetation.

What if she leaned in now and kissed him again? He was right: it had felt darn good. She'd watch his grey eyes turn smoky. She'd let her tongue slide over his, warm and decadently rich, like rum-flavoured chocolate…

And she'd be the one to pull back first, she thought darkly. Just when his mouth responded to hers. Payback time.

Or was it all too long ago to matter?

His hands dropped away. And maybe a corner of his mouth tipped up in a hint of a smile, maybe his eyes flickered with a one-step-ahead-of you glint. Or maybe it was the barely veiled cynicism of a man all too experienced with women's ways. She couldn't be sure because she was still finding her way out of her little daydream.

'Goodnight, Queen Bee.' He rose, giving her an eyeful of male crotch. 'I'll lock up behind me. Pleasant dreams.'

Then he left.

As he should, Mariel told herself, pouring the rest of her beer into the fountain. Judging by the impressive bulge at the front of his jeans, one moment more might have been too late.

Pleasant dreams? Hours later Mariel lay on her bed, staring up at the familiar ceiling. Night air chased goosebumps over her naked body, pebbling her nipples and making the hairs on her arms stand up. The draught through the window was an uncomfortably warm northerly. But the heatwave conditions weren't the cause of her shivers.

Linen *shwupped* beneath her restless feet as she shifted for the zillionth time. Her lips still tingled from their encounter with Dane's; she could still smell his scent in her room.

She frowned into the dark. Despite her attempts to put tonight to the back of her mind, stubborn images—make that one stubborn image—refused to co-operate.

She'd first locked eyes with Dane when Justin had kissed her and tipped her off that he was there. She'd been subjected to that familiar cool and casual gaze he was so good at.

Ah, but at other moments his eyes had blowtorched her with such searing heat she'd wondered how her skin hadn't blistered.

It was still there between them, that connection, like the ghost of Christmases past. She'd thought she was over it; she'd even put it behind her and moved on with Luc, but had she been fooling herself all these years?

She'd come to Dane, her closest friend, looking for comfort and support on the eve of her first solo overseas adventure. He'd come upstairs to help her close her suitcase. Then, in a fit of nerves and excess energy, she'd decided to rearrange her furniture…

They shifted the shabby-chic dressing table she'd bought at a little French provincial shop in town, relocated her blanket box, then she'd flopped back on her bed.

She'd stared up at the ceiling and told him she'd paint it indigo, like the night sky. And that she'd paint gold stars and suspend a crescent moon over the mirror. If she was staying.

He'd watched her in silence, but her young heart had been sure…

She'd taken his hand and pulled him down onto the bed so that they were both staring up and sharing her sugarplum dreams. Then, in that typically female way, she'd succumbed to the tears she'd been fighting all day.

Yes, she wanted to study overseas. She wanted a career. But she was coming back. Because she had someone to come back to. Dane.

She just hadn't told him that.

She'd thought she was in love… And then they'd shared the most dreamy, most poignant kiss of all…

She shook the memories away. She was over it. Over him. Teenage heartache was always the most painful. The most memorable.

Years later she'd allowed herself to be swept away by another man. Flattered by his promises to make her a celebrity. Seduced by his smooth European looks, charm and attention. She'd thought she was in love again.

Just went to prove she couldn't trust her heart. From now on she'd make decisions with her head and leave emotion out of it.

She sighed into the darkness. Dane had changed, too. He was more remote, more cynical. More attractive. Just as she wasn't that starry-eyed girl any more, who'd spun impossible dreams around a moonlit night and a goodbye kiss.

Dane rolled over and picked up the bedside phone, checking the clock's digital readout as he did so. Seven a.m.

'Good morning, Mr Huntington.' A cheery male voice greeted him.

He leaned up on one elbow. 'Who is this, and how the hell did you get this number?'

'The name's Bronson; I'm a reporter with—'

'I don't care who you're with—'

'Is it true that your reunion with Ms Davenport last night has you rethinking your Bachelor of the Year status?'

What the...? He shot up, swung his legs over the side of the bed. 'No comment.' He slammed the phone back on its cradle.

So they hadn't wasted any time digging up the past, had they? Running both hands through his dishevelled hair, he peered through his upstairs window. The high security wall bordering his North Adelaide home kept intruders out.

Mariel. She was alone out there in her parents' house.

Damn. He needed to get out there ASAP.

Mariel didn't deserve to be dragged into the media circus his life had become since he'd been named Bachelor of the Year. His gut told him she was dealing with some heavy-duty stuff right now. Since he didn't have her mobile number, he punched in the Davenports' home number. It went through to the answering machine. Swearing a blue streak, he disconnected and headed for the bathroom.

Setting the showerhead to massage, he let the tepid water pummel his flesh while he cursed the day he'd allowed Justin to persuade him into what was rapidly becoming a *cirque des femmes*.

Teenage groupies who followed the Bachelor of the Year as if he were some kind of rock star rather than a respected businessman and charity patron. Babes from the magazine e-mailing him, contriving to bump into him outside his office, in the supermarket. He'd even had to give up training on his favourite running track along the River Torrens.

He was tired of the endless parade of women who'd manoeuvred their way into his life over the past few months, but he was Bachelor of the Year for another six months unless he made some kind of formal commitment with an eligible female, and that was never going to happen.

Unless… His thoughts turned to Mariel again as he poured on shampoo and lathered his hair. It didn't have to be a formal commitment… A regular date might just take the pressure off. A classy woman at his side. And Mariel was accustomed to the press. She had style and elegance and intelligence. Maybe they could come to some arrangement…

But did he want to get involved—in any way—with

the woman he'd never quite been able to get out of his system? He rinsed off his hair, reached for a towel. It was a moot point in any case. She'd never go for it.

Mariel woke to the musical warble of magpies outside her window. Pushing her hair off her face, she rose, reached for her robe. Last night's clothes lay in an untidy heap beside the bed. Not the way to treat her latest designer dress, which had cost her more than some people made in a year.

The knowledge that it might well be her last indulgence had her picking it up and slotting it into the wardrobe, before padding to the window and staring out at the bushland beyond the property.

The sun already had its claws into the day, scoring the rapidly drying undergrowth for any hint of remnant moisture. Heat and light. She stretched her arms open in welcome after the hibernation beneath heavy, restrictive clothing the European winter necessitated.

She rummaged through her partially unpacked suitcase. Fifty quick laps up and down the pool was just what she needed. Since she couldn't find her swimsuit, and she had the house to herself, she pulled out the first matching set of underwear she found: sapphire, with little cherries all over and a red satin trim.

At the edge of the pool she paused, then in a moment of madness decided skinny-dipping was the way to go and stripped off.

She plunged into the refreshing coolness and angled straight to the bottom, then up. As she sliced through its mirrored surface, she concentrated on the tang of chlorine, the pool's aquamarine lining and the burn of her muscles as she headed for the far end with long, slow strokes.

The last time she'd been swimming had been during a photo shoot on the Riviera in August, but she'd been working, and her enjoyment had been marred by the hordes of beachgoers and photographers. This morning she had the pool to herself. Pure luxury.

She knew almost before she surfaced that her notion had been premature. A ripple of sensation, as if someone had run their knuckles down the length of her spine, was her first and only warning.

Dane stood near the edge of the pool, a folded newspaper under one arm. Unlike last night's sinful black, today he was wearing white. Casual white shorts. White body-hugging T-shirt. Old. Worn. Soft. She imagined it against her fingers. Or her cheek. Her pulse tapped a wild, irregular rhythm. Unlike his top, his shorts were loose. They gave her a far too detailed and up-close view of tanned, hairy and very muscular legs. And, from her lowly position, more than enough exposed thigh…

She jerked her eyes to his. He'd slipped his sunglasses on top of his head and seemed to be rooted to the spot—

And then she remembered… Oh, God, she was stark staring naked.

She inhaled, gulping in a mouthful of chlorinated water, and managed, barely, to sputter, 'What are you doing here?' She glanced at her clothes and towel. Impossibly out of reach. Her cheeks filled with heat and the already irregular pulse picked up speed.

Stepping closer, to the very edge of the pool, he studied her with those piercing grey eyes. 'Watching you. Do you need rescuing?'

'No!' Oh, God. Oh, no. She sank as low as she could,

crossing her arms over her chest and struggling to stay afloat while every skin cell vibrated as if he was physically stroking her. The water was as clear as glass; no part of her was hidden from his powerful gaze. 'How long have you been here? Never mind. Pass me my clothes.'

'No need to panic; I've already seen you naked.' His mouth quirked and his eyes crinkled up at the corners. Lucky for her—or him—depending on one's point of view, right now they were focused on her face. But for how long?

The heat in her cheeks rushed to every tingling part of her body. 'Seven years old does *not* count. And I'm still traumatised by it.'

He picked up her underwear, held the items out over the water for her. Just a fraction too high, she knew— and he knew. She remained as she was.

'Wasn't my fault you forgot your towel and risked running bare-assed down the hallway.'

'Whatever you say. Hurry up.'

'Nice undies, by the way.'

She was acutely, devastatingly aware that he wasn't looking at her undies. A shiver rippled through her. The water suddenly felt chilled against her overheated flesh.

Just when she thought he wasn't going to play nice, he released them. They hit the water with a plop, floating on the surface just far enough away so that she had to uncross her arms and manoeuvre sideways a fraction. She snatched them to her with a murmured, 'Thank you. Now, if you'll be a gentleman and turn your back…'

'Thing is, Mariel, I'm no gentleman.'

For a few seconds the air hummed. The tension between them crackled. She couldn't reply, could only think that if she reached out she could wind her fingers around that calf and feel how hard that muscle really was. Then pull him closer and sink her teeth into that flesh. Fair punishment.

He took a step back, as if he'd anticipated such a move, then—finally—turned away. 'Did you realise there's a photographer a couple of hundred metres down the road?' His casual comment was followed up with an equally casual, 'They could have a long-range camera set up for all you know.'

Oh, hell. With shaking fingers she struggled to pull on the meagre covering—no easy feat underwater. 'Maybe they're just keen birdwatchers,' she said hopefully. Half decent at last, she hauled herself out of the water.

At the sound, he turned to her once more. 'You should be more aware of security when you're on your own. I could have been any stranger.' She snatched up her towel and blotted water from her face, bemoaning the fact that her complexion was winter-lily pale without its make-up mask.

'But you weren't. And you remembered the gate's security code—clever you.'

'Have you seen this morning's paper?' He tossed it on the little glass table between two loungers.

'No.' In a brisk flurry of movement she scrubbed the rough terry towel down one arm, then the other. 'Is it bad?'

'I'll let you decide.'

She felt his gaze on her and realised she was holding the towel in front of her as if she wasn't totally comfortable in her own skin. As if she wasn't used to men looking at her.

She wasn't used to *this* man looking at her.

His gaze drifted lazily down to her breasts, barely covered by her cherry-splashed blue bra, then lower, over the high-cut bikini briefs. 'If you don't watch out you'll burn that tender European-climate-accustomed skin.'

Burn? Her skin already felt singed and raw and tingling. Her nipples, already pebbled from the cool water, contracted painfully.

She swiped the towel over her body one last time, then swung it around her neck, fisted her hands and lifted her chin. Their eyes connected across the stone pool surround. 'So is it the society pages or the ghastly gossip column?'

'Check it out for yourself. Page twenty-three.'

There was a shot of the two of them leaving the wedding, and a smaller one of Dane's car parked in her parents' driveway.

The mystery woman on Dane Huntington's arm last night appears to be none other than Mariel Davenport, daughter of wealthy land-owner Randolph Davenport, Europe's latest modelling sensation. Ms Davenport flew in from Paris and, it seems, straight into the arms of her old friend and flame. Could this cosy reunion signal the end of Adelaide's most popular Bachelor of the Year's reign?

Bad. Bad. Bad. She didn't bother with the small print underneath. She tried to laugh, but the sound came out parched. 'Local gossip. You don't pay any heed to that rubbish, do you?'

His enigmatic expression didn't change. 'How do *you* feel about it?'

She shrugged and headed towards the house, the hot concrete burning the soles of her feet. 'It'll settle down in a day or two.' *When Dane resumes his regular playboy lifestyle.* 'I'm going to take a shower. Have you had breakfast?'

'I picked up croissants on the way, figured you'd want to share. They're in the kitchen when you're ready.'

She thought about the article while she took her shower. Being seen with Dane had cast her in a spotlight when she absolutely didn't need it. It wouldn't take much digging for someone keen enough to unearth the dirt on Paris and Luc and fling the mud at her. She'd never be able to set up a successful business here with that negative publicity. Hopefully the attention would fade when they realised there was *nothing going on.*

CHAPTER FOUR

DANE found coffee, a plunger and mugs, switched on the kettle and studied the business pages while he waited for Mariel to take a shower. He could hear the water running and schooled himself not to think about all that gorgeous flesh and warm soapy water.

Safer, much safer, to think about making that date he'd promised the robust blonde surfer chick he'd met in the bar last week. The fact that he'd had no intention of following up was irrelevant.

He looked up when Mariel appeared, and his gaze drifted over her of its own accord. She wore a navy mini sundress with a bright floral pattern and a white lace trim. It hugged that sensational figure and left miles of bare leg. Heaven help him.

'That feels much better,' she said, taking a seat opposite, her enticing still-damp fragrance wafting across the table.

He didn't agree. Ignoring his body's wayward but inevitable response, he poured them both a coffee, then, remembering, he withdrew a small plastic self-sealing bag from his pocket. 'I was cleaning out my car the other day and found Phoebe's diamond earring.'

'She lost her earring? In your car?'

He noticed Mariel's complexion fade, her green eyes taking on the hue of winter's frost-covered paddocks. Interesting.

'A couple of weeks ago, yes.'

She stared at him. 'You and Phoebe…?'

'Me and four women, actually. Drunk as skunks, talking dirty to me and giggling themselves silly.'

'Yeah, right.' She picked up her mug, but there was a smidgeon of uncertainty beneath the scorn.

'Ever tried to ferry a gaggle of women home from a hen night?'

'Hen night?'

'Amy's do. Drunk on Mai Tais, Screaming Orgasms and a male stripper. Well-endowed, too… Their words, not mine. The bride-to-be appointed me chauffeur for the evening.'

Mariel's expression didn't alter, but he saw something flicker in her eyes. She reached for a croissant, broke it open. 'I bet that put a dent in your social calendar.'

'Not at all.' He took a croissant himself. 'I'd do it for you if you asked.'

'Strip and ply me with Screaming Orgasms? No thanks.' She raised her mug, took a gulp, then set it down with a chink. Her crisp retort made him smile on the inside. But only for a pulse-beat, because the image she conjured with her sharp retort hit him right between the thighs.

He lifted his mug to his suddenly parched throat and took a long, slow swallow. 'I meant chauffeur duty. You don't have a car yet, do you?'

'Actually, I do. A pretty yellow hatchback. I'm picking it up today.'

He watched her eat in silence a moment, considering his words before speaking again, but he had to know for sure. 'What's the deal with your business partner?' He rolled his mug between his fingers. 'He isn't only your business partner, is he?'

'No. He—' She shook her head, pressed her lips together as if she was afraid of saying too much. 'And the word's *was*. He's history. Leave it at that.'

She drank her coffee greedily, then finished off her croissant in three quick, careless bites. 'It's handy you're here; you can put those chauffeuring skills to work and drive me to the car dealer. If you're not busy with any other…ah…commitments, that is.' Without looking at him she rose, carried the dishes to the sink.

'Clear schedule today.' And wasn't that handy? 'When do you want to leave?'

She rinsed the dishes, put them away. 'I'll be ready in a few moments.'

'That's what they all say.'

While he waited he finished off the business section of his newspaper. Twenty minutes later he folded it and wandered over to the window. What had happened between Mariel and her lover? He told himself it was none of his business. He was still pondering when he heard her footsteps cross the tiles.

She'd accessorised the sundress with hot-pink sandals and matching beads.

She looked fresh. Fun. Gorgeous.

His fists tightened in the pockets of his shorts. Once he'd have told her, but now, with this current friction like a live wire between them, it was probably wiser to keep the verbal admiration to a minimum lest it be misinterpreted.

She stared at him a moment, a small frown marring her forehead, as if disappointed to find him lacking in the compliments he'd have once voiced without thought.

Then she spotted his car keys on the kitchen table. Their eyes met and duelled in the familiar battle he'd all but forgotten. 'Uh-uh, I'm driving.' She got to them first, swept them up with a laugh and jingled them above her head. 'Your Porsche. All the way to town.'

'You think so?' He was behind her in a second, fingers tangling with hers, wrestling for possession.

Mariel's laugh snagged in her chest as his familiar deep voice vibrated against her ear and between her shoulderblades. The smell of healthy male sweat and Dane's own brand of scent seemed to wrap around her. She leaned back…or did he shuffle forward?…and his body bumped against hers and her grip on the keys faltered.

All movement ceased. Even her heart seemed to stop for one long breathless moment. His T-shirt shifted lightly against her bare back so that she was oh-so-aware of the hard abdominal ridges beneath. Over the whisper of the air-conditioning she heard the grandfather clock ticking in the hall. Felt Dane's hand locked over hers. The rough edge of a fingernail. His breath on her hair. The power he could wield over her, both body and mind… If she let him…

She hesitated a beat too long. She sucked in a breath, but it whooshed out again as he spun her round. She glimpsed the molten steel in his gaze before his lips clashed with hers. Hard, impatient. If she'd been able, she'd have used her hands to push him away but they were trapped between them. His heart pounded heavily against one palm; his car keys dug into her chest in the other.

She had no time to think as sensations battered at her. The heat of his hands on her bare back, her breasts flattened against his rock-solid chest, the sound of her pulse thundering in her ears.

As if he commanded it, her lips opened beneath his, softening and allowing his tongue entry, duelling with hers in an erotic battle of wills. His taste swirled through her mouth, the after-taste of coffee, and something darker, richer, smoother.

There was nothing gentle about it; this assault on the senses was nothing like last night's getting-reacquainted-and-see-how-we-like-it kiss.

It thrilled her. It terrified her. It gave her the strength she needed to push him away for the second time in as many days. She glared up at him, at the sharp angles of his face, harsh with a desire that had nothing to do with tenderness. Colour slashed his cheeks, his lips. She sucked in air, found it rich with his scent.

His eyes…she couldn't read them behind the storm she saw there. 'Who do you think you are, manhandling me that way?' she demanded, and was appalled at the breathy, *needy* sound of her voice.

'You're over him or you wouldn't have let me kiss you. Not last night. Not now. And definitely not like that.'

Like he really meant it.

Rather than tingly, her lips felt swollen and numb. She ran an experimental finger over them to check that they were still there. He'd told her last night that he'd enjoyed it, and that she had, too.

'Why did you come back, Mariel?'

'I told you, I—'

'Aside from catching up with family.'

She forced herself to take a slow, steadying breath. To take a mental step away from what had just happened here and focus on Dane's much more important question. 'I want to create my own fashion label, set up my own boutique.'

'You could have done that overseas.' His voice lost some of its hard edge. 'Or didn't you think Paris was big enough for the two of you?'

Because her legs barely supported her, she sank onto the nearest chair. 'It wasn't that.' She stared at her hands in her lap. He had to ask, didn't he? Better to get it over with.

He took a chair, turned it around and sat astride it, leaning his forearms on the back. 'Tell me.'

'Luc's a fashion photographer; smooth and sophisticated, and he swept an innocent girl like me away.'

At the low, throaty sound she looked up to see Dane's jaw knotted. He nodded brusquely. 'Go on.'

'He liked my designs, but he liked my face better so I modelled for him. We went into business together. The money rolled in, we got involved, I moved into his apartment. It never occurred to me not to trust him. But it turns out Luc's a drug dealer *and* he was having a fling on the side. I was just a useful addition to his cashflow. He was arrested on Christmas Day. I was taken in for questioning, too, and fingerprinted before being released.'

'The bastard.'

'Yes.' Remembered humiliation washed through her. 'My family knows nothing of this, and I want to keep it that way.'

'You have my word on that.'

The reassuring touch of his hand on hers threatened

to open the floodgate on unshed tears. And unwanted desire. She tugged her hand away, swiped at her eyes. 'So…anyway, I want to set up business here, but finances are a little tight right now.'

His brow lifted. 'I'd have thought you'd be laughing all the way to the… Don't tell me…'

'Yep. It's gone.' She rubbed at the tension in her neck. She felt like such a fool. 'And I'm afraid now my name's been in the press here—and linked with you— that they'll dig up the dirt I left behind.'

'Not if we give them something else to focus on and write about. Keep them interested in the here and now.'

'What do you mean?'

'We give them the impression we're a couple.'

'Couple?' she choked out.

'With eyes only for each other.'

A strangled noise escaped her throat. *As if.* 'There must be another way.'

'If you can think of one I'd like to hear it.'

Thing was, she couldn't—because her stunned mind was on overload, trying to process his outrageous idea. Still, maybe if they went on a few dates. Movies, theatre, a dinner or two…

'I need a regular companion to take some of the heat off this Bachelor of the Year thing,' he continued. 'Someone to accompany me to functions. It'll be good publicity for you, too, and if they do find anything about Paris my influence with the media here could come in handy. As for finance—I have an empty ground-floor room near my office that you can use rent-free to get your business started.'

She was still stuck on 'regular'. 'How regular are we talking?'

His eyes were like charcoal now, and intense. 'You'll move in with me—'

'Whoa. Hold it. *Move in with you?*'

'It's safer that way.'

'Safer for who?' Her gaze narrowed. 'And what's your definition of safe?'

'Your parents are away; you don't want to be up in that big house all by yourself. No one has to know what goes on behind closed doors, Mariel.'

Not an answer. Not an answer at all. 'So in the public's eyes we're a couple?'

'Lovers,' he corrected.

Heat spurted through her veins at the mental image. 'So we've gone from companion and a couple of dates to *lovers*?'

His gaze remained steady on hers. 'I won't pretend not to want you in my bed, Mariel.'

'What makes you think I'd want to be there?' she shot back.

What made her think she could resist?

'Vibes,' he said. 'Zings. Whatever you call them, they've been humming between us since last night. Can't say I'm happy about it. It complicates things.'

'For once we're in total agreement.'

'Problem is, we both want the same thing—but I'm the only one here willing to talk about it.'

Pressing her lips together to stop herself from giving in, she willed herself to look at him. Were his eyes a deeper colour?

'Your eyes are answer enough.' His gaze lowered to her breasts, which suddenly felt full and heavy. 'Then there's the way your body respon—'

'All right, stop right there.' She struggled to find air.

Why was there no air in here? Damn him for making her feel vulnerable.

For making her feel more alive than she had in years.

His expression didn't change, she noted with envy. How could he sit here so cool and casual and discuss the term 'lovers' and what amounted to a business arrangement in the same sentence?

She took another swift breath. It didn't matter; let him think what he liked about sleeping arrangements. Getting her business up and running was the most important thing right now. Good publicity and a place to set up. Forget vibes. And zings.

And if that meant living in Dane's house and masquerading as his lover… *An affair.* She swallowed… She'd bite the bullet and do it.

'Okay. Two sophisticated people like us should be able to pull it off without too many dramas. But this is a business arrangement. I'll pay you back once my business starts making money.'

She reminded herself he wasn't the type of man she dated. She loved glitz and glamour, and sophisticated men with a sense of style, whereas Dane still obviously didn't give a hang about appearances.

She needed to keep that in mind and put this unwanted, unhelpful attraction she had aside. For her career's sake.

For her sanity's sake.

As for Dane and his women… 'Though this is not in any sense a proper relationship, I do have a proviso.' She wanted to jump up and pace, but made herself sit still, lean back and meet his eyes. 'Men are very low on my priority list at the moment, so it won't be a problem on my part, but I won't tolerate any indiscretions from you while we're…together.'

'That goes without saying.'

'No. It doesn't. I won't be made a fool of again.'

'You've got it wrong, Mariel. The Frenchman was the fool.' Dane rose, returned the chair to its proper place and, with a gesture obviously aimed at taking her mind off her troubles, jangled the keys in front of her face.

'Oh…' Somehow he'd managed to steal them away. How had she allowed that to happen?

He opened her hand, dropped them in her palm. 'Let's go look at your new business premises and pick up this car of yours.'

Moments later Mariel ran her fingers over the Porsche's polished silver finish. 'Nice.'

'*Nice?* It's a 911 Carrera. A very expensive piece of precision machinery.'

'So am I, darling.' His eyes met hers over the bonnet and she wished she could unsay the flirty words which once would have brought a laugh to his lips. This time his lips didn't even begin to crack a smile.

She slid into the driver's seat, adjusted the mirrors while Dane made himself comfortable beside her—if sitting ramrod-straight *and* listing her way like a sinking ship could be termed comfortable.

'Relax, I'm not seventeen any more,' she reassured him.

'You've been driving in Europe for ten years. Don't forget which side of the road you're supposed to be on,' he told her. 'And remember, driving a car's like making love. You handle her gently.'

'Really?' She caressed the steering wheel a moment, studying him closely until he turned a quiet shade of pink. 'That's where I disagree with you. I'd say it's more about passion. Fast and furious.' She flashed him a quick grin and pressed her foot hard on the accelerator.

'What's the dress code for tomorrow night's do?' she asked ten minutes later as they coasted down the freeway towards the haze-covered city. 'Black tie? Formal?'

'Yes.'

'I'll need to buy a dress.'

His head was tilted back on the headrest, and his sunglasses hid his eyes, but she felt his gaze on her. 'Just keep in mind that I want to be able to slide my hands down your spine when we smooch on the dance floor.'

The way he said it—slow, sexy and appreciative— sent hot and cold shivers down her back. To make sure he didn't get the wrong idea, she said, 'To give everyone the impression we're a couple, right?'

He didn't answer.

She cleared her throat. 'Any further requests? Colour?'

'Surprise me. But make sure the zip glides easily. I wouldn't want to snag the fabric.'

Her pulse did a fast blip.

'When we get to town we'll organise a credit card for you,' he said. 'I'm guessing you'll want the whole deal: shoes, hair, etcetera. It's an important occasion for me, so don't skimp.'

'I never do.' Rather, she never had. 'So what's the evening about?'

'It's the year's major fund-raiser for a charity I founded a few years ago called OzRemote. This dinner and ball raises funds to support kids in the Outback with no access to computers or modern technology.'

'So you donate computers?'

'It's more involved than that. Money raised can pay

experts in the field to visit remote stations, instal equipment and offer technological support. I've got a trip coming up soon which will take me as far as the northwest corner of the state.'

'As I remember, Bachelor of the Year entrants have to raise a certain amount of money before they're eligible for judging and the "fun" part with the babes.'

'Correct.' He named a figure that had her nodding with approval.

'Impressive. I'll be sure to choose something appropriate to the occasion.'

The office space Dane was offering her was small, but Mariel focused on the positives. She had an address for her business when she eventually opened. Somewhere to store stock, spread out her designs and create in the meantime. She could renovate the little space at the front, dress up the window to attract customers. Employ her own tailor. Dreams, she thought. But they were *her* dreams, and Dane was going to help make them happen.

After he dropped her at the car dealer she collected her car, then drove back to her parents' home and packed her stuff to take to the city. She planned to spend the rest of the day on the all-important purchase of that evening gown.

Since this was an annual event, before leaving home she surfed the Internet for information on last year's ball. There she found a photograph of Dane and a prominent politician's daughter.

Blonde, big-breasted, statuesque. Naturally. Her full-length gown was an elegant sweep of crimson and the neckline dipped low. Very low. Dane's hand was curled around the woman's bare shoulder, hugging her close. Mariel ignored the little twinge. Her emotions were *not* going to become involved in this…*affair* they were embarking on.

It was late afternoon when she pulled up outside the address he'd given her in one of North Adelaide's leafy upscale streets and rang him to say she'd arrived. No pesky reporters that she could see as the high gates swung open.

She took a moment to admire the magnificent two-storey villa, with its bay window and its intricate detail in the veranda columns, stark white against the dark stonework of the nineteenth-century dwelling. A stone cherub cavorted in the midst of a circle of carefully tended low shrubs.

She manoeuvred her car into the empty spot beside Dane's Porsche and sat a moment, rolling her head back on the headrest. She was smart enough to know this arrangement couldn't lead anywhere. Dane wasn't her type, and he didn't do long-term relationships. But, oh, he only had to stand in the same room with her and her libido responded with a kind of sit-up-and-beg.

She didn't have time to ponder further because Dane appeared to help her unload her car. She followed him through a back door in the garage and around to the rear of the house.

Greenery and a variety of colourful flowering bushes filled an area enclosed by high stone walls. An in-ground pool mirrored the sky. A wall of glass doors, clearly a modern addition, opened onto the deck. He led her inside, through a kitchen boasting the latest appliances while retaining its old-world charm. They passed comfortable-looking dark leather couches and a ver-milion rug on a polished blonde-wood floor. But it was

the stunning chessboard on the coffee table that commanded her immediate attention.

'Oh, wow! This is magnificent.' She wandered over
for a closer inspection.

'Black and white crystal. Handcrafted. One of a kind.'

Mariel picked up the king. It was comparable to a
shampoo bottle in height, and like the other major
pieces was tipped in gold. Dane flicked a switch on the
side of the board, which was inlaid with mirrors and
frosted glass, and the whole thing lit up from beneath.
Another switch changed the colour of the light.

'That is one of the most magnificent boards I've
ever seen.'

'I don't suppose you've learned to play?' he asked
hopefully.

'You know me—couldn't sit still long enough.'

'Pity. Nothing I like better than a challenging game
of chess.'

And obviously he didn't get the opportunity often,
she thought, noting the fine layer of dust covering the
entire thing. 'Your father taught you, didn't he?'

'One of the few lessons of any value that I learned
from him.' His clipped, cold tone didn't invite further
conversation on the matter.

Thoughtful, she set the piece down. It saddened her
to think that after all these years there was obviously
still bitterness between them. Not that she blamed
Dane—it was just sad.

Upstairs, they passed an open doorway. 'Is this your
home office?' Without waiting for an invitation, she
wandered to the balcony. Adelaide's high-rise buildings
jutted into an azure sky smeared with orange in the
lowering sun, its reflection in the glass of the buildings

flashing over the nearby golf course's casuarinas and pine trees. She breathed in the scents of summer foliage. Someone was cooking something Oriental; the fragrance of lemongrass and chilli wafted to her nose.

She turned to study the room. An over-crammed bookcase towered against one wall; an antique green lamp sat on the desk beside a modern computer. School trophies and a collection of model cars were displayed on another shelf.

'Come on, you can explore later.'

Dane opened another door and set her small rolling suitcase down. A breeze drifted through a partially open window.

Mariel saw a pair of French doors that opened onto the balcony, maroon drapes tied back with tassels, black lacquered furniture, a matching antique full-length oval mirror on a stand. The bed was covered in a quilt of the deepest merlot. He'd added a black throw and a couple of overstuffed turquoise cushions.

'There's air-conditioning if you prefer.'

'Fresh air's fine.'

'The bathroom's next door down the hall. You'll have it all to yourself; I had my own *en suite* built into the master bedroom.'

'Thanks.' She laid the day's purchases on the bed.

'Come down when you're ready and I'll fix us something for tea.'

As in they'd be dining in? With all these undercurrents swirling them into dangerous waters? She wanted, *needed*, to be amongst people. Lots of people. To go to the city and smell hot Adelaide pavement and hear familiar Aussie accents.

'Let's eat out,' she said. 'I know just the place.'

CHAPTER FIVE

THE SETTING sun had turned the sky gold. The city streets still held the day's heat. Tourists and locals strolled along North Terrace, past the lovely old railway building, now home to a casino and Hyatt hotel, where fairylights sparkled in trees. Others were enjoying drinks at open-air bars on the other side of the busy street.

From their little table Mariel glared at the spot where she and Dane had enjoyed many a meal—only the old pie cart wasn't there. A line of waiting taxis now filled the kerbside. 'But it was a more-than-century-old Adelaide icon,' she grumbled. 'I was going to shout you a pie floater for letting me drive…and for being a good sport about the close brush with the foliage…the very *soft*, very *overhanging* foliage.'

He tossed back a mouthful of beer. 'It's not really pie weather.'

'Any weather is pie floater weather, and I haven't tasted one in ten years.' She pursed her lips to suck lemonade through a straw. 'You know, I tried explaining it to Luc… How do you convince someone, especially a French someone, with vast gastronomic experience, that an upturned meat pie swimming in thick green pea soup and smothered with tomato sauce is a culinary delicacy? And has to be eaten standing at the kerbside, rubbing shoulders with cleaners to cops to politicians come rain or shine?'

He tipped back his glass, swallowed, then nodded. 'I guess you have to experience it.'

'Yeah…' She dropped her chin on an upturned palm and sucked on her straw some more, and for a moment they were kids again, shovelling pie and soup into their mouths, arguing over who had more sauce, waiting for the piecrust to turn sodden…

She didn't notice him move until the warmth of his hand touched hers. He slid his thumb over the inside of her wrist. 'So we'll make our own.'

The way he said that—as if he wasn't talking about pies, but something much more pleasurable. Her gaze darted to his and she found herself drawn unwillingly into the sensuous promise she saw there.

The guy watching her wasn't that teenager she'd known. Dane, the man, wouldn't hesitate to take what he wanted, be it in business or pleasure, and the knowledge shivered down her spine. She tried to tug her arm away, but his grip tightened.

'Don't,' he said, and lifted it to his lips, laying a line of kisses from the middle of her palm to her elbow, watching her with that heated gaze as he did so.

Sensation sparkled along her skin—much too brightly.

Her pulse beat a tattoo beneath his lips—much too loudly.

'We're meant to be lovers, remember?' The low timbre of his voice vibrated against her flesh.

Drawing a breath, she shook her head, as much to

clear it as to negate his words. 'No one's watching. You don't have to…do that.'

'Not true—you never know who's watching, and you should be as aware of that as I. Let's go home.'

'Dinner is served, *mademoiselle*.' Dane set the steaming, aromatic plates down on the French-polished dining room table. Two pies floated in a sea of pea-green, looking incongruous amidst the room's old-world elegance.

'*Ah, merci, garçon, c'est très magnifique.*' She smiled at him, a smile that reminded him of long-ago days, and said, 'But it's traditional to eat it standing.'

'To hell with tradition,' he said, pulling out a chair for her. He passed her a half-empty bottle of tomato sauce with the instruction to, 'Leave some for me.'

'You'll be lucky.'

Dane watched her up-end the bottle over her meal, then pass it to him. Only Mariel Davenport could eat a soggy pie dripping with red and green and maintain some modicum of elegance.

She sipped at her glass of wine. 'So your dad hasn't moved to the city?'

'No.' He stabbed his fork into the pie, hacked off a corner.

She frowned, censure in her eyes. 'I know it was bad for you as a kid. But he's old—he must be in his late seventies now. How does he manage on his own?'

'You know my father—he has a fit and healthy forty-year-old woman drop by to help him *manage*.' He chewed more vigorously, making his jaw ache.

'Oh.'

'Exactly.'

Mariel knew his circumstances. How both his

parents had indulged in extra-marital relationships. How his mother had left to live interstate with a new guy when Dane was seven. And how his father had paid for his only son to board at the exclusive school he and Mariel had attended because he didn't want the inconvenience of a son underfoot.

'I've done okay without his support,' he said into the silence. He'd worked his way through uni like any regular guy, waiting tables to pay his own way until he and Justin had set up their own business. It had exploded—way beyond their expectations. Five years, and financially he'd achieved what some would take a lifetime to do.

He didn't need family. Didn't need anyone. The women who flitted into his life either flitted right out again when they realised he wasn't there for the long haul, or understood where he was coming from and were happy with a temporary arrangement.

Wealth was happiness.

Strange, but tonight he didn't feel as happy about that as he'd thought. He set down his cutlery with a rattle of silver on china, reached for his wine, took a long, slow swallow.

'So I take it you've never changed your mind about settling down and having kids?'

Had she read his thoughts? His fingers tightened on his glass. 'You know me: terminal bachelor. As for kids—never in a million years. No way. No how.'

'That's sad, Dane. You're letting your own child-hood rule who you are now. There's nothing more precious than family. If you do want to talk about anything, at any time…' Mariel set her own cutlery to one side of the plate and met his eyes in the intimate lighting.

He nodded once. Mariel. Sincere, honest, caring. Soothing his mood the way she'd always done. The one person he'd always been able to count on. Unfortunately, right now he wanted her to soothe a lot more than his current mood. And with a lot more than words.

Forget it, Huntington.

Reining in his runaway libido, he straightened, flipping his linen napkin onto the table. 'I've got some fresh peaches, or a frozen—'

'Nothing more for me, thanks.' Patting her mouth on her own napkin, she rose. 'I'm going to be lazy and not help you with the clearing up. I haven't finished exploring yet.'

'Do you want coffee?'

'I'd rather have ice water, thanks.'

When he'd cleared the dishes, he found her in the adjoining family room, where she'd discovered his photographic equipment and was fiddling with his camera. She snapped his picture a few times in rapid succession, checked the results in the little screen. 'Definitely male model material. I didn't think so earlier, but I've changed my mind. I'll borrow this for a while,' she went on. 'Upload these pictures on your computer. Do you have a website?'

'No.' He set their glasses on the coffee table and began walking towards her.

'Not even for your business?'

He narrowed his eyes at her. 'You would *not* want to put those pictures on my business website.'

'You must be on a networking site?'

'Don't have time for gossip.'

'For socialising and sharing,' she corrected. She snapped him again, studied the image. 'There was a time when you used to share everything with me.' Her eyes met his, then cooled. 'Well, almost everything.'

Shadows of their youth swirled in those green depths, and for a moment he was lost in another time, another world. Shared hot fudge sundaes at the movies. Beach towels and barbecued sausages. The time she'd cheated on a test. The day he got his driver's licence and took her for a spin in his father's BMW without his knowledge and put a ding in the passenger door…

He reached for the camera but she'd already whipped it behind her back. 'Getting slow in your old age,' she taunted.

'Or you're getting sneakier.' He closed the gap till their bodies were a handspan apart. Breathed in the scent of her honeysuckle shampoo.

'How do you mean?' She blinked up at him, all innocence.

He set his hands on her shoulders, felt the fragile bones beneath the smooth firm flesh. 'You know exactly what I mean. Using your eyes and the *you-used-to-share-everything-with-me* line as a distraction.'

As if the shoestring straps beneath his fingers weren't distraction enough. Not bra straps, he noted. Just dress straps…

Barely touching her, he slid his fingertips down her arms and felt tiny hairs on her skin rise as a shiver trembled through her. Imprisoning her against his body with one hand, he reached over her shoulders for the camera with the other, and down…

The reason for the clinch was forgotten. Everything was wiped clean from his mind except the sensation of her breasts snug against his chest and the fragrance of her skin. His free hand slid over the smooth flesh of her naked back, each vertebra in turn, as he slipped beneath the edge of her dress and the crisp fabric.

Her head tipped back and her lips were right there, smack bang against his throat. Warm, soft. Mind-numbing.

Anticipation tingled on his lips, danced on his tongue…

Damn.

This wasn't some nameless woman in a dark unfamiliar room where the slaking of lust was the only thing they had in common. He swore silently. Hell of a moment for his better self to show up. He wanted to throw back his head and howl.

Unlike last night or this afternoon, he knew he'd not stop this time until he had her writhing in pleasure beneath him. And she wasn't ready for that. Nor was he willing to take the risk with the ball happening tomorrow night.

So this time it was he who took a step back, kissed her lightly on those waiting lips with their sweet promise of passion and said, 'I've got some last-minute details to go over for tomorrow night; I'd best be getting on with them.'

She blinked at him as if she'd just woken up. 'Don't let me keep you.' Her husky voice dragged like barbs across his over-aroused senses.

'You might want to turn in early. Tomorrow night will be a long one.' He let the suggestion hang.

She nodded. Didn't say a word.

He turned away before he could change his mind, and climbed the stairs to his study. A man of his experience with the opposite sex knew when it was better to wait.

* * *

When Mariel came downstairs next morning Dane was already dressed. A suitcase and a suit bag sat by the kitchen table. He was standing at the breakfast bar, reading the newspaper and drinking coffee.

'Good morning.'

He looked up at her greeting, his brow puckering as if he was uncomfortable seeing her there. 'Good morning.'

He resumed skimming his paper, but she could feel the tension emanating from him like vibrating wire. 'Did I break a house rule or something?'

He flicked to the next page. 'No. Of course not.'

'What, then?'

He looked up again, met her gaze. 'I've never shared breakfast with a woman in this house; it caught me off guard.'

'You're kidding me. Dane Casanova Huntington has never had a sleepover?'

He studied the paper once more. 'I didn't say that.'

'So, what—they're the Cinderella kind?'

'I have a penthouse apartment in the city.' He tossed back his coffee, set his mug on the counter with a snap. 'I'm going to be busy all day, organising for this evening.' He stared through the window at the pool. 'I've booked a suite for us at the hotel, so I'll arrange a car to pick you up when you're ready to leave here.'

She was still processing the first bit. 'You keep a city apartment for *sex*?'

He exhaled slowly. 'I want to keep my private life exactly that. Private. I've also made appointments for a massage, spa treatment, hair and make-up,' he continued, as if she hadn't interrupted him with a question he obviously wasn't comfortable answering. 'Did I forget anything?'

She was still catching up. 'I don't think so,' she said slowly. 'I could do with a little pampering. Do all your partners get the star treatment?'

She saw nothing in his gaze, as if he'd deliberately blanked it. 'Tonight's important, Mariel.'

'I know that.'

'We'll be staying overnight, so if there's anything else you might need…'

Like her contraceptive pills? 'Overnight?'

'We want to give them something to speculate about. Isn't that what we agreed?'

Oh. 'Of course. The *press*.' The reason for this charade.

The press hadn't been the reason he'd kissed her yesterday.

Picking up his bag, he headed for the door, jingling his car keys. Impatiently or edgily? 'I'll join you in our suite at six-thirty.'

Mariel's entire afternoon session in the hotel's spa and beauty rooms were pure bliss. Courtesy of Dane, she was massaged and exfoliated, buffed and polished until her skin tingled, her complexion glowed, her hair shone and her nails sparkled. She had *The Best* in facial and hair treatments.

But beneath the pampering she couldn't stop thinking about this public affair she was rushing headlong into. She considered herself worldly enough to understand that mutual desire sometimes came without strings.

Except when it involved Dane.

She considered herself sensible enough to accept that it was possible to enjoy sexual intimacy without falling in love.

Except when it involved Dane.

And when a high-profile celebrity like Dane and she went their separate ways, as they inevitably would, she was going to have to live with the media attention for a long time.

She would *not* think about the other bad stuff she might have to learn to live with. Bad emotional stuff. Maybe she should make an advance booking for meditation or psychotherapy? She was likely to need it.

At six o'clock, in one of the suite's bedrooms, she stepped into her dress. A one-off European designer gown, it fitted so snugly it took a few moments to shimmy the silky white fabric up her body. As she tugged the zipper in the side seam closed the final wrinkles smoothed out.

But her nerves didn't. They tied knots in her stomach as she stepped into her sparkly stilettos, added a final touch to her upswept hairstyle and make-up. A delicate necklace of black diamonds flashed at her throat; a matching bracelet adorned her right arm. Her long platinum earrings swung as she studied her reflection side on.

Satisfied, she sorted her bag, then paced to the window to watch the late sunlight turn the River Torrens primrose.

She turned at the sound of the keycard being swiped in the door. Ridiculous to feel her heart pounding as if she was on her first date. She knew she looked fine, that this was exactly the type of gown his partners wore. Anyway, what did it matter what Dane—the king of dressing down—thought?

It mattered.

Taking a steadying breath, she turned. How did he manage to snatch her breath away every time? He wore black trousers and a made-to-measure white silk shirt that once again emphasised his shoulders and clung to his broad chest. His hair was still slightly damp and curled over the collar.

She fought the temptation to walk right on over there and smooth it with her fingers. To lean in and press her lips to that distracting V of tanned skin at his throat. Instead she kept her cool. 'No tie to a formal function— why do you ignore your own rules, Dane?'

'Because I can.'

Dane's answer was vague as his eyes swept down Mariel's body. God help him. How was he going to function tonight with that siren's temptation beside him? Because he suddenly seemed to have momentarily lost the power of speech, he motioned her to turn around with his fingers.

White. Floor-length. Skinny. Backless—below backless, in fact, revealing the lower indentation of her spine. Low scooped neckline that dipped…and kept on dipping. Which made him wonder how she kept the whole thing from sliding off her shoulders. A slit up one side that looked as if it had been created by an over-zealous pirate's sword. He had to wonder if she wore panties at all…

'You want to talk rules?' he murmured, unable—unwilling—to tear his hungry eyes away. 'That dress is a rule-breaker. In fact, it should be illegal. One of your creations?'

Dismissing his suggestion with, 'I don't wear my own designs,' she whirled to face him again, the split in the fabric parting to show the long length of one leg. 'You think it's too much?'

'More like not enough.' He frowned, perplexed at his own reaction. He'd never been a conservative man, and enjoyed a good-looking woman as much as the next man.

'It's the latest Veronique design—*Sophisticated Style*. What's your problem?'

Problem? He'd always been more than happy to have the object of every man's desire on his arm. But was he *sophisticated* enough to make it through the evening knowing every guy would be falling over themselves to catch another eyeful of all that exposed skin? Because it was Mariel's skin. His own flesh tightened, tingled as heat simmered beneath its surface.

Weird. He didn't understand himself. On any other woman the gown would have looked stunning. *Did* look stunning. If tonight hadn't been so important, if he hadn't been the one who'd organised the event, he'd have called the whole thing off and suggested a night in. Just the two of them.

Fact was, he didn't want everyone ogling what he suddenly realised he wanted to ogle himself in the privacy of their own suite. What the hell was happening to him?

'Don't you have something…more? A wrap, perhaps?' *Blimey, just listen to yourself.* He needed to change his attitude fast if he wanted this evening to go smoothly.

Of course she looked lovely. Gorgeous. He'd be the envy of every man, and possibly every woman, in the room. And he intended to make sure everyone knew it was him she'd be with at the end of the evening.

Mariel stared at the grim-faced man before her. She knew she looked good, the dress wasn't vulgar, just sexy, so she refused to feel hurt or embarrassed or any of those vulnerable emotions. Temper was preferable, but it wouldn't be wise moments before they were due downstairs. 'No, I don't have a wrap. I don't need one.' She barely restrained herself from raising her voice. 'And, to use your own words, I'm going to wear this dress *because I can*. And I can—very well.' She snatched up her bag.

She had to pass him to get to the door, but a light hand on her arm stopped her.

'I apologise,' he said stiffly. 'You took me by surprise, that's all. You look sensational.'

Too little, too late, she thought, but she could try to be gracious—they had an entire evening in the public eye to get through. 'All right.' She let him curl her hand around his arm. 'We'll put it behind us and try to enjoy the evening.'

But how would the evening end, when the ball was over and an annoyed Cinderella retired to her suite with her suddenly stuffy prince?

CHAPTER SIX

MARIEL watched the floor numbers blink as the elevator descended. They stood apart, but their respective fragrances mingled, their breathing the only sound in a stilted silence until the doors opened and Dane took her hand and wrapped it around his arm once more.

The hotel lobby was alive with light and movement. Airline staff checking in, tourists heading out for the city's nightspots. Photographers snapping their arrival and that of other important guests, interviewing Dane about this evening's event and, as expected, their renewed acquaintance.

'What are your plans now, Ms Davenport?' asked a journalist, shoving a microphone in her face.

'I intend to start my own fashion label.'

'And your relationship with Mr Huntington?'

She met Dane's eyes and smiled coyly, allowed him to pull her a little closer and encircle her waist. *For the publicity.* 'We're just good friends.' Let the press put whatever slant on that they chose.

They passed a glorious Chihuly glass sculpture on their way down the pink marble staircase to the ballroom, where black mirrors on the ceiling reflected the glitter from crystal chandeliers, candlelight and a fortune in jewellery. An orchestra was playing light classical, and the scents of fresh flowers mingled with the latest French perfumes while several prominent politicians, including those holding the youth and education portfolios, mingled with society's elite.

Their table was the closest to the podium and filled with The Important People. She didn't feel up to any in-depth conversation tonight, and to Mariel's relief Justin's wife, Cass, was seated beside her, looking chic in a simple black halterneck gown, her chestnut-brown hair curling softly about her face.

'I've seen your photo in magazines, but it's exciting to finally meet you in person,' Cass said when Dane introduced them. 'And that's the most stunning dress I've ever seen.' She smiled ruefully. 'I wish I could get into something like that.'

'Thank you,' Mariel replied, unable to resist tossing a glance over her shoulder at Dane, who was standing behind her chair with Justin.

Leaning close, he ran his hand lightly over the nape of her neck and halfway down her spine and murmured, 'I think the challenge will be in the getting out of it.'

'I heard that, Dane Huntington,' Cass said, her eyes twinkling up at him.

As she was supposed to, Mariel knew. 'Indeed it will be,' she murmured back, then turned to Cass with a smile. 'So, you and Justin are recently married? I love weddings; tell me about yours.'

As Mariel had predicted, Dane moved away at the mention of nuptials and began conversing with a distinguished elderly man at their table. Justin sat down beside his wife and slung an arm around her shoulders, happy to join their conversation.

The food began arriving. Dane was busy between courses, introducing Mariel to people at the thirty or so tables skirting the dance floor. They ranged from colleagues in IT to contacts that might be useful to her in the fashion business. Everywhere he escorted her he made some sort of physical contact. A brush of his knuckles against her cheek, a finger-to-finger caress, a meaningful glance, a whispered word.

She couldn't say when the contact became more intimate. The glances hotter, the caresses more meaningful. Later, when he excused himself to talk business, she was aware that she knew where he was at any given moment. She'd look up and somehow there he'd be. And more often than not his gaze would meet hers. How long could you continue to play a game when the rules threatened to change?

During coffee he made an inspiring speech about the social, economic and technological disadvantages faced by people living in remote areas of the country, and how OzRemote was helping to address these issues.

Mariel couldn't take her eyes off him—along with every other woman there, she suspected. He was by far the most charismatic man in the room. He spoke with knowledge, passion and eloquence. She could understand why he wanted to shrug off the *Babe*'s Bachelor of the Year association; his respected business reputation didn't deserve it. He'd only participated in the contest to help raise funds for his charity.

'How long have you known Dane?' she asked Cass as they wandered back from the ladies' room later.

'Five years. I met him around the same time I met

Justin. They were just getting their business off the ground.'

Cass stopped, took a seat on a sofa, and Mariel joined her.

'I've never seen him look at any of his other dates the way he does you,' Cass said.

Mariel couldn't allow herself to think about that. She dismissed it with a half-laugh. 'That's because we've known each other for years. I'm not his usual type.'

'No. You're not a blondie, for a start. And he can't seem to leave you alone. This is the first time I've ever seen him look remotely serious about anyone since Sandy. But that crashed in a big way.'

Instantly curious, Mariel shifted closer. 'Who's Sandy?'

Cass lowered her voice and said, 'You didn't hear this from me, but Sandy was a woman Dane was dating a couple of years back. We all thought it might have been serious but then, as Justin tells it, Sandy tried to hurry things along by getting pregnant.'

Her words ricocheted through Mariel's body like a volley of bullets and lodged deep in her own womb. 'Dane has a *child*?'

Cass shook her head. 'Turned out she wasn't pregnant—just out to snare herself a rich husband. But he wasn't the happy father-to-be she expected. She changed her story quick, but it was too late.'

'She never understood him, then.'

Mariel understood. His childhood experiences were preventing him from taking the risk of making a family life of his own, and that, in her opinion, was incredibly sad.

The band struck up a lively nineties party tune as

they returned to their table, and couples took to the dance floor. Dane leaned close and said, 'My father's here. He's leaving in a moment, so we'll go say hello together. For appearances' sake.'

'Oh, Dane, he's supporting you here tonight? That's fantastic. Isn't it?' She looked up at him, but his face was a blank wall. At least his father had made an effort, she thought as he escorted her through the crowd.

'Mr Huntington.' She shook his hand, leaned in and dropped a quick kiss on his whiskered cheek. 'Lovely to see you again.'

'Mariel. And for God's sake call me Daniel.' His handshake was firm, the skin paper-thin. He smiled, and the heavy lines around his mouth deepened. 'Haven't seen you in years. This is Barbara.' He turned to the woman beside him, who was dressed in a low-necked frilly blouse and a long black skirt.

'Barbara. How do you do?' Mariel extended her hand and estimated 'Silicone Barbie' to be in her mid-forties.

Barbie's botoxed lips curved. 'It's nice to meet you.' Then her gaze rolled up to the stiff-necked man beside Mariel. 'Hello, Dane.'

He inclined his head. 'Barbara.'

'Oh, this is one of my favourite songs, and Daniel's not up to dancing tonight—just one dance, Dane?' she said, blinking her false eyelashes at him.

Dane could have refused, but he had a few things to say to his father's live-in lover. Now seemed as good a time as any. He turned to Mariel, let his lips linger on the sweet curve of her cheek. 'Excuse me, Queen Bee. This won't take long.'

'It's fine.' She waved him away. 'I'll keep your dad company.'

'I'm glad I've got you alone,' Barbara said the moment Daniel and Mariel were out of earshot. 'I wanted to explain about that night. The man you saw me with was my financial adviser.'

'Yeah.' Dane laughed without humour and leaned close so only she could hear. 'Since when did financial advice extend to a candle-lit rendezvous? A very intimate rendezvous, from where I was sitting.'

'I—'

'I'm glad you have a financial adviser, Barbara, because you're going to need one.' Not wanting to attract the nearby dancers' attention, he kept his voice low. 'You've wasted eight years of your life waiting for Dad to depart this world, because he's not going to leave you a cent. You're *not* going to get your greedy, *cheating* hands on the Huntington fortune.'

Her nostrils flared, her eyes widened and she tried to pull away, but Dane tightened his hold. 'He hasn't told you he lost everything he owned in the share market crash, has he? *I* bought the family property from him, to get him out of financial ruin. The home you're living in is *mine*. In fact, the dinner you just enjoyed was at *my* expense.'

The skin around her pumped-up lips turned white. 'You're lying.'

'Ask him.' Watching shock bleach the colour from her face was one of his life's more satisfying moments, and his smile was genuine as he escorted her back to her table. 'Thanks for the dance and the chance to talk, Barbara.'

Instantly she was forgotten as he turned to his partner for the evening. 'May I have the pleasure of this dance?'

Without waiting for an answer, he took Mariel's hand and led her to the dance floor. The band switched to a slow, romantic number and he came to a halt in the middle of the room, drew her close. So close that he could see tiny flecks of navy amongst the emerald in her amazing eyes.

He'd never noticed that before. He was discovering a lot of things about Mariel that he'd never noticed before. The tiny mole at the outer corner of her right eye. The way her eyes turned dark—midnight in a deep forest—when she was aroused.

They were dark now.

She stepped in closer, so he could no longer see her face, but her fingers stole up his shirt, the sides of his neck, then beneath his hair, where she stroked lightly with her fingernails.

The music throbbed in time with his heartbeat as his hands drifted over her bare back, absorbing the silken warmth of her skin, the fine hairs at the nape of her neck. She smelled like a fantasy of fresh flowers rather than of her black rose trademark perfume, and he nuzzled beneath her ear to inhale deeper.

'Dane…'

He thought she whispered his name. Like a sigh. But he couldn't be sure over the sound of the music. Did she make that soft sensuous sound when she made love? he wondered.

He could find out tonight.

Her cheek against his felt cool and soft, and his lips tingled as he turned his head slightly to taste.

He couldn't resist—he traced the graceful curve of her spine, down to where it arched against him. 'You were right. This is an excellent choice of gown,' he murmured.

'*I* thought so,' she murmured back, and he felt her cheek bunch against his as she smiled.

The music faded, or perhaps he just stopped hearing it. With his hand still on her back he pulled her closer, so that their bodies touched, breast to chest, thigh to thigh. She melted against him like butter on hot toast.

His body tightened, his pulse thrummed. He wanted to stay just this way, locked in this embrace, until the room was empty and they were alone.

But he was the host, and if he didn't pull away now he'd be an embarrassment to both of them.

He drew back and looked at her. Dark, *dark* eyes. Full lush lips that begged to be kissed. The pulse-point in her neck beat frantically, matching his own. 'I think that convinced them,' he muttered, a rueful smile pulling at his lips. 'It damn well convinced me.'

Her small smile took a while coming. 'Me, too.'

He escorted her back to their table, and then to give himself a moment to cool down excused himself and headed for the men's room. On his way back he saw his father, sitting alone on a sofa outside the ballroom.

He rose slowly as Dane approached, looking older than the last time he'd seen him a few months ago in the solicitor's office.

When Dane had purchased the family home so that his father could continue living there.

'Can we have a quiet word?' his father asked.

'What's on your mind?'

'I just wanted to tell you you've done a magnificent job here tonight. Thank you for inviting me and Barb to be a part of it.'

'You're welcome.' Dane's voice sounded brittle to his own ears. When his father didn't speak he asked, 'Was there something else?'

'Yes. There is,' he said slowly. 'And it's been a long

time coming. I haven't got many years left, and I've taken a good look at myself lately.' He glanced down at his feet, then looked up at Dane. 'It would have been easier to decline your invitation. Son.' He paused. 'Maybe we could let bygones be bygones and move on?'

Son. Dane wrestled with his emotions. It was the first time he could remember hearing his father acknowledge him as such. All those years when he'd wished his dad would toss him one crumb of affection. Dane had never wanted for money, privilege, social standing, but he'd have given it all away for family.

'Why now, Dad? Because I saved your ass? And you know that in the end I'm the only one who gives a damn? We both know Barbara's not going to stick around. I told her about the sale, Dad. It's time she knew.'

His father didn't answer. Just continued to watch him with tired eyes.

Despite all that had happened, deep down where it was only him and his maker, Dane yearned for the connection. But the past pain and the fear—yes, *fear*, dammit—of being hurt again was an impenetrable wall. Instead, he blocked all emotion and said, 'We've never been big on family; you're just getting sentimental in your old age.' He jutted his chin towards the woman he'd just noticed standing like an ice statue at the bottom of the marble staircase. 'Barbara's waiting.'

His father searched in his pocket for a handkerchief, then mopped his face. 'I'll be going, then. Goodnight.' He turned and began walking towards Barbara.

Shaken at his own callousness, Dane caught up, touched his father's shoulder. He was shocked at the frailty he felt beneath the shirt. 'If you need anything…'

His dad nodded without turning. 'I know.'

And as Dane watched him shuffle towards the stairs that lonely little boy inside him ached.

He'd never been so impatient for a night to end. With Mariel never far from his side, he discussed the upcoming trip north with those involved, made small talk with people he barely knew.

Outwardly he maintained his calm, professional façade, but anticipation sharpened his focus on the night ahead to a pinpoint. He couldn't wait to get Mariel alone upstairs.

Finally his hand tightened on Mariel's as the few remaining guests drifted out of the ballroom. They remained where they were while staff bustled in and out, glass and metal tinkling as they cleared tables, stacked chairs.

He looked at her. She looked back. Awareness glimmered in her eyes, desire softened her mouth. She drew a breath, drawing his attention momentarily to the amply displayed cleavage. But it wasn't only her body and the delights he knew that were awaiting his discovery that drew him to her and held him in thrall. It was the whole package.

Words were irrelevant. The whole evening had been building to this moment. Tension gripped him when their linked hands accidentally brushed his trousers. His kiss, when he leaned in, was restrained and chaste. He motioned to the door with their joined hands. 'Shall we?'

'Good idea.'

Still holding hands, they reached the door to their suite. He swiped the keycard and tugged her inside. City lights filtered through the window, casting an amber glow about the room. Even before the door clicked shut his lips were feasting on hers, and they went right on feasting as he whirled her around, pinning her against the wall. He didn't know where to put his hands first, so went with her shoulders. Smooth and fragile-boned. He barely lifted his lips to mutter, 'I can't be gentle, not tonight.'

'I never said I wanted gentle. Those were your words, not mine.' She laughed, a lightly hysterical sound. 'And you were referring to a car.'

She didn't object, and that was all he needed to know.

Tonight she was his, to pleasure and enjoy. The knowledge careened through his mind, through his limbs, as he gorged himself on her sweet honey taste. Like a crazed bee in a field of clover, he left her lips to sample every patch of bared skin, finally settling to suckle the tender spot between neck and shoulder.

Her fingers rushed up his shirt, popping buttons. Yanking the hem from his trousers, she spread the fabric wide to rub circles over his chest. The heat from her palms scorched and seduced, their impatience thrilled and tantalised.

There was no sound in their thick-panelled room save for the sounds they made themselves. It accentuated his harsh breaths, her desperate moans, fabric abrading fabric, skin rasping skin. The urgent sounds detonated small explosions inside him that reverberated like gunfire through his limbs. What they'd begun as a foil for the press had become something else entirely.

Or had they already known this was how it would be?

Impatience born of desires too long denied made his hands clumsy as he pushed the dress from her shoulders, leaving her breasts dazzlingly, breathtakingly exposed. Pale, creamy flesh. Dark, erect nipples.

Greedy now, he wanted more. He wanted all. He met her eyes, dark in the dimness. 'How does this creation come off?'

'Here.' She guided his fingers to the zip. 'It's tight.' He fumbled for a frustrating moment, then came the satisfying sound as it shirred downward. She helped him shimmy it over her hips. Her panties—if she was wearing any—went the same way as the dress. All she wore were sparkly stilettos.

Sweet heaven.

She reached out, flicked his belt buckle open, wrenched his zip down… In seconds he was as naked as she.

He toed off his shoes. His pulse was jack-hammering, his heart felt so huge, so tight, he thought it might be going into cardiac arrest. Was it possible to die of anticipation?

He twisted his fingers into her hair, pulling out pins, letting them drop wherever. Lifting her arms, she teased the silken mass out with her fingers so that it tumbled over her shoulders.

And then she was twining herself about him like a vine, gyrating her hips against his throbbing erection. She was all lean limbs and strong lines, and if his heart didn't give out he was probably going to spontaneously combust.

He'd never wanted like this, never burned this way. Tomorrow, that might concern him, but at this moment the only thing in his mind was their mutual goal. All the years till now, all the women till now, had been a dress rehearsal for this command performance.

Seemed he'd waited half a lifetime.

She'd waited a lifetime. Dane Huntington, teenage fantasy, here. With her. Mariel rubbed her lips over his, opened her mouth and drugged herself with his taste. Heat, desire, impatience. Dragging her towards oblivion. She couldn't think; her head was too filled with his scent. She could only feel. Sensations, lovely sensations, streaking over her skin and zapping through her body like golden lightning.

The ache low in her belly grew, expanded, until she was a writhing mass of wanton need. 'Now,' she demanded, arching her hips against his pulsing hardness. Instinctively she reached down between them.

His answering groan, harsh against her ear, had her shuddering. 'Protection?'

'On the Pill.'

He hefted her higher and her thighs wrapped around his waist. And he snapped, tension tearing free, his eyes smoking in the half-light, the hard planes of his body taut beneath her hands. No preliminaries—she didn't want them this time, didn't need them.

Still watching her, he shoved inside with one long thrust. They stared at each other for what seemed an endless moment, while needs and desire pulsed through their bodies and the air softened around them.

Then he withdrew a little, but only to push again, harder. Again. In a rhythm they both knew how to move to. He took, he possessed, and she met him hunger for hunger, greed for greed.

Her climax shot her into the realms of dark pleasure and bright chaos. She clung to him as he crested the wave and joined her in the sheer mindless joy of shared delight.

CHAPTER SEVEN

DANE was roused from sleep by a pounding on the door. Instantly awake, he grabbed one of the hotel's robes, stepped around last night's discarded clothing and padded to the suite's door.

Room Service with their requested breakfast. 'Good morning, sir.' The waitress smiled as he stood back to let her enter.

'Good morning.' He pushed a hand through his bedroom hair. 'It's nine o'clock already?' He'd slept like the dead. Hadn't slept like that since he didn't remember when. He did remember they'd finally found their way under the bedcovers together.

'Yes, sir. Five past, actually. We're running a little behind this morning.'

He found his wallet, dug out a tip while she set the tray on the table in the entertainment area. 'Thanks.'

'You're welcome. Have a nice day.'

'And you.'

Picking up the tray, he headed to the bedroom. Mariel blinked owlishly at him in the morning's golden light, then sat up, pulling the sheet modestly over her breasts and securing it firmly beneath her armpits.

'Good morning.' The words sounded formal and stilted to his own ears. He followed it up with a more congenial, 'I hope you're hungry.'

'Morning.'

Her hair was a wild dark halo around her face, and there was a glow in those cheeks this morning. He held himself personally responsible. But a thread of something approaching morning-after nerves wound through the satisfaction. He couldn't remember the last time he'd felt that way with a woman. Awkward. Clumsy with words.

Determined to banish it, he climbed onto the bed and set the tray between them, poured two coffees, handed her one. He figured they might both need it. He'd never felt the need nor the inclination for inane morning-after chit-chat. He either left a lover's bed before dawn or called her a taxi as soon as she woke.

'We slept in the same bed,' she said, surprising him. 'All night.' She didn't sound happy about it.

'There wasn't a lot of night left.' Thoughtful, he sipped the thick black brew. 'And, since there's only one bed, after we…' He drew back from the words. 'I figured you'd share.'

'A one-bedroom suite.' She added sugar, stirred. 'So…you *planned* this?'

Seduction 101: Never leave a woman feeling she's been taken advantage of.

He went with a smooth, 'Yes. I told you—the press want details.' He lifted the cover on a plate of fried eggs and bacon. 'We give them details—that was the plan we agreed on. Whether I slept here or on the daybed, the press will assume what we want them to assume.'

She sipped at her coffee. 'Okay. Fine.'

He was unsettled by this strange tension that had sprung up between them. He didn't understand her emotional tug of war. Last night she'd been molten lava in his hands. She wouldn't be thinking this was more than it was. Would she? She'd made it clear that after her Frenchman she wasn't going to get emotionally involved with anyone again.

'Why don't you tell me what the problem is?'

'There's no problem.' Her reply was quick, brisk, the tone casual. She smiled, but it didn't reach her eyes, and took another sip of coffee.

'We used to be able to be honest with each other—'

'Not completely.'

'Okay, you'll probably never forgive me for that, and I accept it. But I never deliberately lied to you. If we can't deal with issues that arise with our new relationship, then we *will* have a problem.'

She was silent a moment, and he thought she wasn't going to answer, but then she said, 'This is going to sound totally gauche, but I woke up and you were lying next to me naked and I don't know how to deal with this…us.' Colour bled into her cheeks and she looked down at the cup in her hands.

'Okay.' He took their cups, set them on the tray. 'I'll let you in on a secret. That makes two of us.'

'Really?'

She felt insecure. He heard it in her tone, saw it in her eyes as she darted a glance at him. 'Yes, really.' He tucked a finger under her chin. 'And don't look so surprised. I think the best thing now is to finish our breakfast, take a shower and head home. Maybe we both need some breathing space.'

'Good idea.' She took a token nibble of toast, then

dusted off her fingers in quick jerky movements. 'I think I'll just go and have that shower now.'

'Slow down.' He reached for her hand, lifted it to his lips and pressed a chaste kiss to the pulse racing at her wrist. 'Just slow down. You haven't tried your eggs. You were always crazy about cooked breakfast, if I remember correctly.'

She seemed to relax some, and managed a smile. 'And I remember you had an appetite big enough for both of us.'

He lowered her hand to the sheet. 'Still have.'

There was something dark, almost primal, in his gaze, and it had Mariel wondering whether he was still talking about food. A night's worth of stubble shadowed his jaw, and his untamed hair fell over his brow. Her heart started up the irregular beat that had become almost familiar over the past couple of days.

Clutching the sheet to her, she slid to the side of the bed. 'Good. Okay…' Her limbs went to water. She simply couldn't do sophisticated this morning—not with Dane watching her with those eyes. Eyes that soothed, yet excited. She even struggled with casual. Dane had seen every exposed inch of her last night, but in the light of day…

'I think I'll take this out onto the balcony,' he said, hefting the tray without giving her so much as a glance. Giving her privacy. Allowing her to keep her dignity. 'Nice view of the river from up here.'

She could have kissed him. No. *Erase that thought.* Before he changed his mind, she dashed naked to the wardrobe, grabbed her change of clothes and high-tailed it to the bathroom. Closed the door. Let out a ragged breath.

So much for her woman-of-the-world reputation.

She was immediately faced with her own reflection in the large mirror above the vanity. Sweet Lord, was that tousled woman with the thoroughly loved look really her? She stepped closer, staring at the wide eyes smudged with last night's mascara. The rest of her make-up had rubbed off hours ago. She explored her cheeks with her fingertips. Was that afterglow or whisker burn? *Emotion or lust?*

She whirled away and turned on the shower, waited for the room to steam up. Why couldn't she be as casual about last night as Dane? No mention of whether he'd enjoyed what they'd done—he'd been more interested in breakfast.

Not that she'd expected pretty words or a tender declaration of feelings. Not from a man like Dane. The truth was she didn't know what to expect from a serial playboy. After one short-lived relationship with a fellow Aussie she'd met while on a weekend in London, she'd only ever slept with Luc.

Dane's lifestyle was light-years from anything she'd ever experienced. She might have a glamorous career and international exposure, but he was still way out of her league. Nor did she believe for one moment his confession moments ago that he was still coming to terms with their altered relationship. He'd just said that to soothe her pride.

It hadn't, but it had been thoughtful of him to try.

She stepped into the black-tiled cubicle with its gold fittings and double showerhead to see if the soft spray could do the job instead. If she felt confused and somehow hollow and…dissatisfied, that was her problem, not his. She didn't know what he expected of her today or tonight. Tomorrow or even next week. Whether whatever he felt for her had changed in the past few hours.

Her head fell back against the tiles as the water caressed breasts still tender and tingly from last night. She only knew how he'd made her feel when he'd been inside her. Like nothing she'd ever felt before. Strong, fragile—a contradiction. It was too much.

It wasn't enough.

Desire—even overwhelming desire—could never be compared to love. And what Dane felt for her was desire.

But love... Love could make a fool of the most rational of people. It could tempt one to throw away every belief, every plan, every dream, and swallow you whole.

She should know.

She stepped out of the shower with renewed resolve. Love would never make a fool of her again. From now on it was logic and reason.

From the beginning of this arrangement it had been a tacit acknowledgement that they'd end up becoming lovers. It had been inevitable.

Just as it was inevitable that they'd end up going their separate ways.

They returned home together, then Mariel spent the next couple of hours at her new business premises a few moments' drive away. Not to avoid him, she told herself, but because it was vital to make a start.

The little room was bland, cramped and would need extensive renovations if she intended to use it for retail purposes. For now she concentrated on arranging the meagre furniture Dane had supplied, sorting through stock she'd brought with her from Paris and setting up her sketching easel. Since it was Sunday, she opened her laptop and made a list of potential suppliers and tailors to contact in the coming week.

Mid-afternoon, unable to concentrate, she gave up trying to work on her latest design and headed home again. She wanted to talk Dane into some photos of her work for advertising and display purposes. And it was time he was fully informed about her work.

She found him in the pool. He was stretched out on an inflatable raft, wearing brief black bathers and apparently asleep behind those sunglasses, because the only movement coming from the pool was the gentle lilt of the raft in the light swirl of air.

And, oh, my… She might have seen him naked last night, but it had been shadowed and frantic. She hadn't seen him like this, in full daylight. He was long and lean and liberally sprinkled with black masculine hair. The sun gods had hammered his skin to a burning bronze and spun streaks of fine gold through his unruly dark mane. Broad shoulders, six-pack abs, firm, flat abdomen…

She breathed in a lungful of searing heat and he must have heard it, because his head swivelled in her direction.

'Hi.' His deep voice rippled across the water. She still couldn't see his eyes, and wondered if he'd been awake and watching her the entire time she'd been staring like some infatuated schoolgirl.

She shifted inside her sticky blouse, laid her tote bag on a nearby lounger. 'Hi.'

Tossing his glasses onto the side of the pool, he

rolled off the raft and disappeared into the blue depths, then popped up again at the edge, hauled himself out.

Water sluiced off his practically naked body, leaving rivulets in the dips and hollows. Droplets snagged on his chest hair. She noticed because he was walking towards her, his shadow looming ahead of him on the cement. She took another breath and lifted her gaze.

Perhaps it was the sun's glare behind his head, but she saw nothing except that wicked grin. She recognised that look. She'd seen it too many times as a teenager to dismiss it. It stunned her that he could change from lover to friend just that casually.

'No.' She took a step back.

He grinned, revealing even white teeth. The crease in his right cheek. A black sense of humour.

She backed up another step. 'Don't be ridiculous. We're not kids…'

Grabbing her around the waist, he rubbed his wet body against hers and shook his hair, scattering drops.

She screamed, wriggling out of his grasp, her breasts grazing hard, muscled body. 'Not fair!' She glared down at her wet-splotched blouse, then at him, and grinned despite herself. For a moment—deliberately, she thought—he'd made her forget the morning's awkwardness. It calmed her, settled her. Almost. To her surprise, she found herself playing his game. 'You idiot—just look at me.'

'I am.' His voice dropped a notch, and his eyes turned from mischievous to molten, but he reached for a towel and rubbed it over his chest. The rasping sound reminded her of how that crisp masculine hair had felt last night, rubbing against her breasts. Her nipples tightened against her bra.

To divert his attention from her wet blouse, and to give herself a moment to steady, she yanked the towel from his hands and used it to swipe at her linen trousers. Then hunted a tissue from her pocket and dabbed moisture from her face and neck.

'Just for that, you can pour me a drink.' She sank onto the nearest recliner under a large green umbrella. A moment later ice chinked as he poured lemonade into tall glasses and set the pitcher back on the little ceramic table beside her.

He handed her the tumbler. 'How did you go?'

'Good. Thanks.'

He leaned down and moved in to touch his lips to hers, lingering. 'You should have let me come and help you.'

'You already helped, letting me have the room. And I didn't want the distraction,' she murmured against his mouth, while the fingers of one hand grazed the side of her face.

Dane was tempted to let his fingers drift lower. To unbutton her blouse. To unzip her trousers and make love to her here in the sunlight. Instead he drew back, planted a kiss on her nose and straightened.

He retrieved his sunglasses, slid them on, and sat on the other lounger, enjoying the sun's heat on his water-cooled body while he watched Mariel reclasp her hair on top of her head. The action pulled her blouse tight across her breasts.

He turned to study the sparkles dancing on the water's surface. She didn't know the outline of her filmy bra and two aroused nipples showed clearly through her damped-down blouse. He could smell her—a blend of make-up, perfume and sun-warmed skin. He also sensed her need for space right now. Closing his eyes, he made an effort to unwind.

'Dane?'

'Hmm?' His eyes snapped open to see a camera shoved near his face.

'Smile and look sexy.'

'What is it with you and photography nowadays?'

'It helps in my line of work.' She squinted up at the sun, then moved in, slid his sunglasses off his face, set them aside. 'Okay, go ahead and be surly. It only adds to the appeal. Women adore that look. You have perfect male model potential. If you'd just polish the rough edges a little.'

'I happen to like my rough edges. On second thought...' His gaze snagged hers and his attempts to unwind came to an abrupt halt. 'Depends on who's doing the polishing.'

'That would be me. Maybe a facial...' Leaning over, she caressed the side of his face with cool, slender fingers.

'A facial? Not in a million years.' But it felt so damn good he allowed her to continue. Maybe she didn't need as much breathing space as he'd thought.

She pushed his pool-damp hair off his brow, her lacquered nails doing incredible things to the front of his scalp. 'Definitely a haircut.' She aimed the camera again.

'I'm missing something here,' he muttered as she snapped off a few more pictures.

'Okay, I'll let you in on a little secret.' She checked the camera's images. 'I want some publicity shots for my work and I'd like to use you.'

'*Me?*' Incredulous, he slid upright. 'Me in a fashion catalogue, posing as some woman's accessory? That'll be the day hell freezes over. Make that the day *after* hell freezes over.'

'No women. Just you.'

'Just me.' He squinted at her smile, frowned. 'What are you up to?'

'Okay. One of the reasons I wanted to work alone today was because I didn't want you to see my designs until I told you. I switched to designing men's fashion before I got involved in modelling.'

'*Men's* fashion? Why would a woman like you want to design men's clothing?'

'What do you mean, a woman like me?' Setting the camera aside, she sat down and looked at him with a kind of luminous excitement that made her eyes come alive. 'I happen to be very good at it. And I love the challenge. The preciseness, the detail, the perfection.'

Green eyes studied him, one perfectly arched eyebrow raised as she cast a disconcerting gaze from head to toe. 'Texture and style. I'm thinking of you in a steel-grey cashmere V-neck jumper. Something to show your shoulders to advantage.' She leaned forward. 'Will you?'

'Be your model? Not on your life.' He flopped back again to digest the new information.

She laughed lightly—an amused, tinkling sound. 'Sure you won't change your mind, Mr Eligible Bachelor of the Year?'

He slung an arm across his eyes because he didn't want to see the smirk playing around her mouth. 'I'm getting very weary of that line.'

'Why? Most guys would find it a hoot.'

'I'm not most guys. Frankly, I prefer to date women with more than half a brain in their head.'

'That's a sweepingly generalised statement. Not all the babes are blonde bimbos, surely?'

He raised his arm briefly, so he could see the smirk and give it back. 'You don't read the magazine. Obviously.' He paused. 'Besides, blondes are on hold for now.'

The atmosphere changed. He felt the sexual zing hum across the space between them.

'Okay,' he muttered. He might as well get it out of the way, because Mariel wasn't one to give up. 'What do you want me to do?'

'We'll take the formal shots here, then drive to Victor Harbor and do some more casual shots. Relax. It'll be fun.'

Fun? He could think of a lot better ways they could have enjoyed themselves this afternoon.

CHAPTER EIGHT

'I WANT your honest opinion.' Mariel selected a charcoal deep V-necked sweater from the pile of garments spread across his living room and held it up for Dane's inspection.

He ran a hand through his hair, feeling as out of place as a microchip in a blancmange. 'Nice?'

She shook her head in disbelief, her eyes twinkling with mirth. 'Too right it is. It's the finest quality cashmere. Feel it.'

She lifted it to his face, stroked it over his cheek. 'Light, yet warm.'

He'd never felt a more sensuous fabric. His imagination ran along the lines of how it would feel to lie with her on a rug made of the stuff and make love. 'And you want me to put it on. In thirty-five-degree heat.'

'Without a murmur of complaint.'

He scowled at the disarray. 'What else have you got lined up?'

'Relax, every piece here's casual. Except one.' She moved to a plastic suit bag, unzipped it to reveal a classic dinner suit.

'There's always got to be one,' he murmured, eyeing it with malice.

'Wait till you see the shirt…' She opened another bag, pulled it out.

'Let's get it over with it, then.'

Moments later he was staring at his reflection in a full-length mirror. He studied himself for several long seconds. It *looked* like an ordinary formal shirt, but…

'The front's transparent.'

'The *bib's* transparent,' she corrected. 'It's sheer, but not too sheer. Just enough to hint at all that gorgeous skin underneath…' Her gaze stroked down his torso like a hot silk glove. 'We'll set up in the front garden.'

Instant heat flooded his groin and he shifted his stance. 'If you look at me that way for much longer the picture will be unusable.'

She smiled, her luscious glossed lips full and inviting. 'Maybe I'm thinking I'll keep the picture for myself. As a memento.'

Smiling back and catching her hands in his, he leaned in, brushed his mouth over hers and murmured, 'Why keep a memento when you can have the real deal?'

As soon as the words were out, he realised why. She was one step ahead. Anticipating the day they'd go their separate ways. He fought the sensation that she was tearing him up on the inside. Permanence wasn't part of the deal. He liked his life fine the way it was. Had been. Would be again.

Backing up, he eased the tension in his fingers so he could let go of hers and cruise his hands up the slender columns of her arms.

'Dane…' She looked up at him. Desire still darkened her eyes, but the humour faded. 'Can we keep things light today? It's really important to me to get the business part of this right.'

'Sure.' He shook off conflicting emotions. 'Let's get this photo shoot out of the way so I can divest myself of this instrument of torture.'

Half an hour later, in his own jeans and T-shirt, Dane headed south along the coast with Mariel. They passed low rolling hills the colour of dried toast and a blue summer sea. The road, busy with tourists eager to reach the resort town, stretched out before them.

'Have you read the article in this morning's paper?'

'No time.' She reached for the paper at her feet, flicked through it until she came to the society pages and the photo of the two of them descending the staircase that led to the ballroom.

'Well?' he said into the ensuing silence.

'"New Year's latest celebrity couple,"' she read aloud. '"How long will it be before our popular Bachelor of the Year steps down?"' He heard the slide of denim as she rubbed her knuckles over her thighs. 'It gives the impression we wanted.'

She read on in silence for a moment. 'Plenty of publicity for OzRemote. It says you're heading north in just over a week.' She folded the paper, set it at her feet.

'I arranged it around my work schedule. Justin's going to hold the fort. Come with me.' He didn't realise he had voiced the thought until he felt her gaze on him.

She paused, then said, 'No.' Another pause. 'This is your big moment. Our relationship shouldn't overshadow the great work you're doing. Besides,' she went on in a brighter tone, 'I'll be flat out with my own schedule.'

He reached out, touched her hand. 'Last night worked in your favour, too. You'll be a runaway success.'

'Speaking of last night…tell me about Barbara.'

'Barbara?' He shook his head. 'She's poison.'

'You two seemed to be having a heavy-duty conversation on the dance floor.'

'I said what I should have said years ago. She didn't take it well.'

'And that was…?'

'That she's a manipulative, deceitful bitch.'

'Strong words. How so?'

'I saw Barbara outside a restaurant several years back in a clinch with some other young guy, even though she's supposed to be devoted to my father.'

'Why didn't you warn him?'

'I tried. He accused me of interfering in his life and told me to stay the hell away.' His body tensed and his fingers tightened on the steering wheel. 'Haven't set foot on the property since.'

'He was talking about you while you were dancing. And I saw the two of you outside the ballroom later. There's regret there, Dane. And more.'

A tight ball of emotion rolled up from his chest and lodged in his throat. 'He made overtures about putting the past behind us.'

She touched his shoulder. 'Family, Dane. Forgiveness. Do you think you might be able to mend some bridges?'

He swallowed, forced the ache down and kept his eyes on the road. 'Do you think Adelaide's going to be rocked by an earthquake this afternoon?'

That evening Mariel sat cross-legged in one of Dane's big T-shirts in front of his main computer, uploading the day's pictures. As she scrolled through the images she couldn't stop anticipation trickling through her at the thought of what tonight might bring.

As long as she kept this arrangement strictly casual. Focused on the present. Took it a day at a time. They'd done okay today, she thought. He'd been attentive and considerate. Sweet, really. On the occasions he'd hugged her there'd been warmth and affection. Their interaction had been open and uncomplicated. Just as she'd asked him.

But the sensual promise in his eyes had been enough to keep her blood on a low simmer all day.

She glanced up, that simmer upping a few degrees as Dane sauntered into the room with a bowl in his hand. She snapped her eyes back to the computer screen and the task at hand. Ordered herself to focus. Plenty of good-quality shots to choose from. She was surprised at how well they'd turned out. Luc's photography skills had taught her something useful after all.

'Can I tempt you with ice-cream?'

'In a minute.' Her eyes didn't leave the screen, but her other senses instantly focused on the man behind her—she could multi-task, couldn't she? The velvet timbre of his voice caressing the nape of her neck. The heat of his body. His tangy soap smell.

The simmer heated to a rolling boil, and without thought she leaned back so she could rub her head against his abdomen. Absently, she tried to remember a time when she'd craved physical touch quite so intensely. 'This one.' She clicked the mouse for a closer look.

It was a shot of Dane in a dove-grey polo neck jumper with one foot braced on a rock, the turquoise ocean and white sea spray a magnificent backdrop. She'd taken the photo on a forty-five degree angle.

'Not bad.'

'Not bad? It's bloody brilliant. Okay…' She saved it to a folder she'd created, then clicked to the next shot. 'What were you saying about temptation? Wait…' She leaned forward, mesmerised at her own talent. Uncurled her feet and planted them on the floor. 'This one. Oh…yeah…'

In the picture Dane's arms were crossed and he was leaning against grey-brown weather-smoothed rocks on the seaward side of Granite Island. He was wearing a dark V-neck sweater over jeans and looking out to Antarctica. 'You do that brooding look like a professional model. Look out website, here he comes.' Even his long hair blowing in the constant wind that battered the island suited the image. 'You're okay with that? Being on my website? When I get one, that is.'

'We'll talk about it. Later.'

'Whatever, that one's a definite.' She saved it to her folder. Then squealed as a cold sticky tongue laved the side of her neck.

'Ice-cream.' He held a mouthful on a spoon in front of her lips.

'Is it honeycomb?' She darted her tongue out to taste.

'Is there any other kind?'

She closed her mouth over the spoon and let the cold creamy taste roll around on her tongue. When she'd savoured every last drop and licked her lips she said, 'I thought temptation was mentioned.'

'Ice-cream was mentioned.' His tongue laved her neck again, then his lips and teeth joined in, nipping and sucking her flesh. 'Is that not temptation enough?'

She closed her eyes and arched her neck for more, then moaned when a cold, moist tongue slid along her collarbone. 'It might be. It really depends on who's offering the ice-cream.' She could almost feel herself melting, sliding off the big leather chair and onto the floor. She gripped the edge of the desk. 'And what else they might be offering…'

She heard the clunk as he set the bowl beside the computer, and her body shivered in the delight of anticipation. His hands glided over her shoulders and then down. Inside the loose neck of the supersized T-shirt and over her breasts. Around her nipples in ever-decreasing circles until she was practically begging. Her head lolled back on the chair.

She heard the sound of tearing seams and the T-shirt's neckline disintegrated. In one quick movement he ripped the whole thing apart down the middle, leaving her naked but for her panties. Hot palms massaged her belly. Her head lolled forward and she saw her own body. The contrast of his hard, dark hands on her pale and practically quivering flesh.

Then she watched, breathless, as both his hands slipped beneath the flat band of purple lace over her hips. The erotic sight nearly tipped her over the edge.

A distant siren wailed. She was vaguely aware of the computer's hum, that someone along the street was playing party hits. Then she wasn't aware of anything much at all.

The muscles in her stomach tensed, then spasmed. Her arms fell away from the desk to hang limply at her sides. Her thighs fell apart as her feet skidded away on the polished floorboards.

Oh, dear heaven… How had she let herself become

so submissive so quickly? she wondered dimly. The little voice in her head warned her that allowing another man to take command of her in this way was a prelude to disaster. And, because this was Dane, he wasn't only taking her body—he was taking her heart. The heart she'd sworn no man would take again. But for the life of her she couldn't move, could only lie helpless and let him continue.

One large hand rose, tapped a couple of keys. The screensaver disappeared; an image of herself flashed onto the monitor. 'What do you see?' said the voice behind her.

She stared at the green unfocused eyes, the slack-jawed mouth, and managed to close it. Barely. She saw a woman who'd well and truly lost it.

She saw the glint of fear in the passion-dark depths of her gaze.

'Not me,' she whispered, shocked. As she watched the monitor she saw his face join hers as he bent down next to her. 'That woman is *not* me…' She tried to struggle up, but Dane's gaze was as captivating as any physical restraint.

'Yes,' he murmured. 'It is.'

His eyes smoked with intent as he parted her liquid heat with his fingers, then pushed inside, a long slide to paradise. His jaw chafed the place between shoulder and neck; his breath whispered over her breasts.

He withdrew slowly, circled the throbbing centre, then plunged inside again. Wherever he touched, heat followed. Pleasure. Hot endless waves rippled through her while the computer's inbuilt camera reflected it back.

Then she saw nothing but the bright sparkle of her climax as it carried her away.

The cheerful tones of Dane's mobile brought her back to reality with a jolt. The air stirred and his heat dissipated. He moved to the other end of his L-shaped desk to answer it.

'Hi, Jus,' she heard him say, as if he'd just been working over a particularly absorbing computer problem rather than her. 'No, nothing important.'

He chuckled, and her sparkle faded. Had he been referring to what they'd been doing? Biting her lips, she pulled the torn edges of the T-shirt together, clicked off the monitor so she couldn't see herself.

'I guess so.' The easy humour drained from his voice. 'What's so urgent?' He nodded, then a lopsided grin creased his face. 'In that case, how can I refuse?'

She heard him flicking through papers and stole a glance at him. He jotted something down, then said, 'Yeah. She's staying here for now.' He'd turned away from her as he spoke. He could have been talking about the weather. 'No...' His shoulders lifted, one hand fisted on the desk. 'That's the official line we're taking, yeah.' Silence while Justin spoke, then a low laugh. 'I don't think so.'

Did he already regret not being free to pursue whatever lady of the moment took his fancy? A shiver cooled the sparkling warmth she'd been enjoying just minutes ago.

She wanted him to look at her the way he'd been looking at her before. To show some indication that he'd enjoyed what they'd just done, that it wasn't all one-sided.

Her legs had recovered just enough to support her, so she rose and crossed to him, rolling the chair with her. He fumbled the pen as she inveigled her way between his body and the desk, but he managed to catch it mid-fall and jotted something else on his notepad.

His jaw was bristly when she ran her fingertips over it. 'What?' she mouthed, capturing his gaze with hers. His pupils swallowed up his irises until only a thin rim of molten silver remained. His confident business persona slipped. Whatever he had started saying to Justin slurred to a stop.

Finally she had his attention. She had Dane where she wanted him. Not Mariel his childhood friend, not Mariel who'd agreed to this arrangement for mutual benefit, but the sexual woman he'd made love to last night.

He shook his head. 'Can you repeat that, Jus?'

She'd ruffled that smooth exterior, distracted his ordered mind. She'd never felt such rush of feminine power before. It swam through her limbs like the most potent brandy until her head was dizzy with it.

High on the elixir, she smiled and prodded his chest, so that his body tipped back onto the chair. It rolled back a little.

'I'll…ah…need you to e-mail me that info tonight.'

On a wave of confidence she shrugged out of the tattered T-shirt and stood before him in nothing but her lace panties.

'When do we…um…when…?' His voice trailed away.

She slid her palms down her hips, stepped out of the last remnant of clothing, flung it over her shoulder. It landed on his desk with a quiet plop.

His eyes glazed over. 'No. Everything's fine. Just fine,' he choked out as she worked deft fingers over the front of his shorts.

Without breaking eye contact, Mariel took the phone from his hand—as easy as taking candy from a baby.

'Goodbye, Justin,' she said, and disconnected. She straddled Dane, satisfied she'd achieved her intended outcome. Oh, yes, she saw desperation and desire, both sharp as a sword and glittering in those grey depths.

'Right now…' she tugged down the zip, grasping his throbbing length with both hands '…I've a craving for more than ice-cream.'

Dane's brief chuckle turned ragged. His blood hammered through his groin, his ears, and every place between. 'So I noticed,' he muttered, before she crushed her lips to his and possessed him with fast, greedy bites. Long, luscious licks on fevered skin that cooled in the air as she feasted on his jaw, his neck, a shoulder.

She took him inside her with a cry that bounced off the walls and echoed like the thunder of horses' hooves in his ears. Conquest, triumph, victory. He saw it in the emerald fire in her eyes. He took her mouth and tasted it on her lips.

In turn, he possessed her with restless hands and frantic touches. Gave her what she wanted, took what she offered. Urgent, reckless, primitive.

There was no gentleness, no finesse. Just the frenzied race to the finish. And when it was over, and she collapsed against him, still it wasn't enough. He wanted more. He wanted to burrow beneath her skin, steal inside her mind. All. One.

Dangerous—this insatiable appetite. This all-consuming need. He enjoyed sex. But this sudden craziness was like an addiction that knew no limit. Which made him wonder: what the hell was it?

For one insane moment a couple of years back he'd even thought himself in love, but it hadn't lasted. It never lasted. The ability to love simply wasn't in his genes.

He drifted a hand over her hair, breathed her scent of sex and warm skin. He squeezed her nape so that she looked up at him with over-bright eyes.

'Wow,' she breathed. 'I'm good. I mean, I'm really, really good.'

The laugh that bubbled up from his throat was a mix of amusement and affection. 'Here I was, thinking it was me.'

Amusement and affection. He should have known with Mariel it would be that simple.

And that complicated.

His humour faded. 'I have to go in to work tomorrow.' He smoothed a thumb over Mariel's jaw.

'I thought you were on leave?'

'I was. But there's a problem with a computer system we installed a few weeks ago. Which means a quick trip to Mount Gambier.'

A day trip. 'And Justin can't go?'

'Jus and Cass are busy trying to make a baby, and it's Cass's fertile time, apparently. According to Cass's calculations tomorrow morning's the charm.'

Her eyes widened, incredulous. 'She's pinpointed it down to the hour? Are you for real?'

'That's what Jus told me.' The thought made him smile. 'What could I say?'

She grinned, too. 'Nothing but yes, I guess.' Her mouth softened, her eyes took on a sparkle, dew on spring leaves. 'Making a baby…'

Without warning the cunning image stole through his mind. Mariel, round with a child. With *his* child. He clenched his jaw against an unfamiliar crushing sensation in his upper chest.

He shook his head to clear the unsettling thoughts

that struck too close, too deep, and somehow messed with his perception that he had this situation with Mariel under control.

'That's convenient, then,' she went on, as if she hadn't noticed his silence. 'I want to work on some ideas, sketch a few designs. Acquire a tailor… I might even get some work done with you out of harm's way and unable to distract me.'

His brows rose. 'Me? Distract you? After what just happened here?'

'You only have to be in the same room to distract me, Dane. It's always been that way. But now I've discovered I do the same to you.'

His gaze drifted over her naked perfection. Already his body stirred with desire again. Fighting the irrational emotion that there was more to it, he shrugged and said, 'I guess we'll get it out of our systems eventually.'

Her delicate shoulders tensed. A weighty silence seemed to thicken the air. 'I darn well hope so.' Her voice was clipped as she climbed off him. She swiped her panties from the desk, shrugged into the remnants of his T-shirt and breezed towards the door.

He wished she'd turn so he could see her expression. 'I'll join you in a few moments.'

'Not a good idea.' She paused at the door. Only then did she face him, and her eyes were unreadable. Her compressed lips, however, told a story. She forced them into something approaching a smile when she saw him looking at them and said, 'We'd spend all night keeping each other awake and I'm totally knackered. Goodnight, Dane.'

He sat for a long time, staring at the darkened

doorway. He could hear her moving about in her room, could still smell her fragrance on the air. How the hell was he going to get back to normal without her when this was over?

CHAPTER NINE

MARIEL plopped face down onto her bed. She deserved an Academy Award for that performance, but she was pretty sure he'd bought it. Except for the fatal way she'd nibbled her lips. He'd seen it. Damn, he knew her too well.

Holding her pillow to her chest, she rolled over and stared up at the darkness. She'd managed to keep her tone as blasé as his. That was what it was all about, after all.

Her mouth twisted with grim humour. So she'd downplayed the intensity she knew they both felt by purposely bringing it up in conversation. He'd bought it, hadn't he? She needed to keep up the façade because that was what they'd agreed on.

Besides, she tried to tell herself, they'd never make it as a couple. They'd never see eye-to-eye on any damn thing—from personal appearance and TV shows to family and kids. Or commitment.

She also needed to make it clear they weren't going to do overnighters. If he saw her before she was wide awake she'd be vulnerable, and he'd see through her as easy as glass. It would be far too dangerous, because she was falling. Out-of-control falling.

Her heart seemed to curl in on itself; her fingers

clenched against her pillow. Time for honesty, she decided. She'd already fallen. Head over heels. Big-time. All the way. She was in love with Dane. Always had been.

Now she knew every intimate inch of his body, knew the sounds he made in passion, the feel of him deep inside her. Friends would never be enough, and 'lovers' was a temporary arrangement.

She sent her pillow sailing through the air, heard it slump heavily against the dark antique wardrobe.

But it was done now. And it was vital that she keep up the charade, that he never knew what she felt deep in her soul, because that would put him in an impossible situation. He didn't want permanency. He'd want to get back to his free lifestyle and bosomy blondes.

The bastard.

So she'd keep it light and easy. She'd make the most of the time they had and then…and then she'd walk away with the memories even if she walked away without her heart.

The following morning she kept to her plan. It wasn't as hard as she'd anticipated because Dane was in a hurry. He didn't stop for breakfast, grabbing a coffee on the run. But he did kiss her goodbye at the front door. A toe-curling kiss that went on and on and on, until the driver of the chauffeured limo waiting at the kerb to take Dane to the airport coughed discreetly.

Dane lifted his head and searched her face for a long moment. The early-morning sun struck his hair with gold, and heat blazed in his eyes, searing her cheeks. 'Tonight,' he promised.

She shook her head. 'You'll miss your flight.' It occurred to her then that they were saying goodbye as if they were a married couple, and she backed away, unsettled. 'Have a safe trip.'

'I'll call you.'

Blowing him a breezy kiss, she turned and walked back inside. Already she couldn't wait to see him again. To hear his voice again. To feel his body against hers again.

It felt odd, walking through his house alone. A reminder that she was here only because they'd agreed it was the best way. It was vital she keep those impatient wants in perspective, because she couldn't afford to want him this much.

If it were possible, their sexual relationship grew in intensity over the coming week. Because she wanted to work—and because she privately worried that they were becoming too close—Dane went about his business during the day and they only met up again in the evenings.

If he had a function to attend, she accompanied him. The press followed. They were a popular couple in the society pages. Speculation in the media mounted as to how long Dane would remain Bachelor of the Year, but he refused any interviews that involved talking about Mariel, insisting again that they were 'just good friends'. Nor did he give Mariel any indication that his status as bachelor might change.

They shared quiet evenings at home, took a moonlit walk on the beach late one evening after a particularly hot day, relaxed by the pool. Doing ordinary things couples did.

And every night, they came together with a passion that gave no indication of slowing down or fading. A love affair, she told herself.

And affairs ended.

But they cared about each other, respected each other. She refused to think beyond each day, determined to enjoy it while it lasted.

Mariel learned that Dane owned a string of buildings within the central business district. There were tenants to deal with, a minor plumbing emergency, renovations to approve. He made preparations for his upcoming Outback trip. It seemed he'd purposely filled his life with distractions to keep him busy.

And it bothered her that he'd turned his back on the only family he had. She lay in bed one night, staring at the ceiling, unable to sleep. She knew they'd had their problems in the past, but the remorse in his father's eyes on the night of the ball had convinced her there was hope, if only she could get Dane to see it.

Slipping out of bed, she grabbed her robe and padded downstairs. She poured herself a glass of milk, then carried it outside into the fragrant night air. Moonlight bathed the high stone walls and the luxury enclosed within. She turned to study the heritage building that was Dane's home.

Dane was a proud man, bordering on arrogant. Independent. Stubborn. Too damn stubborn to admit he might be as fallible as any other mere mortal. Everyone needed family, even Dane. She sensed that deep down he was a little boy, still yearning for that connection.

So he had women, acquaintances, business associates, but when things fell apart or tragedy struck, what then? If she could do one thing for him, it would be to try to reunite father and son.

'What are you doing out here?'

Startled out of her thoughts, she turned to see Dane standing in the doorway, a pair of loose boxers low on his hips. 'Thinking.' She walked towards him, pressed her head against his chest, listened to his heartbeat, strong and steady in her ear. 'Just thinking.'

'I can't sleep either.' His arms slid around her waist. They were silent a moment, while the crickets chirped around them and something rustled in the bushes.

Dane was relearning how to sense her moods, the way he had when they'd been younger, but tonight... What had brought her outside in the middle of the night? Had he upset her in some way? No. Mariel wasn't backwards in coming forwards. If she had a problem with him she'd let him know. So he laid his head against her bed-mussed hair and just held her.

She felt deeply, he thought, his hands wandering over the silken robe to absorb her body heat. Unlike the women who'd shared his bed over the years. Or perhaps he'd never known them long enough, or cared enough, to notice. No, that wasn't quite true. He'd had relationships that had lasted as long, if not longer, than this current relationship with Mariel. But this was different. Almost as if they'd become more than lovers.

No. He couldn't do that. Not to Mariel. He didn't want to hurt her. Would not hurt her. She meant too much, she was too important. Possibly the most important person in his life. He'd do anything to spare her the pain of falling for a man who couldn't commit. Which meant keeping to the same path they'd started out on. Smooth, level. Practical.

She shifted and relaxed against him. He squeezed her shoulders before taking her inside.

* * *

From behind the glass doors overlooking the pool Dane watched the low-slung canary-yellow sports car pull up under the carport beside his Porsche.

It was Sunday afternoon, the day before he was due to fly north. He'd be away for a week. Mariel had told him she had a surprise, and had made him promise to be home and not to argue with her when she got back.

The driver's door opened and he was treated to the mouth-watering sight of yellow stiletto sandals. As they touched the ground he noted that the sandals were attached to long shapely legs. No argument there. White-frosted toenails peeked out from beneath the straps and sparkly bits arched over her ankles.

Mariel climbed out, her dark hair tied back with a yellow ribbon. It looked as if she'd chosen the car to accessorise another neat little sundress, and it occurred to him that not many months ago maybe she would have.

He admired the shape of her bottom as she leaned over the back seat, then straightened with a box from the Chocolate Choices shop in her hands. Couldn't argue with that either.

She looked as delicate and deliciously cool as a slice of lemon meringue pie. Heat stirred deep in his loins and a primal growl rose up his throat.

Until the passenger door opened and his father climbed out.

The gut-punch knocked him back a step. Good God, what the hell was she doing? His body tensed as he watched Mariel walk with his father towards the door where Dane stood, hand frozen on the door catch. A ball of something thick and hard crawled up his throat. Straightening, he slid the door open before she reached it.

'Dane,' Mariel said before he could get a word out. Nerves flitted across her eyes. 'I've brought your dad to town. I know how much you both like chess and…thought you could get reacquainted over a game.'

His gaze swung from Mariel to his father. 'Dad.'

His father stopped an arm's length away. 'Hello, Dane. Mariel invited me, but if you want she'll drive me straight home again.'

Avoiding her gaze, Dane was tempted to tell her to do just that. He flexed his fingers. 'You're here now.'

There was anguish in his eyes, Dane knew, because there was empathy and understanding in Mariel's when he finally looked. He felt as if she'd stripped away his pride and confidence and left him naked.

He gestured stiffly to the sofa. 'What are you drinking these days?'

'I'll have a beer, if you've got one, thanks.'

Mariel switched on a CD. Light music filled the room. She slipped past Dane with an, 'Okay, then, I'll leave you two to—'

'Not so fast.' Dane grabbed her arm and practically frog-marched her to the adjacent kitchen. As soon as they were out of earshot he spun her to face him. Her eyes were moist. And angry.

She was angry? 'What the hell are you doing?' he demanded, his voice killingly low.

'I'm thinking about you, Dane.' She set her box of chocolate goodies on the counter. 'Your father needs you, and whether you know it or not you need him. I thought bringing him here for a friendly game of chess was a good starting point.'

He dropped her arm, strode to the fridge and pulled out two beers. 'I'd rather face a firing squad.'

'I might be able to arrange that.' He didn't need to look at her to feel her knife-edged gaze, as sharp as a slap. 'In fact, I might just perform the favour myself.'

His temper boiled over. 'You brought him here to play chess? Fine. You play. I'm not ready for this.'

Mariel hugged her arms around her body as he passed her, set the beer in front of his father and strode outside. The door slid shut with a thud that vibrated along the wall.

Ah, God. Had she made a really bad mistake? Her heart raced, her legs felt weak, but she made herself cross the room to face Daniel. Tension dug grooves in his already lined face. She'd upset not one person, but two people.

'He'll come round,' she murmured, then pulled her lips into a smile, pulled up a chair so that they both faced the chessboard. 'Meanwhile, why don't you explain the game to me?'

Daniel took three long gulps of beer then scrubbed a hand over his jaw. 'I should go.'

'Give him a few moments.' To distract Daniel, and settle herself, she picked up one of the beautiful black crystal pieces. 'What's this one called?'

Daniel exhaled a slow breath. 'It's a bishop. It can only move diagonally.' He picked up another. 'Whereas the knight can jump over any other chess pieces. The object of the game is to checkmate your opponent's king.'

'And what does that mean, exactly?'

'It's when—' He broke off when the door slid sharply open and Dane stepped back inside.

His expression gave nothing away. It was as if he'd

pulled on a mask. But he was calmer, Mariel noted. The tension in his shoulders had loosened; his hands weren't balled into fists any more. Some of her own tension ebbed. But only a little, because he was too cool. Too controlled.

He wasn't finished with her yet, she knew. She'd stepped way over the boundaries they'd set. She was his lover; that was all. Temporary at that. Which gave her no right to interfere in his personal decisions. Or his life.

Just because family meant everything to her, and she wanted one of her own some day, it didn't mean she had to inflict her lifestyle choices on anyone else. Not even Dane. Even if her motives had been purely for his benefit.

She sprang off the chair, nerves jangling. 'I've got things to do. Upstairs.'

Dane watched her go, then took the chair she'd vacated, set his empty beer bottle on the floor beside him. Outside, he'd been tempted to keep walking, to leave Mariel to clean up the mess she'd made. Until he'd realised she only had his interests at heart. Since when had anyone done anything like that for him? He quite simply couldn't remember. And he'd reacted like an angry schoolkid.

But he was a grown man, so he'd just have to suck it up and act like one. Didn't mean he was going to like it. 'Let's get it over with, then. White?'

His dad shook his head. 'We don't have to play.'

The beginnings of a smile tugged at the corner of Dane's mouth. 'You never did like to lose, as I recall.' He moved the clear crystal king's pawn two spaces.

His dad mirrored the move. 'I haven't played in years.'

'No excuses.' Dane made his second move. Queen, four spaces.

'Barbara left.'

'I know.' Both men studied the board. 'That's the kind of woman she is. I tried telling you that.'

'Women. You can't trust them.'

'Generally, I'd agree with you.'

'But Mariel's different, right?'

Dane felt his father's gaze on him. 'Mariel's not up for discussion.'

'Why not? She's living here. I read the papers. *Just good friends.*' His chuckle turned into a loud throat-clearing and he reached for his beer again.

Dane resisted the urge to defend their relationship. His father made it sound cheap. He studied the board but didn't see it. What they had could never be termed a cheap affair. He'd never known anyone like Mariel. Never would. The fact that he'd have to let her go at some point in the not-too-distant future suddenly loomed, and just for a heartbeat everything inside him stilled and nothingness yawned before him.

More rattled than he cared to admit, he pushed the thought away and made his next move.

Mariel remembered the chocolate cookies she'd intended offering them about ten minutes later. Chocolate always soothed troubled waters. She didn't want to interrupt or distract, so she'd put them on a plate, set it on the table and leave. She stole barefooted downstairs.

Male voices floated up the stairwell as she descended. 'You think you and Mariel might get—?'

'No.'

Mariel froze on the step at the categorical denial, fingers tightening on the smooth, worn banister.

'She wants to play happy families some day. Big old house, kids of her own.'

She'd always known he was going to end it, but to hear it spoken of in that detached and decisive way cut to her core like broken glass.

'Kids were never big in our family,' she heard Daniel say.

'We're not family,' Dane shot back. 'Being biologically related doesn't make a family.'

Well, at least Dane understood that much, Mariel thought. But she didn't want to hear any more. She climbed the stairs back to her room. Closed the door and lay down to wait for the afternoon to be over.

CHAPTER TEN

JUST on dark, Dane switched off the ignition. He had to admit it hadn't gone as badly with his father as he'd first thought. He climbed out of his car, but came to a halt at the garage door.

Mariel sat by the pool in the mellow circle of light. Right at home in the spotlight, he mused. Her long lashes rested on those fabulous cheekbones; her hair flowed over her shoulders in a stream of sable. At some point the sun had kissed the exposed skin of her shoulders and turned them rosy—strawberries and cream.

His mouth watered. One taste. Just one…

She'd probably still be mad with him. But she didn't look angry. She looked sexy. His blood heated at thinking about it, rolling and heaving through him like the restless summer thunder over the hills in the distance.

She moved, dipping her feet into the water, sending ripples across its smooth surface. A strange sensation hooked at his chest, snagging the breath in his throat and momentarily rooting him to the spot.

Growing up, she'd always been his port in a storm, keeper of his secrets. His best friend.

Now they were having an affair.

Nothing permanent, he reminded himself, watching her lean on her arms and tilt her head back so that her breasts thrust upward as if in invitation. A primal growl threatened to erupt, but he fought it down for another moment to watch her—she was so rarely still.

He walked towards her. 'Hi.'

Her head turned slowly towards him. 'So you've finally decided to come home.'

'I helped Dad fix a sticky door.'

Her lips softened into a smile. 'That's good. That's great.'

His bare feet made no sound as he crossed the pool surround. He stood a metre away, breathing her in, watching the rise and fall of her breasts, her nipples tight little buds against the buttercup fabric. Arousal, he knew. Just as he knew that if he bent down and touched the inside of her wrist he'd find her pulse as rapid.

'Shall I tell you what you're thinking?' he said.

She blinked once at him, but didn't answer right away. Finally she said, 'I'd rather you show me.' She tilted her head, and an echo of her thoughts lingered on her curved lips like honey.

The urge to drink that sweet temptation from her mouth consumed him. 'I thought you might still be mad. I take it from your response that you're not.'

'It's a waste of time holding on to anger, don't you think?' Dreamy emerald eyes stared up at him. 'I'd rather make love than war.'

He sat down on the deck beside her, picked up her hand, grazing his thumb over her fingers. 'Wise thoughts.' He brought her hand to his lips before setting it on her thigh and releasing her, then leaned back on his elbows.

His touch seemed to set off an explosion of energy.

She pushed up. Dane made to follow suit, but Mariel's bare foot in the middle of his chest prevented him. He could see her eyes clearly. Green and direct and aroused.

She wiggled her toes against his shirt. 'Make mad passionate love with me. Right here, right now.'

'Okay…' He admired the view of Mariel from this unique angle and said with a quirk, 'But it looks like you have the upper hand at this moment.' He scraped a fingernail under the erotic arch of her foot.

She jerked it away and let out a shuddering gasp as the first warm drops of rain speckled the deck. 'Damn you, that *tickles*.' Lifting her face to the sky, she flung her arms wide. 'Hey, it's raining.'

Her eyes clashed with his and she lurched as if drunk, except he knew she wasn't. His hands shot to her hips, as much to prevent her doing him an unspeakable injury as to steady her. 'I've got you.'

'Have you?' She crossed her arms and an unreadable expression crossed her eyes. He wasn't sure who'd manoeuvred what, or where, but he found her feet planted on either side of his torso. 'Maybe *I've* got *you.*'

He curled his fingers around her ankles. 'You sure about that?'

Anticipation filled the hiatus that followed, as if the evening, too, held its breath. He stared up at the clouds a moment, their heavy underbellies ruddy with the reflected city lights. Lightning flickered in the distance, followed by the restless grumble of thunder.

She glanced towards the darkening heavens, too. 'We should—'

'Yes. We should. Slowly this time. Very slowly.'

He tightened his grip on her ankles and looked into the smouldering depths of her eyes. They were dark, mirroring the approaching storm. Flicking her hair over her shoulders, she stared down at him, all glorious sparks and energy.

'Mariel…' Gazes locked, he trailed his hands up those smooth, firm calf muscles.

She didn't move or react in any way, but the pleasure of watching her eyes darken further with arousal while soft summer rain spangled her hair was like nothing he'd ever experienced. Though need pummelled at him, and urgency beat like a drum through his blood, his plan remained the same. Take. It. Slow.

Skin-warmed fabric slithered against the backs of his hands as he memorised the shape of her legs the way a blind man might learn Braille. The indentation behind her knees, the soft inner thigh.

She was silky heat and trembling need. His own fingers trembled when they brushed the damp cling of cotton at the juncture of her thighs. Anticipation, hunger. Both clawed at him as he slipped a finger beneath the flimsy barrier to find smooth female flesh. Slick. Wet. Hot…

For one paralysing moment Mariel felt her whole body go rigid. If the future of world peace had depended on it, she would have still remained where she was, eyes fused with Dane's while she absorbed the exquisite pleasure of his finger there. As if they'd never made love before, as if it was *different* this time. Chained by her own rampant desire, she was scared speechless. Motionless. Mindless.

Then his hand moved away, and *that* panicked her infinitely more. 'No. I—'

'It's okay, Queen Bee.'

'I know. I know it is.' She blew out a breath, pushed both hands through her dampening hair as she struggled against a tide that threatened to drown her. 'Now you're back, and I'm here, and it's slow and easy, and I'm still getting goosebumps. Because it's you.'

Feeling dazed, she looked down at the shoulders she'd slung her arms around in easy friendship, the familiar grey eyes she'd known since childhood. Except now those shoulders seemed impossibly broad and his eyes smoked with desire. 'It's been over a week and I still can't get my head around it.'

'Don't try. Don't think at all.' His tone was light as he touched his palms to the backs of her knees, but she sensed the tension hum through his body like a low electric current. 'Come down here.'

Easy, since her legs and every other body part were melting. Simple to slide, boneless, on top of him, to put her lips on his and drink him in. Slowly. He tasted of berries and beer, midnight and man.

She raised her head to stare at him in wonder. And amazement. Tangled her restless fingers in his over-long hair and pushed it off his face and behind his ears, breathing in the scent of his skin on the moisture-laden air. She lifted a hand to his eyelashes, caught a single crystal raindrop on her finger.

His fingers fumbled a moment behind her hair, then her zip was being lowered, baring her feverish skin to the refreshing rain. He was sliding the fabric away and she was lifting her arms and helping him, every movement, every shivery rasp of fabric against flesh, skin against skin, dreamlike in the softness of the night, until she was naked but for a scrap of ivory lace bikini.

He rolled her onto her back beside him and leaned up on one elbow. Backlit by the pool's underwater lights, his hair was haloed by a silvery rain mist. His gaze took a leisurely but scorching journey down her body—she could almost feel the moisture on her skin turning to steam, and barely stopped herself moaning.

'Yes. Now,' was all she could say.

He shook his head, his eyes glittering in the dusky dimness. 'You do everything at light-warp speed. Not tonight.'

He traced the side of her face with his knuckles, the barest touch.

And she forgot to breathe.

Forgot everything but the pleasure he promised.

Slow. He was true to his word. He cupped a breast in his palm, rolled the excruciatingly sensitive nipple between finger and thumb, then dipped his head to take it into his hot wet mouth and suckle, drawing the exquisite moment out like warm spun toffee. And again, as he paid the same loving attention to her other breast.

Languid. His palm, hot and heavy, was leaving her breasts to glide across her belly and down, slipping beneath the waistband of her panties.

Lazy. The long, liquid pull as he slid one finger over her moist centre. Deeper, until she moaned his name, the throaty murmur stirring from somewhere deep inside her.

Unable to help herself, she moved her legs and arched into his hand, restless, aching. Wanting. She'd never wanted this way with any other man. 'Dane…I—'

'Shh…' He rubbed his lips over hers, obliterating what she'd been about to say, then stared down at her. His face was part shadow, his hair haloed by the moisture's silvery mist, but his eyes… They were almost cool—unlike his kiss—and direct. 'Just lie there and be quiet.'

'But I—'

He kissed her again, drinking the words from her mouth slowly, the way he'd savour a rare vintage wine, until she couldn't remember a single one.

When he left her lips to nibble his way down the column of her throat and over the pounding pulse in her neck, she couldn't breathe. When he shifted and his tongue delved into her belly button, she couldn't move. When he laved his way slowly and sinuously over her abdomen to the edge of her bikini, she couldn't think…

He was smoothing the cling of lace away, the arousing ridge of callus at the base of his fingers chafing her skin as his hand slid down her thighs, over her calves until he'd divested her of the last shred of clothing.

And, oh… Ah… Yes… His mouth was hot heaven on her air-cooled flesh as he parted her legs and worshipped the swollen knot of need with his tongue. Hands alternately fluttering and fisting in Dane's hair, she floated somewhere between paradise and dawn.

The murky atmosphere dewed her skin with sweat and rain while a restless sky flickered and rumbled. Pressure, thick and white-hot, building, burning. Rising on a cumulonimbus crescendo that echoed within her.

She arched against him, the torrid shock of climax shuddering through her, a primitive sound issuing from her throat, tearing the sultry air.

But he didn't give her time to come down. Before she could draw breath he was plunging a finger inside while his mouth continued to suckle, relentlessly pushing her further, faster, higher. Gasping, she slid over the hot and slippery edge again. She closed her eyes on a moan.

Slowly she became aware that the plush-prickly sensation on her belly must be Dane's chin. She opened her eyes again and met his over the pale expanse of naked flesh. 'Oh. Wow.' Her lungs couldn't seem to find any oxygen, and she seemed to be incapable of muttering more than one word at a time.

'My sentiments exactly.' His voice was thick as he reared up, flicking open his belt buckle.

She laughed raggedly, struggling for breath as she wiggled down, beneath his body, until she felt the rasp of denim and the hot swell of his erection against her sensitised flesh. Buttons popped as she leaned up, tore open his shirt and rubbed greedy hands over hard, hairy flesh.

He snagged her fingers. 'Slow, remember?'

'Okay. But make it quick.' Slow had never been in her vocabulary. But she lay back while he yanked off his almost buttonless shirt, tossed it aside. He stood to shuck off his jeans and jocks.

And… She'd seen him naked, but it had always been in a fevered rush. Now… What could one say about perfection? Every feminine cell rolled around and lay down and begged at that magnificent display of aroused masculinity, and her pulse, which had almost steadied, picked up again at double time.

Dane. In the flesh. Glorious, touchable, within reachable flesh.

He lowered himself to the deck in one deft manoeuvre that swept what little breath she had left from her lungs, rolled her beneath him, almost crushing her in the process.

'Some women like to be smothered,' Mariel murmured, struggling for air and space. 'I'm not one of them.'

'Quit complaining.' But he took some of his weight on his elbows and stretched out over her, the lines of his body like some sleek and muscular predator. The hard length of his erection prodded against her pelvis. His chest rubbed up against her breasts as he coaxed her with light, flirty kisses over her face, her neck, her ear, where he whispered, 'We'll discuss personal preferences another time.'

He pressed his lips to hers, the kiss turning from playful to passionate in less time than it took for Mariel to form a response. Streams of sensation flowed over her skin as his fingers traced her brow, her cheeks, her jaw. His tongue delved inside, coaxing hers to join in with a sensuality she couldn't resist.

Reaching down between their bodies, she wrapped her fingers around him. He jerked in her hands, stopped kissing her to pull back and stare into her eyes. They remained that way for an eternity, gazes locked as she slid her fingers slowly from silky tip to throbbing base, then back to the tip once more. She smoothed the drop of moisture she discovered there with her finger before guiding him between her thighs.

No words. In the deep well of midnight, with the one person who knew her almost better than she knew herself, speech was unnecessary. Time was irrelevant. Their eyes met in accord. She understood him, his vulnerabilities, his fears, his needs. Just as she knew he understood hers.

The rain had almost stopped, leaving only the pungent smell of freshly damp vegetation and the remnant moist heat from the day. She heard the rhythmic *plop* as water rolled off a broad-leaved plant nearby. A patch of sky peeked through the clouds, its silver-gilded edge lit by an invisible moon.

A different kind of heat seduced her now, as he pushed his blunt satin tip inside her. A slow, delicious friction stroked and rubbed her inner muscles. A moan escaped her. The long, liquid glide to paradise.

Urgency grew, need sharpened as he urged her higher. She followed, and with fingers, lips, teeth and tongue she urged him, also, to pursue her.

She met him stroke for stroke, matching demand for demand, as their bodies moved in a choreographed dance. Like a perfect storm, he whipped them away together on a flood of sensation until they washed up on some distant shore.

Dane groaned—maybe she did, too; she couldn't be sure—and collapsed on top of her. Their eyes fused on the other's, lips close, breath mingling. His heart was drubbing like a piston against her own.

When he made to pull away, take some of his weight off her, she yanked him back with what remaining strength she had. 'Don't go.'

'I wasn't leaving.'

His silky hair brushed her skin as he smiled at her in the dimness. 'I was thinking we should go inside and find somewhere more comfortable. Maybe get some sleep.'

'Okay.'

Pushing up, he swept her into his arms and headed for the door. She clung to his neck as he climbed the stairs, barely raising a puff. And just this once she was content to let him play hero.

The cool, smooth sheets beneath her body lulled her towards slumber. Resting her cheek on the pillow of his broad chest, she breathed his scent and listened to his heart return to a regular rhythm. Heard his breathing settle and knew he'd fallen asleep.

So easy for him, she thought. He probably went to sleep with strange women beside him all the time. Why would it be any different with her?

Because he'd told her he'd never brought a woman here to sleep.

She lifted her head to watch him and her heart tumbled. He looked like the boy she'd known, innocent and sweet. Rather than disturb him, she kissed her fingers, laid them lightly against his lips.

When had she ever felt this fulfilled? The answer was easy. Never. Maybe it was because she'd never made love before in so many ways. Body, mind, heart.

But fear snuck through the hazy contentment. If she wasn't very, very careful her heart would be the loser. Big-time. She wasn't going to let anyone hurt her again. Not Dane, not anyone.

She could not allow uncontrolled emotions and past dreams to cloud what was supposed to be a practical arrangement.

And yet she'd allowed him to set this dangerous precedent by bringing her to his bed tonight. She should have insisted he take her to her own room. She'd leave. In a moment. Carefully sliding off him, she shifted to the edge of the bed, closed her eyes to shut out the reminder of his robe hanging on the back of his door.

Somehow she must have slept, because when she pried open her eyes again the pearly light of dawn was pushing back the darkness. Dane's body was sprawled against her, a heavy palm resting on one breast. Every place their bodies touched was slicked with sweat. Neither had thought to switch on the air-conditioning and a blanket of thick air swamped them.

Too late to slip away to her own bed now.

The vague tingling low in her belly sharpened and spread upward, tightening her nipples into hard peaks. The large-palmed hand covering her breast obviously registered that fact and squeezed gently, then rolled the sensitive nub between his thumb and finger.

'You're awake.' His hand moved lower—a slow, lazy glide that had her arching into his big body.

'Mmm… Uh…' Heat blasted her skin and her breath caught as he reached between her legs and slid a finger over still swollen flesh. Her whole body throbbed, tensed.

'Good morning.' His eyes, smudged with sleep, smiled at her.

He was doing it again, driving her up. Driving her towards the edge. And she had to admit she liked it—especially when he did that thing with his thumb… She was even prepared to let him play there a little longer…

But she had her own ideas…

Twisting, she dragged her body up and over his until she was sitting astride him. She saw him blink, watched his jaw drop as she grasped his sex in both hands and impaled herself. His eyes weren't sleepy now. They were wide and opaque and involved.

'And a good morning to you, too,' she said. Then she slid down on him in one slow, smooth glide. 'Now, pay attention. It's my turn.'

Dane left for the north of the state later that morning. Because she didn't want to appear needy or clingy

Mariel made sure she'd already left for her little office when it was time for him to leave. Of course she gave him a long goodbye kiss.

She spent the next few days in a frenzy of activity, interviewing potential tailors, sketching new designs and preparing patterns.

He called her every night. She missed him. She tried hard not to, because sooner or later he was going to call it off. She knew that. So she focused on her work. The way to success was so clear she could almost taste it.

Unless…

Instead of writing up her order for new stock one morning, she forced herself to confront the impossible and made an appointment with her family doctor. She'd finished the active tablets in her packet of Pills. Her period was nearly two weeks overdue. She didn't want to start a new pack until she knew why.

Dr Judy explained, 'If you haven't missed a Pill, vomited or used other medication, it's unlikely you're pregnant, Mariel.'

Mariel bit down on her lip while she looked at the older woman who'd treated her for all the childhood illnesses over the years, and felt like throwing up. She'd read the Pill's accompanying leaflet. She knew the advice by heart… Now. And *now* was a little late. A lot late. 'I was airsick on the way back to Australia. And somehow I miscalculated the time difference and ended up with a spare Pill…'

Dr Judy scribbled something on Mariel's case notes, then smiled at her over her rimless glasses in a grand-motherly way that made Mariel want to crawl onto her lap and cry like she'd done when she was five and she'd had stitches in her knee.

'In that case,' she said, 'why don't we do a blood test?'

CHAPTER ELEVEN

PREGNANT.

Mariel dived off the edge of Dane's pool and sliced through the blue water with smooth, powerful strokes. Pregnant. She increased her speed as if she could outpace her problem.

Dr Judy had assured her it was a definite positive, and outlined the next steps Mariel should take. Choice of hospital, antenatal classes, vitamins. She'd directed her to a couple of websites that showed images of the foetus virtually from the first week. Imagine that?

Except Mariel could barely remember a thing. A shocked numbness had invaded her body so thoroughly she'd driven back on autopilot and wondered how she'd made it from the hills town of Stirling to the city without an accident. Now, with the refreshing sensation of cool water over her, the shock was dissipating and stark reality was creeping in.

Flipping, she backstroked her way to the middle of the pool, focusing on the sky's cloudless blue bowl above her, keeping her mind on her breathing, her strokes.

Not focusing on the place in the centre of her belly that suddenly seemed to practically pulse with its own

self-awareness. She couldn't think about the baby…
Oh, God, she was having a baby. Dane's baby.

'Dane,' she murmured. The man who didn't want
marriage, who didn't want children.

The man she loved.

Rolling over, she dived deep, listening to the cascade
of bubbles past her ears, trying desperately to outrush
her emotions. She knew how dramatically everything
was going to change.

At the moment Dane was blissfully ignorant, and
likely to remain that way for the next couple of days.
There was no way she could tell him something that important,
that devastating, over the phone. She wondered
how long she should let that state of ignorance last.
Maybe she could get away with it a little longer while
she decided the best way to tell him.

But a secret like that wouldn't be a secret for long.

Finally exhausted, she swiped water from her face
as she pushed up out of the water and onto the deck.
She shook her head, scattering water, then wrapped her
hair in a towel and sat on the edge of the pool.

He'd think she'd manipulated him, the way his former
lover had. He'd been prepared to use contraception but
she'd told him she was on the Pill. He couldn't have
made it clearer that he didn't intend having kids. Ever.

So she'd make it clear she didn't intend to force him
into something that would bring unhappiness to both of
them. To all of them. Anger, resentment, and finally indifference
would follow. And nobody had the right to
bring a child into the world to live under those circumstances.
Of all people, Dane would understand that.

A sense of surrealism surrounded her as she reached
for another towel and, wrapping it around her body,

trudged upstairs to take a long, cleansing frangipani-scented bath. She still hadn't examined her own feelings—couldn't. Deliberately she didn't look at her naked body in the mirror as she turned on the taps. Her maternal instinct must have gone AWOL, or maybe it was simply self-preservation or denial, because she could *not* touch her belly and think about the miracle happening in there.

And she had two days to get used to the idea before Dane came home.

In Alice Springs Dane keyed in his home number and switched on his laptop the moment he reached his hotel room. It had become a nightly ritual at seven p.m. over the past week. They'd talk a moment and then, if the reception was clear, switch to computers, where they could see each other while they talked over the day.

It had been a buzz, watching the animation in her face as she told him about her steady journey towards realising her goals. And it gave him an added buzz knowing he'd helped.

Tonight anticipation surged through him. He'd worked it so that he could go home earlier. This time tomorrow he'd be able to say hello to her in the flesh—a surprise he wanted to keep.

He'd never had a woman waiting for him at home. A smile tugged at his lips. Not that Mariel was the kind of woman to wait around.

But tonight she took longer than usual answering. 'Hello?'

Her voice was breathless and intimate and right up close against his ear, but he picked up on something else, too. He couldn't identify it, but it sent a chill skittering over his spine despite the hotel room's ambience. 'Hi, there, Queen Bee.'

'Dane… Oh…is it seven o'clock already?'

'You sound out of breath. Where were you?'

'I was…in the pool.'

He dismissed the hesitation as breathlessness—she'd told him she was swimming, hadn't she?

'Turn on the computer,' he said. 'I want to see you.'

Definite hesitation this time. 'You want me to leave a trail of water on the stairs, too?'

'It'll be worth it, I promise.'

'Not tonight,' she said. 'I'm not feeling the best.'

He blew out a slow breath, swallowed his disappointment. 'I'm sorry to hear that. What's wrong?'

'I must have picked up a bug or something.'

'Why don't you take something for it, climb into bed and get some sleep?'

'I already am. Will be.'

He frowned. Less than a minute ago she'd said she'd been in the pool. They'd never lied to each other. At least he hadn't lied to her. They'd promised each other open and honest communication. What had changed that? 'Are you sure that's all it is?'

'Yes, I'm sure.'

'I'll say goodnight, then, and let you get some rest.'

'Okay. Goodnight.'

The way she disconnected he could have sworn he heard the bedside table rattle halfway across Australia. If she *was* in bed? Something had rattled. He felt a little rattled himself.

He stretched out on the hotel's crisp quilt cover. Yes, she was in bed, he assured himself. In *his* bed. Apart from that last night they'd shared, she'd not slept the night with him in his home, yet he could see her there as clearly as if he were lying next to her.

Her dark hair, smelling of flowers, fanned out across his pillow and tickling his nose. Moon-glow spilling through the tall window, painting her glorious silk-clad body silver.

But in that same moon-glow he saw a single crystal tear track down her cheek.

His smile faded.

Dane thanked the chauffeur, unfolded his body and stepped out onto the footpath in the late-afternoon sun. Outwardly, his home looked the same as it always did.

Ah, but inside there was a woman, delicate and strong, beautiful and sometimes aloof, that he couldn't wait to see.

Dumping his gear inside the front door, he walked through the house, seeing evidence of Mariel's presence: her handbag, an international designer jacket draped over a chair. She'd cooked something with chilli and cumin and coriander, the aroma reminding him he hadn't enjoyed home cooking in over a week.

In all his adult years he'd never come home to another living soul. He'd learned independence and self-reliance the hard way. He needed no one; he was satisfied with his own company. But this…contentment was all he could think about. Having someone waiting for him, that was something new.

He stopped at the glass door that led to the patio. Mariel was wearing a sexy one-piece crimson swimsuit and lying in the shade on a slatted recliner with a magazine over her face.

His heart constricted. Not painfully, but quietly, with

certainty. As if it knew something he didn't. Which gave him a second's pause. Had her strange mood of last night altered?

Impatient to find out, he stepped onto the sun-drenched patio. A wave of heat rolled up from the decking, enveloping him in the smell of chlorinated water and sun-bleached wood.

He crossed the deck soundlessly, sat on the shaded recliner beside her so that their hips bumped, and slid the magazine from her face. 'Hello, gorgeous.'

Sleepy eyes blinked up at him. He watched emotions flicker through their depths as awareness crystallised. Pleasure, then confusion…and something like dismay. But her voice was composed when she said, 'Either you're a day early or I've been sleeping here a lot longer than I thought.'

He grinned. 'I managed to finish up early.' He laid his hand on her belly.

Her eyes instantly flared at his touch, and if he didn't know Mariel better he would have said he saw a glint of something close to fear in their depths.

'I was concerned about you last night.' Justifiably so, he thought now, as she jerked. Her stomach muscles tightened beneath his palm before she swung her legs onto the deck and stood, facing away from him. He stood, too, to meet her on an equal footing.

'No need,' she said breezily, then turned, smiling, and waggled manicured fingers at him in a flippant manner. Too flippant. 'I'm fine. I just wasn't up for talking.'

This woman standing before him wasn't the Mariel he knew. What had changed her? Something like panic flitted through his system. 'You want to explain why?'

Narrowing his eyes, he scoured her features against the low sun's glare. That perfect but slightly aloof smile was her trademark, the smile she showed the world. It wasn't the one he wanted to see. Not here alone with her. Not as her lover.

He wanted to see the smile that lit a glow in her cheeks and sparked fireworks in her eyes, that emanated a soft radiance that filled up an entire room. The smile that shut the rest of the world out and made him the centre of her universe.

'Not particularly,' she said. 'Not right now.'

Since her voice had grown husky on the last words and she was still smiling, albeit not the smile he wanted to see, he took that as an invitation and moved closer, ready to forgive and forget if he could just reacquaint himself with the taste of her mouth.

He refused to try and interpret the tremble he felt in her lips as they met his. He coaxed her gently, cupping her neck, angling her jaw for a better fit when he felt her spine soften, her body turn pliant. Her hands crept to his shoulders, curving around his neck like ropes of silk.

Satisfaction slid through him on a rising tide of desire. He could lure her with one persuasive kiss. Wasn't she already right here with him? All the way?

He hauled her against his burgeoning erection, her damp bathers slick and cool against the front of his T-shirt, and his hands tingled at the thought of how her skin would feel when he peeled the fabric from her.

She moaned against his mouth, whatever was bothering her obviously forgotten as she poured herself into the kiss, arching against him so that he splayed one hand against her back to support her.

Everything forgotten as he lifted his mouth from her lips to roam across the smooth curves of her face. Cheeks, eyes, brow, jaw. Her long twist of ebony hair slithered damply over his forearm; her fingers dug little grooves into his neck.

Now, *this* was coming home. While he could still stand, he leaned down and, with one arm beneath her knees, swept her into his arms and headed for the door.

Her softly fluttering eyes were startled open.

'Relax,' he said, kissing her brow as he reached the staircase. 'I've decided that from now on carrying you upstairs is going to become part of my daily exercise routine.'

Mariel's heart stuttered. Not when he knew what she had to tell him, it wouldn't.

Steel eyes met hers as his footsteps stalled on the stairs. 'What's wrong?'

'I smell like chlorine,' she whispered. 'My hair's still wet.'

'You think I care?'

'I guess not…' Weak with wanting, and powerless to resist what she knew was coming, she allowed herself to be carried up the stairs—again—like some modern-day Scarlett O'Hara.

Because she knew it would be the last time.

One last time to know how it felt to be made love to by Dane.

The sheen of the day's heat reflected on the ivory-coloured walls as he laid her on his bed.

Yanking his T-shirt over his head, he stripped naked in ten seconds flat, then crawled onto the bed. She'd never seen such passion in his eyes as he slid the straps of her bathers over her shoulders and down her arms.

Her nipples, already hard from desire and damp, puckered further as he drew the fabric away.

Then he was tugging it from beneath her bottom and sliding it down over her thighs, her knees, her ankles. He reached out, traced the curve of one breast. 'I'd say you were beautiful, but you've heard it before.'

Mariel heard the casual tone, rather than the compliment, and her heart constricted. 'Not from you, I haven't. Not this way.'

His eyes met hers, a long, lingering hold that imprisoned her with silent and steely intensity.

'So tell me.' Her voice was edgy with impatience. Just once, she wanted to hear it from Dane's lips.

His eyes crinkled up around the edges for a moment, then his expression turned serious once more. 'Ninety-nine percent of the time beauty's an accident of birth. That's what men see when they look at you. So when I tell you you're beautiful I'm not only talking about the softness of your skin or the colour of your eyes. It's inside you, Queen Bee, where it counts.'

As he spoke, his palm seared her skin, rubbing slowly beneath her left breast, then over her concave belly.

Over his unborn child.

Tears gathered in her heart. She wanted to weep. She sensed something more in Dane's voice today. More in his eyes, more in his kiss. Over the past few days her vision had cleared, as if a curtain had been lifted. It didn't matter that they argued and disagreed. That there'd always be vocal and noisy differences of opinion. Who was right and who was in control?

It didn't matter.

Under different circumstances she'd have asked him if it was the same for him, no hesitation. If nothing else they'd always had trust and honesty between them. With time and patience *maybe* she could have had it all, but she'd carelessly thrown that chance away. Because there was no negotiation where children and Dane were concerned.

So take this moment and this man, she told herself. Take the rest of tonight and make it special. Memorable.

She might possibly die of a broken heart, but his was made of stone and she'd told him so and he hadn't denied it. He'd be okay. He'd get over the shock and the anger and they'd sort everything out, and maybe they could still be friends the way they'd always been.

Friends sharing a child. That wasn't so impossible. Was it?

'Perhaps I shouldn't have told you after all,' he murmured in his deep, husky voice, and she realised her mind had wandered off. 'It seems to have made you sad.'

She shook her head against the pillow. 'Make love with me,' she whispered. 'No one ever made love with me the way you do.'

He bent his head, grazed her lips once, twice. 'Because no one knows you the way I do.'

She wanted to tell him she loved him, right here, right now, while the moment sparkled with truth. But the only truth around here tonight was his truth. And her untold secret proved him wrong. He didn't know her as well as he thought. It spun a web of guilt around her, but when he covered her body with his she lifted her arms and gave herself up to him.

Tonight was lingering looks, slow, sweet passion, the languid glide of flesh on flesh. A lazy touch. A tender kiss. She took him inside her wordlessly and with all the love she had to give.

The lowering sun turned the room orange, his skin to bronze. His eyes were dark, almost black in the fading light, and his day's worth of stubble shadowed his jaw and rasped against her hand when she reached out to absorb, to stroke.

Dane became her only reality in a room she no longer saw. The sound of his murmurs, the thump of his heart against hers. The intoxicating scent of man. This man.

And she clung to that reality, to Dane, and in those all too short precious moments, lived that lifetime she was going to be denied.

CHAPTER TWELVE

MARIEL woke first. It was full dark, and the city's twinkling lights cast a dim glow across the walls. Angry with herself for falling asleep, she turned to watch Dane. She'd wanted to stay awake and think. To lie beside him and listen to his breathing while she prepared herself to tell him.

As if he sensed she was awake, his eyes blinked open in the semi-darkness. 'Hi.'

'Hi.'

He moved an arm, stopped. Then pulled a silk night-gown from beneath him and dangled it in front of her with a grin. 'What's this?'

'Oh…' Mariel felt herself flush. 'I…'

Damn it, she hadn't expected him back tonight, and now her secret indulgence to sleep where he slept and feel close to him was out in the open for Dane's scrutiny.

'You slept in my bed.' It wasn't a question.

'Yes. Is that a hanging offence?'

He kissed the tip of her nose. 'I don't think so. Wait here.' He slid off the bed and disappeared downstairs.

He was back in less than a minute with a small swing bag. He switched on the bedside lamp, filling the room with a soft ambience. 'A present from Alice Springs.' The mattress dipped as he climbed back onto the bed with her.

With trembling fingers she pulled out a sexy black bra and matching thong. Her heart soared briefly, then sank as she stroked the flimsy material. How long would she be able to wear it? 'Thank you, they're beautiful. How did you know what size?'

His eyes twinkled and he cupped a breast in his palm. 'You think I don't know the size of your breasts by now?'

'I guess you do. They're lovely.' He didn't suggest she model them, thank heavens, and she set them aside. The tremor in her fingers increased. 'Dane…'

'Mmm?' He shifted closer, nibbled her shoulder. 'I'm hungry; how about you?'

She breathed a tremulous sigh of partial relief. Off the hook a little longer. And they needed to eat before she knuckled down and told him. 'I could do with a cheeseburger and fries.'

His brows rose. 'You want junk food? You never eat junk food.'

'I do. Just not often.'

'What was that yummy dish I smelled in the kitchen when I came home?'

'I didn't know you were coming; there's only enough for one.'

'We could share…'

'We could. But you'd still be hungry. And I haven't cooked the rice yet. It'll take—'

'Okay, okay, I get the message. Pull on some clothes and we'll do take-away.'

* * *

Dane wanted to take their meal and sit by the River Torrens, where it was cooler, and watch the lights reflect on the water. But Mariel didn't seem keen, so they ate at home on the sofa in front of the TV. She was giving her earlobe a workout and his unease flooded back.

When he'd finished his meal, and eaten Mariel's half-finished burger, he stuffed the cardboard containers back into the carry-bag, tossed it on the table. He shifted to a forty-five-degree angle so that he could see her properly. 'Okay, Mariel, what's the problem?'

She bit on her lip, then lifted her chin, took a breath. 'You're not going to like this…'

His stomach bottomed out, but he remained outwardly calm. 'Try me.'

She heaved another breath, as if garnering courage. 'I'm pregnant.'

His brain took a couple of seconds to process the information. It took another couple to get his tongue to work around the word he'd never imagined associated with their lives. His life. 'Pregnant.'

His vision blurred, and the only sound he could hear was the rasp of air as it caught on his tonsils on its way to his rapidly deflating lungs. 'Pregnant.' He blinked to clear the haze that he found himself enshrouded in and saw Mariel, pale-faced, eyes too big, too vulnerable, her hands clenched tightly in her lap.

'Yes.' She worried her bottom lip again. 'I found out yesterday.'

Rational thought began to surface, along with denial. 'How is that possible? I thought you were on the Pill? That's what you told me.' He heard the accusation in his own voice.

Déjà vu. Flashback to another woman, another time. Had Mariel planned it? He shook it away immediately.

'I *was* on the Pill…' She rubbed her arms as if cold. 'I was due to start another packet but I never got my period. So I went to see Dr Judy at Stirling to ask her advice.'

Unable to sit, he pushed up and paced. 'So when you told me last night that you had a bug, you were lying?'

'I couldn't tell you that kind of news over the phone. You would *not* have wanted me to tell you over the phone. Something this important has to be said face to face.'

He acknowledged that with a stiff-necked nod. 'So, what are your plans?'

'*My* plans?' Her eyes narrowed. 'Oh, that's just great. So it seems when things get too hard you're a typical irresponsible male after all. This is your baby, too, so it's *our* plans. Like it or not, this is about *us*.'

'You're missing my intention. I'm giving *you* the option. It's your call. But you'll have my full support whatever you decide.'

She stared at him. 'You…you…' She pushed off the sofa, all white-faced fury, and stood before him, fingers clenching and unclenching at her sides. 'If you're thinking what I think you're thinking—'

'You haven't a clue what I'm thinking,' he shot back. 'How could you when I don't know what the hell I'm thinking myself?' Why did she have to look at him that way, her eyes brimming with tears and censure? 'Oh, no… No, Mariel, I didn't mean…'

And then it hit him—a bolt from the sky, a tsunami, a super cyclone all rolled into one.

His baby.

A part of him.

Growing inside Mariel.

Adrenaline spiked through his veins and bled like fire into already tight muscles. His heart pumped so hard he thought he'd burst a valve.

Seemingly of their own volition his eyes sought and found Mariel's flat belly. Hidden beneath a lolly-pink mini-skirt…his baby.

Some insane, primitive part of him wanted to beat his chest and shout it to the ends of the earth. He dragged his eyes away and turned to stare blindly at the night-darkened window, his mind assaulted by a barrage of *what-the-hell-do-I-do-now?* scenarios.

He could feel her eyes drilling into his back. She was waiting for more from him, expecting more from him. And she *should* expect more. 'I have to think.' Shoving his hands through his hair, he locked them behind his head as he continued to stare into the night. 'I need to get my head around this.'

He heard the shift of fabric and a soft footfall on the polished boards. Something like panic gripped him at the thought that she'd leave without a word and, worse, that he'd allow it.

'Mariel…' He crossed to her in four quick strides, grabbed her fingers. Her hands felt chilled, the bones fragile. He ran his thumb over them and looked into her over-bright eyes. 'When I suggested this arrangement I thought it would help you.'

Mariel saw his pain etched in every furrow, every facial muscle, felt it echo in her heart. She knew he was in shock. That he was still a long way from dealing with the news. But he hadn't told her what she wanted to hear. *We'll get married.* Or even, *I won't leave you* or *We'll raise it together*. And why would he? They'd never agreed to that. And now he'd be leaving not one person but two people.

Pressing her lips together, she nodded, unable to speak lest she blubber—and she didn't want to blubber and reveal how desperately needy she felt right now. How much she wanted him to hold her closer and kiss her and tell her everything was going to be all right.

But it wasn't going to be all right. Because no matter how close they were, or how much she loved him, when it came to the important ever-after stuff they were at opposite ends of the spectrum.

He squeezed her hands once, passed a whispered caress across her lips. 'Go on to bed. You need to take care of yourself now. I'll see you in the morning.'

His kiss was as sweet as ever, and he sounded as sincere as he always did, but a chasm had opened up between them and she knew they'd ever be the same again.

The following morning Dane left before Mariel was awake. He might have opened the door to check on her, but she didn't hear him. She tried to focus on work. She'd need some sort of income to maintain her independence. She didn't have a clue about where she'd live, what Dane would provide—if anything—so she couldn't make plans.

You'll have my full support. His words. But how far did that extend? she wondered. And what had he meant? Financial? Emotional?

Bringing her pregnancy out in the open with him seemed to have sparked her maternal instinct. She thought of Dane's mother, who'd left him. Did the woman not realise all she'd missed out on?

Well, Mariel didn't intend to miss out on a minute of

raising her baby. She'd always dreamed of kids of her own, a man who loved her to share the joy with. But if the father wasn't going to be around, so be it. She'd still have a little reminder of Dane that she could love for ever.

Everything was on hold, like suspended animation. She hated it, but she marked time. She had to wait. Maybe tonight. Would he come and tell her he'd decided he wanted to make a go of it?

But when he came home from the office it was eight o'clock, and she was already in bed, emotionally and physically exhausted. She heard his footsteps hesitate outside her door, then he moved on.

No. She wouldn't let herself weep for the man she loved and would walk away from. Nor was she going to wait around for him to make a decision. She had some pride left, and she refused to be a victim again.

Slipping out of bed, she opened her door. Light from his study cast a strip of light across the polished boards in the passage. Placing one foot in front of the other, she moved towards it.

His phone rang as she was about to enter.

'Huntington.' Pause. 'Yes. I meant to get back to you. There's—' He rolled his head back and studied the ceiling. 'Tonight?' From behind him Mariel saw him rub his temple. 'Okay.' He glanced at his watch. 'Twenty minutes. Don't worry, I'll be there.'

A faint creak in the floorboards alerted him to Mariel's presence. His hand jerked—almost guiltily, she thought—then he disconnected and slipped the phone in his pocket. 'I thought you were asleep, I didn't want to wake you.'

'You didn't wake me. I wanted to talk.'

'I would, but I'm sorry, now's not a good time. I've got an urgent matter I need to deal with.'

She felt her mouth go dry, felt her tongue stick to the roof of her mouth, but she managed to say, 'Now? What's more important than our baby?'

Dane stilled, and something flickered behind the still gaze. 'We'll talk. We will. But it's business. A client.'

'A client.'

'Don't do this, Mariel.' He turned away to shut down his computer, then riffled through an untidy pile of papers. 'You'll have to trust me on this.'

Trust him? The way she'd trusted Luc? He'd had 'business appointments', too. She fought back tears.

He rose and, still folding whatever it was he'd been looking for, walked towards her. He tilted her chin up, gripped it between tense fingers. '*Do* you trust me?'

She thought of his women, his playboy lifestyle. She remembered their childhood and shared secrets, the last couple of weeks they'd spent together here in his home. Arguing, making love. She wanted to trust him. How she wanted to. He was her baby's father; nothing could change that fact. And they were bound by it for the rest of their lives.

'Well?' he demanded. His eyes swirled with some emotion she couldn't read.

'If we don't have trust, Dane, we have nothing.' She couldn't deny it. She couldn't deny him the chance to prove it. If she didn't, there was no future for them at all.

His shoulders relaxed as some of the tension there eased. 'Go to bed. Get some sleep. You look like you need it.' The kiss he laid on her lips was sweet but brief.

Whether he crept in without a sound or whether she was sleeping—though she was sure she'd not slept a wink—Mariel didn't hear him come home.

CHAPTER THIRTEEN

THE following day started out as the day from hell and grew worse with every passing hour. Mariel heard the wind pick up soon after dawn, seething through the casuarinas over the road. From her bedroom window she could see that the sky had turned a dull brown, with raised dust obscuring the rising sun.

Dane left soon after. She waited until she heard his car start, then went downstairs. She tried to eat, but even the thought of putting anything in her stomach made her feel ill. The onset of morning sickness? she wondered.

The radio's weather bulletin was dire. Forty-five degrees, with gale force winds. Hills residents were being advised to ensure their bushfire action plans were in place: to leave now, or stay and be prepared to fight if a fire broke out. It was shaping up to be a day reminiscent of Black Saturday, that horrific day Victoria had burned.

Mid-morning the phone rang. 'Ah, Mariel,' the agitated voice said when she picked up. 'Daniel Huntington here. Is Dane about?'

'He's not here, Daniel. Have you tried his office or his mobile?'

'He's not answering either of those numbers.'

The tone of his voice worried Mariel as she rubbed absently at her empty tummy. 'Are you all right? Is there something I can help you with?'

'It's blowing like the devil up here. I don't like the looks of it, Mariel. Bloody arsonists about. One spark…'

She closed her eyes and wished she didn't have to offer, but… 'Why don't you come down here for the day?'

His blunt, 'I'm not leaving the house,' worried her more.

'It's only a house, Daniel. Material things can be replaced. You're what matters.'

'This is Dane's house, and I'm not leaving it to burn down.'

Dane's house? What did he mean by that? 'There's no fire there now, is there?' Holding the phone in one hand, she clicked on the Internet to see if there were any reports.

'No. But I was just outside, and damned if I can't smell smoke.' There was a shuffling sound on the line, then a thud.

Mariel pressed the phone closer. 'Are you there, Daniel?'

'I'm here. Just trying to shut…the door. It's blowing like the devil. In these conditions if a fire catches hold, we're done for.'

Mariel chewed on her lip in an agony of indecision. He was in his seventies and alone, and in the danger zone on a major bushfire alert day. He sounded out of breath and out of sorts. She couldn't leave him there. She could *not*.

'Listen, Daniel. I'm going to drive up there now and pick you up.'

'No, girlie, I'm not leaving.'

'Okay,' she said, keeping her voice low and soothing. 'I'll come, and we'll talk when I get there.'

Another silence, then a sigh that sounded like relief. 'You're a good woman, Mariel. I'll put the kettle on.'

Mariel disconnected. Great. A joyride to the hills to spend the day from hell with an old man who was as stubborn as his son!

And that old man was her baby's grandfather.

If that wasn't a good enough reason, she didn't know what was.

She tried Dane's phones before she left, to let him know her plans, but the office was still unattended and his mobile was switched off. She knew he had an early breakfast meeting. No point in bothering him now. She'd call him again when she got there and let him know what was going on.

Fifteen minutes later she was on the road.

With a sharp expletive, Dane slammed his foot on the brake. Two elderly women skirted the bonnet, glaring at him as they crossed the driveway outside his office. 'Sorry, ladies.' He smiled an apology. At least he thought his lips moved. They felt a little numb. The oldies kept right on glaring.

'If you'd had as little shut-eye as I have over the past couple of nights you'd be sleep-walking, too,' he muttered.

He waited till they'd taken their sweet time, then zoomed into his personal parking space, killed the engine and let his head roll back on the headrest. His seven-thirty a.m. meeting with a new client had finished early, which now gave him time to check in at the office before heading out again for another meeting and to upgrade a system east of the city.

Not far from the freeway, he thought. His conscience pricked at him. Inconvenient thing, conscience. But he'd drive out to see his father afterwards, just to check he was okay on this hellish day. Wouldn't take long.

Justin's car was nowhere to be seen, and their shared PA was on leave for another week, so the office blinds were shut against the heat, the rooms relatively cool and dim when he entered. He sank into the plush chair behind his desk, checked the office phone and mobile for messages. He returned three calls, left a message in answer to another.

That done, he stuck his feet on his desk and closed his eyes. But he couldn't find the relief he sought. *Mariel.* Her name rippled across his mind like cool, clean water. He should have made time for her, but somehow he just hadn't been able to deal with it. Pain crawled up his chest and into his throat. Worse, he'd let her down when she most needed him.

'Jeez, man, you look like crap.'

His eyes jerked open at the familiar voice. Justin, wearing a fresh white business shirt and pressed trousers, frowned at him from the doorway. He screwed them shut again. 'Go away, Jus.'

'No can do. I'm your business partner, mate.'

Dane could feel his disapproval clear across the room. When he didn't leave, Dane opened his eyes. 'What?'

'Don't tell me you just tried to woo a new client in that sorry excuse for a T-shirt.'

'Okay, I won't tell you.'

'What's with the excess facial fuzz? And the hair— isn't it about time for a trim? A little professional—'

'If I need someone to nag me I'll get a wife,' he

snarled. He picked up a rubber band, stretched it till it broke and snapped against his fingers. He welcomed its sting.

Justin walked right into the room, rested one hip on the corner of Dane's desk. 'Does Mariel realise what she's let herself in for?'

'If she doesn't like the arrangement she's free to leave. In fact I'm expecting the kiss-off any time now. I'll be sure to let you know when it happens, so you won't worry about her.' He snatched up another rubber band, aimed it at the trophy on top of his filing cabinet and fired. 'Probably be the best decision she ever made.'

'Blimey, Dane.'

Dane glanced at his friend, then had to turn away from the accusation he read in his eyes. 'You know me. Commitment was never my strong suit.'

'A blind fool can see that you love her. She only has to walk into the room and that steel in your eyes melts. What the hell happened?'

A baby happened.

Nerves jittered. His heart tightened. 'Fact is, I…' he began, but his vocal cords wouldn't work properly. 'Fact is, we…' He swallowed over the lump in his throat.

Suddenly everything fell into place. This baby was an innocent in all this. Dane knew how it was to grow up without a father's love, without any parental affection. He'd learned from it, was stronger because of it. But did he want the same for his own child? Hell, no. He'd been given a chance. A real chance. And he'd been given it with Mariel. His best friend.

The woman he loved more than anything or anyone. Was he just going to let the only genuine woman who had ever entered his life, the only woman who could blow away the storm clouds he saw in his eyes every time he looked in a mirror, walk away? Could he let the child they'd created together grow up without knowing its father? Without a father's love?

Not if he could help it. He'd just been handed the greatest challenge of his life and he wasn't backing down.

He jack-knifed out of his chair, snapping open his mobile while he walked to the door, barely aware of Justin staring at him as if he'd just lost his mind. Maybe he had lost it for a moment, but now he had it back.

'Mate. Friend. You're just what I needed.' With a headflick, he motioned Jus out. 'Excuse me, I need to make a very important call.' Maybe the most important call of his life.

The instant Justin stepped out, Dane slammed the door shut behind him while he punched in his home number. No answer. He slapped a thigh as impatience simmered through him. Now he knew what he had to do he couldn't wait to get on with it. He tried Mariel's mobile. No answer; his call was directed to her voicemail.

Clenching his fist, he paced to the desk and spoke into the phone. 'Mariel, I've been a bloody idiot. Call me when you get this. I need to see you. ASAP.' Something this important had to be said face to face. He checked his watch. Damn. 'On second thought, don't, I've got a meeting coming up. I'll phone you when it's finished.' He closed his eyes. *I love you, Queen Bee.*

Mariel clenched her hands around the steering wheel, struggling to keep the car in a straight line. The thermometer indicated that it was forty-two degrees outside. Even the air-conditioner failed to cool the interior as hot wind snuck in through the cracks and a hazy sun glared through the windscreen. A branch skidded across the road in front of her. Her mouth was dry, but she dared not let her tensed fingers stray from the wheel to reach for her bottled water.

Finally she parked outside Daniel's house. And stepped out into hell on earth.

A relentless January sun had baked the sky bone-white and sucked the earth dry. She stood a few seconds, her pulse stepping up as she stared in rising horror at the shimmering dust haze shrouding the usually beautiful landscape.

A tinderbox. *One spark...*

'Oh, my God,' she murmured. But the wind, a terrifying banshee of blistering heat, whipped the words from her mouth with the same fury as it ripped through trees and sent debris flying through the air like missiles.

She reached the front door, but no one answered her frantic knocks so she ran to the back. Dane's father was lying in the full sun with the hose in his hand, water spraying on the muddy earth beside him. 'Daniel!' she heard herself scream, and dropped to her knees beside him. 'What are you doing out here?'

'Don't want the house to burn. Mariel?' He peered up at her with pale watery eyes.

'There's no fire, Daniel,' she soothed, but her pulse was hammering in her throat. 'Come on.' She tried to tug him up, but he wasn't going anywhere on his own. She levered herself beneath one shoulder and dragged him a few metres into the shade. The effort left her dazed and breathless, but she unscrewed the top on her water and held the bottle to his lips. 'Here, drink.'

He gulped a couple of mouthfuls, then lay back. She poured the rest of the water onto a wad of tissues she found in her bag and wiped his face, then felt for his pulse. It galloped beneath her fingers. She pulled her mobile from her bag and rang for an ambulance. Then she phoned Dane. Damn him, why wasn't his bloody phone on? She left a message to inform him about his father, then hauled herself up, swaying a little as spots danced before her eyes.

'I'll be back in a moment,' she told Daniel, dry-mouthed, then ran inside and found a towel, soaked it in water and rushed back outside.

'You're a good woman for Dane,' he mumbled while she laid the towel across his body. 'Dane's all I have. Should've been a better…father…' He frowned. 'Head hurts.'

'It's going to be okay,' she told him, closing her eyes. But she didn't feel a hundred percent herself, and that queasy feeling was back. 'Help's coming.'

Finally she heard the wail of the siren over the screaming wind. Dragging herself up, she staggered to the driveway to usher the ambulance around the back.

The paramedics jumped out and checked Daniel over. 'Mild heat exhaustion,' the older man said. 'Lucky we got here when we did. Is he your granddad?'

'No. My…partner's father.'

'So you don't live here?'

She shook her head. 'He lives alone. I came by to check on him.'

'Lucky break. We'll take him in for observation, get some fluids into him, but it looks like he's going to be okay.'

The younger guy glanced at her. A small frown

creased his brow, concern in his light blue eyes. 'You okay? Here. Drink this.' He handed her a bottle of water.

'Thanks.' She drank deeply, swiped the sweat off her neck, her face, took a deep steadying breath. She shifted her stance to relieve the dull ache in her abdomen. 'I'll be okay in a minute.' She watched, sliding sweaty palms together while they loaded Daniel into the nearby ambulance.

Dane, where are you?

'Hey,' said a deep voice near her ear. 'I think you should ride along with us and let me check you over, too.'

'I'm fine.' It was like trying to breathe in an oven. Spots danced in front of her eyes. Firm hands helped her up. He passed her handbag to her. 'You want to call your partner? Let him know what's going on?'

She nodded. 'I'll leave a message.'

An hour later she stood looking out at the dust-ravaged panorama from the fourth-floor hospital window while Daniel slept. He was staying in overnight and going to be okay, but he couldn't go back home. He needed rest and care and monitoring over the next few days. And she was going to ask Dane if his father could go home with him. No, she wasn't going to ask. She was going to demand. There were plenty of spare rooms. If necessary he could have her room.

And if Dane refused she'd go home with Daniel herself, if only to show Dane what an idiot he was. What both men were, when it came to that. It was so important for them to re-establish some kind of a relationship. He was going to be her child's grandfather, and somehow it had fallen on her shoulders to take the first steps towards making a family unit, even if that 'unit' was likely to be spread in three different locations across the city.

Abruptly she felt the floor heave beneath her. She sank onto the visitor's chair, blinking away an encroaching grey mist. The twinge she'd barely noticed this morning suddenly took on a more sinister meaning. *No!* Tears gathered in her eyes as the mist grew darker. She'd had little sleep and a rough morning; that was all. That. Was. All.

She reached out and pressed the nurses' call button before she crumpled over.

CHAPTER FOURTEEN

DANE marched through the hospital foyer, his sneakers squeaking on the linoleum, the smell of antiseptic filling his nostrils. He could barely contain his frustration. Mariel hadn't called back—a situation that didn't bode well for the resolution he'd hoped for.

He'd put his heart on the line in that phone call. But obviously that wasn't enough. She expected him to grovel. And right now he was desperate enough to do just that. Once in a lifetime monumental measures were needed to achieve a monumental outcome. He hoped. By God, he hoped.

So while he waited for the elevator he arranged for a delivery of flowers. He made a reservation at one of Mariel's favourite restaurants while the lift carried him to the fourth floor.

At the nurses' station the petite nurse blushed when he smiled at her. He enquired about his father's room, then promptly forgot her. He could be out of here in ten minutes once he saw his father and assured himself the old goat was okay. The problem of care could be sorted out tomorrow—

'You're Mr Daniel Huntington's son?' a voice asked

behind him, before he'd taken more than a few steps. Barely curbing his impatience, Dane turned his head, continued walking. 'Yes.'

'Dane?' It was the same blushing nurse, with her efficient-looking clipboard in her hand, but this time she appeared more flustered than dazzled. 'And Ms Mariel Davenport is your partner?'

His mouth tightened infinitesimally. Had he met her somewhere? A function? He couldn't recall. 'Yes to both questions,' he clipped.

She nodded, Ms Cool and Professional now. 'Will you come with me, please?'

'Is Mariel here?' He stopped, swivelled to look at her.

She didn't meet his eyes; they were focused on the board in her hands. 'If you'll just come with me…'

'Where are we going?' he asked as he entered the elevator with her.

'To the first floor.' She watched the numbers light up as they descended. He sensed her relief when the doors whooshed open. 'Just speak to one the nurses here; they're expecting you,' she said, pointing to the nurses' station. 'They'll answer all your questions.' He stepped out and she shuffled back. He had a fleeting glimpse of her watching him as the doors closed again.

'Hey…' He turned his attention in the direction she'd indicated, saw a couple of staff glance his way, then lean confidentially towards one another, speaking quietly.

He ran a hand around the back of his neck to soothe the sudden tension there then strode towards them. He wanted answers, but he had a gut feeling he wasn't going to like what he heard.

A middle-aged nurse with sheep's wool hair and

purple-rimmed glasses met him halfway. 'Mr Huntington.'

He nodded curtly. 'What's going on?'

'Ms Davenport has been admitted.' She started walking. 'She's through here.'

'Admitted? Why?' he demanded. 'What happened? How is she?' Good God, didn't anyone around here know how to give a straight answer?

'She'll be fine,' the nurse reassured him when he ran out of words, stopping at the door to a private room. 'She's awake. I'll let her tell you.'

He came to a halt beside the bed. Mariel was one strong woman, and seeing her in a pink and white striped hospital gown, hooked up to a drip, face pale, eyes dull, looking vulnerable and lost, nearly brought him to his knees.

He dropped into the visitor's chair. It scraped across the linoleum as he pulled it close. 'What happened— and why the *hell* didn't someone call me?'

'Because I told them not to.' She looked away, to the dull sky thickening with ominous clouds. 'I didn't want to see you. I wanted to be alone. I still want to be alone.'

His chest tightened further. 'No. I'm not letting you be alone, because you don't really mean that.'

'I do.' Her fingers tightened on the sheet. 'You'll be relieved to know I lost the baby.'

No. Not that. A black hole opened inside him. His heart dropped to his shoes. He'd been offered something precious and he'd been too blind to see it until it was too late. Worse, much worse, he'd hurt the woman he loved with his unspeakably selfish behaviour. 'Mariel. Sweetheart…I'm sorry.' Such inadequate words to express the mountain of emotion, his pain.

Her pain.

He took her hand, chafed it between his. It felt small and fragile, the way she looked right now. She never looked fragile. But at this moment she did. Her face was too pale, her eyes too haunted. 'If I could change anything in the world I'd turn back time—just one day, if that's all I could have, and start over.'

She lifted a shoulder. 'A pretty fairytale. So why say it? Because you think you might magically change your mind about being a father? Hardly. Because you think it'll make me feel better? It doesn't.'

He leaned closer, breathed in the scent of her skin. 'When I rang you it was because I wanted to see you. I wanted to tell you something important.'

'You didn't ring me.'

'I left a voice message. You didn't get it?'

She shook her head and her lips thinned. 'It may have escaped your attention, but I was far too busy dealing with an emergency to check for messages. Your father could have died out there alone today.'

'He didn't—thanks to you.'

'So…what was it that was so *important*?' She weighted the last word and turned away as she spoke. Her cold dismissal was like a kick in the gut.

'Damn it, Mariel.' He pulled her bag from the bedside locker, switched on her phone. 'Here.' He shoved it in her hand. 'Listen.'

He watched her face. Nothing but cool remoteness in her eyes. 'So…the "bloody idiot" bit I already know. Apart from that, your message doesn't tell me a thing.'

'You didn't pay attention to the way it was delivered. What I really wanted to say couldn't be said over the phone. And you understand that as well as I.'

She gave an infinitesimal nod. 'Okay. Tell me now.'

'I wanted to tell you that I wanted to make a life with you and the bab—' He bit his tongue so hard he tasted blood.

He saw her chest—a quick movement, as if she'd gasped—but her face remained an impassive mask, her eyes fixed somewhere outside the window.

Appalled. He was appalled. 'I'm sorry. But I meant what I said. With all my heart, I meant what I said.'

A long silence filled the room. 'It's easy to say that *now*, isn't it?'

'You think it's *easy*?' He jerked off the chair, pushed his hands through his hair and told the ceiling, 'Nothing with you is easy.'

Frustration consumed him. He could understand where she was coming from. With no pregnancy, his words were empty words. No longer applicable. Some might say he was off the hook.

He didn't want to be cast off. He wanted everything back the way it had been this morning. With the woman he intended spending the rest of his life with, raising their child.

And somehow he was going to make at least the first part happen.

He spun back to the bed, sat down on the covers and reached for her hand. A sense of urgency hammered at him. He had a plan, a last chance, but he needed a little time to put it into action. 'You saved Dad, sweetheart. Life is priceless.'

'Yes. It is.' Her eyes filled. 'Do something for me.'

'Anything.'

'Go and see your father.'

He nodded, pressed a kiss to her cheek. 'I'll be back.'

* * *

'Dad.' Dane sat down beside the old man. 'You've had an eventful day, I hear.'

His father opened his eyes. 'Dane.' His bony shoulders visibly relaxed and his papery lips curved just a little.

'And we have Mariel to thank for that.' He clenched his jaw around the words.

'She's a jewel of a girl, that one.'

So…his dad didn't know Mariel had collapsed in his room? 'She is. So what the hell were you doing, watering the garden in forty-plus degrees?'

'Protecting *your* assets. One spark and it could've all been gone.'

'I never asked you to protect it,' Dane growled, then softened when he saw his father's expression. 'It's just a house, Dad. I've been thinking of selling it. Too many bad memories.'

His father's eyes searched his, then he nodded, seemingly defeated.

Dane picked up the water pitcher, refilled his father's glass. 'You shouldn't be there on your own. You could move down to the city. North Adelaide. Lots of history. Convenient. Plenty of parks and shopping close by.'

'Well, now.' He scratched his jaw. 'Maybe.'

Dane wandered to the window and looked out over the night-drenched Botanic Gardens, crouched in shadow. Heard himself saying, 'Plenty of spare rooms at my place.'

A long silence. 'You'd do that? For me? After everything that's happened?'

The wonder, the hope in his father's voice, made him

want to reach out. He dug his hands in the back pockets of his jeans. 'Maybe.'

His father had made the first move on the night of the ball. They'd made progress over that game of chess. 'It would come with conditions.' He turned to his father, but didn't step closer. 'The brewer who had the house built back in the 1870s raised nine children there. It's a good old-fashioned family home. With good old-fashioned family values.' He nodded to his father and walked to the door. 'Think long and hard about that.'

'Good morning, Mariel.' A young nurse with a mass of red hair and a row of studs in her left ear set a tray on the bedside table. 'My name's Tara and I'll be looking after you this morning.'

'Good morning.' Pushing her hair out of her eyes, Mariel glanced at the clock. 'Six o'clock already? That sedative last night put me right out.'

'The doctor didn't prescribe you a sedative last night.' Tara smiled as she did her morning obs and jotted notes on the clipboard at the foot of the bed. 'Spare a thought for your poor guy. He didn't look like he'd slept a wink.'

Mariel knew that look. Long mussed hair, thirteen-o'clock shadow. Soft mouth, hang-dog eyes that made you want to push him back onto the mattress, cuddle into that warmth and make love till—

'Dane was here?'

Tara lowered the sheet. 'All night on that chair, according to the night nurse. You just missed him. He left about twenty minutes ago.'

He must have gone home at some point, Mariel realised, because she spotted her cosmetic bag and a change of clothes on the shelf in front of the mirror.

Tara pulled the sheet back up, patted Mariel's leg. 'Bleeding's stopped.'

'Does that mean I can go home today?' she asked, with a listless glance towards the window. Where was home? She no longer knew.

'Dr Martinez will let you know when she makes her rounds this morning. She's requested a blood test first,' she said, preparing a syringe.

Mariel leaned back against the pillow. 'Oh, goody.'

'And then she wants you to have an ultrasound.'

A short time later Mariel watched the unreadable image on the monitor.

'Baby?' Mariel stared at the monitor, then looked at the technician. 'I'm still pregnant?'

'You are. It's not recognisable yet,' the technician said. 'But see this thickening here?'

'I'm still pregnant?' Her heart thundered with renewed hope. With joy. 'But I had bleeding...' She couldn't read the blur, but she couldn't take her eyes off the monitor.

Dane. What would he say now? What would *she* say?

Dr Martinez appeared at her side. 'Good morning.' She turned to look at Mariel. 'How are you feeling this morning?'

'Last night I was told I'd had a miscarriage.' To her shame, tears welled up and rolled down her cheeks, and her voice trembled when she said, 'Will someone please explain what's going on?'

'You were carrying twins,' Dr Martinez explained. 'One foetus aborted, but the other one's fine.'

Mariel rubbed her chest to ease the nerves rioting

through her system. 'I've never heard of anyone having a miscarriage and still being pregnant. Is that normal? Is it dangerous?'

'It happens. It's known as Vanishing Twin Syndrome,' Dr Martinez explained. 'With IVF now, and very early monitoring, we're finding it happens more often than we once thought.'

Still unconvinced, Mariel looked back at the monitor. 'Is this one at risk now?'

The doctor touched Mariel's hand. 'There's no reason why it shouldn't be a normal pregnancy. And the other good news is you can go home this morning.'

At nine-thirty the nurse entered Mariel's room to bring in the discharge forms for her to sign. She was ready to go home, but where would 'home' be for her now? 'Thanks, Tara.'

Tara smiled and placed the papers on the table. Mariel stood at the window, looking out at the misty rain. Some time last night the cool change had blown in. She ran a damp palm down the side of the dress Dane had brought in with its matching jacket and paced back to the bed. She was jittery. Tara had told her Dane had left strict instructions at the nurses' station that she was not to leave until he came to fetch her.

She had to tell him about the baby.

She had to go through that agonising moment again.

'Are you and your fiancé planning on having kids?' she asked Tara as the nurse walked to the door.

'Not for a couple of years. We— Oh…wow. Oh… my…' Tara trailed off, looking down the corridor. 'Oh, my goodness.' She fanned her hand in front of her face. 'What a man.'

'What's happening?'

Dane was happening, Mariel realised when he appeared in the doorway. Filled the doorway.

And he really *was* happening.

At least she thought it was Dane. Except this man had neatly trimmed *short* hair, and a clean-shaven face, and he was wearing a *tux* and carrying the biggest bunch of pink and white roses she'd ever seen.

Beyond the door she thought she heard a couple of feminine sighs, but she was too busy taking in the view, trying to calm her racing heart, and backing up to the bed before her legs gave way to pay any attention.

His eyes fused with hers like an electrical short-circuit. Held. Without breaking contact, he closed the door with one shiny new shoe. It shut with a heavy thud. He walked to the side of the bed, went down on one knee before her. His tux—her own design, she noted through the haze—was dusted with a fine sheen of rain, his hair damp. The scent of misted roses and some sexy new aftershave wafted to her nose.

But it was the naked emotion in his eyes that nearly did her in. This man knew her, often better than she did herself. He'd travelled childhood's tumultuous journey with her, shared the ups and downs of their teenage years. They could argue the point till the sun switched off and still not give in. He knew her idiosyncrasies and delighted in holding them up to her.

But in the end he respected her, gave her space when she needed it, let her be herself. He understood her because they came from the same place.

He was the only man she'd ever truly loved.

And he was kneeling before her like some knight to his lady. Like one of her teenage fantasies. Her heart was blossoming with so many emotions she didn't know how she could possibly hold them all in. But a thread of pain ran through the beauty.

'Dane, I have to tell y—'

'Not a word,' he said. 'Not. One. Word.'

He laid the flowers aside and pulled a shiny box from his pocket, opened it and held it up for her inspection.

A solitaire diamond as big as her little fingernail sparkled in the light. Heavens. 'Dane…' She pressed her lips together to stop the tremble. 'What are you doing?'

'My God, woman, what do you think I'm doing?' His voice boomed in the small room.

'There are sick people here,' she whispered.

His expression darkened. 'And I might very well be one of them if you don't let me get this over with. I told you to zip it. Mariel…'

He took the ring between finger and thumb and held it up to her. 'This ring's like you. It's bright and beautiful and one of a kind. And it'll be the one you hand down to our oldest grandchild.'

Grandchildren? Shock struck her speechless for one stunned moment, then a wave of happiness rolled up and swamped her. 'Do you mean that?' she whispered.

'I was never more serious. But that's down the track a bit. When you've recovered.' He smiled briefly, then reached for her hand and slid it on. 'Perfect fit. Like us, Queen Bee.'

Tears sprang to her eyes. 'I have to tell you—'

But he stifled her words with a finger. 'Not done yet. I love you. I always have. I always will. I've loved you since that first day at school, when I saw you standing in the sandpit in your new brown and yellow uniform. The Queen Bee surrounded by her faithful swarm of little boys.'

'You marched up and pulled the ribbon off my pigtail.'

'I wanted your attention.'

'And you got it, all right. I beat the living daylights out of you *and* got my ribbon back.'

His smile faded. 'When you told me you were pregnant I couldn't come to terms with it. I couldn't imagine being a father. I needed time. I didn't give a thought to the fact that you'd be needing time, too. That we could have supported each other the way we always have and got through it together.'

'Yes, we could have. We should have. You shut yourself off, but I should have tried harder to reach you.' Mariel reached out to stroke his smooth, tight jaw, then patted the bed beside her in invitation.

'You know my take on commitment,' he said, rising. He sat beside her and searched her eyes. 'But I know now that my heart was waiting for you. It just didn't relay the information to my brain.'

She shook her head. 'I always loved you. Even ten years ago when I saw you with Isobel I loved you. And hated you.'

His smile sobered as quickly as it had come. 'You were so set on going overseas. I didn't want to stop you from doing what you needed to do. And I was afraid to start anything with you, to show you how I felt, because everyone I loved either left or turned their back on me.'

She fingered his newly cropped hair. 'You've made a start with your father, Dane.'

'We've still got a long way to go. But I've got some

ideas that I want to discuss with you. Later.' He cupped her face in one large warm palm. 'We weren't ready ten years ago. You needed to follow your dreams first and so did I. But children…'

He shook his head, and in his expression Mariel saw the old wounds which had never quite healed.

'After my own miserable childhood I was convinced family wasn't for me. I was wrong. I want you to have my babies. I want to watch them grow inside you, see their first smile, be there when they take their first steps. Support them as they grow to adulthood. We can have more babies, Mariel, if you'll marry me.'

She smiled at him through a mist. 'I guess I'll have to marry you, Dane, and as soon as possible—because I want this baby to be born to loving parents who've made a lifetime commitment.'

His eyes widened, then dropped to where Mariel's hand touched her belly. 'Run that by me again—the bit about this baby.'

'I'm still pregnant.' She sniffed, unable to contain her emotion any longer. 'I saw it on a monitor. It's real, Dane.'

Grasping both her hands, he jack-knifed off the bed. 'You're going to marry me and you're having my baby!'

The sound of clapping issued through the door as he hauled her against him and kissed her. And, wow, what a kiss. She cupped his smooth jaw and ran her fingers over his short-cropped hair. Again. To acquaint herself with its feel.

At last they came up for air, and she stepped back so she could admire the man who'd walked North Terrace on a weekday morning wearing a tux and carrying flowers. The man who'd changed for her. 'You are *so* the man for me. You always were. I have everything—a man who loves me, a baby on the way and a promising business.'

'Ah, yes, speaking of which… Let's get out of here. I have something to show you before the press catches on to all this news. There's a cab waiting at the service entrance.'

The taxi took them to a street near the centre of town.

Mariel walked with him until Dane stopped and gestured to an empty shop just off Rundle Mall. 'What do you think?'

'About what?'

He produced a key, handed it to her. 'Your new business premises.'

'Oh. Oh, goodness.' Her fingers trembled so much she couldn't get the key in the lock.

He grinned, took the keys from her and did the honours. 'I think this is where we started not so long ago. Fumbling with keys.'

The smell of fresh paint and new beginnings met Mariel as she stepped inside.

'There's a big room out back for supplies, tailors, anything else you want,' Dane said beside her.

'It's beautiful. Just beautiful.' Honey-toned wooden counters gleamed. Empty racks lined the walls. A large shiny window faced the mall, waiting for the shop's name to be painted on it.

She spun a circle in the middle of the newly fitted-out room. 'I can't wait to move in. When did you do all this?'

'Finished yesterday. It was hard trying to keep it a secret and organise it from up north. That's why I had to go out the other night. There was a problem with the lighting.'

'Ah... The night you asked me to trust you.'

'And you did.'

'Thank you. For this...' She swept her hand to en-compass the room. 'And this.' She took his hand, pressed it against her belly.

Dane pulled her tightly against him. 'Let's go home,' he murmured into her hair. 'I want to celebrate our good fortune in *our* bed.'

She smiled, listening to the gallop of his heart against her ear. 'Yes, let's go home.'

EPILOGUE

Two years later

'COME on, Danny, walk to Grandpa.'

Mariel smiled as fourteen-month-old Daniel Hunt-ington the Fourth's toothy grin widened. His chubby hands were outstretched as he toddled the last few steps into the waiting arms of his grandfather.

Since Dane's father had moved in with them the pair had become inseparable. Mariel couldn't have been happier. Dane and his father had been given a second chance, and they'd grabbed hold of it with both hands.

Family, she thought. A blessing. She smoothed a hand over her still-flat belly. This time she wanted a girl, to even things up a bit. As for Dane—he was too happy about her announcement to care.

'You sure you'll be okay, Dad?' Dane asked as he shrugged into his suit jacket.

'You're only a few minutes and a phone call away. Of course we're all right—aren't we, Danny boy?'

The child gurgled up at him happily.

'He'll be fine.' Mariel opened her compact, checked her make-up. 'They'll both be fine. Stop worrying.'

'This is the first time we've left them together,' Dane murmured.

'He can change a nappy as well as you, if not better. Come on. The restaurant booking's for eight and I don't want to be late. Justin and Cass have got news, I just know it. Oh… Have you read my review?' she asked nonchalantly as she adjusted his silk tie to her satisfaction.

He didn't even seem to mind her female fussing. 'I have. Twice.'

'Read it again. Aloud, so I know.'

Fashion designer Mariel Davenport's latest showing last night has been hailed by the fashion industry as a rousing success. Her label, Dane, is at the cutting edge of men's fashion, with its subtle French influence and effervescent use of colour.

Ms Davenport's advice: 'A man should stay true to himself rather than following fashion blindly. My husband is a prime example.'

That's why Dane Huntington is often seen in worn jeans while sporting the latest in cashmere jumpers.

He's the luckiest man in Adelaide.

Twinkling eyes lifted to meet hers. '*That's* why you wanted me to read it aloud.'

She tilted her nose at him. 'No. I just wanted to hear it again, Mr Luckiest Man. You don't need to read it to know it's true.'

'You're right. This time.'

'I'm always right.' She leaned in for a quick kiss. 'That's why you married me.'

His eyes danced with laughter and he yanked her back for an encore. 'No. That's why you married me.'

RED WINE AND
HER SEXY EX

BY
KATE HARDY

Kate Hardy lives in Norwich, in the east of England, with her husband, two children, one bouncy spaniel, and too many books to count! When she's not busy writing romance or researching local history, she also loves cooking—see if you can spot the recipes sneaked into her books. (They're also on her website, along with excerpts and the stories behind the books.)

Writing for Mills & Boon has been a dream come true for Kate—something she wanted to do ever since she was twelve. She's been writing for Medical Romance™ since 2001, and also writes for Cherish™; her novel *Breakfast At Giovanni's* won the Romantic Novelists' Association's Romance Prize in 2008. She says she loves what she does because she gets to learn lots of new things when she's researching the background to a book: add warmth, heart and passion, plus a new gorgeous hero every time, and it's the perfect job!

Kate's always delighted to hear from readers, so do drop in to her website at www.katehardy.com.

For Maggie—
who helped me see the wood for the trees—
with love and thanks.

CHAPTER ONE

SHE was back.

Xavier's heart beat just that little bit faster as he put down the phone to his lawyer.

This was ridiculous. He was completely over Allegra Beauchamp. He'd been over her for years. So of course it wasn't nerves making his pulse race like this. It was anger—anger that she was planning to walk in after all this time and interfere. He'd put his heart and soul into the vineyard for the last ten years, and he was damn sure he wasn't going to let her flounce in and ruin all his hard work.

He didn't trust her a single millimetre. Not any more. Quite apart from the way she'd broken his heart, dumping him when he'd needed her most, she hadn't come back to support her great-uncle—the man who'd given her a home every summer while she was growing up—when he'd been old and frail and needed her. She hadn't even made it back to France for Harry's funeral; but she'd come straight back to claim her inheritance of fifteen hectares of top-quality vines and a big stone *mas.*

Her actions spoke volumes.

But in some ways it also made things easier. If Allegra was only interested in the money, then she'd be happy to sell her half of the vineyard to him, despite what she'd claimed to his lawyer this afternoon. Right now, she might have some romantic idea of what it was like to run a vineyard, but Xavier knew that as soon as she had a taste of the real thing she'd run straight back to London. Just as she had ten years ago—except this time she'd only be taking his money with her, not his heart. And this time he'd have no regrets.

He grabbed his car keys from his desk drawer, locked his office door and strode off towards his car. The sooner he faced her, the better.

Allegra sipped her coffee, but the dark, bitter liquid did nothing to clear her head.

She'd been a fool to come back after all this time. She should've just agreed with the lawyer's suggestion of selling Harry's half of the vineyard to his business partner, stopped off briefly at the tiny church in the village to lay some flowers on her great-uncle's grave and pay her respects, and then gone straight back to London.

Instead, something had made her come back to the old stone farmhouse where she'd spent so many summers as a child. Whether it was an impulse to do right by her great-uncle or something else, she wasn't sure. But now she was here in the Ardèche, she regretted the impulse. Seeing the house, smelling the sharp scent of the herbs growing in their terracotta troughs by the kitchen door, had made her feel physically sick with guilt. Guilt that she hadn't come back before. Guilt that she hadn't been there to take the call telling her that Harry had had a stroke—and that he'd died in hospital before she'd even found out that he was ill. Guilt that, despite her best efforts, she hadn't made it here for the funeral.

Everyone in the village had already judged her and found her wanting. She'd been aware of the glances and mutters from people in the square as she'd put the flowers on the greening-over mound in the churchyard, next to the little wooden cross that would mark Harry's grave until the ground had settled enough for it to support a proper headstone. And the coldness with which Hortense Bouvier had received her, instead of the warm hug and good meal that the housekeeper had greeted her with all those years before, had left her in no doubt as to the older woman's disapproval.

Walking back into the kitchen had been like walking straight back into the past, ripping all of Allegra's scars wide open. All she needed now was Xav to walk into the kitchen and drop into the chair opposite her, with that heart-turning smile and the sparkle in his silver-green eyes as he reached over to take her hand, and…

No, of course not. He'd made it quite clear, ten years before, that it was over between them. That what they'd shared had simply been a holiday romance, and he was off to start a high-flying career in Paris—a new life without her. For all she knew, he could be married with children now; once she'd taken that first step to heal the breach between herself and Harry, they'd had an unspoken agreement never to talk about Xavier. Pride had stopped her asking, and awkwardness had stopped Harry telling.

Her hands tightened round the mug of coffee. After all these years, she really should be over it. But then again, how did you stop years and years of loving someone? She'd fallen for Xavier Lefèvre the very first time she'd met him, when she was eight years old and he was eleven: he'd been the most beautiful boy she'd ever seen, like one of the Victorian angels in the stained-glass windows at school, but with dark hair and silver-green eyes. As a teen, she'd followed him round like an eager puppy, mooning over him and wondering what it would be like if he kissed her. She'd even practised kissing against the back of her hand so she'd be ready for the moment when he finally realised she was more than just the girl next door. For summer after summer, she'd wished and hoped; even though she must have driven him crazy, he'd been kind and treated her the same way that he treated everyone else, never teasing or rejecting her outright.

But, that very last summer, it had been a kind of awakening. Xav had finally seen her as a woman instead of an annoying little urchin trailing around behind him. They'd been inseparable. The best summer of her life. She'd honestly believed that he loved her as much as she loved him. That it didn't matter that she was going to do her degree in London while he was starting a new job in Paris—she'd spend the holidays with him, and he'd maybe come and spend weekends with her in London when he could get the time off work, and then when she graduated they'd be together for the rest of their lives.

Granted, he hadn't actually asked her to marry him, but she'd known he felt the same way she did. That he was as crazy about her as she was about him.

And then it had all disintegrated.

Bile filled her mouth and she swallowed hard. For pity's sake. She was an adult, now, not a dream-filled teenager. A realist. Harry's business partner was Jean-Paul Lefèvre—Xav's father, not Xav himself. Xav wouldn't be here; as far as she knew, he was still in Paris. She wouldn't have to see him again.

'Monsieur Lefèvre called,' Hortense said coolly, walking into the kitchen. 'He's on his way back from the vines. He's calling in to see you.'

Allegra frowned. Their meeting wasn't until tomorrow. Then again, the French had impeccable manners. Jean-Paul was probably calling on her out of politeness, to welcome her to Les Trois Closes.

And then the kitchen door opened abruptly and Xavier sauntered in, as if he owned the place.

Allegra nearly dropped the mug she was holding. What the hell was *he* doing here? And why hadn't he knocked? What made him think that he could just walk into Harry's house—*her* house, she corrected herself mentally—whenever he pleased?

'Xavier! *Alors*, sit down, sit down.' Hortense greeted him with all the warmth she'd refused to bestow on Allegra, kissing him on the cheeks. She settled him opposite Allegra with a mug of coffee. 'I'll leave you to talk with Mademoiselle Beauchamp, *chéri*.' And with that she swept out of the kitchen.

Allegra was too stunned to say a word. At twenty-one, Xavier Lefèvre had been a good-looking boy. At thirty-one, he was all man. A little taller, unless her memory deceived her, and his frame was broader—though his T-shirt showed that it was muscle rather than fat. His olive skin made his grey-green eyes seem even more piercing, and he had the beginnings of lines round his eyes, as if he smiled a lot or spent most of his time in the sun. His tousled dark hair was overlong; the style, she thought, was more in keeping with a rock star than a financial whiz-kid. And the fact that he hadn't shaved made him look as if he'd just got out of bed, leaving his lover asleep and totally satiated.

Just the sight of him made Allegra feel as if the temperature in the room had soared by ten degrees—and she could still remember just how it had felt to fall asleep in Xav's arms, warm and satiated in the sunshine after making love all afternoon.

Oh, hell. How was she supposed to think straight when the first thing that came into her mind where Xavier Lefèvre was concerned was sex—and the second thing was how much she still wanted him?

She needed her libido strapped into a straightjacket. Right now. Before it started wrestling with her common sense.

'*Bonjour*, Mademoiselle Beauchamp.' Xavier gave her an enigmatic smile. 'I thought I'd better come and say hello to my new business partner.'

She stared at him, shocked. '*You* were Harry's business partner?'

His look told her just how stupid that question was.

'But…' Xavier was supposed to be a financier in a sharp suit, not a vigneron in faded denims and an ancient T-shirt. 'I thought you were in Paris.'

'No.'

'Monsieur Robert said Harry's partner was Monsieur Lefèvre.'

'Indeed.' Still seated, he pantomimed a half-bow. 'Allow me to introduce myself. Xavier Lefèvre—at your service, *mademoiselle*.'

'I know who you are.' For pity's sake. Of *course* she knew who he was. The man to whom she'd given her virginity—and her heart, only to have it thrown back in her face. 'I thought he meant your father.'

'You're five years too late for that, I'm afraid.'

'Your father's…?' She sucked in a shocked breath. 'I'm sorry. I had no idea. Harry didn't tell me, or I would've—'

'Don't tell me you would've come to my father's funeral,' Xavier cut in. 'You didn't even turn up to Harry's.'

And he thought he had the right to call her on it? She lifted her chin. 'I had my reasons.'

He said nothing. Waiting for her to fill the silence? Well, she didn't have to explain herself to him. 'So, what—you thought that as you're his business partner Harry should have left the vineyard to you? Is that it?'

'No, of course not. There's no question of that. You inherit his possessions because you're his closest family.' He paused. 'Not that anyone would have guessed, these last few years.'

'That's a cheap shot.' And it had landed dead on target. Smack in the middle of her guilt, like a hard blow on an already spreading bruise.

'Just stating the facts, *chérie*. When was the last time you came back to see him?'

'I spoke to him every week on the phone.'

'Which isn't the same thing at all.'

She blew out a breath. 'You probably know Harry and I fell out pretty badly after I went to London.' Over Xavier—not that she was going to tell him that. 'We made it up eventually, but I admit I was wrong not to come back and see him.' Especially as half the reason had been the fear that she might have to see Xavier again. Not that she had any intention of admitting that to him, either. She didn't want him to have a clue that she still had a weak spot where he was concerned. That seeing him again had knocked her for six and the old, old longing hadn't died at all—it had just been sleeping, and now it was awake again and desperately hungry for him. 'If I'd had any idea that he was so frail, I would've come back. He didn't give me the faintest clue.'

'Of course not. He was a proud man. But if you'd bothered visiting,' Xavier said coolly, 'you would've seen it for yourself.'

There was no answer to that.

'You didn't come back when he was ill,' Xavier continued.

'Because I didn't get the message that he'd had a stroke until after it was too late.'

'You didn't even turn up for his funeral.'

And he seriously thought she wasn't bothered about that? 'I intended to be here. But I was on business in New York.'

'Not good enough.'

She knew that. And she didn't need him to tell her. She lifted her chin. 'We've established that I'm firmly in the wrong. And it's not possible to change the past, so there's no point in rehashing it.'

He simply shrugged.

Infuriating man.

'What do you want, Xavier?'

You.

The realisation shocked him to the core. After the way Allegra had let him down, he shouldn't want anything to do with her. And she was no longer the *petite rose Anglaise* she'd been at eighteen, sweet and shy and a little unsure of herself and then blossoming under his love. Right now she was impeccably groomed and as hard as diamonds beneath that smart business suit. Her mouth was in a tight line, not soft and promising and reminding him of the first roses of summer.

This was crazy. For pity's sake, he was supposed to be working out how to get the woman to sell her half of the business to him, not looking at her mouth and remembering how it had felt to kiss her. How it had felt to lose himself inside her. How it had felt to see her expression soften and her eyes sparkle with love when she looked up from the book she was reading and caught him watching her, on those drowsy summer afternoons.

Oh, *Dieu*. He really had to get a grip.

'Well?'

'I just happened to be on my way back from the fields. I called Hortense to see if you were in, because I was going to be neighbourly and polite and welcome you back to France.' That was true—though it wasn't the whole truth. He'd also wanted to see if he could gauge her reactions. To work out a plan for persuading her to sell the vineyard to him. 'But, seeing as you raised the subject, let me give you something to think about. You haven't been to France in years and I can't see you being interested in the vineyard now. I'm more than happy to buy you out. Consult whatever qualified oenologist you like to get a price and I'll abide by his or her decision— I'll even pay the survey fee.'

'No.'

She wanted more than a fair price? Well, if it would keep his vineyard safe, it was worth paying over the odds. 'How much do you want?'

'I'm not selling the vineyard to you.'

His stomach turned. 'You're planning to sell to someone else?' To someone who would neglect the vines, so they'd end up diseased and it would spread into his fields? Or, worse, to someone who decided to use pesticide sprays and to hell with the neighbours—when it had taken him years to get organic certification for the vineyard. All that work could be ruined in a matter of weeks.

'I'm not selling to anyone. Harry left me the house and his half of the vineyard. The way I see it, this was his way of telling me it was time to come home,' Allegra said.

He waved a dismissive hand. 'That's guilt talking.' Guilt that he'd just encouraged, admittedly. 'You know as well as I do, the practical thing to do here would be to sell your share to me.'

She shook her head. 'I'm staying.'

He stared at her, incredulous. 'But you know nothing about viticulture.'

'I can learn.'

'I don't have time to teach you.'

'Then maybe someone else can.'

Over his dead body.

'And in the meantime I can deal with the marketing—it's what I'm trained to do.'

Xavier folded his arms, goaded into reacting. 'I don't care what you're trained to do. You're not dabbling in my vineyard. You'll get bored within a week.'

'No, I won't. And it's my vineyard, too.' She folded her arms, reflecting his own defensive body language, and glared at him. 'Harry left his half of the business to me, and I owe it to him to make it work.' Her blue eyes were distinctly icy, and Xavier realised that she was serious. She really did want to make this work, for Harry's sake.

Impossible; but, right now, she looked too stubborn and defensive to listen to common sense. So it would be better to leave now, think about the best tactics to make her see reason and talk to her again tomorrow.

'As you wish,' he said. He pushed his chair back and stood up. 'Did Marc tell you the time of the meeting tomorrow?'

She blinked. 'You're on first-name terms with Harry's lawyer?'

'Actually, he's my lawyer, too.' Xavier judged it politic not to mention that Marc had been his best friend since university. Though he did owe it to Marc to be fair. 'Although, I should add that he isn't acting for me in this case and he hasn't discussed you with me. Marc's the most professional man I know.'

'He said eight o'clock tomorrow morning.'

'Better make it midday,' Xavier said. 'I'm sure you're tired after all your travelling.'

Her eyes narrowed with suspicion. 'You don't think I'm capable of getting up early, do you?'

'I didn't say that.' Though he'd thought it. 'Actually, it would suit me better, too. Here, we work to *l'heure solaire.*'

'The time of the sun?' Her translation was hesitant.

'Sun time,' he corrected. 'Working on the vines in the middle of a summer day is the quickest way to get sunstroke. I do my admin in the hottest hours of the day and I work outside when it's a little cooler. So—midday. My office, at the chateau. And I will provide lunch.' He thought about kissing her goodbye on the cheek, just to unsettle her a little more—but then thought better of it. Given his body's earlier reaction to her, there was just as good a chance that it'd unsettle him, too. Instead, he gave her a formal bow. '*À demain*, Mademoiselle Beauchamp.'

She nodded in acknowledgement. '*À demain*, Monsieur Lefèvre. Midday it is.'

CHAPTER TWO

THE next morning, Allegra spent a while looking at the vineyard's website and jotting down some ideas before setting out for the Lefèvre chateau. The building had barely changed in the years she'd been away; it was still grand and imposing, pale stone punctuated by tall, narrow windows with white shutters. She remembered the formal lawn in front of the chateau, though she didn't remember there being lavender fields flanking the long driveway. And she was also fairly sure there hadn't been a rose garden at the back—although she couldn't see it when she got out of the car, the scent of roses was strong enough for her to guess that there was a mass of blooms somewhere behind the house.

Xavier's wife's idea, maybe?

Not that it was any of her concern. And she couldn't exactly have asked Hortense without it seeming like fishing—which it wasn't. Yes, Xavier Lefèvre was still the most attractive man Allegra had ever met. If it was possible, he'd got even better-looking with age. But, even if he wasn't involved with anyone, she wasn't interested. Wasn't going to give him a second chance to stamp on her heart. This was strictly business.

She glanced at her watch. Two minutes to midday. Not so early that she'd seem desperate, but early enough to tell Xavier that she was professional and punctual. Good. She straightened her back and rang the doorbell.

She had to ring twice more before the door was opened abruptly by a young man with a shock of fair hair who looked annoyed that he'd been disturbed.

'We're not—' he began with a scowl, then stopped and gave her a beaming smile. '*Mon Dieu, c'est* Allie Beauchamp! How long has it been? *Bonjour, chérie.* How are you?' He leaned forward to kiss her cheek.

'*Bonjour*, Guy. About ten years—and I'm fine, thanks.' She smiled back. 'It's good to see you. How are you?'

'Fine. It's good to see you, too. Are you here on holiday?' he asked.

'Not exactly.' She grimaced. 'I'm your brother's new business partner.'

Guy raised an eyebrow. 'Hmm.'

'Care to elaborate on that?' she asked.

'No. You know Xav.'

That was the point. She didn't, any more.

'At this time of day, he'll be in his office,' Guy said.

'I know.' Allegra shifted her weight to her other foot. 'I, um, forgot to ask him whereabouts in the estate his office was.'

'And he forgot to tell you.' Guy rolled his eyes. 'Typical Xav. I'll take you over there.'

'Are you going to be at the meeting?'

'Is it about the vineyard?'

She nodded.

'Then, no. The vineyard's Xav's department, not mine. I just laze about here at weekends, drink his wine and insult him.' He gave her an unrepentant grin. 'By the way, I'm sorry about Harry. He was a good man.'

Allegra had a huge lump in her throat. Guy was the first person in France who'd actually welcomed her warmly and used her old pet name. Maybe he remembered their childhood, when she'd persuaded Xav to include his little brother in their games. And he was the only one who hadn't treated her as a pariah for missing Harry's funeral. 'I'm sorry, too.'

Guy led her round the side of the house to a courtyard, which she remembered had once been stables and a barn but had now been turned into an office block.

'Thanks for bringing me over,' Allegra said.

'Pleasure.' He smiled at her. 'If you're going to be around for a few days, come and have dinner with us.'

'Us' meaning him and Xavier? She knew he was only being polite. Xavier definitely wouldn't second that invitation. 'That would be lovely,' she said, being equally polite.

'See you later, then. À bientôt, Allie.'

She echoed his farewell, took a deep breath, and walked into the office block. Xavier's door was wide open and she could see him working at his desk, making notes on something with a fountain pen. He looked deep in thought, with his left elbow resting on his desk and his forehead propped against his hand. His hair was tousled—obviously he'd been shoving his fingers through it—but today he was clean-shaven. The sleeves of his knitted cotton shirt were pushed up to his elbows, revealing strong forearms sprinkled with dark hair. Right at that moment, he looked approachable. Touchable. She had to dig her nails into her palms to stop herself doing something rash—like walking over to him, sliding her hand up his arm to get his attention, cupping his chin, and lowering her mouth to his, the way she once would have done.

For pity's sake. He wasn't her lover any more, the man she'd thought she'd marry one day. He was her business partner. And, even if he hadn't been her business partner, she had no idea whether or not he was already committed elsewhere. That made him absolutely off limits.

She took a deep breath, then knocked on the door.

Xavier looked up at Allegra's knock. She was clearly still in businesswoman mode, wearing another of those sharp suits. No way would she fit in here; at this time of year, everyone had to help out in the vines, maintaining the shoots and weeding under the vines. Next month would be pruning and then letting the grapes ripen, ready for harvest in late September. Among the vines, her business suit would be ripped to shreds, and those patent high-heeled shoes were completely unsuitable for the fields.

She really had no idea, did she?

'Thank you for coming,' he said, rising politely from his desk. 'Take a seat.'

She sat down, then handed him a gold box tied with a gold chiffon ribbon. 'For you.'

Now that he hadn't expected.

'I thought this might be more suitable than flowers. Or, um, wine.'

So she remembered French customs, then, of bringing a gift for your host. '*Merci*, Allegra.' He untied the ribbon and discovered that the box held his favourite weakness: thin discs of dark chocolate studded with crystallised ginger. She remembered such a tiny thing, after all these years? And she must've bought it this morning: he recognised the box as coming from Nicole's shop in the village. She'd made a real effort, and it knocked him completely off balance.

'Thank you,' he said again. 'Would you like some coffee?'

'Yes, please.'

To his surprise, she followed him into the tiny kitchen area. 'Anything I can do?'

Yes. Sell me your half of the vineyard and get out of my life before I go crazy with wanting you again. He just about stopped himself saying it. 'No need.'

'Aren't you going to ask me if I take milk and sugar?'

'You never used to, and it's obvious you still don't.'

She blinked. 'Obvious, how?'

He spread his hands. 'You wouldn't be so thin if you did.'

Her eyes narrowed. 'That's a bit personal.'

'You asked,' he pointed out.

'Gloves off, now?'

'They were never on in the first place.' And now his mind was running on a really dangerous track. Gloves off. Clothes off. Allegra's shy, trusting smile as he'd undressed her for the very first time and she'd given herself to him completely.

Oh, *Dieu*. He really had to stop thinking about the past and concentrate on the present.

He finished making the coffee and placed it on a tray. He fished a bowl of tomatoes and a hunk of cheese from the fridge, then took a rustic loaf from a cupboard and placed them next to the coffee, along with two knives and two plates, before carrying the lot back to his office.

'Help yourself,' he said, gesturing to the food.

'Thank you.'

When she didn't make a move, he raised an eyebrow, broke a hunk off the bread, and cut himself a large slice of cheese. 'Forgive me for being greedy. I'm starving—I was working in the vines at six.'

'*L'heure solaire.*'

He smiled, oddly pleased that she'd remembered. He could still hear England in her accent, but at least she was trying. No doubt she hadn't spoken French in a long, long while.

'So what's the agenda?' she asked.

'We'll start with the sensible one—when are you going to sell me your half of the vineyard?'

'That's not on the agenda at all,' she said. 'Xav, why won't you give me a chance?'

How on earth could she not know that? Did he have to spell out to her that, the last time he'd needed her, she hadn't been there and he didn't want to put himself in that position again? He certainly didn't trust his own judgement where she was concerned. He'd spent a sleepless night brooding over the fact that he still wanted her just as much as he had when he was twenty-one; it was a weakness he really didn't need. 'Because you're not cut out to work here,' he prevaricated. 'Look at you. Designer clothes, flash car...'

'A perfectly normal business suit,' she corrected, 'and the car's not mine, it's a rental. You're judging me, Xav, and you're being unfair.'

Unfair? *He* hadn't been the one to walk away. The sheer injustice stung, and he had to make a real effort to hold back the surge of irritation. An effort that wasn't entirely successful. 'What do you expect, Allegra?'

'Everybody makes mistakes.'

Yes. And he had no intention of repeating his.

Clearly his thoughts showed in his expression, because she sighed. 'You're not even going to listen to me, are you?'

'You said it all yesterday.' And ten years ago. When she hadn't given him time to deal with the way his life had just imploded, and she'd dumped him.

'This isn't just a whim, you know.'

And then he noticed the shadows underneath her eyes. It looked as though he wasn't the only one who'd spent a sleepless night. No doubt she'd been reliving the memories, too, the bad ones that had all but wiped out the good. And he had to admit that it had taken courage for her to come back, knowing full well that everyone here would have judged her actions and found her very much wanting.

'All right,' he said grudgingly. 'Explain, and I'll listen.'

'Without interruptions?'

'I can't promise that. But I'll listen.'

'OK.' She took a sip of her coffee, as if she needed something to bolster her—though her plate was still empty, he noticed. 'Harry and I fell out pretty badly when I first left for London, and I swore I'd never come back to France again. By the time I graduated, I'd mellowed a bit, and I saw things a bit differently. I made it up with him. But I was settled in England, then. And I…' She bit her lip. 'Oh, forget it. There's no point in explaining. You wouldn't understand in a million years.'

'Now who's judging?'

She gave him a wry smile. 'OK. You asked for it. You grew up here, where your family has lived for…what, a couple of hundred years?'

'Something like that.'

'You always knew where you were when you woke up. You were secure. You knew you *belonged.*'

'Well, yes.' Even when he'd planned to go to Paris, he'd always known that he'd come back to the Ardèche and take over the vineyard. But he'd thought he'd have time to broaden his experience in business, first, see a bit of the world.

'It wasn't like that for me. When I was a child, I was dragged all over the world in my parents' wake—the orchestra would be on tour, or my mother would do a series of solo concerts and my father would be her accompanist. We never settled anywhere. The nannies never lasted long—they'd thought they'd have an opportunity to travel and see the world, but they didn't bargain on the fact that my parents worked all the time and expected them to do likewise. When they weren't on stage, they were practising and didn't want to be disturbed. My mother would sometimes practise until her fingers bled. And then, just as somewhere started to become home, we'd move on again.'

He could see old hurts blooming in Allegra's expression, and her struggle to keep them back. And suddenly he realised what she was trying to tell him. 'So once you'd settled in London, you had your own place. Roots.'

'Exactly. And I could run my life the way *I* wanted it to be. I wasn't being pushed around and told what to do by someone else all the time, however well meaning they were.' She looked relieved. 'Thank you for understanding.'

He blew out a breath. 'No, you were right in the first place. I still don't understand. Surely your family always come first?' It was what he'd always believed.

The way his family—with the notable exception of his mother—had always done things. If there was a problem, you worked together to fix it.

'I didn't say it was logical.' She looked away. 'There were other reasons why I didn't want to come back to France.'

'Me?' He really hadn't meant to say it, but the word just slipped out.

'You,' she confirmed.

Well, at least it was out in the open now. They could stop pussyfooting round the issue.

She clearly thought the same, because she said, 'I was hoping you wouldn't be here.'

He rolled his eyes. 'I've been Harry's business partner since Papa died. Surely you knew that?'

A muscle flickered in her jaw. 'We never discussed you.'

Was she saying that her falling-out with Harry had been over him? But he couldn't see why. It was pretty clear-cut: she'd been the one to call a halt to their affair, not him. And Xavier couldn't imagine Harry breaking Jean-Paul's confidence and telling Allegra what had been going on here—about the problems with the business and Chantal's desertion. Had Harry perhaps counselled her to give Xavier some space and time, and she'd reacted badly because she felt he was trying to push her around, the way she'd been pushed around as a child?

But he needed to know the answer to the most pressing question first. 'Why are you here now, Allegra?'

'Because I owe it to Harry. And don't waste your energy giving me a hard time over missing his funeral. It wasn't intentional and I feel guilty enough about it.'

'I don't have the right to judge you for that,' Xavier said quietly, 'but Harry was my friend as well as my business partner, and I think he deserved better.'

'I know he did.' Colour stained her cheeks.

'Surely your business wasn't *that* urgent? Why didn't you tell your boss or your business contact that you had a family commitment?'

'I did. The client couldn't move the meeting.'

'Couldn't someone else have gone in your place?'

'According to my boss, no.' Her tone was dry, and Xavier had a feeling that there was more to this—something she wasn't telling him. 'I did my best to wrap everything up as quickly as I could, but the meeting overran and I missed my flight.'

'And that was the only flight to Avignon?' he asked. As excuses went, that was a little too pat for his liking. Too convenient.

'Nice, actually,' she corrected. 'It was the only flight to France from New York without a stopover, until the next day. The reservations clerk spent an hour on the computer, trying to find me a flight that would get me somewhere on French soil at some time before breakfast, French time.' She spread her hands. 'But there simply wasn't one. Not even to Paris.'

'Your parents didn't turn up, either.'

'I know. They were in Tokyo. Coming to the funeral would've meant missing a performance. You know what they're like.' She lifted her chin. 'And, yes, you could say I fell into the same trap. I put business before family, and I shouldn't have done.'

'At least you admit it was a mistake.' He paused. 'So, where do you suggest we go from here?'

'You trusted Harry's business judgement, yes?'

Xavier inclined his head.

'And Harry trusted me to take over from him, or he wouldn't have left me his part of the business.' She looked him straight in the eye. 'So are you going to do the same?'

Tricky. He didn't trust his judgement at all, where she was concerned. And trusting her was one hell of an ask. He took refuge in answering a question with a question. 'What do you know about making wine?'

'Right now? Very little,' she admitted. 'But I'm a fast learner. I'll put in the hours until I know enough to be useful. In the meantime, maybe I can be useful in another part of the business.'

'Such as?'

'As I told you yesterday—marketing. I was Acting Head of Creative at the agency where I worked. I can put an effective promotional campaign together on a shoestring budget. Though I'll need some information from you before I can analyse how things are done now and where I can make a difference.'

'What kind of information?' he asked warily.

'The business plan for the next five years. I need to know what we produce, how much we sell it for, who our main customers are and how we get the wine to them.' She ticked them off on her fingers. 'I also need to know who our main competitors are and what they produce. And what kind of marketing campaigns you've done in the past. I know the vineyard has a website, but I want to look at that and compare it with the kind of thing our main competitors produce. And then I'll give you my analysis and recommendations.'

'Strengths, weaknesses, opportunities, threats.' He raised an eyebrow at her obvious surprise. 'Do you think I don't know what they are already?'

She looked deflated. And suddenly Xavier could see the vulnerability in her. On the surface, she was bright and polished and professional. But underneath she was as fragile as hell.

He could break her right now and make her sell her half of the vineyard to him.

But he'd hate himself for doing it. And, weirdly, he suddenly found himself wanting to protect her. How ironic was that? She'd broken his heart, and he still wanted to protect her; even though he couldn't protect himself from her. 'So are you telling me you're planning to run half a vineyard from London?'

'No. From here.'

She was planning to live here? So he'd have to see her every single day? *Dieu*—that would take some coping with. While she'd been in another country, he'd been able to push any thoughts of her to the back of his mind. But living next door to her, working with her...that would be a completely different matter.

And something didn't quite add up. 'Two minutes ago you were telling me that your roots were in London.'

'They are.' She sighed. 'I didn't say this was rational, Xav. It's just how it is. I want to step into Harry's shoes. As you just suggested, I can't do that from London. And the Ardèche was home to me in the summer, many years ago. I can settle here.'

Ten years too late. He'd wanted her here, by his side, back then. As his wife. Now, he'd be a lot happier if she flounced back to London and left him alone.

'What about your job?'

'Ex,' she said succinctly.

'Since when?'

'I resigned yesterday. After my meeting with my lawyer.'

So she was using the vineyard as some kind of get-out? In some respects, Xavier knew he could relax because it meant she wasn't planning to sell the land to someone else; but, in other respects, her statement made him even more tense. Was that how she reacted to pressure—by walking out and launching herself into something else? So what would happen if the going got tough here? Would she bail out, the way his mother had bailed out on his father? 'What about your notice period?'

'In my profession, you can do too much damage if you stay. If you decide to leave, you leave there and then.' She shrugged. 'My assistant's clearing my desk for me and I'll pick up my personal effects later.'

'Bit of a spur-of-the-moment decision, isn't it? How do you know this is going to work out?'

'Because I'm going to make it work out.'

Stubborn and determined: both were points in her favour. In this job, she'd need them. But he still couldn't believe that she'd stick to this. 'Running a vineyard isn't a nine-to-five job,' he warned. 'There are times when we all need to muck in and work on the vines—and what you're wearing right now is completely impractical for working in the fields. Your clothes will be shredded and your shoes—well, you'll turn your ankle or get blisters. And then there's the risk of sunstroke.'

'I'm not afraid of hard work or putting in the hours. Show me what needs to be done, and I'll do it. And I've already told you, I can do jeans and boots and a sunhat, if I have to.'

And doubtless hers would all be designer.

'I don't have Harry's knowledge or experience, so of course I'm not going to be able to fill his shoes,' she said. 'But I learn fast, and if I don't know something I'll ask—I won't just muddle through and hope for the best.'

'Perhaps I should also tell you that Harry was a sleeping partner in the business,' Xavier mused.

Her face shuttered. 'So you're *not* going to give me a chance.'

'That isn't what I said. Allegra, he was almost eighty. I was hardly going to make him work the same hours that I do. And he was happy to let me run the vineyard my way.'

'So what are you saying? That I can stay, but I get no input in anything?' She shook her head. 'No deal.'

'I wasn't offering you a deal. I'm telling you the way it is. Sure, I asked Harry for advice on some things—but I can't do that with you because, as you just said yourself, you don't have his knowledge or his experience.'

'And I also told you that I have other skills. Useful skills. If you give me the information I asked for, I'll work up some proposals. I can bring other things to the vineyard. Added value.'

Xavier took a deep breath. 'The information you're asking for is commercially sensitive.'

'And, as your business partner, I have no intention of letting that information out of my sight—because if it affects the business, it affects *me*.'

She really wasn't going to give up. He stared at her for a moment, weighing her up: could he trust her, this time round?

Harry had obviously trusted her, or he would've left instructions to handle his estate differently.

This was a huge, huge risk. But Harry had never steered him wrong before; and Marc had argued in her favour, too, in their phone call the previous day. And

Guy had actually left his precious lab for a few minutes to bring her over to the office. Harry, Marc and Guy were the three people Xavier trusted most, and they didn't seem to share his wariness of Allegra. So perhaps his best friend and his brother could see things more clearly, their judgement of her not clouded by emotion and the ghosts of the past. Maybe he should let them guide him, here.

Or maybe he was just making excuses to himself, looking for reasons why he should let her back into his life. Because, damn it to hell, he'd missed her, and seeing her again made him realise what a huge hole she'd left in his life. A hole he'd told himself was filled perfectly adequately by work, and now he knew for certain that he'd been lying to himself all along.

'What's it going to be, Xav?' she asked softly.

Knowing that he was probably making a huge mistake, he nodded. 'I'll print out the papers for you now. Read through them, call me if you have questions, and we'll see what you come up with.'

'Thank you.' She paused. 'You won't regret this.'

He'd reserve judgement on that until he'd seen her in action. 'It's two months until harvest. Let's use it as a trial. If we can work together, then fine. If we can't, then you sell your half of the vineyard to me. Deal?'

'So you're expecting me to prove myself to you?' Her eyes widened. 'Even though I own half the vineyard?'

'I'm saying that I don't know if we can work with each other,' Xavier said. 'Look, if you took a job somewhere, you'd have a trial period to see if you and the new company suited each other. This is no different.'

'And if it doesn't work out, I'm the one who has to walk away? I'm the one who loses?'

'My roots are here,' he said simply. 'Would you rip me from them?'

She was silent for a long, long time. And then she stood up and held out her hand. 'Two months, and then we'll discuss our options. Including the possibility of me selling to you, but also including the possibility of dissolving the partnership and me keeping my part of the vineyard.'

Xavier wasn't sure whether he wanted to shake her for being obstinate, or admire her backbone. In the end, he stood up, too, and took her hand.

And the feel of her skin against his took him straight back to the days when he'd driven her to all the beauty spots in the region, and they'd wandered round, hand in hand, admiring the views. Days when the summer seemed endless, the sky was always blue, and the only time he'd stopped smiling was when his mouth was busy exploring Allegra's body.

It would be so, so easy to walk round the table, draw her back into his arms and kiss her until they were both dizzy. And it would be so, so stupid. If they were going to have a chance of making this business work, she needed to be off limits.

He went through the motions of a formal handshake, then released her hand. 'We should perhaps drink to that.'

'I can't. I'm driving.'

'And I'm working in the fields this afternoon. So let's improvise.' He raised his cup of coffee. 'To Les Trois Closes.'

She clinked her cup against his. 'Les Trois Closes. And an equal partnership.'

CHAPTER THREE

ALLEGRA spent the rest of Saturday afternoon looking through the papers Xavier had printed off for her, checking things on the Internet and making notes. He'd given her his mobile number, but not his email address, and she could hardly text him a report—not if she wanted to include charts or drawings.

She sent him a quick text. *Off to London tomorrow. Back Tues, maybe Weds. Will email report, but need address. AB*

It was late evening before he replied—very briefly and to the point. Xavier had clearly turned into a man who didn't waste words; she made a mental note to keep her report extremely brief, with information in the papers behind it to support her arguments.

And she was going to be seriously busy for the next few days, sorting out loose ends in London as well as coming up with some ideas to convince Xavier that she could give something back to the vineyard.

She smiled wryly. So much for telling him that she had nothing to prove. They both knew that she did. To herself as well as to him.

'Sorry, Guy. I'm just not hungry.' Xavier eyed the slightly dried-up *cassoulet* and pushed his plate away.

'If you'd come back from the fields when I called your cellphone the first time, it might've been edible,' Guy pointed out.

'Sorry.'

'So what is it? A problem with the vines?'

'No.'

'Your biggest customer's just gone under, owing you a huge amount of money?'

Xavier shook his head impatiently. 'No. Everything's fine.'

'When you work yourself into exhaustion and you've still got shadows under your eyes because you can't sleep, everything's not fine.' Guy folded his arms and regarded his brother sternly. 'I'm not a child any more, Xav. You don't have to protect me, the way you and Papa did when we had two bad harvests on the trot and the bank wouldn't extend the vineyard's credit.'

When life as he knew it had imploded. 'I know. I'm sorry. I'm not trying to baby you.'

'If it's money, maybe I can help. The perfume house is doing OK right now. I can lend you enough to get you out of a hole—just as you helped me out a couple of years back.'

When Guy's ex-wife had cleaned him out and he'd almost had to sell his share of the perfume house. Xavier gave him a weary smile. 'Thanks, *mon frère*. It's good of you to offer. But there's no need. The vineyard's on an even keel financially, and I'm being careful about credit—even with my oldest customers.'

'Then it's Allie.'

Yeah. He couldn't think straight now she was back. 'Of course not. I'm fine,' he lied.

'You waited just a little too long before you denied it,' Guy said. 'You never really got over her, did you?'

Xavier shrugged. 'I dated.'

'But you've never let any of your girlfriends close to you—not the way you were with Allie that summer.'

'It was a long time ago, Guy. We've both grown up. Changed. We want different things out of life.'

'It sounds to me,' said Guy, 'as if you're trying to convince yourself.'

He was. Worse, he knew that he was failing. 'It's just the surprise of seeing her again. Let's drop this, Guy. I don't want to discuss it.'

'OK, I'll back off,' Guy said. 'But if you decide you do want to talk about it, you know where I am.' He patted Xavier's shoulder, then topped up their glasses. 'Just as you were there for me when it all went wrong with Véra.'

Long nights when Guy had ranted and Xavier had listened without judging.

'Maybe Lefèvre men just aren't good at picking the right women,' Xavier said. 'Papa, you, me—we've all made a mess of it.'

'Maybe.' Guy shrugged. 'Or maybe you and I just haven't met the right ones yet.'

Allegra had been the right one for him, Xavier thought. The problem was, he hadn't been the right one for her. And he needed to remember that, if he was to have any hope of a decent working relationship with her.

In London, Allegra didn't have a minute to breathe. Between sorting out a marketing plan for the vineyard; offering the lease of her flat to Gina, her best friend at the agency; sorting out what she wanted to take to France immediately and what could stay until she'd decided what she needed at the farmhouse; picking up her things from the office and trying not to bawl her eyes out when Gina threw a surprise leaving party for her and the whole of the office turned up except for her much-loathed ex-boss… There just wasn't a spare second to think about Xavier.

Until she was on the train from London to Avignon. That gave her seven hours to think about him, and to fume over the fact that he hadn't even acknowledged the receipt of her proposals, let alone asked her when she was coming back.

Getting angry and stressing about it wasn't a productive use of her time; instead, she mocked up the content for her proposed changes to the vineyard's website and a running feature about being a rookie vigneronne. But when she arrived at the TGV station, prepared to find a taxi to take her to the old central station to catch the local train through to the Ardèche, she was surprised to see Xavier leaning against the wall.

Though she wasn't surprised to see that he was attracting glances from every female in the place. Even when he was scruffy from working on the fields, he was a beautiful man. Today, he was dressed simply in black trousers and a white shirt, with an open collar and his cuffs rolled back slightly; his shoes were perfectly shined, too, she noticed, and he looked more like a model for an aftershave ad than a hotshot businessman.

He seemed to be scanning the crowds, waiting for someone. When he saw her, he lifted a hand in acknowledgement before coming to meet her.

He was waiting for *her*?

She set her cases down. 'What are you doing here?'

'Hello to you, too.'

'*Bonjour*, Monsieur Lefèvre,' she chorused dutifully. 'Seriously, what are you doing here?'

'I had business in Avignon and you need a lift back to Les Trois Closes. So it seemed sensible for me to wait for you.'

Served her right for thinking, just for one second, that Xav might've made a special trip to Avignon to pick her up. Of course not. He'd admitted to working crazy hours, and he certainly wouldn't let up the pace for her. This was the man who'd pushed her away and broken her heart. He hadn't wanted her then, and he didn't want her now. 'Thank you. How did you know I was going to be here?'

'Hortense told me.'

Allegra blinked.

Xavier shrugged. 'Now, are you going to stand there and argue all day, or can we go?' He lifted her suitcases.

'I can handle them myself,' she protested.

He shot her a look. 'Men in London might no longer have manners, but this is France.'

She subsided. 'Thank you.'

Another Gallic shrug. '*Ça ne fait rien.* How was London?'

'Fine.'

'And this is all you've brought with you?'

'I put some of my things in storage.'

'In case it doesn't work out here.' He nodded. 'It's sensible to play it safe.'

It sounded like a compliment, yet it felt like an insult. She decided not to rise to the bait. 'Did you get the proposals I emailed you?'

'Yes.'

'And?'

'I'm thinking about it.'

In other words, he was going to be difficult. 'How was your business meeting?' she asked.

'Fine, thank you.'

She coughed. '*Vineyard* business, would that be?'

'No, actually.'

Infuriating man. Would it really kill him to tell her?

As if he read her mind, he smiled. 'All right, if you must know, I bunked off for the afternoon and had lunch with Marc.'

'Marc, as in Monsieur Robert? Harry's—*my* lawyer?' she corrected herself.

'We didn't discuss *you*,' he told her loftily.

She scowled. 'You know, sometimes you can be so obnoxious.'

'No, really?' He slanted her a look as he put her cases into the back of his four-wheel drive. There was the tiniest, tiniest quirk to his lips, a hint of mischief in his eyes—just like the Xav she remembered from years ago, rather than the wary stranger he'd become—and suddenly she found herself smiling back.

'Welcome back to France. Come on, I'll drive you home,' he said.

Home. Was he being polite, or did he mean it? She wasn't sure.

'What happened to your sports car?' she asked as she climbed into the passenger seat. The one his father had bought him for passing his driving test, an ancient classic car with a soft top. The one in which he'd driven her all round the Ardèche, showing her all the beauty spots—from the natural wonder of the Pont d'Arc, a huge stone arch across the Ardèche river, through to the Chauvet Grotto with its incredible thirty-thousand-year-old cave paintings, and the beautiful lake in an old volcano crater at Issarles.

'It wasn't practical,' he said, surprising her. 'This is.'

'Practical?' She didn't follow. Practical had never been a consideration. Xav had loved that car. He'd chosen it in favour of a new one, and restored it with the help of Michel, who owned the garage in the village and had sighed with Xavier over how beautiful the car was. She and Guy had teased him mercilessly about the amount of attention he gave the car, but he'd never risen to the bait. He'd simply smiled and polished the chrome a little bit more.

'Sometimes I need to use my car off road, and sometimes I need to take a few cases of wine to a customer.'

'This has rather expensive upholstery for a delivery van,' she remarked.

'What do you expect me to do, use a pushbike and trailer?'

She had a vision of him doing just that and smiled. 'Well, hey, that'd be the eco way of doing things.'

'This car is as eco as a four-wheel drive gets, right now.'

'This is an eco car?' she asked, surprised.

'It's a hybrid,' he explained. 'I put my money where my mouth is. The vineyard's organic. I carry the ethos through to the rest of my life, too.'

A life she'd once thought to share. A life she knew nothing about.

Not that she wanted to tell him that, so she subsided and looked out at the countryside as Xavier drove, the fields full of sunflowers and lavender becoming hillier and full of vines and chestnut trees as they travelled deeper into the Ardèche.

Two suitcases really weren't much. Xavier knew women who needed more than that for a week's holiday, and Allegra was supposed to be here for the next two months. Was she going back to London again to bring more things over, or had she arranged to have things shipped? Or wasn't she planning to stay? 'What are you going to do about transport while you are over here?' he asked.

'I assume Harry still has his 2CV. I'll get that insured for me to drive.'

Harry's old banger? She had to be joking. 'He hasn't used it for years. You'll need to get a mechanic to look at it and check it over before you drive it—that's if it's still driveable.' He gave her an enquiring glance. 'Why didn't you bring your car over from England?'

'I don't have a car. I don't need one in London; I use public transport,' she explained.

'What if you had to go away?'

'If it was on company business, I used a hire car.'

Knowing that it was none of his business, and yet unable to leave it alone, he asked, 'So why did you resign? Why not just take a sabbatical?'

'I don't think the MD would have been too keen on that.'

'Your boss?'

Her lip curled. 'For the last six months, anyway.'

'You worked elsewhere before then?'

'No.' She sighed. 'Peter took over the agency, about a week after my boss—the Head of Creative—went on sick leave. I was Acting Head in his absence.'

'And now your boss is back?'

'He didn't come back,' Allegra said softly. 'He decided it was too much stress, so he took early retirement, two months ago.'

'And you took his place?'

'That was the idea. But Peter brought someone else in. Clearly he'd been planning it for a while.'

Her words were cool and calm, but he could hear the hurt in her voice. In her position, he would've been furious: doing a job for months, on a promise that it would be his, and then having it snatched away. Why hadn't Allegra fought back? 'Peter being this MD?'

She nodded.

The expression on her face told him more. 'He was the one who made you go to New York before Harry's funeral.' It was a statement rather than a question.

She swallowed. 'He said I had to prove myself to the company.'

'But you'd been Acting Head for…?' He paused for her answer.

'Five months.'

'So you'd already proved that you could do the job.'

She shrugged. 'That wasn't how he saw it. And he's the MD. What he says, goes.'

'And everyone else in the agency gets on with him?'

'No, but they put up with him. It's not exactly easy to change jobs in the current economic climate.'

'So if Harry hadn't left you the vineyard, what would you have done?' Xavier asked, curious.

'Probably found myself another job. And worked out where I could get a reference.'

Xavier blinked. 'He refused to give you a reference?'

'Not *refused*, exactly. But he could have written a reference that would've made any prospective employer have second thoughts about me.'

'Then you could have sued him for defamation.'

'Mud sticks,' she said. 'And would you employ someone who'd sued her previous employer? Doesn't that just scream "troublemaker" at you?'

'You have a point,' he said.

'I might've gone freelance, worked for myself. This just crystallised it for me—it was time to get out.'

So she *was* running from her job. That didn't bode too well for her working at the vineyard. He'd wondered before what would happen when the going got too tough for her; now, he was pretty sure she'd do exactly what his mother had done. Walk out. Find someone to rescue her.

Just as she was obviously seeing the vineyard as a way of rescuing her from the collapse of her job in London.

'If you sold the vineyard to me, it would give you enough money to set yourself up in business,' he pointed out quietly. 'You could go and do what you really want to do in London, instead of being stuck here.'

'I'm not selling, Xav. I'm going to make this work.' She lifted her chin. 'And I'm not going to let you bully me into changing my mind.'

Bully her? He stared at her in surprise for a moment before concentrating on the road again. 'I wouldn't bully you.'

'Intimidate, then.'

'I'm not intimidating.'

'Actually, you are,' she said quietly. 'You have strong views and you're not afraid to voice them.'

'Which doesn't make me a bully. I do listen. I listened to you, the other day,' he reminded her. 'Without judging. Much,' he added belatedly, trying to be fair.

'And you're so sure of yourself, of where you're going.'

'I see what needs to be done, and I do it without making a drama out of it.' He shrugged. 'If that's intimidating…sorry. It's how I am.'

'Whatever you throw at me, I'll handle it.'

So there was still some fire there, even if it was buried fairly deeply right now. 'Is that a challenge?' he asked, interested.

'No,' she said, sounding bone-deep tired. 'Why do men always have to make issues out of things?'

'I'm not making an issue out of things. Yes, I admit, I'd prefer you to be a silent partner, the way Harry was, but that obviously isn't going to happen. For the next two months, we're stuck with each other. I'll expect a lot from you, but I won't go out of my way to make life difficult for you.'

'Thank you for that. And I do mean to pull my weight. I'm not a slacker.'

Had this Peter accused her of that? he wondered. But for her to have wrapped up all the loose ends in London over the last couple of days and said her goodbyes, as well as emailing him a detailed report that had clearly taken time to research—no, Allegra Beauchamp wasn't a slacker.

Finally, Xavier parked on the gravel outside Harry's farmhouse. He was out of the car and holding the door open for Allegra before she had a chance to unclip her seat belt, and then he took her cases from the back of his car.

'Thank you,' she said. 'Um, would you like to come in for a coffee or something?'

'It's kind of you to ask, but I have work to do.'

'Of course.' And there was something else she needed to know. Her normal skill with words deserted her, and she ended up blurting out, 'Um, is it going to be a problem for your wife, having me as your business partner?'

Xavier gave her a speaking look. 'If you want to know if I'm married, *chérie*, just ask me—don't do that feminine subterfuge stuff. It's annoying.'

She felt the colour flood into her face. 'All right. Are you married?'

'No. Happy?'

Right at that moment, she really regretted accepting the lift from him. 'It doesn't actually make a difference to me whether you're married or not,' she said, looking him straight in the eye. 'I was just thinking, if you were involved with someone, I'd like to reassure her that I'm no threat to your relationship. Out of courtesy to her.'

Xavier spread his hands. 'You wouldn't be a threat.'

Of course not—he'd made it clear years ago that she wasn't what he was looking for. That he didn't have time for her. Though the comment still stung.

It must have shown in her face, because he said, this time a little more gently, 'I'm not involved with anyone. My energy's concentrated on the vineyard. I don't have time for complications.'

'Don't tell me you're celibate.' The words were out before she could stop them.

He raised an eyebrow. 'Asking about my sex life now, Allegra?'

This time, her blush felt even deeper. 'No. I didn't mean to say that aloud. And it was intrusive. I apologise.'

'But you asked, so you clearly want to know.'

'Forget it.'

His smile had a definite edge. 'No, I'm not celibate. I like sex. A lot, if you remember.'

Oh, God, yes. She remembered. And nobody had ever made her feel the way Xav had made her feel. As if she were drowning in pure pleasure.

There was a glint in his eye. 'But, as I said, I don't have time for complications.'

'You've changed a lot in ten years.'

'So have you. Let's leave it that we're both older and wiser.'

'Yes. Thank you for the lift, Monsieur Lefèvre,' she said politely, and picked up her cases.

She heard the sound of his car moving away on the gravel as she opened the front door, and sighed inwardly. So much for being business partners. He hadn't even wanted to discuss her proposals.

She greeted Hortense and took her cases upstairs. While she was unpacking, her phone bleeped. She glanced at the screen, surprised to see that the text was from Xavier. *See you in the office at midday tomorrow. Bring a loaf of white bread.*

It was an odd request, but at least it showed that he was prepared to talk to her about the business. And maybe the bread was meant to be her share of lunch. She finished unpacking before asking Hortense for the keys to Harry's old 2CV.

It was parked neatly in the barn Harry used as a garage. How many times had he picked her up in this from the station in Avignon? It looked cramped and old-fashioned, compared to Xav's sleek grey four-wheel drive, but it was still transport. If it was good enough for Harry, it was good enough for her.

She turned the key in the ignition, but the engine refused to start. It was pointless pulling up the bonnet and looking at the engine, because she knew next to nothing about how they worked; Xavier was right, she'd have to ask Michel—if he was still the local mechanic—to tow it in and inspect it. In the meantime, what? Given that she'd only be going to the village or over to the chateau, hiring a car seemed a bit over the top.

Then she saw the ancient bicycle leaning against the wall.

A quick check of the tyres told her that it was in working order. She experimented by cycling round the yard, testing that the brakes and gears worked. Well, she only needed transport for one. This would do her fine for the next couple of months. If she needed to go farther afield than the village or the vineyard office, she could use the train. And this was definitely a good way to help her get fit. There was even a wicker basket on the front of the bike that was big enough to carry her laptop and a handbag.

Perfect.

And tomorrow was the real beginning of her new life.

CHAPTER FOUR

THE next morning, Allegra cycled into the village and picked up a loaf from the *boulangerie* on the way to the office.

Did Xavier really think she'd be happy just to roll up at midday? No chance. They were partners, so her working day would be just as long as his. She'd told him she wasn't a slacker, and she'd prove it to him. But when she arrived at the chateau, the office block looked deserted. She tried the door: locked.

Oh, brilliant.

That left her three options. She could disturb Guy and ask if he had a spare key—though, as he'd already told her that the vineyard was Xavier's department, he probably wouldn't have one. She could ring Xavier's mobile and ask him to bring the key down—and risk annoying him if he was in the middle of something important. Or, given that she'd charged up her laptop the previous evening, she could find herself a comfortable spot in the gardens and work in the sunshine.

It was a no-brainer, really.

She took her laptop case out of the basket and propped her bike against the wall. There was a large chestnut tree to the side of the office block; she settled herself next to it, leaning back against the trunk, and powered up her laptop. The spot really was idyllic, she thought; she could smell the roses and the lavender, and hear the drowsy hum of the bees on their quest for pollen. Given the choice between this and her desk in a busy London office block, where all she could see from the windows were more office blocks, she knew where she'd rather be right now.

At quarter to twelve, Xavier parked outside the office, then slammed his car door and strode over to her. 'What do you think you are doing?' he asked.

'Working.'

'In the garden?'

She gave him her sweetest smile. 'As my business partner hasn't given me a set of keys to our office, yet, and the door's locked—yes.'

He frowned. 'Harry didn't have an office here.'

'I'm not Harry—and I'm not cycling from my house to yours every time I need a piece of paper. Just so you know, I'll be working here in office hours.'

He folded his arms. 'There isn't a spare office for you to use.'

Oh, wasn't there? 'I seem to remember seeing one on Saturday.'

'That's my secretary's office.'

It sounded plausible, but there was one huge hole in that theory. 'So why isn't she here now?'

'She's on a week's leave. Her daughter's just had a baby and she needs to be there to help.'

Allegra liked the fact he seemed relaxed about his secretary having time off for something so important. But it still left questions. 'Why don't you have a temp in while she's away?'

'Because Thérèse doesn't like people touching her paperwork. So don't even *think* about suggesting you can use her desk while she's away.'

Since when would a powerhouse like Xavier Lefèvre let anyone tell him what to do? She couldn't stop a gurgle of laughter escaping.

'Why are you laughing?' he asked.

'At the thought of someone bossing you about. Your secretary must be seriously scary.'

He rolled his eyes. 'Thérèse doesn't boss me about. And she happens to be extremely good at organising things.'

'I'll take your word for it.' She gave him another sweet smile. 'I take it you've been in the fields this morning? And you'll be there later this afternoon?'

'Yes.'

'Then your desk is free most of the day. Good. I can work there while you're in the fields. Unless you want me to work in the fields with you,' she added, 'in which case a chair in your office will do just fine during our admin period—the middle of the day, I believe you said? It won't take long to add my laptop to your network.'

He stared at her, his expression a mixture of admiration and annoyance. 'You've got it all planned, haven't you?'

'Yup.'

'You're difficult.'

She laughed. 'Pots and kettles.'

'La pelle se moque du fourgon,' he shot back.

'What?'

'"The shovel mocks the poker",' he translated. 'As we say in France. Same thing.'

She rolled her eyes. 'You always have to have the last word, don't you?'

He gave her another of those smiles she remembered from the station: full of mischief, slightly self-mocking, and utterly irresistible. 'Yes. Did you bring the bread?'

'Voilà.' She indicated the loaf in her bicycle's pannier. 'I assume it's my contribution to lunch?'

'No.' He unlocked the office door and shepherded her inside. 'Excuse me. I'm filthy. I had intended at least to have clean hands before you turned up.' He headed to the kitchen and washed his hands thoroughly, then took a platter from the fridge. 'Lunch today is cold meat and salad.'

'I don't expect you to provide lunch for me every day, Xav.' She used the pet form of his name without even thinking about it. 'I can bring a sandwich with me.'

'As you wish.' He spread his hands. 'But we're having a working lunch today, so you might as well share this with me. I see you cycled in.'

She nodded. 'You were right about Harry's 2CV. I couldn't even get it to start. Hortense is going to chat to the local garage for me and see if they can get it going again.'

'I could lend you a car.'

Did he think she was fishing? Wrong, wrong, wrong. And she wanted to prove to him that she could stand on her own two feet perfectly well—that she wouldn't be a burden. 'No need,' she said brightly. 'I'm fine with Harry's old bicycle.'

He raised an eyebrow. 'Even if it rains?'

'I'll just make sure my laptop's in a waterproof bag. Or I can use your computer while you're getting soaked in the fields, and copy it to a memory stick or email it to myself at the end of the day.'

'Stubborn, aren't you?'

'*La pelle se moque du fourgon,*' she threw back at him.

'Now that's cheeky.' But he looked amused rather than annoyed. 'Here.' He fished in his pocket, removed a key from his key ring and tossed it to her. 'Don't lose it.'

She caught it deftly, took her own key ring from her handbag and slid the office key onto it. 'I won't. Is there an alarm code?'

'Yes. Harry's birthday.'

Was he testing her, to see that she did actually know the date? Well, she wasn't going to let him rattle her. 'That's fine. The French format's the same as English, isn't it—two-digit day, then two-digit month?'

'Yes.' He handed her the platter. 'Take this in. I'll bring everything else.'

'Do you normally eat at your desk?' she asked, when he came in carrying the crockery, cutlery, a cobblestone-shaped loaf studded with olives that she recognised as *pavé*, Harry's favourite, and two glasses of iced water.

'It's convenient. And don't start. I bet you usually do the same.'

'Well, yes,' she admitted.

'Right. Help yourself.'

'Thank you.' She paused. 'As this is a working lunch, can we start with the website? I take it you got the recommendations I sent you?'

'Yes.'

His face was expressionless, but the fact that he didn't sound enthusiastic wasn't promising. 'What did you think?' she asked.

'Do you have to go into the heritage stuff?'

She frowned. 'Xav, it's a strength of the vineyard, and we should make the most of it. Your family has grown grapes here for years and years. If you'd tell me when they actually started, there might be an anniversary coming up that we could use to—'

'I don't think we should be going on about the past,' he cut in.

'Why not?'

'Because we haven't always been as successful as we are now. I don't want to drag up the past—any hint of failure, even if it was years ago, could make our suppliers nervous.'

'What failure?'

'It's not important now.'

She wasn't so sure. But he'd made it clear that he wasn't going to talk about it.

'I think we should concentrate on what we do now. What we're good at.' Xavier frowned. 'To be honest, I don't think we need to do any more marketing than we do now. Our customers like what we produce. I'm not planning to buy more land and increase the quantity of our output, so what's the point in making a big fuss?'

'Do you want this vineyard to be a huge success or not?'

He rolled his eyes. 'Don't ask ridiculous questions.'

'Then you need to talk about it, Xav. Tell people what we're better at doing than other producers.'

He arched an eyebrow. 'We?'

She flushed. 'All right, so I haven't done any of the physical work for this year's crop. But I'm learning. And I intend to pull my weight, whatever you think.'

He made a non-committal noise and cut some more bread.

'Who designed the original website?' she asked, curious.

'One of Guy's business contacts.'

Guy, Xavier's younger brother, clearly worked from home but had nothing to do with the vineyard. Years ago, she remembered Guy being the scientific type; she'd always thought he'd become a doctor. Obviously he hadn't. 'What does Guy do?' she asked, helping herself to cold meat and salad and accepting the piece of bread Xavier offered her.

'He's a nose.'

'A what?'

'A parfumier. He's gifted.'

Guy made perfume?

Xavier continued. 'His degree was in chemistry, but, like me, he doesn't have time for distractions. He owns half a perfume house in Grasse and heads up the R and D arm, directing the development of new perfumes. Half the time he lives there, but he also has a lab here—he spends most weekends at the chateau, or comes here when he wants to think and work on fragrance ideas in peace and quiet without office politics getting in the way. Except in harvest, when he drives the tractor for me.'

That, she thought, explained the rose garden. Guy's raw materials. 'Your mother must enjoy trying out his creations.'

'Chantal doesn't live here,' Xavier said, his tone short and warning her not to ask further.

Allegra remembered Chantal Lefèvre as the quintessential elegant Frenchwoman—always dressed in cream or navy, her dark hair beautifully coiffed and her make-up discreet and flawless. Allegra had always felt shy and faintly scruffy in her presence. So why didn't Chantal live at the chateau now? Was it that she couldn't bear to be there without Jean-Paul?

And yet Xavier had just referred to his mother by her first name, as if she weren't actually related to him. Odd. Chantal hadn't exactly been the demonstrative type but, given her own family background, Allegra wasn't really in a position to judge Chantal's relationship with her sons. Best to leave it, she decided, and brought the conversation back to a neutral topic. 'You said yesterday that the vineyard's organic, but the website doesn't say anything about it. How long has it been organic?'

'We've been certified for the last three years. If you want to see the files to see exactly what was involved, fine—though I should warn you it's all in French.'

'My French needs brushing up,' Allegra said. 'I suppose this is as good a way as any of getting back into it.' She looked at him. 'I want to do a blog, too—about learning to be a vigneronne. In French and English. Would you mind looking over my translations for the first few, so I don't make us look stupid?'

'You're here for two months,' he said.

'During which I'm going to bring new ideas to the business,' she said. 'This is an ongoing project.'

'I see.' He looked wary.

'Xavier, I have to start somewhere.'

'Then I suggest,' Xavier said, 'we start with the product. Which is why we need the bread.'

'You've lost me.'

'Already?' He rolled his eyes. 'It's to cleanse your palate between tasting.'

'You mean we're going to taste wine?'

'*You're* going to taste wine,' he corrected. 'What wine do you normally drink in London?'

'You're not going to like this,' she warned. 'New World.'

'So do a lot of our customers, outside France,' Xavier said, seemingly unruffled. 'What's your favourite?'

'New Zealand Sauvignon Blanc.'

He nodded. 'It's a good grape. Why do you like it?'

'Because of the taste.'

He waved his hand in a circle, encouraging her to expand on her answer.

'It's fruity,' she said.

'Good. Which fruit?'

'Sorry, I don't know.'

He sighed. 'When you say fruit, do you mean lemons, gooseberries, strawberries, melon, blackcurrants?'

She was pretty sure that a white wine wasn't supposed to taste of blackcurrants. 'Gooseberries. Is that right?'

'There isn't a right or wrong answer,' he said, surprising her. 'But in a good New Zealand Sauvignon Blanc, I'd expect gooseberries, maybe a hint of melon and citrus. Some are complex, some aren't. It depends on a lot of things. So your first lesson today is that the way the grape tastes has a lot to do with the winemaker—but it also has a lot to do with the *terroir*, the soil it's grown in.' A tiny furrow appeared between his eyebrows. 'Harry must've taught you this?'

'Sort of. I didn't pay as much attention as I should,' Allegra admitted. 'Anyway, he used to water down the wine for me when I was younger.'

Xavier smiled. 'You water it down for the children so they grow up appreciating it—and when they're eighteen they're less likely to go and binge on the stuff.'

She remembered.

'Here in the south, the kind of wines we make are probably closer to the kind of wines they make in Australia and New Zealand.'

'And we produce mainly rosé and white here, yes?'

'Yes. The rosé's *vin de pays*, also known as "country wine", which is a step above table wine. And the best is AOC—*appellation d'origine contrôlée.*'

He actually looked approving, and her heartbeat quickened just a tiny bit. 'I take it you know that wine in France is labelled by the area in which it grows, not by the grape?'

'Yes, but I don't think it's that helpful to consumers. If they know they like, say, Grenache, then why not tell them it's Grenache in the bottle, the way the New World producers do, instead of making them jump through hoops to understand what's in there?'

'Fair point. And, actually, we do say on our labels. Our rosé's mainly Grenache, so it's easy drinking—chill it down to four degrees and it's perfect for lazy summer afternoons.'

He spread his hands. 'I can talk all day but you're only going to learn if you experience it. Which is what we're going to do when we've finished lunch.'

'Why does this feel like taking my driving test?' she asked wryly.

He shrugged. 'It's not a big deal, Allie. It's just setting a baseline. If I'm to teach you what I know, I need to know what you know already so we don't repeat stuff you don't need to go over.'

A tiny frisson shimmered up her spine. He'd slipped back into calling her by her old pet name. And the last time Xavier had taught her something...

She shook herself mentally. That summer was in the past, and staying there. They hadn't talked about it, but they didn't need to: they were both older and wiser, and they weren't going to repeat their mistakes. So there was no point in dragging up the fact that he'd pushed her away, hard enough to make her end their relationship.

This was business. 'Thank you,' she said, hoping her voice sounded steadier than it felt, and concentrated on eating her lunch.

When they'd finished, she helped Xavier take the remains into the kitchen. His desk was already practically clear; he moved his in-tray to the floor, then fished out a white tablecloth from a box underneath his desk and spread it over the wood.

'Why do you need a tablecloth?' Allegra asked.

'So you can judge the colour of the wine properly. Did Harry never do this with you?'

'Not that I can remember,' she admitted. 'We were too busy talking about other things.'

'And you've never been to a wine tasting event?'

'No—but, Xav, hang on. I'm cycling back to the *mas*. I can't drink.'

'You don't actually drink wine when you're tasting—not if you're serious about it,' he explained. 'If you glug down half a dozen glasses on the trot, you won't remember anything about what they tasted like, and that negates the point. You taste, you spit it out, you make notes, and then you cleanse your palate with water and white bread before you try the next one.'

Enlightenment dawned. 'So *that's* why you wanted the bread.'

'*Exactement.*' He took a bottle from another box under his desk and handed it to her.

It was perfectly chilled.

'You use a screw-cap, like the New World producers?'

'For the *vin de pays*, yes. I'd rather have screw-tops than plastic corks because you don't have landfill issues. But for the AOC I use cork—it helps the wine age better, it's a renewable resource and it's biodegradable.'

Xav clearly thought deeply about what he did and its effect on the world; he'd grown up to become a man with integrity.

Pity he hadn't been so thoughtful ten years ago.

He took the bottle back from her. 'I was going to let you read the label,' he said, 'but I don't want to put ideas in your head. I want your gut reaction to the wine.'

He unscrewed the cap and poured her about a third of a glassful. 'This is a tasting serve. This means there's lots of space in the glass so you can swirl the wine around and test the aroma, and also so you have a chance to see the colour.' He tilted the glass over the tablecloth. 'Like this—you need to look at the colour of the body of the wine and the rim.'

She knew she was supposed to be looking at the wine. But she couldn't help looking at Xavier's hands. Strong, capable and slightly roughened by work, they were the hands of a man who saw what needed to be done and did it, not someone who left things to other people. And yet she knew his fingers could be infinitely gentle, too. Sensual. They'd teased a response from her body that she'd never quite managed with anyone else.

'Allegra?'

'Sorry. I was miles away.'

'If you'd rather not do this, it isn't a problem.'

'It's not that.' Though she'd rather dance barefoot across hot coals than tell him what she'd been thinking about. 'You were saying—the colour of the body and the rim.'

'The wine should look clear.'

'It's not as dark as I expected,' she said. 'It's almost pale peach. I thought rosés were pinker than that.' As pink as her cheeks felt, right at that moment.

'It depends on the grape you use and how it's produced. And the blend. Now, you swirl the wine in the glass. This mixes oxygen with the wine and releases the aroma. Your first sniff should be with caution—if it smells burnt, there's too much sulphite. Then do it again, this time with concentration—you're looking to see what aromas you get and the intensity.'

He passed the glass to her and she nearly dropped it when his fingers brushed lightly against hers.

This was crazy.

She'd been over Xavier for years. And she couldn't afford to fall for him again, not now they were business partners. That would be a huge, huge complication; he'd already warned her that he had no time for complications. Neither did she. He was *off limits*.

'So what can you smell?' he asked.

Right at that moment, Xavier reminded her of his younger brother, all intense and serious. She couldn't resist the urge to tease him slightly. She batted her eyelashes at him. 'Fruit?'

'Can you be a bit more specif—? Oh.' He rolled his eyes.

She grinned. 'Gotcha.'

'Very funny.' But then his eyes were smiling right back at her. Warm and sexy and utterly irresistible, and she was seriously glad she was sitting down because her knees turned straight to jelly.

'Cranberries,' she said. 'That's what it smells like. Fruity but dry.'

'Taste it.'

There was just a hint of an accent in his deep voice, and the way he spoke the phrase made her look straight at his mouth. Bad move, because he had a beautiful mouth, with even white teeth and a full lower lip. She could remember just how it had tasted against hers; and how easy it would be to brush her mouth against his, nibbling his lower lip until he opened his mouth to let her explore him.

'You need to swish the wine round your mouth, because different parts of your mouth detect different kinds of tastes,' he told her. 'At the back of tongue, it's bitter. The side is sour. The centre is salt and the front is sweet. Your gums react to the tannin in wine—it makes them feel dry.'

Her mouth felt dry, right now, and she could feel her lips parting. She only hoped that Xavier assumed she was about to taste the wine, not thinking about tasting him. Or was this his way of teasing her back?

'Roll it around your mouth,' he said. 'Think about the body.'

The body of the wine. Not his body. Not about how he'd broadened out, or how powerful his shoulders were now, or wondering whether his skin would still feel the same against her hands.

'The body's how heavy it feels on your tongue,' he added.

He probably meant to be helpful, but it just made things worse. It made her think of the way he used to kiss her, demanding and yet giving at the same time. His tongue teasing hers. His lips coaxing a response.

And she swallowed the wine, completely involuntarily.

Oh, hell. How to make herself look like an idiot. He'd specifically told her not to swallow. She was supposed to be thinking about the wine. But how could she when her head was full of him? How he'd tasted when he'd kissed her, all those years ago… Like the ginger chocolates he favoured, dark and hot and intense.

'Sorry. I, um…made a hash of that.'

'It's OK. Just think about the wine and how long it lingers afterwards—that's the finish. The longer the finish, the better the wine. Does it make you want another taste, or is it too bitter, too sour, not the kind of taste you enjoy?'

'It tastes of berries,' she said. 'Cranberries, raspberries. Maybe peaches, or maybe I'm letting the colour influence me.'

'And the finish?'

It was pointless in bluffing, so she went for honesty. 'I'm not sure,' she said. 'It's not something I've ever really paid attention to before. Can I use this one as a benchmark, and tell you when I've tried another?'

He looked approving. 'That's good—you think logically. Write down your thoughts, then we'll do the next one—and we'll compare what you found with what it says on the label later.' He took another bottle from under his desk, brought out a corkscrew from the drawer, and opened the bottle effortlessly.

'This one's a bit unusual because it's completely Viognier, though I have thought about mixing some Rolle with it and I'm planning to experiment with a blend, this harvest.'

She bit her lip. 'I'm sorry, you're going to think me completely hopeless—but I haven't heard of Viognier or Rolle.'

'Viognier has been neglected for a while, but it's becoming fashionable again,' Xavier said. 'It's one of the older varieties of grapes—it's been grown in Provence since Roman times, maybe even before that. Rolle's another very old variety. I'm growing it in a quiet corner of the vineyard for an experiment.' He poured her a tasting serve. 'Tell me what you see.'

'It's very pale gold—there's almost a green tinge at the rim.' She swirled the wine, then sniffed. 'No burning smell.' She sniffed again. 'You're going to think I'm crazy. It smells of flowers to me.' And one in particular. 'Honeysuckle.'

'I think,' he said, 'you might be a natural at this. Anything else?'

'Pears, I think.' She took a mouthful, let it swoosh over her tongue, then spat it out. 'It tastes of melon and peaches, and it makes my tongue tingle. It's definitely dry—and the finish is longer than the rosé's, though I think I'd prefer the rosé for the garden on a summer afternoon.'

Either she'd been playing him for a fool earlier or she was a quick learner.

Given what he remembered of her, Xavier was pretty sure that it was the latter.

And he really, really had to stop thinking of that summer. Had to stop looking at her mouth and wondering what it would be like to kiss her now.

He had no idea what possessed him to uncork a bottle of Clos Quatre. His baby. But, before he knew it, he'd poured her a tasting serve of the wine.

Her eyes met his. Saw the challenge. Answered it.

And then she picked up the glass. Surveyed it critically.

'It looks like rubies.'

One sniff. A second. 'Berries—but darker than raspberries. Blackberries, maybe, and something else I can't work out. Herby?'

'That'd be the *garrigue*. The scent of scrubland on limestone soil,' he explained.

And then she sipped.

He couldn't help watching her mouth. A perfect rose-bud. She'd moistened her lips slightly before she'd tasted the wine, and the sunlight glinted on the sheen of her mouth.

Did she have any idea how alluring she was?

And it wasn't from make-up, either. Today, Allegra was dressed far more practically; rather than trying to cycle here in a business suit and heels, she was wearing flat, sensible shoes and soft, pale denim teamed with a short-sleeved T-shirt. She was the girl next door and she was dressed like it.

And yet she didn't look like *just* the girl next door.

Something about her kicked his heart rate up a notch.

'Blackberries,' she said.

'Hmm?' He wasn't following. At all.

'It tastes of blackberries,' she said.

And her lips were parted. Sweet and soft and inviting. With the tiniest, tiniest gloss of wine along her lower lip. Just as she'd been when she'd been eighteen and they'd taken a bottle to drink in the evening by the lake.

He couldn't resist any longer. He simply dipped his head and kissed her, touching the tip of his tongue to the spot of wine on her lip. 'You're right. Blackberries.'

Her pupils were huge, and she looked as lost as he felt right at that moment. And then she placed her palm gently against his cheek and stroked his lower lip with the pad of her thumb. Such a light, light touch, but it made his knees buckle and his mouth open. He nibbled her thumb, keeping the touch as light as gossamer.

He wasn't sure which of them moved first, but then she was in his arms, his mouth was jammed over hers, and he was kissing her. And she was kissing him back as though she'd missed him as much as he'd missed her, was as desperate for him as he was for her. Hot and open-mouthed and demanding, yet giving and promising at the same time. His arms were wrapped tightly round her, hers were just as tightly round his, and at some point he'd sat down and pulled her with him so she was straddling his lap.

When she rocked ever so slightly against him, nudging against his erection, it made him gasp into her mouth.

Dieu, he wanted her so badly.

And they really shouldn't be doing this.

He broke the kiss. 'This is a seriously bad idea.' His head knew that. But his body wasn't listening; for the life of him, he couldn't loosen his arms from round her. And hers were wrapped just as tightly round him.

He tried again. 'We know it doesn't work between us.'

'Uh-huh. But I can't move, Xav, because you're still holding me.' Her voice was breathy, her pupils were huge and her mouth was reddened and swollen from his kisses.

And he wanted to kiss her again.

Desperately.

'*You're* still holding *me*,' he pointed out. 'Allie, we have to stop this. How the hell are we going to be able to w—?'

She brushed her mouth against his, stopping the sentence and scrambling his thoughts, and he groaned. 'I can still taste the wine on your mouth.'

'All I can taste is you.' She did it again, taking her time about it and blowing his mind in the process.

If she hadn't realised how turned on he was before, he thought wryly, she'd be in no doubt of it now. He was as hard as iron. And it would take him all of five seconds to strip her naked and bury himself inside her.

With a huge effort, he shrugged free of her embrace, dropped his hands to her waist, and lifted her off his lap. 'We're not doing this.'

'Pushing me away again, Xav?' There was a hint of bitterness in her smile.

Again? What was she talking about? He frowned. 'I've never pushed you away.'

She scoffed. 'You know damn well you have.'

Was she talking about their break-up? Blaming him for it? He felt his eyes narrow. 'You were the one who called a halt.'

'Because you made it clear you'd had enough. That I didn't fit in to your new life.'

He stared at her. 'Did I, hell. I was there, and I remember.'

'I was there too, and *I* remember,' she countered. 'I asked you when you were coming to London. You said you were too busy.'

Yes, because everything had gone wrong at the vineyard. They'd been close to losing everything. And his mother had walked out in the middle of the chaos, leaving his father devastated. Xavier had been faced with a choice: walk away, too, and start his job in Paris, or put everything on hold and support his family. 'And you couldn't have waited a little while, until things had settled down for me?'

'What was to settle down, Xav? You already had a flat sorted out in Paris. You had a job. OK, so it might've taken you a couple of weeks to find your feet, but you…' She shook her head. 'It was obvious to me that you'd changed your mind. That I was just a—a holiday romance for you, so you were making excuses not to see me. Perhaps you'd already met someone else, but you were working up to dumping me.'

'There was never anyone else. If you'd asked me, I'd have told you that.' He blew out a breath. 'I can't believe that you had so little trust in me. And what about you? The second I didn't drop everything for you, you decided it was over.'

'I didn't expect you to drop everything for me,' she retorted. 'But it would've been nice if you'd called me, once in a while, instead of making me call you all the time.'

He felt a muscle flicker in his cheek. 'I told you, there was a lot going on.'

'And you couldn't have spared just a couple of minutes to say you were up to your eyes but you were thinking of me?'

Xavier threw his hands up in disgust. She was just like his mother, and just like Guy's ex-wife. 'What is it with women? If we're not paying you a hundred per cent attention a hundred per cent of the time...'

'I wasn't asking for *all* of your attention. Just a bit of it.' She glared at him, resting her hands on her hips. 'Talk about unreasonable.'

He scoffed. 'Says the woman who called it off.'

'You pushed me into it. I'd had enough of trailing behind you, like some pathetic doormat. So, yes, I called it off. What did you expect, that I'd trot meekly behind you and wait until you dumped me officially?'

'No. I just expected you to trust me. Clearly you didn't, so it's just as well you called it off.' He got to his feet. 'Excuse me. I have things to do in the fields.'

'Running away from the truth?'

'No. Putting space between us, before I say something we'll both regret. What happened just now was a huge mistake—and, yes, I'll take the blame for it. I can assure you that it's not going to happen again. And if you're serious about pulling your weight in the vineyard, then I suggest you work on tasting the wine, making notes and checking it against the labels instead of flirting with me.'

Her cheeks went scarlet. 'I wasn't flirting.'

No? She'd been kissing him back. Intimately. But there was no point in arguing with her. 'I'm going back to work. And you can do what the hell you like.' As long as it meant leaving him alone. 'Excuse me.' He rose from his chair, moved past her—very, very careful not to let any part of him touch any part of her—and left his office.

CHAPTER FIVE

ALLIE sat back in her chair and lifted a shaking hand to her mouth. Did Xavier really think she'd wanted them to break up?

The words of their argument echoed in her head. According to him, he hadn't pushed her away. Was it possible that she'd misinterpreted things back then?

Yet, when she'd said their relationship was over, he'd agreed. He hadn't asked her why. He'd let her go without fighting for her—and she'd assumed it was because she'd saved him the bother of ending it himself.

Then again, he'd taken the blame for that flare of passion between them just now—even though she'd been there all the way with him. He'd as good as admitted how much he wanted her. Just as she wanted him.

But he'd also made it clear he had no intention of letting it happen again.

She blew out a breath. This was a mess. And they definitely had crossed wires about what had happened all those years ago. The way he remembered it wasn't the same way that she remembered it. They needed to talk about it properly; then maybe they could work out where they were going from here.

Especially as they co-owned a vineyard. If they didn't sort it out, working together was going to be excruciating.

She tried ringing his mobile phone—but either he wasn't in a position to take the call or he wasn't in the mood for talking to her, because he didn't answer. So instead, she texted him. *Xav, I'm sorry. I don't want to fight with you. We're both older and wiser and we both want the business to succeed. We can work together.*

Provided they talked properly and cleared things up between them.

I'll see you tomorrow.

She tidied up in the office and restoppered the bottles of wine. There wasn't much more she could do here. Maybe she should take the wine back to Harry's and work on the tasting, as he'd suggested. She could send him her notes, to show that she was serious and she wasn't just playing at being a vigneronne.

And burying herself in work, giving herself something else to concentrate on, might just stop her thinking about the way he'd kissed her. The way her body had responded. The way her blood was still tingling in her veins.

She cycled home and let herself into the empty house. Although in some ways it was a relief not to have to face anyone—not when she was feeing this shaky—in other ways, she wished the housekeeper had been there. How Harry must've rattled around here on his own.

And how she wished she could change the past.

But it wasn't possible. She had to move on, not let the past drag her back.

Look at the labels, Xav had said. So she did—but not just to read the notes. This time, she looked at them with a professional eye, and she didn't like what she saw. The design of the labels just wasn't inspiring. They told the customer nothing about the wine, the vineyard—there wasn't really a brand. They simply contained the vineyard's name, the name of the wine, its classification and the year, and the fact that it was *'mis en bouteille au Domaine'*—bottled at the estate. Everything that needed to be there, without the pizzazz.

The back was a little better, telling her about the wine's bouquet and its taste. But it still had no personality. And Les Trois Closes definitely had a personality.

Letting the ideas bubble in the back of her head, she tasted the wines again, this time taking account of the notes on the label and trying to see where she agreed with them and where she couldn't pick up the scent or taste. She made notes to discuss with Xavier later, then wrote her first blog about tasting wine. Laboriously, she translated it into French and emailed the file with both the English and the French version over to Xavier.

Next, she wrote a design brief. From what Xavier had told her, she had a very clear idea of what Les Trois Closes was all about. They used traditional grapes and traditional methods, and the wine was hand crafted, so she wanted the label to reflect that. Maybe a textured label with hand-drawn lettering. It also needed a strong graphic to go with the text that legally had to be on the wine.

She sent a text to Gina. Can u do freelance job 4 me, hon? Need logo + sample wine bottle labels. Middle next week OK?xxx

Gina replied almost immediately: Sure, email brief @ home, I'll ring u if I have any queries xxx

This was a private job, not something through the agency, so it made sense to email the brief to Gina's home address rather than to work. And of course Gina would ring her with any questions: she was an excellent designer, and good at seeing to the heart of a brief, especially in cases where the client asked for one thing but clearly meant something else.

She was about to text a thank you when her phone beeped again with another text from Gina. U OK?

Far from it. She was as miserable as hell because she didn't want to be at loggerheads with Xav and she wasn't a hundred per cent sure if it was fixable, let alone how to fix it. But Gina didn't need to hear all that. Tres OK, she texted back, adding a smiley face. She emailed the brief to Gina, along with a chatty note saying how much she was enjoying it here in the Ardèche. She told her about Nicole's farm shop and café in the village, the way that the light and the air felt so different here, how fabulous the food was.

What she didn't say was that she couldn't get Xavier out of her head. Or how it could be oh so easy to be lonely, here; in London, she'd always been busy with work and had people round her, never had time to think about whether she was happy. Here, the pace of life was so much slower—and there simply weren't people around. The estate workers reported to the office at the chateau, and Hortense lived with her brother in the village. Harry had always had a basset hound; Allegra had asked Hortense what had happened to the dog and discovered that he'd been rehomed. It wouldn't be fair to bring the dog back here now. And it wouldn't be fair to buy a puppy, either, until she'd convinced Xavier that she was a worthy partner in the business.

All the same, she found herself searching the Internet, sighing over puppy pictures. Xavier didn't have a dog—at least, not that she'd seen. But if she trained her dog well, kept him under control in the fields...surely Xav wouldn't object?

Maybe she could get a rescue dog—to give an unwanted animal a second chance, just as she'd been given one.

Three clicks later, she was looking at the photograph of a dog called Beau in an Ardèchoise animal rescue centre. He was an orangey-brown-and-white dog with the most soulful brown eyes, and it was love at first sight. *Un epagneul Breton.* She grabbed her dictionary to help her with the difficult words; the more she read, the more she wanted him.

Though she could hardly collect a dog on a bicycle. And Xavier *had* offered to lend her a car...

An offer she'd refused. And an offer that might not be forthcoming again.

Half an hour later, her email pinged again. This time it was from Xavier.

I don't want to fight, either. I'm sorry, too.

Good. So let's kiss and make—oh, no. She definitely couldn't mention the *K* word. Not after the way they'd kissed each other in his office this afternoon. Especially as he'd accused her of flirting with him. She deleted the words and typed instead, Truce?

There was a long, long pause—or maybe it just felt as if time were running at a tenth of its usual speed because she so badly wanted to know how he'd react—but finally his reply came through. OK. Truce.

A few minutes later, there was another email from him: a list of Internet links for her to follow, plus a word-processed file with corrections to her French typed in red.

How to make her feel like a schoolgirl.

Then again, this wasn't about her ego. This was about their joint business, and she wanted to get this right. She'd asked for his help, and he'd given it. Besides, he hadn't just marked corrections: he'd added a couple of notes at the bottom, in English, to explain where she'd gone wrong and why.

Xavier Lefèvre would've made an excellent teacher. Then again, she thought ruefully, he would've been excellent at any job he chose. Xav wasn't one to give half measures in anything.

She heard the back door rattle; a moment later, Hortense walked into the kitchen and raised an eyebrow when she saw Allegra sitting there at her laptop.

'Sorry, will I be in your way?' Allegra asked.

Hortense shrugged. 'I can work at this end of the table.'

Allegra tidied up her notes and shoved them into a folder. 'Sorry,' she said again. This really wasn't a good state of affairs. And there was a perfectly good study next door. 'Hortense, would you mind if I go through Harry's study at the weekend?' she asked. 'I was thinking, if I put some of his things away, it would make room for mine—and I wouldn't be under your feet in here all the time.'

Hortense shrugged again. 'It's your house. Do what you will.'

'Madame Bouvier, I'm not that thick-skinned. I don't want to hurt you or ignore your feelings—but I can't keep working at the kitchen table and getting in your way.'

Her only answer was another Gallic shrug.

Allegra sighed inwardly and continued working, becoming absorbed in coding the website.

Half an hour later, Hortense put a large mug of black coffee beside her—a kind of peace offering, Allegra guessed.

'I'm off now,' Hortense announced. 'There's a casserole in the oven—*poulet Provençal*. It will be ready at seven, and there are green beans and broccoli in the fridge.'

'Thank you.' Hortense's *poulet Provençal* had always been one of Allegra's favourites: another peace offering, it seemed. And at least the housekeeper wasn't being territorial over the kitchen and insisting that Allegra didn't touch a thing—probably because she'd learned over the last few days that Allegra wasn't going to take her for granted and had washed up and put things away in the right places.

Allegra spent the evening in Harry's study, looking through his books. There were plenty on viticulture, but they were all in French. She ordered herself the English versions of the ones that looked most well thumbed; just as she finished, an email came through from Gina.

Brief looks fine. I need pics of the vineyard and surrounding area to give me some inspiration for visuals.

Well, that was something for her to do over the next few days—while she waited for Xavier to accept her new role in the business.

On the case, she emailed back.

On Friday morning, Allegra cycled into the village to pick up some bread and cheese, then cycled up to the chateau. Her heart was tattooing crazily at the thought of seeing Xavier again—and how were they going to face each other? They'd agreed to a truce, but there was still that scorching attraction between them. They were going to have to deal with that, too, and she had no idea how.

When she saw that the office block was locked, she wasn't sure if she was more disappointed or relieved. Everything was confusion where Xavier was concerned. She wanted him—and, at the same time, she wanted to be a million miles away from him.

Crazy.

She unlocked the door, then installed herself at Xavier's desk.

It was the first time she'd been in his office without him. Without his presence to command all her attention, she was able to pay more attention to her surroundings. Obviously Xavier believed in a clear-desk policy; it was a million miles away from Harry's cluttered study. And, unlike Harry, Xavier didn't keep anything personal in his workspace. This room could've belonged to anyone.

Maybe that was the way forward. Act on pure logic and keep her emotions out of this. Treat him as a client, as a business associate—and block off everything else that he'd meant to her. Pretend she didn't feel that wild surge of longing every time she looked into his eyes.

Telling herself that this was work, she booted up her laptop and got down to some work.

At quarter to twelve, Xavier parked outside the office. Allegra was clearly there; her bicycle was propped against the wall, his office window was wide open, and she'd also left the front door open—probably in the hope of cooler air circulating.

It wasn't as hot here as it was on the coast, but it was still a good deal warmer than she was used to. She'd always spent a lot of time in the pool in those long-ago summers.

And then he wished he hadn't remembered that, because his mind supplied another image. Allegra bathing naked in a mountain pool, looking like a mermaid with hair the colour of winter wheat spreading out on the surface of the water. He'd loved it when she'd worn her hair long and loose, instead of the glossy, high-maintenance style she had now.

Dieu. He really had to get himself back under control. They'd agreed to a truce—by email—and he'd promised her that he wouldn't let the events of yesterday be repeated. Even though his body was quivering with the need to touch her. He could do this. Keep it strictly business.

Maybe he needed a night out. An evening with someone who'd give and take pleasure in equal measure, and wouldn't expect anything else from him. Hot, mindless sex that would sate his body and stop his mind dwelling on Allegra Beauchamp.

Ha. Who was he trying to kid? He couldn't stop thinking about her. And making love with someone else was completely out of the question. He wouldn't be able to do it.

When he walked in though the front door, he could see her sitting at his desk. She was clearly concentrating hard on what she was doing and hadn't heard him. There was a tiny furrow between her brows; she looked serious and businesslike. And incredibly cute.

How he yearned for her.

But he'd keep himself under control. He wouldn't walk in, lift her out of his chair, take her place and settle her in his lap. Wouldn't touch his mouth to hers, coaxing and teasing until her response flared, the way it had yesterday. Instead, he walked into his office and dropped into the chair opposite the one where she was sitting—the one he reserved for clients. *'Bonjour,'* he drawled.

She looked up and her eyes widened. 'Sorry, I didn't realise you were back. I'll move. Do you always break for lunch this early?'

'At this time of year, yes. It's too hot to work outside now until later in the afternoon.'

She nodded. 'Thanks for correcting my pieces.'

'No problem.'

She gave him a cool, professional smile—though it didn't quite work. Obviously she was nervous around him. Worried that he'd kiss her again, maybe? That he'd break their truce? 'I've set up the blog now, done it in French and English and cross-referenced it, and also linked it to our website. Oh, and I looked up those links you gave me and I've ordered some books.'

'Which ones?'

She told him and he nodded. 'They're good ones to start with.'

'I'd like to take a few pictures of the vineyard. Do you have time to show me round?'

Spend more time in her company? He needed his head examined.

Not to mention a cold shower.

'Give me five minutes to have something to eat, and I'll be with you,' he said.

'It's not *that* urgent,' she said. 'I don't expect you to drop everything for me.'

She'd said something about that yesterday.

So had he been wrong, all those years ago? He certainly hadn't been thinking straight at the time, not with all the chaos going on here. Maybe he'd misunderstood her. Though he couldn't ask her straight out, not without opening a huge can of worms. He needed to think of a way of dealing with this to give minimum discomfort on both sides.

'I'm making coffee. Do you want some?'

She was clearly making an effort, so he ought to do the same. 'That'd be nice. Thanks.'

'And I bought some bread and cheese. If you'd like some?'

'Thanks. There's salad in the fridge, if you'd like to share it.'

And how much this reminded him of lunches they'd shared in the past. Picnics in a shady corner, sprawled out on a rug. He'd loved feeding her choice morsels and stealing kisses from her in between. Especially peaches. How he'd loved feeding her slices of fresh peach, and licking the juice from the corner of her mouth.

Oh, for pity's sake, could he just stop thinking about her mouth?

He waited as she saved her file and vacated his seat. But, when he sat down on the business side of his desk, his chair was still warm with her body heat. And he could smell her perfume.

How to drive a man slowly crazy…

Business, he reminded himself, and switched on his PC. It didn't take him long to find the blog she'd set up and to read through it.

He looked up from the screen as she walked back into the office with their lunch. 'You've made a good job of the blog.' And to his relief she hadn't gone on about the heritage.

She flushed. *'Merci.'*

'So you want to look round the vineyard.' He eyed her critically. 'Your shoes are sensible enough. Do you have a hat?'

She fished a baseball cap out of her laptop bag. 'Will this do?'

'Sure.' He smiled. 'It's not what I expected.'

She frowned. 'What did you expect?'

'Something floaty.' Like the straw boater she'd worn that summer, with a chiffon scarf tied round the brim and trailing down at the side.

'This is practical.'

'So I see.' He took a sip of the coffee.

Somehow they managed to get through lunch, and then he drove her over to the vines. At least driving her meant that he had to concentrate on the road.

'Is it all right for me to take pictures?' she asked when she climbed out of his car.

'Are they for the blog?'

'Yes and no,' she said. 'I want them for myself as well.'

'Any particular reason?'

'I'm a visual learner,' she explained. 'You know the old saying, "I hear and I forget, I see and I remember, I do and I understand"? Well, I see and I understand.'

Visual.

Oh, *Dieu.* How was he going to keep his mind on business instead of remembering what she looked like naked?

Tell her about the grapes, idiot.

'What you're seeing here are the Viognier grapes. We've just passed the flowering stage. Some people start pruning now to let more light onto the grapes but I don't tend to deleaf at this point because the grapes are in full sun here all afternoon. If they get sunburnt, it'll make the skins weaker; if we get heavy rain afterwards, they'll become swollen and split and rot sets in so they'll be useless for making wine.'

'They look like tiny peas,' she said, lifting some of the leaves to look at the grapes and taking a shot.

Her hands were beautiful. Delicate. And he could still remember what they felt like against his skin. How shy she'd been, the first time she'd touched him. How her confidence had grown over the weeks until she matched him heat for heat, passion for passion.

He swallowed hard. 'They'll grow hugely now,' Xavier said. The grapes. Not his body. Though that was reacting, too, and he was glad that he hadn't tucked his shirt into his jeans. It would spare both their blushes.

'Which means we have to keep on top of the weeding,' she said, clearly remembering something she'd read. 'But we're organic, so we don't spray, right?'

'No herbicides or systemic pesticides. We use cover cropping instead.' He indicated the area between the rows of vines. 'Sure, the grass and clover might look a bit scruffy, but it means the soil doesn't erode as much, nitrogen goes back into the soil and we get much more biodiversity. It's a great habitat for insects, which eat the pests.'

'But under the vines it's clear,' she noted.

'We hoe them by hand, to make sure there are no weeds choking the vines.'

By hand.

Allegra could imagine Xavier hoeing, focused on his work. Maybe he'd take his shirt off in the heat, and the sunlight would gild his skin.

She swallowed hard. Clearly the sun was addling her brain, despite her hat. And she really needed a drink of water. Except the film in her head kept unfolding. Memories. Xav, in the middle of a hot summer afternoon, tipping his head back to drink from a bottle of water. His throat working. Closing his eyes, pouring the rest of the water over his head to cool him down. Droplets of water glistening on his bare chest.

Oh, hell. She really had to get a grip. He shouldn't still be able to affect her like this. Though she had to admit he'd grown even better-looking with age. He was still self-assured, but he'd lost the cockiness and arrogance of youth.

'When it's August, it will be *veraison*,' Xavier continued.

'When the grapes change colour.'

He gave her an approving look, '*Exactamente*. Since you've obviously been reading up, do you know how I test them?'

'You taste them?'

The words were out before she could stop them.

Taste.

Just as he'd tasted her yesterday.

Just as she wanted him to taste her, right here and now, under the hot Mediterranean sun.

'I like to check the numbers as well,' he said. 'August is the month when we rest, gearing up for the harvest in September—when things go crazy.'

'You work every single day? And you're in the fields every day?' she asked.

'Mostly, yes—and, no, before you ask, I don't expect you to do the same. It's my land. Part of me.'

He had the sense of belonging that she needed so very much. And how she envied that.

'Though if you're still here in two months' time—'

He really didn't think she would be?

'—you'll be roped into harvest, because we need all the help we can get. We hand-pick because it's better—it does less damage to the clusters and we can select the best bunches. Even Guy joins us in the fields. We'll be working from dawn until late and the days just blur into each other.'

He made it sound like torture, but his expression showed how much he relished it.

'I'll look forward to it,' she said coolly. 'My first proper harvest. I was always back at school when harvest started.' Except that last year, when her parents had been in London in the September before she'd started university, and Harry had encouraged her to leave early and spend some time with them. Build a few bridges.

That last year, when leaving France had been so hard. She'd seriously thought about giving up her place at university and staying with Xav.

And then, when he'd pushed her away, she'd been hugely relieved that she hadn't done anything so rash.

She lifted her camera, doing her best to act as if she were completely casual about this, and began taking photographs. Ostensibly of the vineyard, although somehow Xavier ended up in the frame of a few of them.

'You have a good zoom on that?' he asked.

'Yes, why?'

'Move very slowly, and look to your left.'

She did so, and saw a gorgeous copper-and-black butterfly on one of the leaves. 'It's beautiful,' she whispered, taking the snap. 'What is it?'

'A *papillon petit nacré*.'

'In English?'

He shrugged. 'No idea. You'll have to look it up. But, if you like butterflies, go and take a look in the lavender.'

'It might make a nice picture for the blog. Thank you.'

He drove her down the road to see the Grenache and the Syrah.

'What about the other wine I tasted?' she asked. 'Or was that pure Syrah?'

He blinked. 'Clos Quatre, you mean? That's Marselan.'

'Marselan?' She didn't recognise the name.

'It's a relatively new grape,' he explained. 'A cross between Grenache and Cabernet Sauvignon.'

'I liked it,' she said. 'Do we sell much of it?'

'No. It's my private stock.'

She frowned. 'How do you mean, private stock?'

'It's not part of the vineyard,' he explained. 'Our customers love our rosé and the AOC, but we've made it for years and I wanted to try something a little different. Marselan's grown more in the Languedoc region than here, and it's not a particularly heavy cropper, so it wasn't fair to make Harry bankroll half of my experiment.'

'So you buy the grapes from Languedoc?'

'No. I bought a small clos down the road, about four years back.'

A fourth clos—hence the name of the wine.

And she noticed that he didn't offer to show it to her. That hurt, though she knew she was being ridiculous: it was Xav's personal venture, nothing to do with Les Trois Closes, so there was no reason why he should take her there.

Instead, he took her to the production plant and explained the process of making the wine, from the grapes arriving from the field through to bottling the final blend. Allegra took copious notes as well as photographs: maybe she could do a 'day in the life of a grape' type piece.

'Enough for today, I think,' Xavier said.

'Yes.' Her head was spinning and it'd take a while to absorb all this.

'Any questions before you go?'

This was the perfect opportunity. 'Actually, yes. You know you offered to lend me a car, the other day—did you mean it?'

He looked surprised. 'Why do you want to borrow a car?'

'Because…' She took a deep breath. Given that her dog would spend a fair amount of time on his land, this was something she probably ought to float by him. 'I wanted to go to the animal rescue centre. There's this dog…'

He frowned. 'Dog?'

'Harry always had a dog. And I…' She stopped. Telling him that she was lonely, when she'd only been here a few days, was tantamount to showing weakness.

'You seriously want to get a rescue dog?'

She nodded.

'They'll want to know that the dog is going to a good home. That you know about dogs, how to care for them, and the dog won't be left on its own all day.'

'I thought he could come with me to the office,' she said. 'And, um, I was hoping you might be able to vouch for me, if I need a character reference.'

He blew out a breath. 'A rescue dog needs a lot of attention, Allie. We're gearing up for harvest, the busiest time on the domaine. It's going to be noisy, with lots of people about and machinery going. Is it fair to bring a dog who's maybe had a bad time into that kind of environment, when nobody has time to spend with him and settle him in properly?' He spread his hands. 'And what if you decide this isn't what you want to do, and you go back to London? What then? Does the dog have to go back to the rescue centre and hope that someone else will take him, or are you going to put him in quarantine kennels for months?'

'I'm staying, so that isn't an issue,' she said, lifting her chin.

'You haven't thought this through.' He shook his head. 'Wait until harvest is over. If you're still here and you still want a dog, then I'll help you. I'll drive you to the rescue centre myself and vouch for your suitability.'

He'd been fair. More than fair. And she knew he was right: this wasn't the right time for a dog to settle in. But disappointment lodged in her throat. 'Thank you. I'll see you tomorrow,' she muttered.

'Tomorrow's Saturday. I don't expect to see you until Monday.'

'You'll be working, though.'

He shrugged. 'Just absorb your notes. Maybe do some more tasting—Harry has a good cellar. See if you can tell the differences between vintages.'

'Sure. Um, have a nice weekend.' Feeling that somehow she'd lost some of the ground she'd gained, she packed her things in her laptop bag, secured it in the basket on the front of her bicycle and went home.

CHAPTER SIX

ON SATURDAY morning, Allegra began sorting through Harry's office. He'd always filed everything away neatly, so it wasn't an onerous task—though she had a lump in her throat when she discovered that he'd kept all the letters she'd sent him over the years.

There were photographs, too. A big box full of them, in no particular order. Summers blurred together: when she was eight, fourteen, eleven. Eighteen, all dressed up for a night out in a group with Xav, Guy and Guy's then girlfriend, Hélène. Older pictures, too: a man just recognisable as her father, in his late teens. A younger boy—maybe also her father? And other people she didn't even begin to recognise.

And there, at the bottom, was a photograph in a folder, which was clearly by a professional photographer rather than a family snap. She caught her breath as she opened it and saw the bride and groom smiling into each other's eyes. The groom was Harry, though the bride was a total stranger. Allegra had never seen a photograph of the woman before, and she'd certainly never heard her father talk about any aunt in connection with Harry.

So who was Harry's bride? And what had happened to her?

She went to make herself a cup of coffee and found Hortense in the kitchen, making what looked like ratatouille. '*Bonjour*, Madame Bouvier.'

'*Bonj*—' Hortense began, looking over at her, then stopped with a frown. 'Are you all right, Allegra?'

'Yes and no.' She wrinkled her nose. 'I've just found this photograph of Harry on his wedding day. I had no idea Harry had ever been married—and nobody's ever mentioned his wife.'

'It was a long time ago. I was a child myself,' Hortense said, surprising her. 'They honeymooned here when my mother was the housekeeper.'

'Was she French?' Was that why Harry had left England years ago and settled in France—to please his bride?

'No, she was English.'

'What happened?' Allegra asked, not at all sure she wanted to hear the answer.

Hortense grimaced. 'It was very sad. She died in childbirth.'

'Oh, no.' Allegra clapped a hand to her mouth. She'd thought maybe they'd got divorced—though, given that Harry looked in his twenties in the photograph, the wedding must have taken place in the 1950s, which meant that any divorce would've been seriously messy, not to mention difficult to arrange. But this…this was even more unexpected. And shocking. Poor Harry. 'Did she die here?' Allegra asked. 'And, if so, shouldn't Harry be buried next to her, instead of in a grave on his own?'

'She was buried in London. He came here after it happened.' Hortense lifted a shoulder. 'They'd been happy here.'

Allegra bit her lip. 'I wish I'd known. I mean, I lived in London—I could've put flowers on her grave for him and made sure it was kept clean.'

'He had an arrangement with a florist near the cemetery.' Hortense spread her hands. 'You will need to cancel that.'

Allegra shook her head. 'Absolutely not. I'll keep it going—it's what Harry would've wanted. And I'll make sure I put flowers on his grave, on the same day as flowers go on hers.'

Hortense looked approving. 'He would like that.'

'I really had no idea. I don't even know her name,' Allegra said.

Hortense blew out a breath. 'It was the same as yours, *ma chère.*'

Allegra stared at her, barely able to believe it. 'I was named after her?'

'You'll have to ask your parents.'

Which was easier said than done. Charles and Emma Beauchamp were touring somewhere in Russia, as far as Allegra knew. She could send them an email, but that didn't guarantee a quick answer, especially for something that didn't concern their work. A phone call was completely out of the question; when her parents weren't performing or sleeping, they were practising, and Allegra had learned at an early age never to interrupt their work. She still remembered the day she'd wandered into their practice room and touched one of her mother's violins. The mark of her mother's fingers had been imprinted on her skin for most of that day.

Here was the only place she'd ever really felt accepted as one of the family. And having her around must've been a constant reminder of what Harry had lost. His wife, his child.

'You can't change the past,' Hortense said gently, as if her thoughts were written all over her face.

'No.' Allegra blew out a breath. 'I just wish I'd known.'

She spent the rest of the afternoon sorting methodically through the office, but even after she'd eaten Hortense's excellent ratatouille and an omelette, that evening, she couldn't settle.

This was when she really could've done with a dog to hug. Someone who wouldn't judge her, who'd just be company and accept her for who she was. She knew she could ring Gina and talk to her about it—but then, she also knew what her best friend's response would be. 'Get the next plane home and I'll meet you at the airport.'

It would be, oh, so easy.

And it would be running away. Which wasn't what she wanted. She needed to prove to herself that she could make a go of this.

Why hadn't her parents ever said anything about Harry's wife? Well, that was an obvious one. If it wasn't connected to music, it didn't even register with them. But why hadn't *Harry* ever confided in her?

That hurt.

A lot.

Completely out of sorts, Allegra decided to go for a walk. Exercise was meant to be good for lifting your mood, wasn't it? Given that there was no chocolate in the house and Nicole's shop would be shut, endorphins were about the best she could do. And she might catch some of the sunset, if she was lucky; it might take her mind off things and stop her brooding.

Almost unconsciously, she found herself heading for the small lake that straddled the boundary between her land and Xavier's. It had been her favourite thinking-place in her teens. Though it had also been the place where she and Xavier had made love for the very first time, in the dusk of a summer evening. She remembered every second of it. The way he'd made her feel. Her shyness as he'd begun to undress her, the worry that she wouldn't quite live up to the glamorous girls he'd dated before, and then all the fears dissolving as she'd seen the wonder in his eyes, the tenderness as he'd touched her.

How she'd loved him.

Ten years ago. So much had changed in those ten years.

She sat down by the shore of the lake, wrapping her arms round her legs and resting her chin on her knees, and watched the dragonflies hovering above the water on gauzy wings. The sight was enough to lift her mood and stop the blues settling in too deeply.

Then she became aware of a movement beside her and looked up.

Xavier.

He was the last person she wanted to see right now; but, given that the lake was on the border of their land and she was actually sitting on his side, she couldn't exactly tell him to go away. She was the one who was trespassing.

'Watching *les libellules*?' he asked, gesturing to the darting dragonflies.

She nodded.

'Are you all right?'

'Fine,' she fibbed. Then she sighed. 'Not really.'

He sat down next to her, drawing his knees up and linking his hands in front of his ankles, the way she had. 'What's the matter?'

She opened her mouth, about to tell him that it didn't matter, but the words spilled out regardless. 'I've been sorting through Harry's things. I found this photograph of Harry on his wedding day. His wife shared my name.'

Xavier looked surprised. 'And you didn't know?'

'Not a thing.' She bit her lip. 'Poor Harry. He must've been lonely. If only I'd *known*.'

'Would it have made a difference?'

'Yes,' she said fiercely. 'It would. Because I would've come back earlier. I understand now why he didn't mind me coming here for the summers—I suppose I was as near as he'd get to a grandchild. And maybe there's some family likeness. Obviously not of Allegra herself but of…' She choked. 'I can't believe how bloody selfish my parents were. My father must have known about it. He must've known that Harry had lost his wife and baby in one fell swoop, and yet…' She shook her head, anger curling her lip. 'He just dumped me with Harry for the whole of the summer without giving a damn about how either of us felt about it.'

'Not necessarily,' Xavier said softly. 'Harry must've been in his mid-twenties when it happened. Was your father even born then?'

Allegra thought about it. 'He was a toddler, I suppose—but even so, he must have known the family history. Surely my grandparents told him. And why didn't any of them ever tell me?' She stared at him. 'How come you know about it?'

Xavier shrugged. 'Papa was fifteen when Harry first came here. He once told me that when Harry arrived, he was the Englishman with the sad eyes. Papa overheard his parents talking one day about how Harry had spent his honeymoon here, and his wife and baby died in London the following year. He came back here because he had only happy memories of the place.'

'To be a widower so young, to lose the love of your life and your child in such a way—that's terrible.' Unshed tears stung her eyes. 'And I had no idea.'

'He loved you,' Xavier said drily, 'so he didn't want you to be upset. That's probably why he made the effort to keep it from you.'

She glared at him. 'If I'd known, things would've been different. They *would*, Xav. I would never have been so stubborn. I wouldn't have fallen out with him. I would've come back.' She dragged in a breath. 'I know everyone around here thinks I'm a gold-digger who only came back for my inheritance, but this was never about the money. I don't need the money or the farmhouse. This was about...'

Coming home.

She couldn't bear to say the words.

'I know.' He shifted closer to her and slid his arm round her, drawing her against his side. This time, there was nothing sexual about the contact. It felt as though his strength were wrapped round her, giving her courage. Yet she couldn't speak, couldn't thank him—her throat felt as if it were filled with sand. And she wasn't going to bawl her eyes out in front of him. She wasn't going to let him see just how weak and needy she was.

The misery in Allegra's face told Xavier that she was genuinely angry and upset with herself that she hadn't done more for her great-uncle.

'It's not your fault,' he said softly. 'Your family's as dysfunctional as mine.'

'Yours?' She gave him a scornful look. 'Your parents were always there for you when you were growing up—and Guy adores you. He always has. How's that dysfunctional?'

'*Laisse tomber.* Forget about it,' he said. She didn't need to know about the mess of his parents' marriage, the lies and the deceit. But he didn't pull away from her. It was obvious that Allegra was upset, trying to put a brave face on it, and really needed someone to comfort her. And, right at that moment, he was the only one who could do that. There wasn't anyone else. Harry was dead, her parents were away somewhere on tour—and, even if they'd been here, they would've put their music first— and her friends were on the other side of La Manche, in England.

He couldn't just leave her to stew.

Though sitting there with his arm round her made the last ten years melt away. He remembered another evening when she'd been all wide-eyed and trying to keep the tears back as she'd stared at the lake. The end of June. When she'd been anxious about the A level exams she'd just sat, worrying if her grades would be good enough for university. When she'd worried that maybe university would be a mistake, that she'd face the same pressure there that she'd faced at school to follow in her parents' footsteps. That evening, he'd given her a cuddle, to comfort her—and the moment he'd touched her he'd stopped seeing her as the girl next door. He'd seen her as a woman. *Ma petite rose Anglaise,* he'd called her.

He turned his head slightly to look at her, and it was like a replay of that moment. She was looking straight back at him, her whole expression unsure. He could feel the tension in her body.

'We've been here before,' he said softly. Ten years ago, he'd leaned forward and kissed her. And the way she'd responded had blown his self-control to smithereens. Comfort had turned to passion, and they'd both been carried away.

'Don't blame yourself. I was there too,' she said, accurately reading the guilt on his face. 'I wanted it as much as you.'

'It was your first time.'

She nodded. 'And you made it good for me.'

He smiled wryly. 'You don't have to flatter me, Allie.'

'I'm not.' She returned the smile. 'I must have driven you crazy when I was a kid—an annoying little brat who followed you about and cramped your style with all your girlfriends and made a nuisance of herself.'

'That night,' he said, 'I didn't see you as an annoying little brat. I saw you as a woman.' And he'd fallen deeply in love with her over that summer. His arm was still round her now, but for the life of him he couldn't move away. 'You still have those amazing eyes. Deep and dark as the lake at Issarles.' Later that summer, he'd taken her to see the lake in the old volcanic crater, with water the deepest shade of blue he'd ever seen, and they'd made love among the wild flowers. Even now the memory stayed with him. Even now, the scent of wild flowers brought it all back. The softness of her skin against his. Her warmth. And how he'd felt as if he were a different person when he was with her—as if he could conquer the world.

'Your eyes are amazing, too. You always used to make me think of a pirate king.' She gave him a small smile. 'You still do. Especially with that haircut.' She reached up and placed her hand against his cheek, her fingertips moving lightly against the burgeoning stubble on his cheeks.

'Careful, Allie,' he warned.

When she didn't move her hand away, he turned his face and pressed his lips to her palm. Unable to help himself, he curled his free hand around hers. How soft her skin was, unlike his own work-roughened palms. He kissed the pad of each fingertip in turn, then drew a tiny path of kisses down over the heel of her hand to her wrist. He could feel her pulse beating hard against his mouth, and his senses were filled with the light floral scent she wore.

Oh, hell. This had happened yesterday and it had all gone wrong. Badly so.

He had to stop this right now.

But, for the life of him, he couldn't. It seemed the most natural thing in the world to lean over Allegra, drawing her gently down onto the soft grass. Just as he had all those years ago. Now, as then, her eyes were wide and trusting. Her pupils were huge, telling him that this was affecting her exactly the same way that it affected him. That she wanted him just as much as he wanted her.

His hands were on either side of her body, and he was careful not to squash her with his weight—but right now he really, really needed to kiss her. Properly. Even though his head was saying that they shouldn't be doing this, that he'd told her he wouldn't kiss her again, and here he was doing exactly that. Breaking his word. How dishonourable could he get?

But then her hands slid under the hem of his untucked shirt and splayed against his back, feeling the play of his muscles. Skin to skin. And Xavier lost it completely.

He bent his head and touched his mouth to Allegra's. Her lips parted, opening under his, and he deepened the kiss, sliding his tongue against hers. Her mouth was warm and sweet, and her hands were drawing him closer, her fingertips pressing against his back. She tasted of summer and it made his head swim.

How long had it been since he'd last wanted someone this much?

He couldn't remember and didn't care. All he could think of was Allegra and the fact that she was kissing him back.

When he finally broke the kiss, he traced the outline of her jaw with his mouth. She tipped her head back, offering him her throat, and he responded with hot, open-mouthed kisses all the way down her throat, swirling his tongue against her skin.

She gave a tiny whimper of need—the smallest, smallest sound, but it was enough to shock him to his senses.

Feeling guilty, frustrated and out of sorts, he pulled himself away from her and shifted to a sitting position.

'Sorry. That shouldn't have happened. It was…'

Mad. Crazy. Irresistible, and he wanted to do it all over again, except this time take it to its proper conclusion. With her naked and in his bed.

'We were supposed to have a truce.'

'Uh-huh.'

'It wasn't meant to involve kissing.' And he didn't dare look at her, because he knew he'd just yank her into his arms and kiss her again. 'You and me, it's complicated,' he said ruefully.

'There's a lot of unfinished business,' she said. 'We need to talk. Properly.'

'But not tonight. You're upset and I'm tired. If we're going to do this, really sort it out between us so we can move on and have a decent professional relationship, we need to be on an even keel before we tackle it.'

'You're right.' She sighed. 'Why can't things be simple?'

They were, in one sense. He wanted her, and the way she'd responded to him told him that she wanted him.

But as soon as he started thinking, things started to get complicated. A mixture of resentment and anger and guilt and yearning and… The emotions made his head spin.

'Come on. I'll walk you home,' he said.

'There's no need. I'll be perfectly safe.'

He knew that. He could see the farmhouse from here. But he'd still feel better if he saw her home. 'Humour me?'

She clearly saw it as the request it was, rather than an order, and nodded.

Though he didn't help her to her feet. And he made absolutely sure there was distance between them, enough so that his hand couldn't accidentally brush against hers and then end up with his fingers twined with hers. Because if he touched her now, just once, his control would snap completely.

'Would you like to come in for a coffee?' she asked politely as they reached her front door.

'Tonight, I think that would just make things more complicated.' Because it wouldn't stop at coffee. He could see it in her eyes. She needed comfort—comfort he could give her physically, but then all the past would get in the way and make it even harder for them to move on. 'We'll talk on Monday. And maybe things will be easier.'

'Monday,' she repeated softly.

'*À bientôt,*' he said—and left, before he gave in to the temptation to hold her close and kiss her until the shadows in her eyes vanished.

CHAPTER SEVEN

ALLEGRA slept badly that night; her single bed felt way too big and, even though the night was hot, she felt as if cold radiated all the way through her.

You and me, it's complicated.

He could say that again.

But at least he'd agreed to talk things through with her.

On Sunday, Gina emailed her three different logos and half a dozen different label designs. Smiling, she emailed back, *Thanks, you're a genius and these are brilliant.* Obviously she'd need to discuss it with her co-vigneron and take his views into account, but the one she liked most was the simplest. Three stylised vine leaves, the stems making a knot, with 'Les Trois Closes' in a simple script next to it. With any luck, Xavier would think the same.

And with any luck, things would start to get simpler between them.

On Monday morning, Allegra cycled to the *boulangerie* and the farm shop to pick up her lunch—including a punnet of irresistibly juicy cherries that Nicole told her came from one of the farms outside the village, and a box of *galettes* for the office, which she hoped would give her a friendly start with Xavier's allegedly formidable secretary. She settled herself at Xavier's desk with her laptop and had just started roughing out a list of possible PR activity when she became aware of a shadow by the front door.

She looked up to see a middle-aged woman with steel-grey hair walk in. Thérèse? But she didn't look formidable or bossy, as Allegra had expected; rather than being severely elegant, she was slightly plump with unruly hair and a kind, maternal smile.

'*Bonjour*,' Allegra said with a smile. 'I take it you're Thérèse?'

'Yes, and you must be Allegra. *Bonjour*.'

'I was just about to make some coffee. Can I get you some?' Allegra asked.

'*Merci*, that would be nice.'

When she'd made the coffee, she took the *galettes* through to Thérèse's office as well; half an hour later, they were firm friends. Allegra had made it clear that she didn't expect Thérèse to look after her as well as Xavier, and had cooed over the pictures Thérèse carried around of her five-year-old granddaughter, Amélie, and her brand-new grandson, Jean-Claude. In return, Thérèse had reassured Allegra that having someone to challenge the way he did things would be good for Xavier.

Xavier arrived in the office at his usual time, just before midday. He greeted Allegra with an English, 'Good morning,' but Thérèse was treated to three loud kisses on her cheek and exclamations in rapid French that Allegra couldn't quite follow but, from the smile on his face, it was clear that he was pleased to see his secretary again.

Which was a good thing—but the conversation they needed to have really had to be in private. Clearly it wasn't going to happen in the office. She saved the file on her laptop and shifted to the chair in the corner, letting Xavier have his desk back. He clearly had a lot of admin to do, because he barely acknowledged her for the next hour. He didn't even stop to eat his lunch, instead taking mouthfuls of a sandwich between phone calls.

So much for having a chance to talk to him about the logo and labels and being able to make some decisions. And so much for setting things straight between them.

The next time he put down the receiver, she seized her chance. 'Xavier, there are some things I need to discuss with you about the vineyard. I can see you're busy right now, so would you be free for dinner tonight?'

'Tonight.' His expression turned wary. 'Yes. We need to discuss things.'

'Work things, too,' she said softly.

'OK. Do you want to eat here?'

'I think somewhere neutral might be easier,' she said. 'Somewhere quiet where we can have a decent-sized table in a corner so we can spread papers over it.'

'And discuss things.' He nodded. 'I'll book a table. Though there are some things I need to do in the vines late this afternoon. I'll pick you up at half past six.'

'No need. I'll meet you at the restaurant. Just give me the address.'

'And you'll know how to get there?'

'I can look it up on the Internet.'

He rolled his eyes. 'Don't be difficult. Your bicycle will fit in the back of my car so, better still, we'll go from here and I'll drop you home afterwards.' He glanced at his watch. 'I need to be elsewhere. I'll be back at five, which will give me enough time to have a shower and change.'

She gestured to her jeans. 'And I don't need to change?'

He spread his hands. 'You're not going to be in the fields getting messy. So, no. The place I have in mind doesn't have a strict dress code. See you later.' He said goodbye to Thérèse, then headed out of the door.

Thérèse left at four to go and pick up her granddaughter from school. Xavier turned up at quarter past five. 'Sorry I'm late. And I'm filthy from the fields. I'll shower and change, and then we'll go.'

'Come and get me when you're done,' she said, striving for offhand.

He raised an eyebrow. 'You've been in the office since before Thérèse arrived and you didn't have a lunch break.'

'Neither did you,' she pointed out.

'We're going to work through dinner, so would it not be better to pace yourself?'

When it was put like that, she could see the sense of it.

She waited while he locked the office, then walked over to the chateau with him. 'Guy will be in his lab; there's no chance he'll come out and be sociable,' Xavier said. 'But if you want a drink, there's coffee, juice and chilled water in the kitchen, through there.' He gestured to the door at the end of the hallway. 'The library's nice at this time of year. There's a good view over Guy's roses if you want to go and sit in there and relax while you're waiting for me.'

'Thanks. I will.'

'I'll be as quick as I can.'

Allegra didn't know the inside of the chateau particularly well; as children, they'd usually been shooed outside by the housekeeper, and when she'd been older Xavier had always picked her up from Harry's. But she duly went into the kitchen. It was a huge room with a terracotta tiled floor, a range cooker nesting in an enormous inglenook and a large scrubbed wooden table in the middle of the room. The cabinets lining the walls were painted cream, and it looked very much as if they were handmade. Next to the inglenook there were open shelves with a rack above it from which hung copper pans; cast-iron cookware sat on the shelves. Another rack contained plates; next door to that was a glass-fronted cabinet containing glassware, and next to the enormous fridge was a tall wrought-iron wine rack filled with bottles.

The worktops were as clear as Xavier kept his desk. She could try to find a coffee maker, but it felt like snooping; instead, she took a tumbler from one of the glass-fronted cupboards and filled it with water from the tap. And she tried not to think of Xavier upstairs, naked and in the shower.

She wandered back into the hall. The first door led to a formal dining room; next was a sitting room; and another opposite that. Again, she was struck by how tidy everything was; every single piece of woodwork was beautifully polished. Clearly Xavier had a housekeeper, because just keeping up with the housework in the chateau would take a full week's work—no way would he have time to do this himself as well as putting in the hours at the vineyard.

At last she found the library. The shelves were filled with an eclectic mixture of volumes in several different languages; there were comfortable sofas either side of an open fire; and the French doors did indeed overlook Guy's rose garden, as Xavier had told her.

On the mantelpiece there were photographs in silver frames: Xavier and Guy at their graduation ceremonies, and a picture of them both with Jean-Paul. But none, Allegra noticed, of Chantal. Which seemed very strange; she knew that family was important to Xavier. Something had obviously happened—though it was none of her business, and she had a feeling that Xavier would be sensitive about it. Given that they already had a tough discussion ahead of them, it would be better not to complicate matters by asking.

But then the baby grand piano in the centre of the room caught her attention. Her upright piano was still in London, and Harry had got rid of his a couple of years ago, according to Hortense.

The lure was irresistible. And hadn't Xavier told her to relax?

She set her glass down on one of the low tables and sat down at the piano. Experimentally, she played a couple of scales. The instrument sounded slightly sharp and needed tuning, but it didn't bother her; this was better than not being able to play anything at all. She began with Lizst's 'Liebestraum', stumbling a little at first and then relaxing into the music. How she'd missed this. Closing her eyes, she let the music flow into her head and played entirely from memory. Chopin's 'Raindrop' prelude, then Satie's 'Gymnopédie number one', finally segueing into Debussy's 'Clair de lune'.

Xavier walked down the stairs, his blood turning to ice as he heard the music coming from the library. Debussy. It took him straight back to his childhood. How he'd loved listening to his mother playing the piano—especially this piece, if he was sitting by the window in the library and watching the rain trickling down the window.

Now the notes sounded like the soundtrack to betrayal, and it rattled him hugely.

He strode into the library, half expecting to see Chantal sitting there instead of Allegra. 'What are you doing?'

To his relief, Allegra stopped playing. 'You told me to relax.'

'Not this way.' The words burst out before he could stop them.

She frowned. 'What's wrong, Xavier?'

Everything. 'The piano's out of tune.'

'A bit, yes, but it's not that bad.'

But maybe some of his tension showed on his face, because then she stopped arguing, slid off the seat and stepped away from the piano.

'I should've got rid of it years ago. Guy and I don't play.'

'Xav, this room needs a piano. And this one's gorgeous. It's so right, here.'

It had been. Once. When the world had been a different place.

'I'm sorry, Xav,' she said quietly. 'I didn't mean to be intrusive. Harry got rid of his piano a while back, and—well, I miss playing.'

He hadn't known that Allegra played the piano, let alone so skilfully. She'd been so adamant that she didn't want to follow in her parents' footsteps, he'd been pretty sure that she didn't play an instrument at all.

And now she looked worried, her lower lip caught between even white teeth.

It was hardly surprising, given his hissy fit. He blew out a breath. 'Sorry. I overreacted.'

'And I intruded. So we're both at fault.' She gave him a rueful smile. 'We're not going to talk about things tonight, are we? On Saturday, I was upset and you were tired. Today, you're upset and I'm tired. You're right, it's not a good combination—not if we want to sort it out without having a huge fight.'

'Maybe we should forget dinner and I should just take you home.'

'We both still have to eat,' she pointed out. 'I don't know about you, but I'm not in the mood for cooking. And there really are some business things I wanted to discuss with you. If today's anything to go by, you're in the fields for most of the day and constantly on the phone when you're in the office. The only way we're going to discuss things is if it's in the evening.'

'A vineyard isn't like an office. You can't work nine to five.'

'I didn't say it was a problem.' She reached out towards him, as if she were going to take his hand—and then stopped, as if she'd thought better of it. 'Do you think Guy would like to join us for dinner?'

'You can try getting him out of his lab, but I don't fancy your chances.'

They paused by the door to Guy's lab; Allegra rapped on it, and Guy appeared a minute or so later, looking dishevelled and resembling a mad scientist. Which, Xavier thought with a rush of affection, was exactly what his little brother was.

'Yes?' Guy asked, frowning.

'I was wondering if you'd like to come to dinner with us,' Allegra said.

'Thanks for the offer, *chérie*, but no. I'm sorting out something here.' Guy made shooing motions with his hands. 'Go and enjoy yourselves, children.'

'It's work,' Allegra said swiftly, as if to make absolutely sure that Guy didn't get the wrong idea.

'So you'll be talking shop all night? Absolutely not, then. I get enough of that from Xav as it is—and he drives me crazy, sampling wines and comparing them to the ones he produces.' Guy smiled at her to take the sting from his words. 'Some other time, perhaps, when you're not talking shop and I'm not up to my eyeballs. *Au revoir, petite.*' He blew her a kiss and closed the door again.

Allegra followed Xavier out to his car. 'Don't you dare say, "I told you so",' she warned.

'As if I would.' He opened the passenger door for her, made sure that she was settled, then hefted her bicycle into the back of his car. When he switched on the ignition, 'Waterloo Sunset' blared through the car; he grimaced and switched it off. 'Sorry. Bad habit,' he said. Given that she'd been raised on classical music—and she'd been playing it herself on the piano, rather than an arrangement of a pop song—she'd probably hate what he was playing. Particularly as it was so loud.

'The Kinks, right?' she asked, surprising him. 'Good choice. So it's just the piano you hate.'

The pieces that made him remember things he'd rather forget. To stop her asking questions, he shifted the focus back onto her. 'I didn't realise you played so well. Didn't you ever consider doing a duet with your mother?'

She grimaced. 'You must be joking! I play for fun, and she plays for perfection.'

He remembered. 'What about your father?'

She scoffed. 'He wouldn't be interested unless I practised twenty-four-seven and was note-perfect on all four Rachmaninov piano concerti.'

'Or the Rhapsody, so you could do a double-bill with your mother.'

She rolled her eyes. 'Oh, please. I can see her standing next to me and smacking me over the head with her violin bow if I dared to play a wrong note. And then my father would insist that I worked on something like Alkan's Grand Etude because it's so fast and so difficult to play smoothly…' She grimaced. 'No, I'd never be good enough for him. And working on something until I met with his approval would take all the pleasure out of it for me.'

'Do they know you play the piano?'

'Absolutely not. I swore my friends to secrecy at school, and Harry would never have dropped me in it—given that he was the one who actually taught me.' She wrinkled her nose. 'I just enjoy playing for me. Sad stuff when I feel blue, happy stuff when the world's full of sunshine. And, actually, I most like playing the Beatles' music. "Eleanor Rigby", "Yesterday"—pieces with a good melody.'

He'd had no idea that their musical tastes meshed so well. They'd never really listened to music, all those summers ago. As children, they'd been too busy playing elaborate games, and when he was old enough to drive, his beloved ancient sports car hadn't actually had a sound system that worked. Jean-Paul had insisted that both Xavier and Guy learned the value of money by paying their own car repair bills, and there was always something on the Alfa that needed fixing rather more urgently than the radio.

'Do you mind if we change the subject?' she asked. 'We're supposed to be discussing the vineyard, not me.'

'Sure. What did you want to run past me?'

'Logos and labels. My best friend works at the agency where I worked—she's a really talented designer. I gave her a brief last week and she's come up with some samples.'

'You gave her a brief. Without talking to me first.' He gave her a speaking look. 'So I get no say in the branding of my own vineyard.'

'You were busy, and I wanted to…' Her voice faltered.

'You wanted to prove yourself,' he finished for her. 'OK. You're the one with the qualifications in marketing.'

'Xav, I wasn't trying to cut you out. I was trying to show you that I can bring something to the vineyard—something different.'

She was trying. And he'd already given her a hard time today, over something that wasn't her fault. 'All right. When we get there, you can show me what she's come up with.'

The bistro he'd chosen was a quiet one. The food was good, the service was unobtrusive, and the chef was an old friend. Once they were settled in a quiet corner, with a glass of wine for her and a bottle of still water for him, and they'd ordered their food, he looked straight at her. 'Right. Talk me through these labels and logos.'

She'd brought a briefcase with her; she took a folder from it and spread four pages across the table. 'These were the ones Gina came up with. I have my favourite, but I'm not going to say which. But I'd like your opinion.'

He picked out the simplest one, the stylised vine leaves. 'I like this one. Three leaves—it fits in with our name, and the colours are for red, rosé and white wine.

Though, strictly speaking, the red I produce is nothing to do with Les Trois Closes.' He studied the piece of paper. 'It's clean. Definitely a case of less is more.'

She looked pleased. 'That's the one I like—for exactly the reasons you just said. Good. We're *d'accord*, then. This is going to be our new logo.'

'D'accord,' he said solemnly, disguising his amusement at the way she'd started sprinkling her conversation with French phrases. She really was trying to fit in.

She put the papers away and replaced them with the sample labels.

Xavier shook his head. 'We have plain type on the back of the label now. It does the job. Why replace it with this spiky handwriting?'

'Because the land here is spiky and uncompromising—we're on the edge of the gorges of Ardèche. And the labels will be hand drawn because our wine is made the traditional way, mainly by hand. So then our label reflects the *terroir* and the process—you're an artisan.'

He raised an eyebrow. 'You're calling me a peasant, now?'

'When you live in an ancient chateau? Hardly—I'm calling you a skilled craftsman.'

He smiled, amused. 'You're making a mental note to check your dictionary when you get home, aren't you?'

'I guess I deserve to be teased.'

'No. You're doing OK,' he said.

The delight in her face was quickly dampened down, as if she didn't want him to know that she was pleased by his grudging compliment.

'All right. We'll use the logo. I'm not sure about the labels, though. What's the point of trying to fix something that already works?'

'You have them printed every year, so it doesn't matter whether you use your old typography or the new,' she said. 'If you're trying to broaden your markets, you need to change the labels to reflect customer expectations outside France—which is what these labels do. Speaking as a consumer, I've tried wines simply because I liked the look of the label. If I liked the taste of the wine, it made me try others from the same producer.'

She wasn't going to give up easily. And what she was saying did make sense. Time to compromise, Xavier decided. 'All right. We'll give it a go.'

'Thank you. I also want to set us up on the social networks.'

'They aren't as big in France as they are in England and America,' he warned.

'Fair enough, but if you're trying to widen your markets in England and the States, you need to use the right communications to reach them,' she countered. 'That means viral marketing and word of mouth. Starting with the blog—and, by the way, our hits are rising nicely there—and maybe the odd podcast.'

'Podcast?' Xavier blew out a breath. 'I think I'm beginning to regret agreeing to this.'

He was saved from an argument by the arrival of their food.

'You're right. The food is fabulous,' she said after the first mouthful.

During the meal, she told him of her ideas for promoting their wine, including talking to the local tourist board about a wine-tasting trail, setting up a wine walk round the edges of the vineyard—'So people get to enjoy the wildlife in the vineyard and then taste what we produce at the end,' she explained—and a series of articles in different magazines, each focusing on a different aspect of the vineyard.

But what really impressed him was that she'd included budgets, and ways of measuring the success of the campaigns so they could decide what to do more of in future and what to drop.

By the end of the evening, Xavier was surprised by how much he'd enjoyed talking business with Allegra and seeing her hit her stride. Her enthusiasm was infectious. And she'd grown into a woman he actually liked. A lot.

It would be oh so easy to let himself fall back into a relationship with her. The way she'd kissed him earlier told him that she, too, still felt that zinging physical attraction.

But the past could still get in the way. Mess things up again. He didn't want to risk that.

'It was my idea to go out for dinner, so it's my bill,' Allegra said as the waiter came over.

'You're assuming that I'm a modern Frenchman. Wrong. My bill,' he corrected.

'You can't have it both ways, Xav. You can't see me as the money-grabber who's only come back to France to strip her share of the assets from the vineyard, and then refuse to let me pay for dinner.'

In answer, he simply raised an eyebrow.

'Equal partners, remember,' she said. 'And we have a truce. No fighting.'

He gave her a wry smile. 'All right. We'll split it.'

When they'd paid, Xavier drove them back to their own village. He parked outside Harry's farmhouse—

after years of habit, he still couldn't quite think of it in any other way—and opened the passenger door for her, before taking her bicycle from the back of the car.

'You've given me a lot to think about,' he said.

'In a good or a bad sense?'

'Mostly good,' he said. 'Except the podcast. I'm really not convinced about that.'

'If you want people to start talking about you, you need to do something different,' she said. 'And I think doing a sounds quiz—asking people to guess what they hear—would get us a lot of traffic. People might just come for the fun of the quiz, but if we make the pages sticky enough then they'll see the other, more serious side of the vineyard.'

'Sticky?'

'Give them some interesting things to hold their attention. Interactive and dynamic. The longer they stay on our website and the more they enjoy the experience, the better their opinion of us will be. And it might lead to more orders.' She smiled. 'Let me mock up a few things—and then I'll try it out on you.'

'It's going to be easier to give in than to argue, isn't it?' Xavier asked wryly. 'All right. Our rosé's meant to be about summer and chilling out and having fun. Mock it up and I'll have a look at it.'

'You won't regret it, Xav.' She paused. 'You seem more relaxed, now.'

He had been, but the tension snapped back into him. 'And?'

She took a deep breath. 'The longer we put off this conversation, the harder it's going to be.'

'It's not exactly going to be easy now,' he warned.

'It's probably as good as it's going to get.' She took the door key from her handbag. 'I'll put my bike away. Do you want to make the coffee?'

Hot, strong coffee was probably what both of them needed right now. He took the key. 'Sure. Ready when you are.'

CHAPTER EIGHT

WHEN Allegra came back from the barn, Xavier had made coffee and was sitting at the kitchen table, his hands wrapped round his mug. His face was etched with strain, and her heart ached for him. Even though he'd hurt her so badly in the past, she hated seeing him look so upset now. Part of her wanted to wrap her arms round him and hold him close, tell him everything would be fine—just as he'd held her when she'd been upset by the lake.

But she knew that sex would just get in the way. They'd go to bed, comfort each other—and they wouldn't talk, so the problem would still be there. He was right to have set her mug on the opposite side of the table, rather than next to his. They needed space between them to do this properly.

'Have you ever had an infected scratch from the vines?' she asked.

'Yes, a couple of times.' He looked surprised. 'Why?'

'This is the same sort of thing. Dealing with it's going to hurt, but the bad stuff has to come out before you can heal.'

He took a swig of coffee. 'I'm sorry I had that hissy fit on you earlier. I suppose it caught me on the raw, and I wasn't expecting it.'

'What's so bad about playing the piano?'

He took a deep breath. 'Chantal used to play it. It's kind of... I don't know. Bringing back happy memories, but at the same time they feel tainted.'

'I notice you don't call her "Maman" any more. I take it you fell out with her?'

'Big time.' He sighed. 'You might as well know. She had an affair and left Papa.'

'No way.' It was the last thing she'd expected him to say. She couldn't take it in. Chantal had always been reserved and a bit haughty, but Jean-Paul had been such a sweetheart, so easy to get on with. She could remember him sitting on the terrace outside with Harry, laughing uproariously over some joke or other, and envying Xav and Guy for having a father who was so approachable and interested in his children, unlike her own. 'I'm sorry. It must've been a shock.'

'It was. I always thought with marriage you took the rough with the smooth, and most of the time it *was* smooth. She and Papa were happy—they never had huge fights or bickered, and Papa idolised her. He would've done anything for her.'

'Your father was lovely,' she said, meaning it. 'Why on earth would she...?' She stopped herself, wincing. 'Sorry. That was intrusive. You don't have to answer.'

'Why did she have the affair?' Xavier dragged in a breath. 'She said he wasn't paying her enough attention.'

No wonder he'd made that comment during their fight, about women wanting all your attention. Slowly, she was beginning to understand him a little more.

'I'm still not sure which shocked me most—the fact that she left, or the timing.'

'Timing?'

'We'd had two bad harvests—I didn't know it at the time, because Papa kept it from me, too, but he was putting in crazy hours, trying to keep the vineyard afloat, and the bank threatened to pull our credit.'

'That's awful, Xav.' And no wonder he'd been wary about the website, not wanting to talk about the heritage. He'd said to her that the vineyard hadn't always been successful. She'd had no idea that he'd meant in the recent past, rather than the distant past.

Then a seriously nasty thought struck her. *The timing*, he'd said. 'When did this happen?'

'It doesn't matter.'

'I think it might.'

He was silent for so long that she didn't think he was going to answer. But then he looked straight at her. 'Ten years ago.'

The sick feeling in her stomach intensified. 'After I'd gone to London?'

'The day after Guy's eighteenth birthday,' he confirmed. 'I suppose in some respects we should be grateful that she didn't ruin that for him, too, but the fact that she could plan a party, knowing that she was going to leave the next day...' He shook his head. 'I couldn't stomach the deceit, Allie.'

Guy's birthday was in September, just before harvest. Allegra had been invited to the party but hadn't been able to make it, because she'd been finding student digs—plus her parents had been in London and it had been a rare chance to see them, which Harry had encouraged her to take.

So it had all happened just as Xavier had been due to start his job in Paris.

She needed to know the truth. 'When I called you and asked you to come to London, spend some time with me...' When she'd believed he was in Paris. 'You weren't actually in Paris, were you?'

'No,' he admitted. 'I couldn't leave Papa in such a mess. Losing Chantal devastated him, Allie. She broke his heart. I made him talk to me, and then he told me about the finances—the reason why he hadn't been paying her enough attention. He'd been working crazy hours, trying to keep the business going. The way I saw it, he needed my support—Guy was in his Baccalaureate year, and there was no way either of us would let him throw it all in.'

'So you gave up your job in Paris instead.'

He gave a half-shrug. 'I always knew I'd be coming back here to take over the vineyard when Papa wanted to retire. It just meant that I'd do it a bit earlier, that was all.'

She bit her lip. 'Did Harry know?'

'Yes. He went into partnership with Papa a few months later. He didn't tell you?'

She shook her head. 'I told him that you and I had split up. He told me I was pushing you too hard, we were too young to settle down anyway and I should give you some space.'

'And that's when you fell out with him?'

She nodded.

'Over me.'

'Xav, if I'd only known what was going on... But it felt as if everyone was pushing me about. Harry was telling me what to do, and you as good as told me I was just a holiday romance and you were too busy to see me. I thought you'd met someone else.'

'You weren't a holiday romance. And I *was* too busy to come to London. I was working with Papa to stop the vineyard going under. It wasn't just about us, Allie—it was all the people who relied on us for jobs. We couldn't let them down.'

'Why didn't you tell me what was happening here, Xav?' Regret and anger merged—regret that she hadn't had the chance to support him, and anger that he'd shut her out so completely, hadn't trusted her enough to tell her what was happening.

He blew out a breath. 'Because I was ashamed, I suppose. I didn't want you to know that my mother had run off with someone else after nearly twenty-five years of marriage. And I didn't want you knowing that we were in financial difficulties.'

'I would've understood, Xav.' She swallowed hard. 'If you'd told me—OK, I couldn't have done anything practical to help, but I could at least have been there for you. I could've listened. And if you'd told me you needed me, I would've come back. I would've been there to hold your hand.' She dragged in a breath. 'Your life had just been turned upside down and, instead of being there to support you, I dumped you. You must have hated me.'

'I did,' he admitted. 'I thought you'd let me down as much as Chantal had let my father down. All I needed was some time to get my head together, but you went on and on and on, wanting to know when I was coming to see you. I know I probably snapped at you, but I didn't mean it like that.' He paused. 'You really thought I was seeing someone else?'

'No—well, yes.' She raked a hand through her hair. 'I couldn't think of any other reason why you'd suddenly go so cold on me, why you'd push me away and tell me you were too busy to see me. Xav, I was eighteen years old. I still had a lot of growing up to do. And I was tired of being pushed around, never in charge of my own life. I thought you didn't want me. I had some pride left—so I wanted to be the one who called a halt, not the one who was dumped.'

'So you hated me, too.'

'For a while.' She bit her lip. 'I never wanted it to end between us.' Tears pricked her eyes. 'Xav, that summer, I thought all my dreams had come true. I thought we'd…' She dragged in a shaky breath. No. That was a confession too far.

'We'd what?' he asked, his voice husky with emotion.

'It doesn't matter.'

'I think it does,' he said, echoing her earlier words to him. 'Tell me.'

'Once I'd graduated, I thought we'd…' She blew out a breath. 'I thought we'd get married.'

'Me, too. I was going to ask you to marry me that Christmas,' he said. 'In Paris. I was going to sell the car so I could get you a really spectacular ring. And I was going to take you to the top of the Eiffel Tower and ask you to marry me.'

She could see the truth of it in his face. That, back then, he'd loved her just as much as she'd loved him. And he'd been willing to sacrifice his beloved car to get her a flashy ring, because he'd thought that was what she'd wanted? 'You know, a silver ring off a market stall would've been enough for me,' she said. 'I didn't need anything flash. I didn't *want* anything flash. I only wanted you.' He was all she'd ever wanted.

His breath hissed. 'How did we get it so wrong?'

'I misinterpreted the way you were acting. I had a lot of growing up to do. But I wouldn't have hurt you, Xav. Not for the world.'

'And I never meant to push you away, make you feel that I didn't want you.' He sighed. 'I guess I needed to grow up a bit, too.'

'If only we'd talked—really talked—back then. But you can't change the past. There's no point in endless recriminating.' She so, so wanted to reach out to him. Just holding his hand would be enough. But she could still see the wariness in his face; so she held back, keeping her fingers wrapped firmly round her mug. 'Do you see your mother at all?'

'Not much,' he admitted. 'I found it pretty hard to forgive her. Papa loved her so much. Losing her meant he'd lost a part of himself. But he loved her enough to let her go, give her a divorce so she could marry this guy.'

'She married him?'

Xavier shook his head. 'It didn't last. Neither did the next three—I sometimes wonder whether she measured them up to Papa and realised she'd made the biggest mistake of her life.'

'Would your father have had her back?'

'Like a shot. He was still in love with her right until the day he died. But she just stayed away. I wish he'd found someone else, someone who would've made him happy and loved him back the way he deserved. But he only wanted Chantal.' He gave her a wry smile. 'That's the thing about Lefèvre men. They have a habit of falling in love with the wrong woman.'

That stung. And it wasn't true. 'You and I weren't wrong, all those years ago.'

'Maybe. Maybe not. We weren't strong enough to last.'

There was nothing she could say to that. Ten years of being apart said that he was right.

'Papa threw himself into work. I put in the same hours, but it just didn't occur to me that he was so much older than I was—that he needed to slow down. Not until he had his heart attack.'

He blamed himself for his father's illness? 'Xav, it wasn't your fault.'

'That's what he said. So did Guy. But it felt like it,' he admitted. 'I did call Chantal, when Papa was in hospital. I asked her if she'd come and see him.'

'Did she?'

'She said she'd think about it.' He looked away. 'I don't know whether she would've come or not, because he died before she made up her mind.'

'Xav, that's so sad.' And she could understand now why he'd shut off. He'd lost everything except the vineyard and Guy: and that kept him going now.

'I haven't seen much of her since. Guy found it easier to forgive her—I guess because Papa and I didn't tell him about the business problems at the time. We thought he didn't need that kind of pressure when he had exams on the horizon.' Xavier shrugged. 'Guy trained in Grasse, which isn't so far from Cannes, and he saw her again there. It took him a year to admit it to me. I think he thought I might disown him over it.' He gave a rueful smile. 'We had a bit of a fight. But he made me see another point of view. She was a middle-aged woman who panicked when she realised that she was heading for forty, thought my father wasn't paying attention to her because she was old and unattractive—she had no idea that he was trying to save her from worrying about the business—and she made a really stupid mistake.'

'Maybe if your father had shared his worries with her, she would've understood.' Just as Allegra herself would've understood, had Xavier confided his worries in her instead of pushing her away.

'Maybe,' he said. 'We'll never know, and, as you said, we can't change the past.'

'So where do we go from here?' she asked.

'I don't know. Trust is a bit of an issue for me,' he admitted. 'What with my mother lying to Papa and running off, you dumping me and then Guy's wife deciding that he wasn't paying her enough attention while he was building up the perfume house...'

'Guy's divorced?'

'Yes. And Véra took him for every Euro she could.' He gave her a cynical smile. 'You could say, like father, like sons. There's a bit of me that thinks the men in my family just aren't any good at finding "the one".'

'Or maybe they're just too proud,' Allegra said. 'Maybe they need to open up, let their partners close and realise that it isn't weak to share your worries.'

He shrugged. 'Who knows?'

'And you still don't trust me.' She shook her head in exasperation. 'It doesn't help that I only came back here after Harry died.'

'You told me why you didn't make the funeral. I understand that. It wasn't your fault,' he said.

'Actually, it was my fault. I should've been stronger and stood up to my boss. I should've refused to go to

New York and told him that my family was more important, and that people who put their job before their families don't make good employees because they can't empathise with others.' She bit her lip. 'But I wanted that job. So badly.'

'Do you still want it?'

'That's academic—he appointed someone else.'

'Let me rephrase it. If you had a second chance of having that job and keeping it, would you still want it?'

She considered it. 'No. I loved working at the agency, but I wouldn't go back now, even if I was offered the job that should've been mine and a huge payrise.'

'So what do you want?'

Xavier. It had always been Xavier. But was he too damaged to give them another chance? 'I don't know,' she prevaricated. 'Maybe we should take this day by day. Maybe we can become friends.'

'There's a problem with that. I can barely keep my hands off you. My office in the middle of the afternoon, the lake, the other evening… Even now, there's a bit of me that wants to kiss you until we're both dizzy. I want to carry you up to bed, right here, right now.' He blew out a breath. 'And that's not fair to either of us. I'm not looking for a relationship, Allie. I just want to concentrate on building up the vineyard and make wine that people really love.'

'So you're saying that it's going to be business only between us?'

'Business only,' he confirmed. 'It's the best thing for both of us.'

She wasn't so sure. But it was the best he was going to offer her. 'You trust me to work with you, then?'

'Now we've had this conversation…yes. I think we both know where the other's coming from, now. We've got a shot at making this work. As a business.' He stood up, and took his still-full mug over to the sink. He poured the coffee down the drain and rinsed out the mug. 'For what it's worth, I'm sorry I hurt you all those years ago.'

'I'm sorry I hurt you, too.'

'I'll see you in the office. Goodnight, Allie.' And he walked out of the door.

CHAPTER NINE

BUSINESS only, he'd said. And, over the next few days, Allegra seemed to go into overdrive. Every day she had something to show him: a proof for the new wine labels; new word-processing templates for the vineyard's letterhead and compliments slip, bearing the new logo; and more entries in her 'Diary of a Rookie Vigneronne'.

She might not be doing any of the physical stuff, Xavier thought, but she worked just as hard as he did. And she was clearly intent on proving just how much she could bring to the vineyard.

'I've got quite a few magazines interested in features on us,' she informed him on the following Monday. 'There are three definites: one on life as an English expatriate in France; one on the change from a hectic City lifestyle to a rural environment; and one on the biodiversity in our vineyard. We should get quite a bit of interest from those.'

'That's good.' And something he hadn't thought of doing, even if he'd had the time.

'Obviously I need to take photographs to go with the features, so is there anything you'd rather I avoided? I mean, of course I'll ask the team for their permission before I take pictures of them working or what have you, but I'd love to be able to offer a series—something like a year in the life of a vineyard,' she said.

Given that magazines had long lead-times, she was clearly planning much further ahead than their two-month trial. And although Xavier knew that her show of commitment should've made him relax, it only made him feel warier. It was like building a house of cards. The more she put into it, the more it would collapse.

'I'd better take you round to meet everyone properly,' he said.

She positively beamed at him. 'Great. When?'

'Tomorrow morning?'

'Fine. Do you need me here at the crack of dawn?'

If he said yes, he knew she'd do it. But he wasn't going to push her that far. 'Whenever suits you. Just call my mobile when you're ready to leave, and I'll pick you up.'

She shook her head. 'I can't drag you away from work. Tell me where to go, and I'll meet you there.'

'It'll take me ten minutes, tops,' he said. 'But if it makes you feel better, I'll meet you here at the office.'

'OK. I'll call you when I'm here.'

And so he found himself outside the office at half past seven the following morning. Allegra was wearing jeans, sensible shoes, a loose cotton shirt and a broad-brimmed hat trimmed with a chiffon scarf the same shade of cerise as her shirt, the same way she'd dressed years before. Xavier was really glad that he was driving, because it meant that he had to concentrate—and his hands had something to do other than remove her hat and draw her close to him so he could bend his head to kiss her.

Oh, for pity's sake. He was working crazy hours to keep her out of his head. It had to start working soon—surely?

He introduced her to the team working on the field, and the way they responded to her unsettled him further. Even the most taciturn of them talked to her about what they were doing; her questions were sensible and showed her true interest in what they were doing, so they became expansive, showing her how to do things and encouraging her attempts and giving her enough time to make notes. And when she told them about the articles and her blog—in French, he noticed—not one of them refused to have their photograph taken. She'd clearly managed to charm them all.

By lunchtime, she'd made friends with all of them and knew their families and histories—and they treated her as if she'd always been part of the vineyard.

'That was brilliant,' she said as he drove her back to the office. 'They've got great ideas about the kind of wildlife I should be recording and the best time to see them, and what kinds of sounds would be interesting for the podcast.'

'They're a good team.' Xavier had known them for years and trusted them implicitly; but he'd never thought of asking the estate workers for their views on promotion. He'd concentrated on the vines and the produce.

'Xav, I know I'm going to be more of a hindrance than a help at this stage, but I'd like to do my bit here. Even if it's only an hour or so a day, or you just give me, say, half a row to look after. I want to be more than just the woman who sits in the office and talks to people. I want to be a real part of the vineyard.'

Put like that, how could he refuse? It was how he felt about the place, too. 'As long as you pace yourself. It's a lot hotter here in the south of France than it is in England,' he warned.

'I can take direction,' she said softly, 'as long as I know the reasons behind it.'

'In other words, you don't want to be bossed around just for the sake of it.' He remembered what she'd said about being pushed around.

'Exactly.' She smiled at him. 'So would you be happy if I, say, do an hour's work in the fields, then walk around a bit with my camera in the mornings?'

'Happy' wasn't quite the way he'd put it. In the fields, he was at least away from her and didn't have to fight the attraction—unlike in the office, when he was intensely aware of every single movement she made and had to rein himself back all the time. But he couldn't think of a decent reason for her not to be there. She was his business partner, and the best way of finding out exactly how a business worked was to do every job yourself or shadow someone else. Her suggestion made complete and utter sense—except where his emotions were concerned. 'Sure,' he lied.

Over the next few days, Allegra did an hour's work in the fields in the morning, then went round the vineyard making notes, taking photographs and recording sounds before going back to the office and putting in a full afternoon's work there. By the end of the week, he knew he was falling under her spell again, no matter how hard he tried to fight it.

Late on Friday afternoon, everyone else had gone home and Xavier was checking on a row of vines that he'd been concerned about when he became aware that someone was walking down the row towards him.

Without looking up, he knew it was her, because the back of his neck was tingling.

What was she doing here? Why wasn't she in the office, or heading for home? He always sent everyone home early on Friday.

'Hi.' She gave him a shy smile.

The midday heat had died down, so there was absolutely no need for him to feel this dopey. 'Hi.' Damn, and his voice *would* have to croak.

'You sound thirsty.'

He was. For her. Though he kept his mouth resolutely shut; he simply nodded and hoped she'd be fobbed off by it.

'Here.' She handed him a water bottle, chilled to perfection.

'Thanks,' he mumbled, and tilted the bottle to his lips. And almost choked when it occurred to him that she'd probably sipped earlier from exactly the same spot.

She patted his back. 'Are you OK, Xav?'

'Yes. Thank you for the water,' he said, when he'd recovered.

'Pleasure.' She met his gaze, then deliberately drank from the same spot.

Was she *flirting* with him? His libido responded instantly, and he immediately hoped she wouldn't notice his arousal.

'Do you have five minutes?'

If his libido had been a dog, it would've been wagging its tail madly, sitting up and begging.

'I wanted to run something by you,' she said.

Then he noticed that she had her laptop bag with her.

Work. He could manage that. 'Sure,' he said.

He let her lead him to a quiet spot by the trees, and sat down beside her. She powered up the laptop, then slid it from her lap to his. 'Let's see how sharp you are,' she said, giving him a truly sassy smile.

Her 'sounds' quiz, he realised. Definitely something different; and he managed to get eight out of the ten sounds.

'Tut, tut, Monsieur Lefèvre. And I expected you to get a perfect score.'

No, he was far from perfect. But, right at that moment, looking at her with the sun shining on her hair and her eyes sparkling, she was. France had softened her. Without her business suit, she was just how he remembered her, that summer, all warm and sweet and adorable. And, despite her floppy hat, she'd caught the sun slightly and there was a dusting of freckles on her nose. This wasn't the cool-headed businesswoman sitting next to him. This was the girl he'd fallen in love with all those years ago.

'What are you thinking?' she asked.

How beautiful you are. Not that he had any intention of telling her that. Or acting on the crazy impulse to kiss her. *'Ce n'est rien,'* he said, resorting to a Gallic shrug. 'So when's it going live?'

'Next week.'

Once they were back to talking about work, the dangerous moment was averted. But Xavier was all too aware of how easy it would be to let things slip back to how they'd been, ten summers ago. Part of him wanted it; but the cynic in him wondered. If they hit a problem with the vineyard, was she right and talking about it with her would help with his worries? Or would she misinterpret him again and walk out? He didn't know, and that was the problem: until he could trust her, and trust his judgement where she was concerned, he had to keep his distance. For both their sakes.

Another week went by, and Allegra thought that Xavier was starting to lose that wary look with her. She'd taken to dropping in to the café/farm shop on the way home and trying one glass of a different wine, and making notes about it in her tasting diary. Nicole was highly amused by it, but made plenty of good suggestions; and Allegra tried to catch Xavier at lunchtimes and talk her discoveries over with him.

Working in the fields boosted her confidence further; she was beginning to feel a real part of the vineyard now, part of the team. Even the day when she got blisters from hoeing was bearable, because Xavier noticed—he smoothed cream on her hands, and there was a tenderness in his touch that disarmed her. He made her sit in the shade for a while and, as if he noticed how frustrated she was at not being able to do what everyone else was doing, he sat with her and talked through the week's schedule, to make her still feel part of it all.

Late on the Wednesday afternoon, they were walking through the vines together while she took photographs for the blog. Usually it was cool enough to be bearable at that time of day, but right then the air was close and heavy.

'It's going to pour in a minute,' Xavier said, looking up at the sky. 'We'd better head back.'

Allegra put her camera back in its pouch and slung it round her neck before following him back through the vines.

They were half a row from the edge of the field when the rain hit—huge, fat drops of water. Xavier took her hand and ran for the belt of trees at the edge of the field, pulling her along with him. The canopy of leaves was enough to protect them from the worst of the rain, but they'd been far enough into the fields to be drenched already. Allegra glanced at Xavier; the rain had plastered his T-shirt to his body like a second skin, exposing the width of his shoulders and the hardness of his muscles, and no doubt she was equally exposed.

Her heart seemed to skip a beat and all her senses were heightened; she could smell the rich earth, feel the sudden coolness in the air now that the oppressive heat was broken, and hear the raindrops drumming on the earth around them.

She glanced at him again to discover that he was looking straight back at her, his gaze trained on her mouth and then lifting up to her eyes again. She had no idea which of them moved first, but then he was cupping her face in his hands. He lowered his head and brushed his mouth against hers once, twice; her lips were tingling, and it wasn't anywhere near enough to be satisfying. She needed more. As if he sensed it, he dipped his head again and nibbled at her lower lip. She opened her mouth to let him deepen the kiss, and his tongue slid against hers, teasing and exploring and demanding and coaxing and inciting, all at the same time.

When she kissed him back, everything seemed to vanish; she was only aware of Xavier, the strength of his body and the warmth of his mouth. His hands had moved to splay against her spine, holding her close to him, and her arms were wrapped tightly round him. She didn't care that they were both wet; she just wanted him to keep kissing her and touching her, until the tightness in her body eased.

And then he broke the kiss.

She almost whimpered with frustration and need. Until she looked at him and saw the same need and frustration in his expression.

The rain had stopped, and steam was rising from the earth.

'We'd better get you out of those wet clothes,' he said.

'Yes,' she whispered, knowing that she was saying yes to a lot more than just dry clothes. She wanted to feel the weight of Xav's body over hers; and she desperately wanted to wrap her legs round him and urge him deeper inside her.

Xavier's fingers were entwined with Allegra's as they walked back to his car. His head was telling him this was utterly crazy and he shouldn't do it, but for the life of him he couldn't stop now. This had been a long, long time coming. Maybe once they'd made love it would break the tension between them and put everything back to normal, he told himself. Maybe it would get this desperate craving out of his system—and hers. The way she'd kissed him just now told him that she needed this as much as he did.

He opened the passenger door for her, then climbed into the driver's side. And he managed to stall the engine when he tried to start the ignition. Worse, he'd left the air conditioning on, so the blast of cool air against his rain-soaked skin made his body tighten further. Then he made the mistake of glancing at her. The cool air had had exactly the same effect on her body, and her nipples were clearly delineated through the wet cotton of her T-shirt. He couldn't stop himself reaching over and tracing the curve of her breast with one fingertip, swirling it round her nipple.

She murmured her consent, and he lost it completely. He dragged her over towards him and dipped his head, opening his mouth over her nipple regardless of her clothes and sucking hard. Her fingers slid through his hair, urging him on, and her body arched against him.

He had just enough strength left to release her. Heaven only knew how he drove them back to the chateau. But, the next thing he knew, they were standing on the cool terracotta floor of his utility room, and he was peeling off her wet clothes. Getting her exactly how he wanted her to be. Naked.

Dieu, she was so lovely. All woman. And he wanted her so badly, it actually hurt.

He stripped off his own clothes, before bundling them into the washing machine.

But when he turned back to Allegra, he discovered that she'd gone shy on him. Her eyes were wide with worry, and her hands were strategically placed to cover herself.

'What's wrong?' he asked, as gently as he could.

'What if someone comes in?'

'They won't.'

'How do you know?'

'Guy isn't here. He's in Cannes. There's just you and me here, right now.'

She bit her lip. 'What about whoever does your house?'

'She works mornings only.' He took a step closer to her. 'Allie, stop panicking and stop talking. *Just kiss me.*'

He lowered his mouth to hers; this time, Allegra was the one to deepen the kiss. His hands came up to cup her breasts, taking their weight, and he teased her nipples with the pads of his thumbs. Pleasure lanced through her, but it still wasn't enough. She wanted more—so much more. She broke the kiss, arched her body against his and tipped her head back, offering him her throat.

He made a murmur of assent and drew a line of kisses down her throat, hot and open-mouthed; her skin tingled at the contact. One of his thighs was nudged between hers; she could feel the heat and strength of his erection pressing against her. Despite the fact they'd both been soaked in the rainstorm and the floor was cool, her skin felt super-heated. Any second now, she was going to implode.

He dipped his head farther, just as he had in the car, and took one nipple into his mouth. Except this time there were no barriers; and the feel of his mouth against her drove her crazy. She pushed her fingers into his hair, urging him on.

To her shock, he stopped. And then he stooped slightly and scooped her up into his arms.

'Xav!' She clutched at his shoulders.

'It's either carrying you to my bed or taking you on the floor right now,' he warned her, his eyes hot with desire. 'While I have a shred of civilisation left in me, I'm going to give you the chance to say no.'

Absolutely not. She wanted this as much as he did. She wouldn't mind betting that right now her eyes were as wild as his and her mouth looked as reddened and ravaged as his did; and it thrilled her that she'd done this to him, that she'd broken his iron control over his emotions and he was letting go for her.

'I'm saying yes,' she said, and then grinned. 'Whoops, forgot my manners. That's a yes, *please*.'

In response, Xavier carried her straight up the stairs; he kissed her all the way there, and she didn't have a clue whereabouts his bedroom actually was in relation to the stairs. All that mattered was that he'd carried her there and laid her gently on his huge double bed, an old-fashioned brass frame with a thick mattress, deep, soft pillows and amazingly soft, smooth bed-linen that smelled of lavender.

The mattress dipped beside her; he kissed her once, very lightly, then took his time exploring his way down her body, kissing and stroking and inciting until she was burning hot for him. Her breathing was shallow and she was actually quivering with need. He slid his hand between her thighs and stroked her skin, getting nearer and nearer to her sex but stopping a whisper away.

She dragged in a breath. 'Xav, I'm going crazy here.'

'With you all the way, *ma belle*.'

'Please,' she begged.

And then at last he drew one fingertip along her sex. She quivered at his light touch, teasing at first and then more focused, swirling with just the right pressure.

Though it still wasn't enough.

'More,' she whispered.

He slid one finger inside her.

'*Please*.' The word was ragged and didn't even sound as if it came from her. 'I need you inside me, Xav. Now.'

He shifted his weight so he could open the drawer in the cabinet next to his bed and took out a condom. She heard the foil packet ripping; then he rolled it on and shifted so he was between her thighs. She saw his biceps flex as they took the weight of his body—and then finally, finally, he fitted the tip of his penis against her sex and pushed, easing into her.

She could still remember the very first time he'd made love to her, the day he'd taken her virginity by the lake and blown her mind. Then, he'd paused to let her body adjust to the feel of him inside her, and he did exactly the same now. He dipped his head to brush his lips against hers, and whispered, 'OK?'

'Very,' she whispered back. Physically, Xavier was perfect, and he knew exactly how to give her pleasure.

'Hold on, *ma belle*,' he told her, his voice cracked, and began to move. Slowly at first, then harder, faster, sending shocks of pleasure rippling through her body.

She'd forgotten just how good this could be. Sure, she'd had lovers since her relationship with Xavier, but she'd never committed to them, and none of them had been as skilful a lover as Xavier. None of them had ever matched up to the man she'd thought would be her one and only.

She slid her hands round his neck and tangled her fingers in his hair; it was so soft, so silky, beneath her fingertips. Then she drew his head down to hers and kissed him deeply, exploring his mouth with her tongue, mimicking the action of his body inside hers.

The pressure built and built and built, drawing her closer and closer to the peak; she broke the kiss, tipping her head back against the pillow and pushing up hard against him, taking everything he could give and wanting more.

And finally her climax hit, pleasure splintering deep inside her.

She opened her eyes and looked straight into his; she could see the exact moment that he reached the peak, too.

'Xav,' she whispered.

He jammed his mouth over hers, kissing her hard, and she felt his body pulse within hers.

At last, he eased out of her.

She stroked his face, brushed his lower lip with the pad of her thumb and smiled. They didn't need words; what they'd just done transcended all. And now everything was going to be all right. She settled back against the pillows and pulled the sheet over her while Xavier went into his en suite.

But, when he came out, everything seemed different. He'd left the bed relaxed and smiling, but she could see the tension in his shoulders as he walked towards the bed, and his mouth was set.

'What's wrong?' she asked softly.

'I'm sorry.'

She frowned, not understanding. 'What for?'

'I owe you an apology. This shouldn't have happened.'

She stared at him. This couldn't be possible. They'd just made love; and she was pretty sure it had been as good for him as it had for her.

He raked his hand through his hair and sat on the edge of the bed. 'We agreed. We're business partners.'

'It's not as simple as that, and you know it. Xav, just now, you were there with me. All the way. It was completely mutual. We both wanted this—*needed* this.'

'I can't offer you anything other than a business relationship,' he insisted.

She wasn't buying that. 'Only a few minutes ago, I saw you completely lost to pleasure. Inside me,' she emphasised.

Colour slashed across his cheekbones. 'OK, I admit it. I find it hard to keep my hands off you.'

At least he admitted there was a physical connection between them.

But she was pretty sure it went deeper than that. When they'd had that heart-to-heart, he'd told her that he'd planned to ask her to marry him. Their break-up had been a stupid misunderstanding; they'd both been hurt by it, but now they understood each other better. It was time to start healing.

'Xav. I can't keep my hands off you, either. We're good together. So what's the point in fighting it?'

He shook his head. 'This is just physical.'

No, it wasn't. It was more than that for her. She liked the man Xavier had become. Responsible, fair, treating his staff with respect and expecting more from himself than he did from them.

If she was honest about it, she'd never really stopped loving him. She'd hidden it away, not wanting to be hurt any more—but that was the real reason why she'd never wanted to commit to anyone else. Because she loved Xavier. Always had, always would.

And she had a feeling that that was why he hadn't committed to anyone, either.

He was in deep, deep denial.

How was she going to haul him out?

'You want me and I want you,' she said. 'If I kissed you now, you'd kiss me back.'

'And I'd resent you for it,' he said. 'Allie, I told you. I have trust issues.'

'You think I'm going to let you down again?' That hurt. Hadn't he listened to a single thing she'd told him? Hadn't she shown him how it could be? 'Xav, I've worked with you in the vineyard. I've learned a lot from you, and I think I've taught you things, too. We're a good team.'

'I know. Business isn't the problem.'

'Then what is?'

'I can't shake the fear, Allie,' he told her. 'I can't help wondering what will happen if we have another set of bad harvests, like we had when my parents split up, or there's some other problem at the vineyard.'

She couldn't believe what she was hearing. 'So you think I'm going to be like your mother and just bail out?'

'You came back to France to escape your job in London,' he pointed out. 'The day you found out you'd inherited half a vineyard, you resigned.'

She blew out a breath. 'That's unfair.'

'But it's true.'

'Well, yes. But that's different. The problem with my job had been dragging on for months.'

'Business problems can drag on for months.'

'So you're saying we have to keep each other at arm's length because you don't trust me.'

'Or my own judgement. Not where you're concerned. I've got it wrong on so many levels, before now.'

She bit her lip. 'You're not even going to give us a chance, are you?'

'I don't want to hurt you, Allie.'

Too late. He already had.

'What's it going to take to make you trust me?' she asked.

'I don't know.' He raked a hand through his hair. 'God help me. If I knew that, I could fix this. But I don't. I can't.'

She felt her eyes narrow. 'This works two ways, though. Xav, how do I know that you're being open with me—that you haven't still got this weird masculine idea that you need to protect delicate little me from anything difficult, and you're holding out on me?'

'You don't and you can't,' he said simply. 'So now do you get what I'm trying to tell you?'

She hated it…but, yes, she did. And until she could find some way of persuading him to see her point of view—that they could work it out if they took the risk and trusted each other—she'd just have to live with this. 'You have to be the most stubborn, awkward man I've ever met.'

'I'll take that as a compliment.'

'It isn't one, believe me.' She grimaced. 'I would offer to give you some space, but would it be possible for me to borrow some dry clothes, first?'

'My clothes would drown you.' He sighed. 'Look, the washing cycle should've finished by now. I'll go and put your stuff in the dryer.'

'Can I borrow a T-shirt or something in the meantime? Because I'd rather not, um, stay here.' In his bed. Where the sheets were still warm from their bodies joining together.

'Sure.' He looked uncomfortable. 'Um, would you mind looking away?'

'Of course.'

He frowned. 'What's so funny?'

Clearly he'd noticed that she hadn't been able to stop the momentary quirk of her lips. 'We just had sex. Hot sex. Completely *naked* sex. It's a bit late for modesty, Xav.'

'Yeah, you're right.' He brazened it out and strode over to the chest of drawers.

She knew she ought to look away but, heaven help her, she couldn't. Physically, Xavier Lefèvre was the most perfect man she'd ever seen. Utterly beautiful. And she wanted him so badly.

He pulled on his underpants, then went to his wardrobe and dragged out shorts and a T-shirt. 'Help yourself to whatever you want,' he said, gesturing to the wardrobe. 'I'll be downstairs. If you want a shower, there are clean towels in my bathroom.'

Clean towels, and the woody shower gel he used that made her feel as if his arms were still wrapped round her. She washed her hair, wrapped it in a towel, then dried herself and went in search of something to wear. The best she could come up with was one of his white cotton shirts; it would show no more flesh than if she'd been wearing a short dress.

Just as long as she didn't bend over, because there was no way she was borrowing any of Xavier's underwear.

She borrowed his comb to take the tangles out of her hair, then padded downstairs to the kitchen.

Xavier's eyes widened when she walked in, and she could see the surge of desire in his face, quickly damped down.

God, he really was the most stubborn man she'd ever met. Didn't he realise that this thing between them wasn't going to go away? Ten years ago, she'd convinced herself that she didn't care and she was over him, but it wasn't true. And she was pretty sure he wasn't over her, either.

'Coffee?' he asked.

'No—I'm fine, thanks.'

'I would suggest a walk in the garden, but it's raining again.'

She gave him a wry smile. 'Xav, you can talk as much as you like, but it's not going to go away.'

'Yes, it is.'

She walked over to him and rested her hand on top of his. 'Let me do one thing for you.' She could at least make the library and the piano less difficult for him, bring back some of the pleasure he'd once had in it—just as Harry had made music a pleasure again for her.

'What?' he asked, looking wary.

Her heart bled for him. Xavier really couldn't trust anything or anyone, could he? 'Come with me,' she said softly, and led him to the library. 'It's up to you whether you sit next to me or as far away from me as you can—but let me take away the bad memories for you.'

He flinched as she sat down at the piano. 'Just don't play Debussy.'

'I'm not going to.' She started to play 'Waterloo Sunset', stumbled a bit, changed the key, then began humming along. She glanced over at him. 'You're supposed to join in.'

'What?'

'Given how loud the stereo is in your car, you obviously sing along to it. So do it now.'

He looked as if he was fighting himself, but eventually he joined in. And he had a good voice, strong and in key.

'See? It's not so bad. This is how I get rid of the blues, Xav—and it's the best way I know. Now give me another song.'

He blinked. 'You can play absolutely anything by ear?'

'If I know the tune, yes.' She rolled her eyes. 'Don't look at me like that. It's not exactly difficult if you've played for years and know where the notes are.'

'Allie, normal people can't do that.'

'Yes, they can. So don't tell me I've inherited my parents' musical genius. I'm just me. And this is about fun, not relentless pressure.' She started playing a Beatles tune next; looking resigned, he gave in and sang along.

By the time she'd finished playing, he looked a lot happier—though he was still not sitting next to her.

She closed the lid of the piano, walked over to him and laid her palm against his cheek. 'There's good stuff in life, Xav. You just have to look for it and let people in.'

He looked surprised. 'But the way you grew up, practically ignored by your parents and dragged around in their wake...'

'I had Harry,' she said simply. 'And, actually, he was the one who showed me that music could be fun instead of the endless quest for perfection that my parents made it. He used to play like this with me, when I was little. He'd play all the famous songs from musicals. Actually, he could've been a professional musician.' She sobered, and blinked away the threatening tears. 'Ignore me. I'm being ridiculous.'

'No, you're not.' He drew her close, cradling her against his body. 'Allie. I wish it could be different. But something broke in me ten years ago. I'll only hurt you. And I don't want to do that.' He rested his cheek against her hair. 'It's better for both of us.'

'That'd sound more convincing if you didn't have your arms wrapped round me,' she said. And regretted it when he promptly loosened his hold.

'I'll go and check if your things are dry,' he said.

He was being a coward, and they both knew it, but she couldn't bring herself to call him on it. He'd already told her more than she'd expected, and no doubt now he was panicking about how vulnerable opening up to her had made him.

She sat back down at the piano. She was just going to have to take it a bit more slowly. But she'd show him that this could work. That together they could be amazing. It would just take a bit of time until he believed her.

CHAPTER TEN

OVER the next few days, Xavier steadfastly tried to resist Allegra—but even when he was in the fields, he found himself looking out for her, and he despised himself for being so weak. Hadn't he learned from what had happened to his father? No way was he going to put himself in that situation: loving her so much that he'd fall apart when Allegra eventually got bored with the vineyard and decided to leave.

But, God help him, he couldn't take his eyes off her. He couldn't sleep at night, remembering how her hair had been spread out over his pillow and how he'd felt inside her, as if everything was right with the world.

And then an opportunity arose: a meeting in Nice to discuss options with a new distributor. Which meant he'd be miles away from Allegra, that he'd finally have some space to think.

Though Allegra had other ideas when he told her. 'What do you mean, you're going to Nice to talk with a distributor?'

'It's a good opportunity.'

'Then I'm coming with you.'

'You really don't need to.' Although he made sure he sounded casual, inwardly he was panicking. The romantic Côte d'Azur: Cannes, with its sandy beaches and palm trees, its beautiful stone buildings and the harbour, the flower market and the narrow streets in the picturesque old town. Sharing that with her would be irresistible. How was he possibly going to keep his head? He could see himself walking hand in hand with her in the sunset, the sea swishing gently onto the shore.

No, no, no, no, no.

'It's my vineyard too.' She folded her arms and glared at him. 'I'm going with you.'

'You'll be bored,' he said.

'I need to learn about distribution.'

'The discussions will be entirely in French.'

'Not a problem. My French is nowhere near as rusty as it was a month ago. And if I miss anything you can always fill me in later.'

Every single argument he made, she had a counter-argument for it.

In the end, he was forced to agree.

And then it got worse.

'Nice is off,' he told her as he put the phone down.

She looked up from her laptop. 'So when do we reschedule?'

'Not when. Where.' He took a deep breath. 'Paris.' The City of Light was the most romantic city in the world. The Seine and its *bateaux-mouches* all lit up at night, the cafés in the Latin quarter playing jazz, Montmartre with its street artists and the Sacré-Coeur at the top, the Eiffel Tower lit up like a golden beacon at night over the city and sparkling on the hour.

The place where he'd planned to propose to Allegra at Christmas, ten years ago.

'Paris.' Her face went white.

'You don't have to go.'

'No, it's fine.' She lifted her chin. 'Paris it is.'

So, early on the Tuesday morning, he drove them both to Avignon, where they caught the TGV to Paris. He spent the entire journey forcing himself to concentrate on sets of figures on his laptop, though he was intensely aware of Allegra beside him: the floral scent she wore, and the fact that she was humming softly to herself as she worked on her own laptop.

Although she was wearing one of her sharp business suits, he knew the softness that lay beneath, and it was driving him crazy.

When was he going to stop wanting her?

They had just enough time to check into the hotel before their meeting with Matthieu Charbonnier, the distributor. And Xavier found himself clenching his fists when the older man went straight into charm mode and kissed the back of Allegra's hand—particularly when she blushed and responded.

Oh, for pity's sake. He had no right to be jealous. He was the one who'd called a halt on their affair.

But the feelings just wouldn't go away.

When Matthieu realised that Allegra was English, he insisted on conducting their business in English. And he was delighted with the new bilingual labels that Allegra had produced. 'These will definitely help in the English-speaking market,' he said. 'I like the new look. Clean yet traditional, like your wines.'

'Allie's idea,' Xavier said shortly.

'And a very good one. Now, which competitions have you entered, this year?'

'None.'

'Pity, because your wines are good. Even if you only get a silver or a high commendation, it still carries weight on the English and American side of the market,' Matthieu pointed out. 'If you want to widen your distribution, maybe you should think about it for next year.'

'Are we too late to enter for this year?' Allegra asked.

'Not if you sort it out in the next couple of days,' Matthieu told her.

'We don't need to enter competitions. It's all hype. The wine speaks for itself,' Xavier said, feeling even more out of sorts. He steered the conversation back to the wine and distribution options. Finally, they agreed terms, shook each other's hand, and Matthieu promised to have the draft contract sent to their lawyer.

'And how charming it was to meet you, Allie,' he said, bowing and kissing Allegra's hand again.

'You, too.'

He gave her his business card. 'Just in case there's anything else you want to discuss with me. I would have liked to offer you dinner tonight, but I'm afraid I have to be in London. But some other time, perhaps?'

Over Xavier's dead body. And he shook Matthieu's hand just a little too firmly as the older man said goodbye.

'That went well,' Allegra said brightly. 'I'm glad I came.'

'Mmm.' Xavier wasn't glad. At all. He was as jealous as hell, and it unsettled him even more. Why couldn't he think straight where Allegra was concerned?

She glanced at her watch. 'Do we have any more business to sort out this afternoon?'

'No. Why?'

'It's just…it'd be nice to see a bit of Paris.'

He stared at her. 'Have you never been to Paris?'

'Only to the airport and the train station.' She bit her lip. 'I know you probably have tons to do so, if you don't mind me playing hooky, I'll find a tour or something.'

'I'll show you round.' The words were out before he could stop them.

'Really?' She beamed at him. 'Thanks. I'd appreciate it. It's so much better to visit somewhere with someone who actually knows the place and can tell you about it.'

He could hardly disappoint her by changing his mind now. But maybe if they walked everywhere, he'd wear them both out enough to keep their hands off each other. 'Can you walk in those shoes?' he asked.

'Sure I can.'

'We're not going to have time to visit everything,' he said, 'so either we can go and walk around the Louvre or we can just tour the outsides of some of the more favourite buildings.'

'What are the chances of spending tomorrow here and visiting the Louvre properly then?' Allegra asked.

He knew he should say no. But the appeal in her wide eyes was irresistible. 'OK. We'll start at Notre Dame.'

He took her over to the Île de la Cité and let the beautiful gothic cathedral speak for itself.

'Xav, this is stunning,' she whispered, gesturing to the huge rose windows.

'So are the views from the tower. It's the best place to see the gargoyles.'

'Can we?' she asked.

She was delighted by the strange carvings and, although Xavier had seen them several times before, seeing them with her made him see them anew. And not just the gargoyles; all the beautiful buildings in Paris seemed just that little bit more sparkling, seen through her eyes.

'I think we've earned ice cream,' he said when they reached the bottom of the tower stairs again. Though he didn't have just any old ice cream in mind. He wanted Allegra to experience the best of the city he'd loved so much as a student.

He took her over the bridge to the Île Saint Louis and bought her a *fraise de bois* ice cream.

'This is amazing,' she said, after her first taste. 'I've never had ice cream this good before. Thank you.'

'Pleasure.' He smiled back at her. 'It's the best in Paris.'

She eyed his cornet. 'So what's yours?'

'Caramel.'

'Is it as good as this?'

'Would that be a hint that you want a taste?'

She grinned. 'Yup.'

He offered her the cone but, to his shock, instead of licking the ice cream, she reached up and touched her mouth briefly to his.

'Mmm. That's good.'

Her voice was low and breathy, and sent desire lancing through him. 'My control only goes so far, Allie,' he warned.

Her smile told him that she was perfectly aware of that and had kissed him deliberately.

As they walked along his hand kept brushing against hers and his skin was tingling; he could feel his control starting to splinter.

'We're going to the Eiffel Tower,' he said, and shepherded her to the RER station near the Notre Dame.

He'd planned to walk up all the stairs to the first stage, but he'd noticed that she was starting to flag, so they took the lift instead. Though it really didn't help that he was squashed next to her and she fitted perfectly into the curve of his body. How easy it would be to slide his arms round her and draw her back against him. And even easier to dip his head and kiss the curve between her shoulder and her neck.

Even though the whole of Paris was spread out before them, the only thing he could see was Allegra's skin, all soft and smooth. And he *wanted*.

'The view's amazing,' she said softly. 'So why is Paris called the City of Light?'

'*La Ville-Lumière*? Because of the street lighting at night—it was set up earlier in Paris than in most places,' Xavier explained. 'Plus the lighting now. We have so many beautiful buildings, and they need to be shown off.'

'I'd really love to see Paris lit up at night. Do you think we could maybe have dinner somewhere overlooking the city?'

He couldn't resist the appeal in her eyes. 'Sure.' He glanced at his watch. 'They're about to close, here. Let's go back to the hotel and change.'

A cold shower helped his common sense take over again. Waiting for her in the hotel reception also helped. But then she walked into the reception area, and Xavier was really glad he was sitting down because he'd just gone weak at the knees. Allegra was wearing a sleeveless dress in raspberry-coloured silk georgette, knee length and swishy; there was a rose corsage in the same material on the left of the deep V-neck. She'd teamed it with suede high heels in the same raspberry colour with a rose detail on the toe, her hair was up in a chic twist, and she was wearing a choker of black pearls with a black agate rose in the centre. Her make-up was minimal, but in any case her amazing midnight-blue eyes didn't need any emphasis. She was gorgeous just as she was.

This was his *petite rose Anglaise* all grown up.

And he didn't want to take her out for dinner tonight; he wanted to carry her straight to his bed and loosen her hair before taking her clothes off, very, very slowly.

He kept himself in check—just—and took her to Montmartre.

'This is beautiful,' she said as they wandered through the ancient streets.

'It's where many of the artists lived,' he told her. 'Degas, Matisse, Renoir and Picasso.'

'I can see why it attracted them. Do you know the area well?'

'Given that I was a student in Paris?' He slanted her a look.

She rolled her eyes. 'Of course you do. You know it as well as I know London.'

He smiled. 'This is my favourite part of Paris—even though it's pretty touristy in places. And then there's the Place du Tertre—it's just north of here and during the day it's full of street artists.'

'Would we have enough time to come back tomorrow?' she asked. 'I'd love to see the Sacré-Coeur properly, too.' She gestured up to the pure white basilica.

'Sure.' He led her through the back streets to a tiny bistro, somewhere he'd been before and knew the food was good. 'Would you like some wine?'

'Just one glass,' she said.

Something reckless in him made him order champagne.

'Celebrating something?' she asked.

No. He'd just wanted to drink champagne with her. 'Our new distribution deal,' he said.

'To Les Trois Closes,' she said, lifting her glass.

He echoed the toast and clinked his glass against hers.

'So why don't we enter the wine competitions Matthieu talked about?'

He wrinkled his nose. 'It's a lot of admin. It really isn't worth the fuss, whatever Charbonnier says.'

'If you say so.' She smiled at him. 'Though did you notice that he liked the new labels?'

'You're fishing.'

She laughed and sipped her champagne. 'Humour me.'

'OK. I admit that you were right, Mademoiselle Beauchamp, and I bow to your superiority.'

Then he wished he hadn't been so sarcastic when she gave him the most wicked look. 'I'd rather you knelt.'

Oh, *Dieu*, the pictures *that* put in his head.

When their meal arrived he had no idea what it tasted like; he could only focus on her. And it was even worse when the sky started to darken outside and the waiters lit candles on every table. Why had he been so stupid as to think that he could cope with such a romantic atmosphere?

When they'd finished, the waiter came over to ask what they wanted for pudding.

'Will you trust me to order for us?' he asked Allegra.

'Sure.'

'We'll have *le moelleux*,' he said decisively. 'With two spoons.'

She arched an eyebrow when the waiter had left. 'You're sharing a pudding with me, Xav? Isn't that a bit risky?'

Way too risky. He brazened it out. 'It's *the* Parisian pudding, but no way can you eat a whole one on your own.'

'Is that a challenge?'

He smiled. 'No. I wouldn't dare challenge you.'

'Pity.' She moistened her lower lip with her tongue. 'I enjoy a challenge.'

Oh, *Dieu*, she was flirting with him again. And now he was imagining her doing that to his mouth. Astride him. Without that dress.

When the pudding arrived, she smiled. 'Ah. So it's a chocolate fondant pudding.'

'Not "a",' he corrected. *'The.'*

'I love chocolate puddings.' She looked at him through lowered lashes. 'They're so *sensual*.'

He groaned. 'You're doing this on purpose, aren't you?'

'Moi?' She gave him a teasing smile. 'I have no idea what you mean.'

Then she dropped her spoon. 'Oops.'

'I'll get you another.'

'The poor waiters are rushed off their feet. Let's be kind to them and share a spoon.' She eyed the spoon, and then his mouth. 'It's a long spoon. If I lean forward slightly…'

She did so, and he couldn't help following the line of her dress, seeing how her cleavage deepened. And he remembered touching her skin. Tasting it.

He cracked and fed her a spoonful.

She gave a deep sigh of pleasure. 'That's fabulous.' She took the spoon from him—his skin burned where she touched him—and fed him a mouthful.

It took all his control not to let his hand shake when he took the spoon back.

He managed to survive pudding. Just. 'Coffee?' he suggested, intending to order a double espresso. The caffeine might jolt some common sense back into his head.

'Not for me, thanks.' She stifled a yawn.

'My company's that boring, hmm?'

'No. It's the fresh air and lots of walking.'

'I can take a hint. Let's go back.' He paid the bill swiftly, ignoring her attempts to pay her share, and shepherded her out of the bistro. When she stumbled on a rough piece of pavement, it was only natural that his arm should go round her to support her. And even more natural that her arm should slide round his waist. And then they were strolling through Montmartre like lovers...

He stopped under one of the lamp-posts. 'Allie.'

'Mmm?' She glanced up at him.

He spun her round to face him, dipped his head and brushed his mouth against hers. How sweet she tasted. He'd barely touched his glass of champagne, and yet his head was spinning—all because of her.

'Tell me to stop now, or I can't be responsible,' he said.

'Who says I want you to be responsible?'

'My control's at the point of deserting me,' he warned.

'Good. Because I want you out of control. I want the man I know you are,' she told him fiercely. 'All of you.'

Pure desire skittered down his spine. 'You drive me crazy. I want your hair down and spread across my pillow,' he said hoarsely. 'I want you in my bed and wrapped round me.'

'That's what I want, too,' she said. 'Right now.'

Without another word, arms still wrapped round each other, they walked back to the hotel. By mutual consent, they ended up in his room. The second he closed the door behind them, he unzipped her dress, peeled it off her, and hung it carefully over the back of the chair.

Her smile held a quirk of amusement. He pulled her to him and kissed her with real passion, deep and demanding and hot—and suddenly even the flimsy barrier of her underwear was too much.

Her bra and knickers matched her dress perfectly, he noted: a glorious shade of raspberry, in sharp contrast to the sheer ivory of her skin. He hooked his fingers under the straps of her bra and drew them down to bare her shoulders. *Dieu*, she was lovely. He kissed his way along soft, smooth skin, lingered in the hollows of her collarbones and then traced a path of kisses just beneath her pearl choker.

She gasped and tipped her head back, and he took advantage of the position to loosen the fastenings in her hair and let it tumble to her shoulders. 'Allie, you're amazing, so perfect,' he whispered.

He unsnapped her bra with one hand and let it fall to the floor. When he cupped her breasts and teased her nipples with the pads of his thumbs, she quivered. He was gratified to see her pupils dilate, to the point where her irises were the tiniest rim of midnight-blue.

'Xav, I need to feel your mouth on me,' she said huskily.

He dropped to his knees, and teased one breast and then the other with the tip of his tongue. How amazing the contrast was between the puckered raspberry skin of her nipples and the smooth ivory skin of her breasts; and he just couldn't get enough.

She wriggled, moving closer to him; he took the hint and kissed his way down over her abdomen and along the top of her hold-up stockings. As it was, he seriously considered just ripping the seam of her knickers, but exercised enough control to draw them down, stroking her skin as he did so. He nuzzled her inner thighs and drew his tongue oh so slowly along her sex.

'Xav!'

He felt her knees buckle and supported her before she fell. Then he stood up, scooped one arm under her knees and carried her to the bed. It took him all of three seconds to strip off his own clothing. He grabbed a condom from his wallet; his hands were shaking so much that he had trouble putting it on. Then he knelt between her thighs. 'Now?' he whispered.

'Oh, yes.' Her breath was a hiss of pleasure. 'Love me, Xav.'

He did.

He loved this amazing woman with every fibre of his being. He always had. He'd hated her for a while, when he'd thought she'd let him down—but now he knew they'd had crossed wires. If only he could get past this stupid fear and trust her. Trust himself. Love her the way he wanted to.

'Je t'aime,' she whispered, and he stopped being able to think straight; he was so aware of how much he loved her and wanted her and needed her.

Gently, he eased his body into hers; she felt so perfect round him, hot and so ready for him. He pushed deeper and was rewarded by a murmur of pure pleasure. He loved the fact that she was so abandoned to him right now. He kissed her hard; her hands fisted in his hair and she kissed him back, demanding and taking just as much as he was. He felt her body begin to tighten round him, and it tipped him into his own orgasm.

As he came, he whispered, 'Allie, *je t'aime*,' and held on to her for dear life.

Afterwards, she pressed the tip of her finger against his lips. 'Don't you dare say it. I know you're thinking it, but don't *say* it. At least give me tonight.'

He kissed her fingertip. 'I can't think straight any more.'

'Then sleep with me tonight, Xav. I want to wake in your arms tomorrow.'

He wanted that, too. Wanted it so badly.

'Last time…' She dragged in a breath. 'I don't want it to be like last time. I just want you to hold me.'

'I know, *petite*.' He kissed her, and went to the bathroom to deal with the condom. As he came back to bed she propped herself up on one elbow and he could see fear glittering in her eyes. In his head, he knew that this was going to make everything much more complicated—but they'd deal with it tomorrow. Tonight he was going to act on the urging of his heart, not his head, and sleep with her in his arms.

As he slid beneath the covers and gathered her into his arms he could see the relief in her face. '*Tout va s'arranger*,' he said softly. 'Everything will turn out fine.'

Even though he knew he was lying.

The next morning, Allegra woke with her head pillowed on Xavier's shoulder and his arms wrapped round her.

She could hear by his regular breathing that he wasn't awake yet; not wanting to break the spell, she stayed where she was, enjoying his closeness.

When he finally stirred, she smiled at him. 'Good morning.'

'Good morning.'

She could see the panic in his eyes, and stroked his face. 'Hey. This is Paris. It's a stolen day out of time. No discussions, no judgements. We're going to wander through Paris and enjoy it. Hearts, not heads. That's the rule. OK?'

'OK. But we have to get the TGV home this afternoon,' he corrected, 'so I make that half a day.'

'Better get up and make the most of it, then.' She brushed a kiss against his chest. 'Care to join me in the shower, Monsieur Lefèvre?'

His whole body tensed, and she could feel the war going on between his head and his heart. Luckily for her, his heart seemed to win, because he climbed out of bed, scooped her up and carried her to the shower.

After a breakfast of hot, dark coffee and pain au chocolat, they went to the Louvre, and then wandered hand in hand through the Jardin des Tuileries, enjoying the sculptures and the fountains and watching children play with wooden boats on the boating pond. They saw Monet's huge pictures of lilies in the Musée de l'Orangerie then took the Metro back to Montmartre and caught the funicular railway to the top of the hill.

The beautiful white basilica of the Sacré-Coeur was even more beautiful inside, Allegra thought; then Xavier kept his promise to take her to the Place du Tertre, where they wandered through the square full of tables and brightly coloured umbrellas, drinking in the scent of coffee and hot bread from the cafés lining every inch of the square. Over the sound of people chattering, she could hear jazzy guitar playing.

As he'd told her, there were artists everywhere, sketching.

'Can we?' Allegra asked.

'N—' He stopped himself. 'Sure.'

Ten minutes later, she was in possession of an amazing sketch of them together. And Xavier was definitely looking at her as if he cared, she was sure.

Finally, it was time to catch the TGV back to Avignon. Their half a day out of time was over.

As if Allegra was reading his thoughts, she asked, 'So where do we go from here?'

'I don't know,' Xavier answered honestly. 'What do you want?'

She took a deep breath. 'I want a man who wants the same things as me. A man who respects that I'm independent, that I'm an individual and have my own way of looking at things. A man who respects my mind as much as he wants my body.'

He could do that. He could definitely do that.

'And I want roots. I want a man who wants to be in the same place as me.'

Ice trickled down Xavier's spine. 'Which is where? The vineyard?'

'I love it at Les Trois Closes. But…maybe. Maybe not. I don't know.' She spread her hands. 'Right now I'm at a crossroads. I need to make a decision about where I want to be.'

And he could guess what she really wanted. The way she'd spoken to him before about London, about how safe she felt there—she'd want to go back. Back to the safety of her life in London. And her independence was important to her, too: she'd want the place where she could control her own security.

London.

Which meant there was no place in her life for him.

He couldn't settle in London, even for her. The call for home was too strong.

Allegra sighed inwardly. He'd closed up on her again. But she'd been as open as she could with him. She wanted him to see that she was independent and committed, but she wanted a say in things; she didn't want him to run the whole show and dictate all the terms.

'It's your life. Your decision,' he said. 'You're the only one who could make it.'

This was where he was supposed to add, 'But I want you to stay.'

Or was he acting on his head again, convinced that love never worked out and he didn't want to take the risk?

She could slide her hands round his neck, pull his head down to hers, and she knew he'd respond. Physically, they were perfectly in tune.

But she wanted more than just sex. She wanted his heart.

And somehow she was going to have to find a way through all the barriers he'd thrown straight back up.

CHAPTER ELEVEN

THEY drove back from Avignon in silence; with every kilometre, Allegra knew that Xavier was distancing himself from her. When they reached the farmhouse, he took Allegra's case from the back of his car and opened the passenger door.

'Would you like to come in for coffee?' she asked.

He shook his head. 'Not a good idea. You know what will happen.'

She did.

'And you know my feelings about that.' His expression was bleak. 'We agreed that Paris was a day out of time, and now we're back in the real world. Which means we're business partners. End of. Goodnight, Allegra. See you in the office tomorrow.'

Why did he have to be so stubborn about this? She was utterly sure he felt the same way that she did. The night before, he'd even said he loved her, in his own language.

And yet he wasn't going to give them a chance.

The next morning, Xavier was out in the fields when she arrived at the office. She fished Matthieu Charbonnier's card from her handbag and called his mobile. Ten minutes later, she had the information she needed. Twenty minutes after that, she'd entered Clos Quatre into the wine competition online, organised a courier and was busy sticking labels on the wine.

Strictly speaking, she should've asked Xavier first. It was his wine, not theirs.

But she knew he'd refuse, and she wanted to prove something to him. She wanted him to see just how good his wine was and how far he'd come since the days when he'd taken over from his father. And maybe, faced with the proof that she believed in him, he might just start to believe in her.

Over the next week, Xavier avoided her as much as possible. She knew why; this was his way of avoiding temptation. He'd admitted that he could hardly keep his hands off her, and it was the same for her. And yet he steadfastly refused to give in. To the point where he'd even work in the fields during the hottest part of the day rather than face her.

This really wasn't good for him. The second day he did it, she texted him to tell him that she was too hot to work in the office and she was going home for a swim, and for the next week she planned to work just in the mornings at the vineyard office and would be going home in the afternoons.

His reply was brief and to the point. *Merci.*

And she wanted to push him into a pool of icy water, make him wake up. Did he know how unreasonable he was being right now?

Knowing Xavier, he probably did.

She sighed. How could she break the stalemate between them? She was out of ideas, and this was going nowhere. Apart from driving her slowly insane.

In the middle of Thursday morning, Guy walked into the office and sat on the edge of her desk. 'Allie, *petite*. Lovely to see you.'

'Hi. I wasn't expecting to see you. Are you back for a long weekend?' she asked.

'Yes. Are you doing anything this evening?'

She shrugged. 'Nothing important. Why?'

'Just wondered if you wanted to come over for dinner. Right now it's perfect for eating outside.'

'Was that dinner just with you, or with Xav as well?' she asked.

'Both of you. Is that a problem?'

'No,' she fibbed. She'd bet good money that as soon as Xavier found out that Guy had asked her over, he'd make some excuse not to be there. But in a way that would be useful; maybe she could talk to Guy about the situation. He was the most likely person to know what was going on in his brother's head, and he might have some good ideas about how she could persuade Xav to see reason. 'I'll bring pudding,' she said, adding with a smile, 'I wouldn't dare bring wine.'

'Half past seven, then.' He slid off the edge of her desk and blew her a kiss. '*À bientôt.*'

She cycled home via the village and picked up a tarte tatin and a pot of double cream from Nicole. And when she cycled back over to the chateau that evening, Xavier answered the front door.

His eyes widened. 'What are you doing here?'

'I invited her. Don't be rude to my guest,' Guy said, coming into the hall. 'Welcome, Allie. Come in and have a glass of wine.'

'Thank you, Guy.' She handed him the box and the pot. 'I hope tarte tatin's all right.'

'*Absolument*. It's my favourite.' He smiled. 'Given that, resourceful though you are, I doubt you box things up like this, do I take it that this is one of Nicole's?'

'Yes, and she sends her love.' Allegra looked straight at Xavier.

Colour slashed across his cheekbones. 'I'd better get back to the grill,' he muttered and fled.

'Maybe I should just go home,' Allegra said, feeling awkward.

'No. He's been like a bear with a sore head for days. Ignore him.'

Ha. That was easier said than done.

Guy escorted her out to the terrace, putting the apple tart in the fridge on his way, and poured her a glass of rosé. 'I've been reading your Rookie Vigneronne blog. It's great stuff,' he said.

'Thank you.'

'And I like the new labels. Actually, I have to admit I invited you over tonight with an ulterior motive. Would your designer be able to do something for me?'

'I can ask her. It depends how mad things are back at the agency and how big the job is.'

'I'm developing a new perfume and I need a look for it. Maybe you could come to Grasse and I could show you around the perfumery and talk over the brief with you. And maybe if you have some spare time I could ask you to do some work for me, too.'

Being away from Xavier might help. Didn't they say that absence made the heart grow fonder? Or maybe it would be a case of out of sight, out of mind. She glanced over at him—brooding over the grill, and using it as an excuse to avoid her. 'Sure.'

'Thank you, Allie.'

Xavier eventually joined them with a platter of bar-becued meats and bowls of salad, and Guy kept the conversation going whenever Xavier and Allegra fell into an awkward silence.

'Xav tells me you've been hiding your light under a bushel,' Guy said when he brought a jug of coffee and three cups through to the terrace.

'Me?' Allegra felt her eyes widen. What had Xavier said?

'I didn't realise you played the piano.' He smiled at her. 'Any chance you'll indulge me and play for us this evening?'

She glanced automatically at Xavier. Just for a mo-ment, before he made his face carefully blank, she was sure she saw longing there—the same longing that filled her whole heart.

'Of course I will,' she said, rather more brightly than she felt.

Guy undid the French doors to the library; she sat down at the piano. Xavier was sitting as far away as he could, she noticed; but she didn't need him to look at her. She needed him to listen.

She played a couple of upbeat, lively numbers.

And then—looking straight at Xavier so he'd know she was playing this for him—she began playing 'Time after Time'. She sang along with it, straight from the heart, silently begging him to listen and understand what she was telling him. That he could let himself trust her because she'd be there. She'd find him if he was lost. Catch him if he fell. She'd be there every single time.

Except he clearly didn't listen—or didn't want to know—because he walked out in the middle of the first chorus.

She stared at his retreating form in dismay, knowing that she'd lost, and stopped mid-song.

Guy came over and gave her a hug. 'Sorry. My big brother's a total idiot.'

Right at that moment, she didn't trust herself to speak; she just nodded and willed the tears to stay back. She'd cried herself empty over Xavier ten years before, and no way was she going to do that again.

Dully, she closed the lid of the piano. 'Thanks for this evening, Guy. I'm sorry I spoiled it.'

'You didn't spoil it, *petite*.'

He was just being kind, and she knew it. 'I'll be on my way home.'

He sighed. 'I'll drive you.'

She shook her head. 'You can't. You've been drinking.'

'Only one glass, so I'm well under the limit, *chérie*. I wouldn't take stupid risks.'

'But I came on my bike.'

'With my car, that would be a teensy problem—but there's an easy solution. I'll use Xav's.' He shepherded her into the kitchen and grabbed Xavier's keys from a drawer.

He hefted her bicycle into the back of the car, opened the passenger door to let her in, then climbed in the other side and switched on the ignition. 'You really love him, don't you?'

'I never stopped.' Her voice cracked. 'How obvious do I have to be, Guy? I'd give him everything I am. But he's never going to let himself trust me. And my being here isn't good for either of us.' She dragged in a breath. 'So I'm going back to London.'

Guy's eyes widened. 'You're bailing out on him?'

'I can't make him love me, Guy. And I'm only making him unhappy, being here. He can do what he likes with the vineyard—I'm not going to sell it, but I'm not going to get in Xav's way.'

'Ah, *chérie*, I wish things could be different.'

'So do I.' But they weren't. And it was about time she faced it instead of fooling herself and opening herself to further hurt.

Guy drove her home, settled her at the kitchen table and made her a mug of hot chocolate. 'Are you sure you're going to be OK?'

'Yes.' She kissed him on the cheek. 'Thanks, Guy. For looking after me. For caring.'

'Of course I care. You've been my friend since we were little.' He gave her a hug. 'If you need a friend, you know where I am.' He took his wallet from his pocket and pulled out a business card. 'Do you have a pen?'

She found one in her handbag; he scribbled a number on the back of the card. 'This is my personal mobile, as opposed to my work mobile. Call me any time.'

'Thanks, Guy.'

If only it had been Xavier making that offer.

But she knew now it was never going to happen.

Twenty minutes later, Xavier looked up as Guy pulled the plug of his computer from the wall in his office. 'Hey! I was working on that.'

'Tough.'

'I hadn't saved my file.'

'Tough,' Guy repeated, folding his arms. 'For someone usually so astute, you're being really dense. You do realise Allie's in love with you?'

'And?' Xavier drawled.

'Oh, for pity's sake. Don't start spouting that rubbish about Lefèvre men not being able to find the right one. Papa and Maman—they had a lot of good years before it went wrong. And don't bring my marriage into it, either. Véra and I should never have even got engaged because we just weren't compatible. It was my fault as much as hers.' Guy shook his head in frustration. 'Do us all a favour, Xav, and think about it. It's been ten years, and Allie never got married to anyone else. Neither did you. That's because you're meant to be together.'

Xavier rolled his eyes. 'You've clearly been in your lab too long and the chemicals have muddled your thinking.'

'Face it, *mon frère*, you're in love with her and she's in love with you, and right now you're running scared. Stop being such an idiot. It's the chance to get your life back on track, the way it should be, with a woman who's going to give you everything she is and expect everything you are in return. You're lucky you've found the right one.'

'I can't trust my judgement where she's concerned.'

'Then trust mine.' Guy shrugged. 'It's up to you. If you want to be an idiot, I can't stop you. But I'm telling you, if you have a grain of sense left in you, you'll ring Allie now and apologise, tell her you're as mixed up as hell but you love her, and beg her to sort you out. Because, if you don't, she's going to be on the first train back to London.'

'Guy, I love you dearly, but don't interfere in things you don't understand.'

'I might be younger than you,' Guy shot back, 'but I've got a hell of a lot more sense.'

Xavier said nothing, simply plugged his computer back into the wall and switched it on. And he ignored the fact that Guy slammed the door so hard it nearly fell off its hinges.

Allegra didn't come in to work the next day. Which proved what Xavier had thought all along. He spent the next week telling himself that it was her loss, not his; though the fact that neither his secretary nor his brother were speaking to him annoyed him further. It unsettled him, too. Had he pushed her away? Or was he right, and she would never have settled here anyway?

The phone shrilled, and he answered it absently.

'Monsieur Lefèvre?'

'Yes?'

'It's Bernard Moreau from Vins Exceptionnels. Clos Quatre is your wine, yes?'

Xavier started paying attention. How had Vins Exceptionnels heard of his own private bottling? Unless it was something to do with Allegra's Rookie Vigneronne blog. 'Yes.'

'I'm delighted to tell you that it's been awarded a gold medal in this year's competition.'

'I beg your pardon?' How could it possibly have won a gold medal? He hadn't entered it.

'It's still a little young, but the judges think that in a year or two it will be absolutely superb.'

'I…uh… Thank you. I wasn't expecting this.' Because he hadn't known about the entry. But he had a pretty good idea who'd done it.

'We'll be in touch shortly with the official certification,' Bernard said. 'But we just wanted you to know. Well done.'

'*Merci beaucoup.*'

Xavier's head was spinning as he put the phone down. Allegra had entered his wine in the competition—his, not the AOC or the *vin de pays*. His baby. She'd done it without telling him, too, because she believed in him and she wanted the world to know it.

She believed in him.

The world seemed to tilt. He'd been so wrong, it was untrue. Yes, she'd left Les Trois Closes—but not for the reason that Chantal had left his father, or for the reason that Véra had left Guy. Allegra had left because he'd done what she'd thought he'd done ten years ago: he'd pushed her away. And, now he thought about it, he realised that she'd put so much into the vineyard—the new labels, the website and the blog, the tours of the vineyard that she'd publicised with the local tourist board. All that stuff she'd said in Paris about not being sure where she wanted to be had been an elaborate bluff, because she hadn't wanted to put pressure on him. At the time, he'd been too obtuse to take the hint and say to her that he wanted her to stay.

'Xavier? Are you all right?' Thérèse asked, pausing in his doorway.

'No. I'm an idiot.' He dragged a hand through his hair. 'Can you book me a flight to London, please?'

'London?'

'London,' he confirmed. 'And I don't care how much it costs.' He took his credit card from his wallet and handed it to her. 'I want the fastest flight to get me to Allegra. If anyone wants me, tell them to call me next week. I'm going to fetch my passport.'

When he returned, ten minutes later, Thérèse said, 'The quickest flight is from Paris. But you're better off going by train—it'll save you time the other end, too. Your ticket's ready to collect at Avignon.' She handed the credit card back to him.

'You,' he told her, kissing her cheek, 'are wonderful. Thank you.'

En route from Avignon, he called Hortense. It took him a long time to persuade her, but eventually she gave him Allegra's address in London. Then he flicked into the Internet on his mobile phone and checked out the route to Allegra's flat, memorising it.

The rest of the journey to Paris dragged—and the minutes seemed to go by even more slowly on the way to London. But at last he was at St Pancras station. At this time of day, Xavier knew it'd be quicker to take the Tube than a taxi to cross the city. He paused for just long enough to buy an armful of flowers, then headed out to Allegra's Docklands flat.

If she wasn't in, then he'd sit on the doorstep until she came back.

And he hoped to hell that she'd give him the chance to explain.

In Docklands, Xavier rang the bell on Allegra's door and waited; but the woman who answered the door wasn't Allegra.

'Sorry, I must have the wrong address,' he said. Hopefully this woman was a neighbour and would be able to point him in the right direction. 'I was looking for Allegra Beauchamp. I'm—'

'I know who you are,' she cut in, glaring at him. 'I'll see if Allie's available. Wait here.' She left the door very slightly ajar, and he could hear her calling Allegra's name.

On the one hand, he was glad that Allegra had a friend looking out for her. But he could really do without a gatekeeper. Having to relay messages through a hostile third party wasn't going to be ideal.

He could of course just walk straight in.

But he knew he didn't have the right. This was Allegra's territory, and he'd hurt her badly. So waiting was the right thing to do, even though he hated every second of it.

'You'd better come in,' the woman said when she returned to the door.

'Thank you.' He stepped inside and saw Allegra leaning against the wall, looking wary.

'I'll give you some space,' the woman said to Allegra. 'I'll be in the coffee bar across the road if you need me. I'll keep my mobile on.'

'Thanks, Gina.'

Allegra looked terrible. There were shadows beneath her eyes, her skin had none of the lustre it had held in France, and her soft curves had turned to angles again.

And it was all his fault.

He waited until Gina had closed the front door before he handed Allegra the flowers. 'Peace offering,' he said.

'Thank you,' she said. 'They're lovely. I'll put them in water.'

He followed her into the kitchen, where she found a vase and filled it with water.

'Allie, I know I don't deserve it, but I'm asking you to give me the chance I didn't give you. Would you hear me out?'

She finished arranging the flowers and turned to look at him. 'What's the point, Xav? You've made your position quite clear.'

'There's something else you need to know about that position,' he said. 'It's completely in the wrong.'

Allegra stared at him, wondering if she'd really heard that correctly. Xavier, admitting that he was wrong?

Maybe she was in some weird parallel universe.

'What are you doing here, Xav?' she asked. 'I mean, really?'

'I've come to apologise. For lots of things.' He blew out a breath. 'For pushing you away, for not trusting you, for not believing in you the way you believed in me.'

Everything she'd wanted to hear from him—before she'd given up and come back to England. 'What changed your mind?'

'A call from Vins Exceptionnels, to say we got a gold medal.'

The penny dropped. 'For Clos Quatre? Your wine got a gold?'

'*Our* wine,' he corrected. 'Yes.'

'That's fantastic!'

He reached out and took her hand. 'You believed in me enough to put my wine in the competition.'

'Without telling you,' she admitted with a twinge of guilt.

'You believed in me, Allie. You thought I was good enough. And it's made me realise something—I believe in you, too. I believe in us.' He took a deep breath. 'I know you like your independence and I know you want roots. I understand that—the way your parents dragged you about means that security's important to you. And

I also know you made your own roots in London. So if you want to live here, that's fine—we'll put a manager into the vineyard, and I'll move here.'

She was hardly able to believe what she was hearing. 'You'll move to London? For me?'

'For you,' he confirmed softly. 'Because France isn't home without you. I love the Ardèche, but without you it just isn't enough. I've been as miserable as hell without you. I know it's taken me too long to realise it, but my home's wherever you are. If that means living in London and getting a job working for someone else, then so be it.'

'You'd give up the vineyard for me?'

He nodded. 'Without you, Les Trois Closes is just an empty shell. I love you, Allie. I know I've hurt you, and I'm sorry. But if you'll give me the chance, I'll make it up to you.'

'You love me,' she said in wonder.

'I've loved you for years,' he said. 'I never really stopped. I realised that in Paris, and it scared the hell out of me. It still does, if I'm honest. Love makes you vulnerable.'

And he was admitting that vulnerability to her. Leaving his heart wide open and giving her the power to hurt him.

To trust her that much, and to put her needs above his beloved vineyard, he really must love her.

'I don't want you to get a job in London,' she said.

He untangled his fingers from hers, his expression grim. 'Too late? Well, I guess I deserve it—it's my own fault.'

She shook her head. 'That's not what I'm saying. You'd hate it here, Xav. You love Les Trois Closes.'

'I love you more, Allie. As long as you're with me, I don't care where I live or what I do.' He paused. 'Maybe we can find a place together. Somewhere of our own, where we can make good memories.'

'Where?'

'Wherever you're going to be happy.'

Although she'd been miserable since Paris, she'd been happy in the Ardèche before. Settled. And she knew how much Xavier loved his home. 'France,' she said. 'I want to live at Les Trois Closes and to make my home there with you.'

He took her hand again and drew it to his lips. 'I could build us a new house. By the lake, maybe. We could make a fresh start. You, me—and, if we're lucky enough, our children.'

He wanted children? With her?

'Allie?' With the pad of his thumb, he wiped away the single tear trickling down her cheek. 'Don't cry.'

'Xav, I...' A second tear spilled over, and a third.

He wrapped his arms round her, cradling her against him. 'Don't cry, *ma belle*. I love you. Whatever it takes to make you happy, I'll do it.'

She swallowed hard. 'I'm not crying because I'm sad. I love you so much, Xav. And I didn't think you'd ever be able to love me back. I thought you were too broken.'

'I was. But you've healed me,' he said softly. He brushed his mouth against hers. 'Come home, Allie. Marry me and make a family with me. And I'll get you that dog you wanted so much.'

Home. A family. With Xavier. Everything she'd ever wanted. She reached up to kiss him back. 'Yes.'

CHAPTER TWELVE

GINA was sceptical when Allegra rang her to break the news, but after she'd returned to the flat and spent an hour or so grilling Xavier, she seemed mollified. 'So you're going to treat Allie as she deserves to be treated,' she said to Xavier, narrowing her eyes at him.

'Yes.' His fingers tightened round Allegra's. 'And, as she's agreed to marry me, I'm planning to buy her an engagement ring tomorrow. In Paris.'

'What's wrong with London?' Gina asked.

'Nothing. But Paris is…' He paused. 'Paris is special. And I have something in mind. But first I need to sort out a hotel for tonight.'

'You're not going to stay here with me?' Allegra asked, surprised and more than a little hurt.

'I didn't come here to impose on you, *ma belle*. I came to ask you to share your life with me. And there are some practical details I need to sort out.'

'What kind of practical details?'

'All I have with me is my passport, so for a start I need to buy a change of clothes.'

'You're telling me you came here on the spur of the moment?' She found that hard to believe; no way would Xavier be that spontaneous.

'I wanted the rest of my life to start right now,' he said, surprising her further. 'So, yes.'

'I have a washer-dryer,' Allegra said.

As if he remembered exactly what had happened when he'd put their wet clothes in his washing machine, Xavier coloured spectactularly.

'I'm not going to ask,' Gina said, laughing.

'Thank you. I think,' Xavier said. 'So, if I can borrow your washing machine later, Allie, can I take you both out to dinner this evening?'

'Normally,' Gina said, 'I'd be polite and say no to playing gooseberry. But as you're going to whisk my best friend back to France tomorrow and I have no idea when I'll get the chance to see her again—yes, please.'

Xavier smiled. 'You have an open invitation to come and stay whenever you like.'

After dinner, Xavier insisted on putting Gina in a taxi back to her own flat. He walked hand in hand with Allegra back to hers. She enjoyed peeling his clothes off and putting them in her washing machine; and he responded by making love to her slowly and tenderly, until she felt as if her bones had melted.

'I love you,' he said softly. 'I love you more than I knew it was possible to love anyone.'

'I love you, too.' She stroked his face. 'And I knew you'd get the gold medal. I told you how good your wine was. Your dad would've been so proud of you.'

'And Harry would've been proud of you. Look at the way you've made people take notice of our vineyard.' He paused. 'Do we have to wait until our new house is built before we get married?'

'No. We can live at Harry's.' She nestled closer to him. 'But if we want my parents to turn up to the wedding, we'll have to fit it around their schedule, so that might be a while in the future.'

'That's up to you, *ma belle*.' He stole a kiss. 'If I had my way, I'd marry you tomorrow. But I thought maybe we could have a ceremony in the village church.'

'So Harry and your dad will sort of be there. I'd like that,' she said.

The next morning, Xavier brought Allegra coffee and toast in bed, then proceeded to book their flights and a hotel room.

'We're staying in Paris tonight?' she asked.

'Yes. I know it's not Christmas, but I always planned to propose to you in Paris. This is…just a little late.'

She smiled. 'Hey. No regrets. We've learned from the past.'

He kissed her. 'I love you. And I'm buying you a dress to wear, so you don't have to pack a thing. Not even your toothbrush,' he said. 'The hotel will deal with everything.'

'That sounds a bit extravagant,' she said. She revised her opinion to 'extremely' when the taxi stopped outside their hotel in Paris and Xavier collected the key to their suite. She'd expected maybe a nice room with a four-poster; she hadn't expected a circular Italian marble bath with a view of Montmartre, a huge bed with a gold silk canopy, a living room with one glass wall and an incredible view over the Seine, and a rooftop terrace with a view over Paris.

'Xav, this is just *stunning*,' she breathed.

'Like you.' He stole a kiss. 'Come on. We have shopping to do.' Which involved the Champs-Elysées, pure silk underwear, and the most beautiful dress and shoes Allegra had ever seen, both in midnight-blue silk.

Finally, he took her into an exclusive jeweller's on the Place Vendôme, where she noticed that the jewellery had no price tags.

'Xav, this is too m—' she began.

He pressed his forefinger lightly to her lips, stopping the words. 'Stop worrying. It's fine. I want you to choose something you like.'

She tried on several different rings, but the one she liked best was a simple twist of platinum with a brilliant-cut diamond in the centre. And it was the perfect fit, not even needing any alteration.

'This was meant to be,' Xavier said simply, and bought it.

They spent the rest of the afternoon playing tourist in the sunshine, sipped aperitifs overlooking the Seine, and then Xavier suggested that they went back to the hotel to change.

Allegra already guessed that he was going to give her the ring tonight. Though where he'd choose to do it was another matter. The top of the Eiffel Tower, as he'd told her he once planned to do? Montmartre, his favourite part of the city? Under the Arc de Triomphe?

'First,' he said, 'I want to share something with you.' He ran a bath, adding a viscous golden liquid that made the water smell of honey and gave the water a deep topping of creamy bubbles. Then he slowly peeled off her clothes, kissing every centimetre of skin as he revealed it. She enjoyed returning the favour, and then he lifted her up and stepped into the bath with her.

The view was incredible: the white basilica of the Sacré-Coeur was in sharp relief against the deep blue of the sky.

'Xav, this is…' She shook her head, unable to find the words.

'This is you and me,' he said softly. 'And I wanted to spoil you a bit.'

He dipped his head to brush his mouth against hers, and his hand slid down her back, smoothing the curve of her spine. She wrapped her arms round him and deepened the kiss; the next thing she knew, he'd shifted and pulled her onto his lap so she was sitting astride him.

'Now that's decadent,' she teased.

'Mmm, and we have to stop.' He kissed the hollows of her collarbones. 'I need to get a condom.'

'No, you don't. I don't want any more barriers between us. I want all of you, Xav.'

'*Dieu*, how I love you, Allegra Beauchamp,' he said, and kissed her hard.

She lifted herself slightly, slid her hand round his shaft, and then eased down on him.

'Oh, yes.' His breath was a hiss of pure pleasure. 'Do you have any idea how incredible you feel?'

'About as incredible as you do.' And, seeing the passion in his gaze, she believed now that he loved her as much as she loved him.

She began to move, and he cupped her buttocks, supporting her as she lifted up and lowered herself down. Her arms were round his neck, his mouth was plundering hers, and the tension inside her was coiling tighter and tighter and tighter until at last she hit the peak. She felt his body surge against hers, and knew he was there with her.

'You're amazing. And I love you more than words can say,' he said.

'Me, too.'

He coughed. 'You could try.'

She rubbed the tip of her nose against his. 'The first time I saw you, when I was eight years old, I decided that you were the man I was going to marry. I've loved you for years and years and years. Even when I told myself I didn't. And I'll love you for the rest of my life and beyond.'

'Glad to hear it,' he said, holding her close. 'We'd better get out of here, or we'll be like prunes.'

'I need to wash my hair.'

He kissed her lightly. 'Then I'll leave you, *ma belle*. Your things are all in your dressing room. Come and get me when you're ready.'

'Count on it,' she said as he climbed out of the bath and wrapped himself in a thick, fluffy bath sheet.

'You look fantastic,' he said when she finally emerged from her dressing room.

'So do you.' In a well-cut dark suit, white shirt and a sober silk tie, he looked every millimetre the Parisian socialite, sophisticated and urbane. And yet she knew the other side of him, the scruffy vigneron who was equally at home making love with her in a meadow of wild flowers. Both sides of him made her heart beat faster.

'May I have the pleasure of your company for dinner this evening, Mademoiselle Beauchamp?' he asked.

'*Bien sûr*, Monsieur Lefèvre,' she said with a smile.

He tucked her arm through his. But just when she thought he was going to open the door to their private lift and take her out to Paris, instead he led her onto the terrace. A table had been set for them with a white damask tablecloth, a silver candelabrum with vanilla-scented candles, and a silver bowl full of the palest pink roses. The shrubs by their table were festooned with tiny white fairy lights.

From the terrace, they could see most of the city, and in the dusk the buildings were beginning to light up.

'Welcome to the City of Light,' he said softly. 'I want it to be an evening you'll remember,' he told her, his eyes glittering. 'Tonight's special.'

The night they were finally committing to each other. A shiver of mingled delight and apprehension rippled down her spine.

The meal was fabulous—a rosette of avocado with grapefruit and shrimps, Sole Meunière with a selection of perfectly cooked vegetables, and the best crème brûlée she'd ever tasted. Particularly as Xavier insisted on sharing a spoon with her, while she was sitting on his lap.

And then finally, after rich, dark coffee, Xavier took a midnight-blue velvet box from his pocket and dropped to one knee beside her. Opening the box and offering her the ring, he asked, 'Allegra—will you be my wife, the love of my life and my equal partner, for the rest of our days?'

'Yes,' she said.

And sealed it with a kiss.

BEDDED BY BLACKMAIL

BY
ROBYN GRADY

Robyn Grady left a fifteen-year career in television production knowing that the time was right to pursue her dream of writing romance. She adores cats, clever movies and spending time with her wonderful husband and their three precious daughters. Living on Australia's glorious Sunshine Coast, her perfect day includes a beach, a book and no laundry when she gets home. Robyn loves to hear from readers. You can contact her at www.robyngrady.com.

For Carol, my beautiful big sister.
Happy birthday!

With thanks to my editor, Diana Ventimiglia,
for your help in making this book so special.

One

One

Tristan Barkley knew danger when he sensed it. As he whipped open the sliding glass door and scanned his expansive backyard, he sensed it in spades.

His heart beat like a war drum against his ribs while the hair on his nape prickled and every muscle in his body bunched tight.

Where was Ella? What trouble was she in?

He'd phoned to speak with his housekeeper twice this morning. Ella wasn't aware of his last-minute plans to attend a gala event in Sydney tonight. Home a day early from a weeklong trip to Melbourne, he'd wanted to be sure his tuxedo was back from the cleaners.

But when she hadn't answered his calls, he hadn't been concerned. Perhaps she was out shopping. Ella Jacob was fanatical about having her boss's every need and want satisfied. It was one of the reasons he valued her—or rather, her dedication to her job—so highly.

However, when he'd arrived home a few minutes ago, he'd noticed her car keys hanging on their hook. A second later, his gut wrenched at the sight of her practical leather handbag and its contents strewn over the kitchen counter. Her uniform had been turned inside out and discarded on the cold marble tiles. One black lace-up shoe lay near the timber meals table, the other had been left upside down near this door.

Now as he shaded his eyes against a single ray piercing the brewing black sky, his heart squeezed like a fist in his chest.

If anyone had entered his house uninvited…if someone had dared to hurt Ella…

He strode onto the lawn and movement beyond the northern courtyard caught his eye. Tristan narrowed his focus and zeroed in on a trespasser's fluid backstroke as the intruder sliced through the cool blue of his Olympic-size pool. Twenty-twenty vision said the long, tanned limbs were female. A flash of a pink swimsuit, and the curves it partially concealed, confirmed she was of his generation or younger.

Tristan let out a territorial growl. There'd been a recent spate of robberies in his neighborhood. The police suspected the work of a couple. One poor grandmother had been assaulted and tied up in her own home. Was that woman in his pool the girlfriend of some brazen burglar? he wondered.

He charged forward even as another scenario came to mind. Might be that Ella had simply invited a friend over. Although, come to think of it, he'd never heard her speak of friends. Or family. And that didn't explain the handbag, her uniform. It didn't explain where she was.

His long strides picked up pace.

Once he yanked that woman from the water, *hell 'n' Hades*, he'd have some answers then.

He reached the pool's edge at the same time the woman in pink climbed out, her hair falling like wheat-colored silk down her back. Her glistening body might have belonged to a swimsuit model—buxom with shapely, tanned legs that seemed to go on forever.

Tristan braced his own legs shoulder-width apart and crossed his arms. Unsuspecting, the woman straightened fully, sliding her hands back over her hair, like some Bond girl from a beach scene. When she finally noticed him, when she looked up with those big blue, suddenly startled eyes…

Tristan's mouth fell open and his arms dropped to his sides like dead weights. Then he dragged a hand down over his mouth and blinked several times.

No, this didn't make sense. The hair was the wrong color. That body sure as hell didn't fit. Still, he ground out the question.

"*Ella*…is that you?"

"Mr. Barkley?" The bombshell's cheeks turned as red as the miniature roses spilling from the poolside terracotta pots. "You weren't supposed to be back until tomorrow."

"I rang this morning." *Twice*.

Driven by testosterone-fueled force, his gaze dipped lower and his blood began to stir. Mother of mercy, he'd had no idea.

She folded her arms over the top of the swimsuit,

which only made her amazing cleavage appear twice as deep and ten times more alluring. This couldn't be the same woman...

"I rolled my ankle on a run this week," she explained. "I like to keep fit. Swimming's a good alternative." Her wet hair sprayed a cold arc on his business shirt as she threw a look at the pool then back. "I didn't think you'd mind."

His brain stumbled up to speed. Ella, his unassuming housekeeper, ran to keep fit? In a dowdy uniform, who'd have guessed she worried about anything other than making sure the bathroom sparkled and her delicious dinners were set on the table on time. Out of uniform, however, in that amazing swimsuit, she looked nothing short of...*sensational*.

As telltale heat flared through his system, he shook himself and squared his shoulders. That kind of reaction was totally inappropriate. Miss Jacob was the hired help—his housekeeper—and she still had more than a little explaining to do.

He cleared the thickness from his throat and stabbed a reproving finger toward the house. "Your uniform and shoes were tossed around the kitchen. Your handbag was tipped upside down on the counter."

What was he supposed to have thought? He'd been worried. Damn near frantic, in fact.

Her sheepish gaze dropped away. "Oh, that."

His brow furrowed more. "Yes. Dammit. *That*."

Dripping over the tiles, she began to move away. "It's kind of hard to explain."

"Like it's hard to explain how your hair's gone from mousy brown to blond?"

Had he landed in Wonderland? What was going on!

"I've only dyed it back to my natural color." She shrugged and explained, "I'm a woman. I wanted a change. This week I wanted to change it back."

He growled loud enough to be heard. She was avoiding his question. He wasn't a hard boss; he deserved her respect. The respect he'd always received from Ella in the past. Unless…

His thoughts froze as a withering feeling dropped through his center.

His voice deepened with concern. "Are you in some kind of trouble, Ella? Trouble you don't want to tell me about?"

When she blinked at him over her shoulder, her full lips slightly parted, she looked so vulnerable.

She curled strands of blond behind her ear. "I'm not in trouble. In fact, it's rather the opposite."

She continued on toward a sun lounger, her step favoring one leg. A very nice leg. Very nice body.

Tristan growled again.

He needed to get to the bottom of this mystery and he needed to do it now!

She picked up a towel from the sun lounger's back and wrapped it around herself, sari style. When she turned toward the house, he barred her way.

His voice was rough, his gaze unremitting. "I need an answer, Ella."

She peered up at him as rivulets of water trickled down her flawless face. Her eyes were the color of Ceylon sapphires. How had he missed that before? Did she usually wear glasses? He didn't think so.

Ella's mouth opened then shut. Finally she blew out a defeated breath. "I was going to tell you tomorrow."

He set his hands on his hips. His patience was wearing out. "I suggest you tell me now."

Her chin lifted slightly. "I'd like to hand in my resignation. I'm giving you two weeks' notice."

Tristan's usually balanced world tilted then slid off its axis. He ran a hand through his hair. Of all the crazy things, this had been the farthermost from his mind.

"You want to *leave*. Is it the pay?" Her wage was more than generous, but if that was the problem, it could easily be solved. "Name your price."

She was the best housekeeper he'd ever had—thorough, autonomous, inconspicuous, or at least she had been until this incident. He wasn't prepared to let her go, particularly not now.

The newly elected mayor of a neighboring smaller city had invited himself to dinner in three weeks' time. A positive impression could only help with an important deal Tristan had been working on, a project upon which he'd spent a vast amount of time and money. Obviously Ella's fine cooking skills wouldn't make or break the deal with Mayor Rufus. However, given the querulous past he and the mayor shared, frankly, Tristan could use all the help he could get.

A quiet strength shone from Ella's jeweled eyes. "Money's not the issue."

A recent memory popped into his head, and then he knew. Of course he knew.

Tristan scratched his temple and replaced the gravel in his voice with a more understanding tone. "Look, if this is about that episode before I left…"

The red in her cheeks spread down the column of her throat. Her chest rose and fell as she shook her head and, dodging him, moved away. "That morning has nothing to do with my leaving."

As his sense of control returned, Tristan eased out a relieved breath. Now that he knew what was behind her resignation, he could fix the situation.

He caught up, fell into step beside her and searched for words to handle this delicate matter.

"Admittedly it was an awkward moment," he said. "But there's no need to be embarrassed or do anything rash." His mind went back to that day. "You thought I'd already left for my week away in Melbourne," he recalled. "You didn't expect to see me in the bedroom, particularly without any clothes…"

His words trailed off as, head down, she limped faster.

That morning when he'd heard her gasp, he'd swung around and Ella's eyes had grown to the size of saucers. In that moment, he had reflexively stepped closer—to assure her not to be alarmed, nothing more. But he'd barely said her name before she'd scurried down the stairs like a frightened deer. After he'd dressed, he'd gone to smooth things over but had discovered that she'd left the house. With him away this week, they hadn't spoken of it…until now.

They lived together. Tricky situations were bound to occur, like her walking in on him buck-naked that morning, like his discovery of her swimming today—

He frowned.

Which brought him back to the original question.

"A resignation doesn't explain what happened to your

handbag." The way it had been upended as if some no-good scum had been in a hurry to get what he'd come for.

Her pace eased as she wrapped the towel more securely under her arms. "My inheritance from my mother finally came through." She flicked him a glance. "Nothing compared to your wealth, but enough that I shouldn't need to worry about money again if I'm careful. The executor organized to have the funds transferred through to my account last night, but when it bounced back this morning, he rang to check the BSB number. After a few minutes, when I couldn't find the book I normally keep in my bag..." Her lips pressed together. "Well, I overreacted and dumped it upside down."

Tristan pictured the scene—Ella taking the call, the executor perhaps growing impatient when she'd kept him waiting. Her heart could have raced, her hands might have shaken. She was normally so composed and ordered, as was he. But having overreacted himself just now, he could better understand how she might have lost control in that moment.

"And the uniform? The shoes?"

Her face pinched, then she shrugged. "When I ended the phone call and knew the money would be in my account on Monday, I had this overwhelming urge to be free of them. I ripped the uniform off where I stood. Then I kicked off my shoes." She focused on her bare feet as she continued walking, moving slowly now. "I'm sorry. I didn't give any thought to where or how they landed."

Tristan slid his hands into his trouser pockets. So

Ella had come into an inheritance. Odd, but he'd never thought of her with parents. She'd seemed such a blank sheet. He hadn't known her business and she didn't ask about his. Not that there was much happening in his personal life these days.

He stood aside as she entered the kitchen through the still open door. "I'm sorry about your mother's passing," he offered.

Her step hesitated as she gave him a look he couldn't read. "She died eight months ago, just before I came to work for you."

As she moved into the kitchen, it struck him again that he knew nothing of his housekeeper's background. She'd shown up on his doorstep, explaining that she'd heard of the job opening. She hadn't presented references, which he usually would insist upon. But he'd taken her on, mainly because of a gut feeling that she would fit. Her reserved demeanor, her unassuming appearance, the way she'd quietly but succinctly responded to his questions—she'd simply felt...*right*.

As a rule he thought through every detail of a decision. He hated making a mistake. Growing up, his two brothers had called him Mastermind and had ribbed him constantly about his meticulous ways. Those days seemed so long ago. Although his younger brother hadn't visited this house in a long time, he and Josh kept in touch. However, he hadn't spoken to his older brother, Cade, in years. Never planned to again.

Ella made her way to the cushioned window seat and, wincing, sat.

He followed and indicated her ankle. "Mind if I have a look?" He'd been a lifeguard in his teens and early twenties and knew first aid. It could do more harm than good limping around when a joint needed rest.

She gave a reluctant nod and he dropped onto his haunches.

"The bruise is fading," she told him as he carefully turned the one-hundred-percent feminine ankle this way then that. "It wasn't so bad."

"Have you had it seen to?"

"No need. It's happened before, since as far back as junior high when I ran cross-country. I wear an ankle support and try not to overdo it, but I can't give up running. It's always been my release."

Well, this was the most information of a personal nature she'd ever offered. Was it because she was leaving? Because she was finally free and out of that drab past-the-knees dress that usually hid those honey-eyed shins. Shins that must feel as smooth as they looked.

When his fingertips tingled to inch higher, he bit down the urge, lowered her foot and pushed from his knees to stand.

Focus, Mastermind.

This was no time to slip up, even if Ella's transformation was one hellova jolt, as was her resignation. He'd gotten used to her living here. Where would she be bunking down two weeks from now?

"Have you arranged somewhere to live?" he asked.

Her blue eyes sparkled up at him. "I want to buy in an affordable neighborhood and rent something in the meantime."

Although he nodded sagely, it was almost painful to

think of not coming home to her. Despite checking her references, the housekeeper before Ella had been less than satisfactory—scorched shirts, mediocre meals. Ultimately, he'd had to let her go. Perhaps that's why he'd gone with gut rather than referees in Ella's case.

And with Ella taking care of his domestic front, all had been as it should be. She knew exactly the right amount of ice to mix with his predinner Scotch. His sheets had never smelled better, of lavender and fresh sunshine. He trusted her, too, never needing to worry that some valuable item might go missing.

Damn.

He rubbed the back of his neck. "Two weeks, huh?"

Her smile was wry. "This is a luxurious setting with wonderful conditions. I doubt you'll have any trouble filling my spot."

"None who can cook like you."

Her head slanted at an amused angle as her eyes sparkled more. "Thank you. But my cooking's really nothing special."

Said who? He could practically smell her mouth-watering beef Wellington now. He particularly liked the way she distributed gravy—from a delicate, gold-rimmed pourer at the table, and only over the meat, never the vegetables. She always asked if there was anything else he'd like.

He'd always said no.

Tristan's stomach knotted and he cleared his throat. Hunger pains. He should've eaten on the plane.

He moved to his briefcase, which he'd left on the counter beside her upended handbag. "Whatever you do, however you do it, I've only ever received compliments from our dinner guests…and requests for invitations."

Most recently from Mayor Rufus.

As he clicked open his briefcase, out of the corner of his eye he saw Ella push to her feet. He could almost hear her thoughts.

"You've invited someone special to dinner, haven't you?"

He put on the eyeglasses he needed to read small print and shuffled through some property plans he ought to go over this afternoon. "I'll get around it."

Did he have any choice? Ella was obviously eager to start her new life, permanently shuck out of her "rags" and into something pretty. If no one else could make pork ribs with honey-whiskey sauce the way she did, he'd have to survive. He only wished the mayor, who had a notorious sweet tooth, hadn't heard Councilor Stevens's compliments regarding Ella's caramel apple pie.

Either way, the mayor had invited himself over, undoubtedly to kill two birds with one stone—sample Ella's superb culinary skills as well as address rezoning problems regarding acreage Tristan had purchased with a vast high-rise project in mind. But Tristan wasn't looking forward to another topic of conversation that would unfold during the course of the evening—conversation concerning a duplicitous and beautiful young woman who also happened to be the mayor's daughter…

Ella's voice came from behind him. "When did you invite them?"

"Really, Ella—"

"Tell me," she insisted.

He pushed out a sigh. "Three weeks. But it's fine."

"I could stay on a little longer, if that would help."

He slipped off his glasses, turned to her and smiled. Loyal to the end. "I wouldn't ask you to do that."

"Another week won't kill me." She flinched at her gaffe. "What I mean to say is, if one last dinner party will make a difference to an important business deal, I'll stay."

"I appreciate that, but as wonderful as your meals are, they're not a deal breaker."

She arched a knowing brow. "But it wouldn't hurt, right?"

Shutting his briefcase, he surrendered. "No. It wouldn't hurt."

"Then it's settled."

When she pulled back her shoulders, his jaw shifted. In the past, she'd never been the least assertive, but given she was only acting in his best interests he couldn't find a reason to object.

The real pity was he couldn't talk her into staying indefinitely. But why would—as it turned out—an attractive young lady remain as someone's housemaid when she had money enough to be independent? He had to be grateful she was willing to help out for an added week.

He swung his briefcase off the counter. "All right, I accept your offer. But I owe you."

Looking defensive, she moved to tidy her handbag mess. "You've already done enough."

"What? Allowed you to cook, clean and do my laundry?"

"You gave me a place to stay when I needed it most."

When she hesitated before dropping her purse into her handbag, Tristan studied her suddenly tight-lipped expression. Her background wasn't any of his business, particularly now that she'd resigned. Still, he was intrigued as he'd never been before. What harm would it do to get a little closer now that she was leaving? In fact, perhaps he could satisfy his curiosity over his unassuming duckling turned swan and at the same time thank Ella in some small but apt way.

He cocked his head. "I insist I repay the favor. What would you say to me supplying dinner for a change?"

Her eyes narrowed almost playfully as she stuffed the last article, a hairbrush, into her bag. "I didn't think you could cook."

"I can't. But I know a few chefs who can."

Her expression froze as a pulse beat high in her throat. She took a moment to speak. "You want to take me to dinner? But I'm your *housekeeper.*"

"Only for another three weeks." But he didn't want to give her the wrong idea. "It's just a small show of appreciation for your efforts in the past, as well as for staying on longer than you'd intended."

It wasn't a date. Truth was he hadn't had a *real* date in a while. He didn't count the run of women he'd asked out once or twice to see if the chemistry worked.

He was thirty-two—time to find a wife and have that family. But with each passing birthday more and more he realized he preferred the old-fashioned type, and the women in his circle were either sickeningly simpering, over-opinionated or flat-out treacherous, as Bindy Rufus had been.

Ella crossed to the pot to make coffee—strong and fresh, just the way he liked it. Head bowed, she curled wet hair behind her ear and answered his question. "I don't think going out to dinner would be…appropriate."

"Then you need to think again." When he made up his mind, no one and nothing dissuaded him. Nevertheless, he put a smile into his voice. "Today's a day to kick off your shoes and let go, remember?"

She chewed her lower lip then, looking up at him, slowly grinned. "I guess it is."

Ignoring the embers that innocent smile stirred in the pit of his stomach, he headed for his study. "We'll make it tomorrow night."

He smacked his forehead and turned back. Where was his mind today?

"Ella, is my tux back from the cleaners? I have an event tonight."

"It's hanging in your wardrobe."

She paled and he read her thoughts as clearly as this morning's newspaper. *The wardrobe where I saw you without a stitch on last week.*

But that was all behind them.

He stole a last look at those legs.

At least he thought it was.

Two

Finished applying her new lip gloss, Ella examined her reflection in the bedroom mirror and let out a sigh.

Life truly could turn on a pin. Only eight months ago she'd buried the poor wasted body of her mother, Roslyn Jacob, who'd finally succumbed to cancer. Later that same day, a man she would revile until the end of time had paid her a visit. A man Ella hoped she would never see again.

She'd first met Drago Scarpini some weeks before the death of her mother. He'd claimed to be her half brother, conceived out of wedlock by Ella's father before he'd married her mother.

Scarpini's own mother, an Italian who'd immigrated to Western Australia many years before, had recently passed away. On her deathbed she'd revealed the name of her son's father, Vance Jacob. Scarpini discovered that Ella's father had passed away long ago but Scarpini had wanted to visit his father's widow to see if he had any brothers or sisters.

A well-packaged story, but from his first, Scarpini had sent chills up Ella's spine. As days wound into weeks and Roslyn's condition and faculties deteriorated more, Scarpini's visits continued and his ulterior motives became clear.

Ella had overheard Scarpini talking to her mother about his difficult life growing up without a father, without money. Although Vance Jacob couldn't make recompense now, Roslyn could change her will and divide the estate between Ella and himself. That, Scarpini had said, would've made her husband happy. After all those years of unwitting abandonment, it was the right thing to do.

Ella had been disgusted at his prodding. Her mother had been so ill, so confused. And there had been no proof Scarpini was who he claimed to be. If she'd had a few thousand to spare, she'd have hired an investigator.

The second time Ella had heard him pushing Roslyn, she'd told him to get out. Roslyn had died the day after, sooner than doctors had anticipated. Scarpini had attended the funeral and had even played the sorrowful, supportive brother. Later, however, he'd arrived on Ella's doorstep demanding she divide the estate. When Ella had reminded him she'd just buried her mother, he'd exploded. He needed money to pay off pressing gambling debts.

As she'd shut the door in his face, he'd shouted she would regret it.

The next day, the police had arrived. Scarpini had alleged Ella had murdered Roslyn with a morphine overdose to head off the change she had been about to make to her will. It had been an hour of horror Ella would never forget, but, of course, no charges were laid. The following day her front window was smashed and a condolence card left on the mantel. Scarpini had phoned—either she agreed to his suggestion, or he would get nasty. He'd said he intended to haunt her until he got what he deserved.

Quaking all over, she'd immediately called the police, who couldn't do much about Scarpini's threats. She could petition for a restraining order, the officer explained, but perhaps it would be better to wait and see if Scarpini would cool down and disappear. If he physically harmed her, she should get in touch straight away, the officer had advised.

Ella hadn't slept that night. She'd given up her job to care for her mother and, after medical expenses, there was no cash to speak of. The house, as well as an investment property, needed to be sold before the estate could be settled. That would take several weeks, if not months.

By dawn Ella had made two decisions. One, she needed a job to survive until the estate came through. Two, she didn't intend to wait around for Scarpini's next sadistic game. She'd bought a prepaid phone, organized a post office box for correspondence from the will's executor—the husband of a longtime friend of her mother's—and dyed her hair a different shade for good measure. Then she'd applied for the housekeeper's position at the Barkley mansion.

It had been a bold move, particularly without references, but she certainly knew how to cook and clean and do laundry. When she had secured the job, she'd settled and kept very much to herself.

She'd heard nothing from her harasser since. She hoped the police were right and Scarpini had slid back beneath the rock from which he'd crawled. Now with the house and investment property sold and all of her inheritance in hand—just over a million dollars—the time was finally right to take a deep breath, emerge from her cocoon and start afresh.

And what a way to mark the occasion…asked to dinner by the thoroughly enthralling, undeniably dreamy Tristan James Barkley.

Tingling with anticipation, she gazed into the mirror and clipped on her rhinestone eardrops.

She'd lived through a nightmare. How wonderful if dreams could come true…

A knock on her bedroom door made Ella jump.

Tristan's familiar, deep voice reached her from beyond the timber frame. "The reservation's at eight. We need to leave soon."

Swallowing against the knot of nerves stuck in her throat, she called back, "Be right there."

She grabbed her clutch bag then took one last look at her cocktail-length white dress and matching sling-backs. Socialite material? Not even close. But, as Mr. Barkley had said, this wasn't a date. It was a thank-you from employer to employee…infatuated with her boss though that employee may be.

"Ella?"

She blew out an anxious breath. Here goes.

When she entered the kitchen—the room adjoining her own—Tristan's expression opened in surprise then appreciation, and delicious warmth washed from Ella's perfumed crown all the way to her polish-tipped toes.

One corner of Tristan's perfectly sculpted mouth hooked upward as his hands slipped deep into his trouser pockets. "Sorry. I'm still not used to seeing you out of uniform."

Crossing to join him, she fought the urge to smooth the jacket that adorned the magnificent ledge of his shoulders. In an open-neck collared shirt and impeccably tailored trousers, he was tall and muscular and held himself as a powerful man would—with a casual air of authority and an easy yet mesmerizing gaze. She'd always felt so safe here in his house. So appreciated.

As a housekeeper, at least.

She pushed the silly pang aside and straightened her spine. "I'll be back in my uniform tomorrow."

He withdrew his hands from his pockets and moved to join her. "But you really don't like your uniform, do you, Ella?"

No use fibbing. "Not especially."

"My parents' house staff wore uniforms, so I've always provided them, too. But if you'd rather wear regular clothes these last three weeks, I don't know a reason you shouldn't."

Ella's heartbeat fluttered.

Wear above-the-knee hems? Pretty colors? Feminine heels that echoed as they clicked upon these imported marble tiles?

She shook her head. "It wouldn't feel right." Wouldn't feel…appropriate.

"It's up to you, but don't think I'll object." The lines

bracketing his mouth deepened more. "Really, it's not a big deal."

Maybe not to him.

Absurd, but tonight, more than ever, she couldn't help but compare herself to the glamorous sorts with whom Tristan had been pictured in glossy magazines. Eleanor Jacob was an ordinary woman who was destined for an ordinary life. She'd best remember that.

Still, this weekend her relationship with her boss had changed, if only slightly. Soon their association would end and it was likely they wouldn't see each other again. In fact…

She let out a breath.

Heck, maybe he was right. Doing away with her uniform wasn't such a big deal.

She smiled. "If you're sure."

She couldn't quite read the look in his dark, all-knowing eyes before he moved away to check the back door. "I'm sure."

As he rattled the handle, she let him know, "I locked it earlier."

He worked the blinds shut. "Can't be too careful."

It was obvious what lay behind his security consciousness tonight. Her impetuous behavior the day before apparently made him concerned that she might have been harmed in some way.

She apologized again. "I'm sorry about giving you that fright yesterday, Mr. Barkley."

"It's forgotten." But he checked the windows, too.

What must he have thought finding her clothes strewn across the room, her handbag dumped inside out? But she'd had no idea he would return a day early from Melbourne or she wouldn't have donned that swimsuit. Some women didn't mind flaunting their bodies, but she wasn't one of them. She was mortified by the thought of exposing herself to her boss, although he clearly didn't share her reserve.

That day a week ago in his bedroom when he'd turned to face her—muscled, bronzed and breathtakingly bare—he'd seemed surprised by her unexpected appearance, but not the least bit self-conscious. And why the heck would he be, with an amazing body like that?

Tristan left the last window and joined her, his face almost grave. "There's one more thing we need to get straight."

She held herself tight. What had she done now? "Yes, sir?"

"No more *sir* or *Mr. Barkley,* particularly tonight. We don't want to confuse the waitstaff." His dark eyes crinkled at the corners. "Deal?"

Returning the smile, Ella relaxed and nodded.

His hot palm rested lightly on the curve of her arm as he motioned her toward the connecting garage door. He couldn't know the wondrous sizzle his casual touch brought to her blood.

Minutes later, she was buckled up in his sleek black Bugatti, surrounded by the smell of expensive leather and another intoxicating scent—woodsy, masculine, clean. Whenever she changed his bed linen, she was tempted to crawl over the sheets, bundle a pillow close and simply breathe in.

She stole a glance at Tristan's shadowed profile.

What would it be like to have that beautiful mouth capture hers? Be held against his hard, steamy body?

When a bolt of arousal flashed through her, her heart began to pound and her hands fisted in her lap. That kind of make-believe could only get her in trouble. She needed to keep her mind occupied—needed to talk.

Pinning her gaze on the passing pine trees beside the drive, she put a bright note in her voice. "So, how was the function last night?"

The automatic gates fanned open and the European sports car purred out onto the street. "If you want to know, it was boring."

She smiled to herself. No interesting women, then.

She sank back more into the leather. "I thought you were home early."

"You waited up for me?"

When he grinned at her, his dark eyes gleamed in the shadows and her cheeks heated all over again. "I was watching an old movie and heard your car."

She hadn't been waiting up for him. Not really.

"Don't tell me you like those Fred Astaire, Ginger Rogers kind of flicks."

She grinned. "Not that old. Do you remember *Love Story?*" The score of that classic weepie was enough to give her goose bumps.

"I know it. You're a romantic, then?"

"Most women are."

He coughed out a laugh. "You think?"

She blinked over at him. What an odd thing to say. Women daydreamed about meeting Mr. Right. They imagined bouquets and church weddings and sparkling diamond rings. It was usually men who had a hard time committing, particularly when they were so desirable

they could enjoy a veritable smorgasbord, Tristan
Barkley case in point.

The car pulled up at an elite restaurant, which sat on
the fringe of their exclusive Sydney neighborhood.
When Tristan opened her car door, Ella asked, "Did you
have a reservation already made for tonight?"

It was common knowledge bookings here were as
rare as hens' teeth.

He winked. "I said I knew some good chefs."

And she wasn't the least surprised when, inside, the
attentive maître d' fairly clicked his heels and showed
them to the best table in the house: by an open window
with a magical view of the twinkling harbor, secluded
from the other guests and a comfortable distance from
the live entertainment—a guitarist strumming the soft
strains of a ballad.

As the maître d' left them, Ella perused the listed
entrées. No prices. She couldn't imagine how expensive each must be.

A waiter nodded a greeting at Tristan as he passed.
Tristan nodded back.

Ella lifted a brow. "You obviously come here often."

He kept his eyes on his menu. "Often enough."

She wouldn't ask with whom. Perhaps a different
lady each time. He never spoke about the women he
dated—she knew only what she occasionally saw in
magazines. Tristan Barkley was a brilliant enigma who
had yet to lose his heart. Frankly, she couldn't imagine
one woman being enough for him. She only had to
look into those dark, hot eyes to know he'd be insatiable
in the bedroom.

When a vision flew into her mind—naked limbs,

glistening and entwined on his sheets—Ella's heartbeat deepened. She gripped her water glass and took a long, cool sip. This evening would be sweet torture.

They chose their meals—prime steak for him, sea-food for her. By the time their food arrived, they'd dis-cussed music, politics and books. He was surprised that she liked mystery novels, too. When he poured their second glass of wine, she realized the nerves in her stomach had settled, almost to the point where she could have forgotten that handsome, intriguing man sit-ting opposite was her boss.

She was interested to know, "How's your steak?" It smelled delicious and appeared to be cooked to perfec-tion.

He dabbed the corner of his mouth with his napkin. "Almost as good as your filet mignon." She laughed, unconvinced, and his brow furrowed. "It's true." He lifted his wine goblet to his lips. "Must be good not to have to think about the dishes tonight."

"I clean up as I go. It's not so bad with a dishwasher."

"Did your mother teach you to cook?"

"She wasn't much of a hand at cooking, even basics." She gave a weak smile. "That's how I got so good." After her mother's accident eighteen years ago, someone had to take care of those things, she thought.

"Bet your father appreciated your finesse."

Her chest tightened and her gaze fell to the flicker-ing centerpiece candle. "He died when I was ten. A coronary. Heart disease runs in the family."

Tristan slowly set down his glass. "I'm sorry about your dad."

"So am I. He was an exceptional man." She smiled

at a memory. "He taught me to French knit. You wind wool around small nails tacked into the top of a wooden cotton reel and pull the knitting down through the hole—" She cut herself off and, embarrassed, shrugged. "Sounds kind of lame now."

He searched her eyes. "It sounds as if you loved him very much. What did he do for a living?"

"He trained horses. We had stables. Dad got up every morning before dawn, even Sundays. His only vice was betting on the track. Not a lot, but always a few dollars each week."

Perhaps Scarpini had inherited his thirst for gambling.

Ella gripped her cutlery tight. She would not let memories of that man intrude tonight.

"I've never understood some people's need to gamble," Tristan said. "If they thought it through, did the research, they'd understand you lose more than you win."

Her smile was wry. "I think it's more to do with the high when they *do* win."

"Like a drug?"

She nodded.

"You like to gamble?"

She shook her head fiercely. "Not at all."

"I'm sure you've already guessed, neither do I. I only bet on sure things."

His gaze roamed her face and a delicious fire flared over her skin. While she fought the urge to pat her burning cheeks, he poured the last of the wine and changed the subject. "Do you have any brothers or sisters, Ella?"

She inwardly cringed. Not her favorite subject. "It's a matter for debate."

One dark eyebrow hitched. "Sounds intriguing."

"It's a long story."

He pushed his nearly clean plate aside. "I'm a good listener."

She studied him across the table, the encouraging smile, the thoughtful dark eyes, and right or wrong she wanted to share—truly be more than the house staff, if only for a night.

As the waiter cleared their plates, Ella searched for words and the courage to say them.

"I have a half brother."

"Doesn't look as though you approve."

"I have my reasons."

His eyes rested on her, patiently waiting for more.

Did she want to get that familiar with Tristan? she wondered. She was a private person, too. The quiet one at school. The wallflower at the dance. But she wasn't sixteen anymore. She was almost twenty-six and dining with a man she didn't know a whole lot about yet trusted nonetheless. If she was ever going to stretch her wings, now was the time.

Her fingers on the stem, she twirled her glass on the table. "Over two years ago I gave up my job to care full-time for my mother when she was diagnosed with cancer. The disease metastasized to her bones and…" Ella swallowed against the emotion swelling in her throat. "It affected her organs," she went on, "including her brain. Toward the end she sometimes forgot what year it was."

Since her fall down the back stairs eighteen years ago, Roslyn had been "delicate." She'd broken her collarbone and both legs and had lain in a coma for six weeks. Her bones had slowly mended, but her cognitive functions never fully recovered. She'd still been a happy, loving person, just a bit…slow.

A pulse beat in Tristan's jaw. "Taking care of your ill mother…that must've been hard for you both."

At times unbearably hard, watching the person you love most withering away, losing any capacity to care for herself. "Finally she begged me to find a place for her in some facility. I couldn't do it."

His voice deepened. "She was lucky to have you."

When he sat back, she could feel him waiting for the half brother to make an appearance.

She'd thought if she could banish that horrid man from her thoughts, memories of him might fade. She hadn't spoken his name in eight months, but the image of his face was as vivid as the day the police had banged on her door, Scarpini smirking alongside of them.

But rather than bottling it up, perhaps talking about it would help exorcise some of the pain, humiliation and anger she still felt.

She concentrated on the candlelight casting sparkling prisms off her crystal glass. "A few weeks before my mother died, a man showed up claiming to be my father's illegitimate son."

"You didn't believe him?"

That familiar battle raged inside of her. Was he? Wasn't he? Did it make a difference if they were related? she wondered. After the agony Scarpini had put her through, she had no desire to find out.

"He was very convincing…" She thought back. "But I didn't trust his eyes."

"The windows to the soul."

She looked from the candlelight across the table.

Tristan's eyes were clear and filled with unswerving strength and sound purpose.

"Drago Scarpini's were empty. He seemed to look right through me. And his smile…" Icy tendrils trailed down her back and she shivered. "His smile was cold. But he charmed my mother and tried to convince her that my father would want her to acknowledge him now." In a lowered voice, she confessed the rest. "I heard him speak with her about changing her will."

Tristan's chin kicked up. "Sounds as if he was an expert at befriending vulnerable women. A real predator."

"The doctors had given her a few months more to live but she died sooner than expected."

"And Romeo didn't get a slice of the pie."

Her throat constricted. She wouldn't tell Tristan the whole story. He didn't need to hear how she'd been accused of murdering her own mother. It was just too ugly. "After a lot of soul-searching, I decided to gift him ten thousand dollars from the estate."

Tristan looked disappointed. "Ella, you're not even sure you share the same father. Even if you do, he shouldn't have expected anything from your mother's estate."

"My lawyer said the same. But right now I don't have any desire to go through the ordeal of finding out if we are related, and the money was something I felt compelled to give." She half shrugged. "I guess to settle my conscience and be done with it."

There was no right answer, just the memory of her father and what he might have done.

"I'm surprised he hasn't hassled you," Tristan said. "Those types usually don't know when to back down."

A chill crawled up her spine. She had the urge to check over her shoulder, but she shucked it off and instead announced, "It's all in the past now."

The waiter took dessert orders and the rest of the evening they spoke about Tristan's work—the same important project he needed to discuss with the mayor. Ella was sorry when the evening ended and they arrived back home.

As they moved through the garage door into the kitchen, she put her bag on the counter and turned around. Tristan stood close behind her, his expression unreadable, his presence overpowering…his kissable mouth almost too close to resist.

Pressing her palms against her jumping stomach, Ella manufactured an easy smile. "Can I get you anything before we go to bed?"

She withered down to her shoes.

Bad choice of words.

"Thanks, no." His brow pinched. "But there's something I want to ask you, Ella. I have a function to attend next weekend. A black-tie affair. I wondered if you'd like to come."

The flock of butterflies she'd been holding released in her stomach. Was he asking her on a real date? Her? Little Miss Ordinary?

"There's a bigwig in property analysis going," he went on. "I'd like the chance to speak with him in a more relaxed setting, but it's a *couples only* night. Would you mind helping me out? After tonight, I realize you'd make the perfect companion for that kind of thing." He laughed softly. "I'll try not to make it too boring for you."

She closed her parted lips and willed the silly stinging from behind her nose.

So this was a business proposition?

Well, of course it was. Ridiculous for her to think anything else. Next weekend he wanted a date who was polite, presentable and knew her place. A platonic someone who wouldn't interfere with the business he wanted to discuss.

The housekeeper in her glad rags.

But she was being overly sensitive, she thought. Tristan was only being honest and it wasn't as if she had anything better to do.

Her lips curved. "Sure. I don't mind helping out."

"Excellent." He smiled but she glimpsed something else swimming in the depths of his eyes.

No, that was pure fantasy. The only stars in this room were in *her* eyes and she needed to see clearly or she was in danger of being hurt—and it wouldn't be Tristan's fault, but hers for being so silly.

And yet Tristan continued to hold her eyes with his, then his head slanted and he came a step closer. When he reached for her, Ella stiffened and her surroundings seemed to recede and dim. But he didn't kiss her. Rather he touched her left earring, his hand near her neck warming the skin.

His voice was husky, deep. "I've wanted to say all night…these are very becoming."

Could he hear her heart thumping? "They're not real," she managed to say.

"Pity. Diamonds would suit you." His gaze lingered, over her ear, down her jaw, along her trembling lips, causing a fire to flicker up her neck and light her cheeks. For a moment she thought he might lean forward and touch his lips to hers, that he might take her in his arms and kiss her as she'd dreamed so often that he would.

The possibility seemed to hang between them, real and weighted with temptation, but then he merely smiled and moved away.

"Good night, Ella," he said over his shoulder.

She let out her breath on a quiet sigh. "Good night."

She was about to float off to her bedroom when the kitchen extension rang. Tristan had gone, perhaps already on the stairs that led to his bedroom. She'd take a message. Nothing could be that important this late on a Saturday night.

"Tristan Barkley's residence." She waited but no reply. "Hello." Ella frowned. "Anyone there?"

As the clock on the wall ticked out the seconds, in a dark recess of her mind she imagined the hand clutching the other receiver. Had a flash of the face smirking at her irritation.

Slamming the phone down, she tried to catch her sudden shortness of breath. She touched her brow and felt the damp sheen of panic.

But she was overreacting. It was the talk of Scarpini over dinner and the fact the inheritance had come through that had her jumping to conclusions. That call had merely been a wrong number.

Still, before going to bed, she checked the back door—not once but twice.

Three

The following Thursday morning, Tristan swung out from behind his desk to greet his brother, who was striding into the city penthouse suite. Tristan clapped his arms around Josh and they gave each other a hearty hug.

When they broke apart, Josh jokingly tried to spin Tristan around. "Do you ever leave this office? I think you might be growing roots."

Tristan laughed, always happy to see his younger, wisecracking brother, who many people mistook for his twin. "Just because you're in love, doesn't mean the rest of the world grinds to a stop."

Josh's dimples deepened. "You sure about that?"

Tristan pretended to cringe. "Ooh, you have it bad."

"Bad enough to propose."

Tristan's jaw dropped. "Marriage?"

"Even got down on one knee."

Tristan took Josh's hand and shook with gusto. "Congratulations. That's wonderful, just…unexpected. How long have you and Grace been dating?"

Looking every bit the high-powered executive in his tailored business suit, Josh crossed his arms and rocked back on his heels. "Three months and I've never been more certain of anything in my life. Grace and I are meant to be. I can't wait to make her my wife."

Just yesterday it seemed Josh had been captain of the under-nines football team and had scrunched his nose up at girls 'cause they smelled funny. Now he was tying the knot? Tristan ushered Josh over to the wet bar. This news deserved a toast.

He found two glasses. "If you can't wait to exchange rings, I can't wait to welcome her into the family."

For some reason, an image of Ella came to mind— the sound of her soft laughter the other night, the subtle yet alluring scent of her skin. He couldn't remember a time when he'd been more relaxed with a woman over dinner. Guess it was par for the course, given she served him that meal maybe five times a week.

Obviously Ella had enjoyed herself, too, but from day one he'd had the impression she'd be easy to please. After hearing her background, he was more convinced than ever. A loyal daughter who'd cared for her dying mother for years…his respect for her had increased tenfold.

As Tristan reached for his finest Scotch, Josh ran a finger and thumb down his tie. "Welcoming Grace into the family brings me to the second reason for this visit."

Tristan stopped pouring. "You look worried."

"We're having a families' get-together Saturday afternoon. I want you to come."

Handing over Josh's glass, Tristan arched a brow. "Let me guess. What you're *not* saying is you want Cade to come, too."

"Besides the fact Cade and I work together, he is our older brother."

Before taking a sip, Tristan muttered, "Unfortunately."

Josh exhaled. "This feud can't go on forever."

Tristan crossed to the floor-to-ceiling windows and a view of the Opera House shells. The surrounding silky-blue harbor glistened with postwinter sunshine. Narrowing his eyes against the glare, he sipped again, clenching his jaw as he swallowed. "You're too young to understand."

"I'm twenty-eight and I *do* understand that Mum would roll over in her grave if she knew about the rift between you two. You both need to get over it and on with your lives."

"Because what Cade did to me wasn't reprehensible, right?" Tristan's voice was thick with sarcasm. If Josh even knew the half of it…

"If you're talking about the board voting him sole chairman over you not long after Dad's death, Cade offered to continue to share the seat."

If Tristan went along with every decision Cade made. In Tristan's book, that was called chronic egomania. No way could he agree to such terms.

Tristan turned to face Josh. "It was better for everyone for me to decline. The arrangement Dad put into place was never going to work."

He and Cade were to jointly run the largely family-owned Australasian hotel chain. Josh was to be incorporated into the combined chairman's role on his twenty-seventh birthday, which had, indeed, happened last year. If it were only himself and Josh running the show, no problem, they were great friends as well as brothers. But as for the eldest of the trio…

Tristan stared straight through Josh to the imagined figure of his adversary. "Cade and I have never got on," he growled.

Too much competition, only one person willing to budge. As the older brother, Cade had always called the shots, won the praise and Tristan had been expected to smile and follow.

"Profits were down," Josh recalled. "You both had different views on how to strengthen the figures. You wanted to borrow to refurbish the older hotels. Cade said the company couldn't afford the debt. The board agreed."

Tristan deadpanned, "Yet he found the money to buy me out."

"If I remember correctly, you were the one who suggested the split."

"And it was the best decision I've ever made."

He'd examined the refurbishment proposal from every angle and had been certain of its viability. But, once again, Cade had played God.

Tristan knocked back his drink and smacked the heavy glass down on a corner of his desk. The echo reverberated through the room like the fall of a gavel.

He'd gotten out from under the Barkley Hotels' weight and had started a property development company. No more kowtowing to big brother. This recent project would be his largest and most successful enterprise yet—*if* he got the nod on rezoning from Mayor Rufus.

Which brought to mind the other reason Tristan couldn't care less if he ever spoke to Cade again—the fact that Cade had slept with Bindy Rufus while she and Tristan had been dating. Minutes before she'd driven off without him and died in that auto wreck, Bindy had announced to Tristan that she preferred his more mature and wealthier brother.

Talk about a kick in the gut.

Thoughtful, Josh swirled the amber liquid in his glass. "Tristan, there's something else… I'd like you and Cade both to stand beside me when Grace and I say our vows."

Tristan shoved a hand through his hair and tried to laugh. It was either that or cry. "You're not making this easy for me."

Josh's smile was hopeful. "I want us to be a family again. All going well, one day soon you'll both be uncles." He pulled a card from his jacket's breast pocket. "Cade asked me to give you his cell number." He grinned wryly. "In case you'd lost it. He said to call anytime."

Tristan put the card on his desk and changed the subject. They chatted for half an hour and, as soon as Josh was out the door, Tristan found and crushed Cade's card in his fist. Taking particularly careful aim, he shot the wad into the trash basket.

He'd sort out something for the family get-together. He was happy for Josh. In fact, he envied him. Would *he* ever be fortunate enough to find a woman who didn't think of marriage as nothing more than an astronomical weekly allowance with a single child to cement the deal? A woman who wasn't a heartless gold digger as Bindy Rufus had so obviously been.

Ideally, he wanted a woman who was in love with the idea of half a dozen kids and believed in the wholesome riches of "family comes first." Wouldn't it be great if he could simply whip up the perfect wife?

Later that day, on his way through his building to a midafternoon meeting, Tristan passed a jewelry store and an item caught his eye. The price tag was horrendous, but the diamond and Ceylon sapphire earrings would look stunning dangling on either side of Ella's slender neck. The dazzling blue stones matched the color of her eyes precisely.

He walked away remembering the impulse that had gripped him when they'd stood in the kitchen after their dinner out almost a week ago. He'd wanted to bring her near and taste her lips, see how they fitted with his. Crazy stuff. She was his *housekeeper.* Yes, he was looking forward to taking her to the black-tie affair tomorrow evening. She certainly was sexy out of that drab uniform. But she was also a simple, unassuming and honest soul.

He frowned, then slowly smiled.

The perfect wife?

At the dining table that night, Ella poured gravy over Tristan's beef Wellington, feeling his lidded gaze not on the gravy boat but her arm—and inching ever higher. She bit her lip trying to tamp down the tingling sensation radiating from her center. What might happen if, instead of looking, he reached out and touched...?

The instant the thought hit, sizzling arrows shot heat to every corner of her body. She sucked in a breath and stepped back. She'd enjoyed their dinner out last weekend...perhaps a little too much. That time together had fed fantasies she'd secretly dreamed of for eight months. Fantasies about being a rich man's bride.

She held the gravy boat before her, a reminder of her place. "Is there anything else I can get for you?"

His jaw jutted before he nodded, and Ella's heartbeat skipped. Every night that he dined in, she asked Tristan that same question. He'd never once said yes. From the ardent look in his dark eyes now, she knew he didn't want more ground pepper on his potato.

He sat back, elbows on the chair arms, tanned, masculine hands laced over his lap. "Have you eaten yet?"

Worried, she examined his meal. Did something look suspect? "I was about to sit down to mine."

One corner of his mouth lifted. "In that case, join me."

Ella could only blink. She ate in the kitchen or in her room. She'd never sat at this long, polished oak table. Never.

Then understanding dawned. He probably wanted to discuss something he needed from her tomorrow evening. Perhaps he wanted to fill her in on some background of the people attending so there'd be less chance of her feeling out of place. But it didn't really matter what he wanted to discuss. If Tristan had suggested she eat with him, whatever was on his mind must be important.

She backed up toward the kitchen. "I'll get my plate."

When she joined him again, he was on his feet. After arriving home, he'd changed into jeans, the faded ones with the rip in the back pocket that sat like a dream on his lean hips. His white oxford was unbuttoned at the collar, revealing a V of hard chest and dark hair. His jaw was shadowed with daylong bristles that gave him a rugged look. A *sexy* look.

Ella swallowed.

And if she continued along that train of thought, she'd start to drool, which was *not* good etiquette.

He pulled out her chair. Holding her plate firmly in her suddenly buttery fingers, she smiled. "Thank you."

He pulled in his own chair and joined her. "I thought you might enjoy a glass of wine with dinner."

Her gaze skated to a bottle of red next to the condiments. He filled her crystal glass, which he must also have placed there while she'd ducked into the kitchen, then his.

After they'd both sampled the smooth-blend Shiraz, Tristan smiled at her. "Well, this is pleasant. We should have done it sooner."

Ella flicked out her napkin. If nerves weren't pummeling her stomach like a drumroll she might agree. It was very pleasant indeed sitting beside this über-attractive man at his dinner table, surrounded by fine things. The scenario was so unbelievable, she couldn't even have daydreamed about the possibility.

Slipping beneath his sheets isn't in the cards, either, she thought, but she'd daydreamed about that, and more often than usual this week…

"Do you have a gown for tomorrow evening?"

Clearing her throat, Ella fumbled to collect her silverware. "I picked up a dress today." It hadn't been overly expensive. She'd set herself a limit and had very nearly stuck to it. "I hope it's okay."

"I'm sure you'll look stunning."

His eyes crinkled at the corners and flames leapt up from the kernel of heat building low in her belly. He could smile at her like that all day.

"What color is it?" he asked, then tasted the beef and made a groan of appreciation in his throat.

"Kind of a lemony-golden shade."

"It'll go with your hair." Like a touch, his gaze trailed her long, loose braid, which lay over one shoulder, leaving a smoldering line in its wake.

She concentrated to stop her heart belting against her ribs and mumbled, "So the sales assistant said."

His lopsided smile lifted higher before his brows drew together, his gaze dropped and he cut his broccoli, which was bathed in a three-cheese sauce. "Were you going to wear those earrings?"

She remembered his hand near her cheek the other night and the buzz of sexual arousal that had ignited a flash fire over her flesh. She would melt if he ever touched her intimately.

She shook herself. As if that would ever happen. Supermodels. Starlets. Billionaire's daughters—they were the breed of women with whom Tristan normally kept company.

"I'm not sure those earrings will suit," she said, "but if you think I should wear them…"

Eyes still on his plate, he chewed slowly, then with a barely perceivable shrug dismissed it. "Totally up to you."

They ate in silence, Tristan deep in thought, Ella still

coming to terms with the current seating arrangements, until the phone on the sideboard rang.

Ella's midsection turned to ice. She hadn't forgotten that curious phone call the other night. Had it been Scarpini or her imagination working overtime? she wondered. Either way, the phone couldn't simply go unanswered now.

Stomach churning, she rose but Tristan put his hand on her arm. The contact was like the charge of an electric current and her heart catapulted and pounded all the more.

"They can call back," he told her.

The tension locking her muscles eased a fraction and her rubber band legs lowered her back into her seat. Letting it ring out was more than fine with her.

As the phone stopped, Tristan refilled her wine glass.

"The other night made me realize how little I know about you," he said, as if he'd suspected something untoward from her body language. But surely that was only her guilty conscience, she thought.

"There's not much else to tell." She slid her laden fork into her mouth.

"No surprises other than that half brother?"

Nothing he needed to know about. She smiled and chewed, letting him take from that what he would, but he wasn't satisfied.

"No royalty in your background," he joked, "Nobel Peace prizes. No axe murders."

She coughed as she swallowed. "Why would you say that?"

His smile was amused and a little intrigued. "Ella, I was kidding."

She let out her breath. Of course he was. He didn't know about Scarpini's wild accusation of murder. No reason he ever should.

She patted her mouth with her napkin and apologized. "I don't know what's got into me tonight."

"I do. You're preoccupied, thinking about starting a new phase in your life. You'll be missed." He collected his fork and explained, "You've been excellent at keeping every aspect of this place running smoothly."

Her cheeks heated. "You're being kind."

"I'm being truthful." He speared some potato. "I'm surprised no man has snapped you up."

It took a few moments for his words to sink in. He meant marriage. She groaned. "Now you *are* being kind."

His eyes hooked on to hers. "So you've never found the right one?"

For a short time, she'd thought she had—a doctor, Sean Milford. She'd been sadly mistaken. "There's a lot that goes into finding the right one."

"At the top of most women's lists would be a man who can support them."

She slowly frowned. "I'd much rather know I could support myself."

"Even if it meant cleaning houses for the rest of your life?"

Her chest tightened with indignation. What was he suggesting? "I worked in a doctor's surgery before I resigned to look after my mother. I could've found other employment if I'd chosen to. And I certainly wouldn't marry someone because they had money, if that's what you mean."

His smile was genuine. "I didn't think you would. But I wasn't talking about you. You're not most women."

Ella concentrated on his wry expression and it dawned. "You think the women you date are after your bank account?" She laughed. Had he looked in the mirror lately? she wondered. She waved her fork. "You're crazy."

"And you're naive." But his tone said he didn't mind. "So you'd be as happy marrying a plumber as a CEO of a conglomerate?"

"It would depend on which one I loved."

His lips twitched. "Ella the romantic."

"Is there anything wrong with that?"

He smiled that smile. "Quite the contrary."

He'd angled toward her, about to say more, when the phone rang again.

With a growl, he set his napkin aside. "Whoever that is, they're not giving up."

"I'll get it." She pushed back her chair.

Already standing, Tristan put his hand firmly on her shoulder. "Tonight you're a guest at my table. Allow me."

But she sprang up and wove around him toward the phone. "I insist."

He frowned then chuckled as he shook his head. "You're doing a lot of that lately."

She wouldn't have insisted if she weren't worried it might be Scarpini. She didn't want Tristan talking to that man, because it would mean explaining that sordid episode. And in two weeks, she'd be gone from this house for good. Tristan need never know about her visit from the police.

But she'd answered the phone dozens of times this week. No wrong numbers, no heavy breathing. No sign of Drago Scarpini. Nevertheless, her palms were damp by the time Tristan was seated again and she picked up the phone.

"Barkley residence."

Three beats of silence then, "Eleanor? That *is* you, isn't it?"

A concrete wall hit and knocked the breath out of her. She blindly reached for the sideboard and held on.

"If you're wondering how I got the number," Drago Scarpini said, "you can speak with the new receptionist at your lawyer's office. Thank you for the ten grand, by the way. It's a start."

The solicitor's office had given out her number? She squeezed the receiver. "I said under *no* circumstances—"

Ella stopped, but she'd already let slip the acknowledgement Scarpini needed. He was indeed speaking with Eleanor Jacob.

"The receptionist stumbled over herself giving me your number so that a brother and sister could get in touch again." He chuckled. "Some people are just so helpful."

She stole a guilty glance at Tristan, who pushed back his chair again.

"Is everything all right?" Tristan asked.

Her brow prickled as perspiration beaded on her upper lip and nausea rolled high in her stomach. Somehow she managed an unconcerned face, nodded at Tristan then turned and, into the receiver, said very quietly but firmly, "Don't call again."

His laugh was pure evil. "Eleanor, you can run but you can't hide. Not forever, anyway. See you soon, *bella*. Very soon."

As the line went dead, the floor tilted under her feet, like the deck of a ship going under. Her stomach twisted and the light seemed to fade.

Tristan materialized beside her, his supportive arm around her waist. "You're not all right," he said. "Who was that?"

Giddy, she gazed up into his stormy eyes. If she told him that was Scarpini, he'd want to know the rest. She didn't want Tristan to know…

Her father had told her once that mud sticks. In other words, bad opinions are darn hard to shift. Ella believed in being truthful, but in this case she didn't want Tristan for even one moment to picture her as her mother's murderer.

She made an excuse.

"It was a friend wanting to meet me for coffee tomorrow." Her voice was threadbare but not trembling, thank heaven. "I'd already told her definitely not. It would have to be next week."

The lie stuck in her throat. Not only did she hate fibbing, even for this good reason, but linking the word *friend* with Scarpini in any sense made her physically ill.

Tristan's brows nudged together. "You didn't seem pleased to hear from your friend."

Her throat convulsed. "We…have some things to sort out."

"Nothing I can do to help?"

She started to make another excuse, but he held her arms and willed her to look into his eyes. "Let me help, Ella."

She held her breath then crumpled and let the whole story spill out.

"The man who says he's my half brother—Drago Scarpini—that was him on the phone. He phoned a week ago, too, after you'd taken me to dinner that night. He said the money I left from the will was a start. He said he'd see me…see me *soon*. I'd hoped he'd go away, but—"

A bubble of panic caught in her throat.

"Hey, it's okay." Tristan brought her close and rubbed her back. His heat and scent wrapped around her like a warm winter cloak.

When she'd almost stopped trembling, he gently pulled away and looked at her more deeply. "Tell me the rest."

She garnered her strength. Since she'd told him this much, she might as well tell him the rest.

"The day after the funeral the police knocked on my door. They wanted to investigate an accusation…"

When she hesitated, he tipped up her chin with a knuckle. "An accusation of what, Ella?"

She swallowed. "Matricide."

"You?" When she nodded, Tristan laughed. "That's absurd." His amused expression dropped. "What evidence did they have?"

"More or less just Scarpini's accusation."

"More or less?"

"I administered morphine to my mother for the pain.

Scarpini said I overdosed her. I had her prescribed supply but he said, because I'd known a doctor, I could access more."

"What reason could you have for killing your terminally ill mother?"

"Scarpini was livid I hadn't given in to his threats. Whether he'd called the police to intimidate me, or he'd hoped that they'd actually charge me, I don't know. But he told them I was tired of looking after her. That she was about to change her will and I wanted it all."

"The worst kind of gold digger," Tristan murmured gravely.

His pupils dilated until his eyes were burning black coals. When he finally spoke, his voice was dangerously low. "How long have you known this man?"

She was a little taken aback. "I told you. Just weeks before my mother died."

He nodded, but the slope of his brows said he needed to absorb it. Could she blame him? His mind must be reeling.

"Tomorrow," he said, "we'll go to the police."

"No. *Please*."

She couldn't forget the way the officers had looked at her the day after her mother's funeral, as if, despite the lack of evidence, she was nonetheless a criminal. All those disgusting questions, the sensation of having her heart ripped out and trodden on again. She'd only ever tried to help her mother, yet she would always remember the cold suspicion shining in their eyes.

Mud sticks.

"Ella, this man isn't going to back off without a less-than-friendly nudge."

"I couldn't bear to go through all that again. The questions, the looks, riffling through the details of my mother's illness…"

He studied her pleading gaze for a long moment then nodded once. "It goes against my better judgment…but, all right. Only on the condition that if he calls again, you tell me straightaway. Now—" his hand curved around her jaw, "—I don't want you to worry, okay?"

She eased out a shaky breath. "I'll try."

And she did feel a little better. But the best remedy for worry, she'd discovered long ago, was keeping busy.

Her gaze skated toward the table. She'd lost her appetite and after that episode she wouldn't be much company. "I'll clear the table."

Crossing over, she swept up her plate, then his. When she turned, he was behind her.

He took both plates and set them resolutely on the table. "The dishes can wait. We have wine to finish."

Mere inches divided their bodies but with that call still echoing through her mind…

She touched her clammy forehead. "I think I've had enough wine."

"Are you that eager to get to the dishwasher?"

"*No.*" He grinned at her quick reply and she smiled weakly back. "It's habit, I guess."

"There'll be a dance floor and music tomorrow night." He paused. "Do you dance, Ella?"

She gave him a knowing smile. "You're trying to take my mind off of that phone call."

His head slanted. "Be that as it may…" He waited for her answer.

"I…have danced," she admitted.

With a playful tilt to his mouth, he measured her hesitant expression. "But not recently."

"Seems like a hundred years."

She bit her lip. Too much information.

"Do you know how to waltz?"

She didn't want to make a fool of herself—or him. "I'm really not very good."

"Then perhaps we ought to practice. I can put on some music in the living room." He took a step closer and the edge of his warm hand brushed against hers. "Or we could practice here."

The intercom buzzed, loud and unexpected enough for Ella's stomach to jackknife to her throat. She swung toward the door.

Oh Lord. It was Scarpini wanting in at the entrance gates, she just knew it.

Annoyed at yet another interruption, Tristan groaned and headed for the intercom panel.

"I can get it," she called after him.

"*I'll* get it. And if it happens to be your Mr. Scarpini, I'm more than ready for him."

Ella's knees turned to jelly. Eight months of calm, now the world was spinning out of control.

She straightened and pinned back her shoulders.

Whatever came, be damned if she would stand in the background, quaking in her shoes.

She followed Tristan to the intercom.

"Hello." Tristan waited a beat before one hand clenched at his side. "Hello, who is this?"

The reply was deep and familiar, but not in the way Ella expected. It sounded somehow like Tristan.

"Tristan," the disembodied voice came back. "It's Cade. We need to talk and we need to talk now."

Four

The relief seeping through Ella's system was so wonderfully intense, she almost laughed.

It hadn't been Drago Scarpini buzzing for access at the Barkley gate. As was true of most bullies, Scarpini was a coward, a cockroach. He wouldn't knock on Tristan Barkley's door and expose himself like that, even to get to the person he obviously still viewed as a worthwhile payoff, she thought.

Then Ella saw Tristan's face, his tanned complexion paler than she'd ever seen it. His nostrils flared as he stared at the floor, then he slammed the back of his fist against the wall.

Her stomach muscles clutched in reaction.

"Tristan?" she murmured.

He turned and glared at her as if she were the

enemy. Then he dragged a hand through his hair and his savage expression eased slightly. "Ella, you can clear the table now."

He stabbed a button to open the gates and seconds later a car rumbled up the drive.

Ella let out the breath she'd been holding. Whoever this visitor was, clearly he wasn't welcome. But that wasn't any of her business. She was an employee with a job to do and despite Tristan now knowing her dirty laundry, that hadn't changed.

Running her hands down her sides, she concentrated on slipping back into professional mode. "Would you like me to bring coffee?"

When Tristan looked at her, his eyes were filled with fire—or was that hatred? "He won't be staying that long."

Tristan strode off to answer the front door while Ella calmed her frazzled nerves. What was the visitor's name? Mr. Cade? She started toward the table and with leaden arms collected the dishes, then moved to the kitchen.

She'd never heard that name used in this house. But Tristan had a lot of business dealings to juggle. Sometimes business relationships turned sour. Ella rinsed the dishes while her thoughts churned over Tristan and his visitor, then Scarpini and his phone call.

She dropped her head and cursed the ache in her throat. Oh, how she wished that man would drop off the edge of the planet.

A blind clattered against a kitchen window. Ella's stomach gripped as her concentration snapped up. Her locked muscles relaxed when the scent of coming rain entered the room. Not an intruder, just a storm on the way.

Tristan preferred fresh air to air conditioning, but Ella hurried to close all the windows now, then remembered there were more open in the main living room where she'd vacuumed today.

A moment later, she thumbed on a living room lamplight and went to each window. After checking that the security system was still activated, she spun around and almost tripped over the vacuum cleaner she'd neglected to put away earlier. When she bent behind the settee to bundle up the cord, a man's raised voice permeated Tristan's closed study door.

Crouched behind the settee, Ella froze as her heartbeat boomed a warning in her ears.

Move, Ella. This isn't a position to be caught in.

About to escape to the kitchen, the study door swung open, slamming against the wall.

"Get it through your skull," Tristan snarled, "I will never agree to your terms."

"Never's a very long time," came that other deep and graveled voice.

"As far as I'm concerned, not long enough."

Curiosity won out. Ella peered over the couch and saw her boss speaking with a man. His hair was a shade darker than midnight. He was tall, with a commanding presence similar to Tristan's. The man stood angled toward her. Even at this distance she noticed his eyes, bright yet at the same time seemingly impenetrable…the color of scorched honey. As his gaze narrowed upon Tristan, the amber eyes flashed. But then he slapped his thighs, a gesture of defeat, and stormed away.

Ella slumped as the tension ran from her body. Seconds later, the front door thumped shut. As the echo thundered down the hall, Ella pushed to her feet at the same time Tristan strode past the room and spotted her.

He pulled up, his handsome face dark with fury. She'd never seen him so wild. In fact, other than last week when he'd thought some harm had come to her, Tristan had always kept his emotions well under control.

"Ella," he growled.

She forced her rubbery lips to work. "Yes, Mr. Barkley?" How easily she slipped back to formalities. Suddenly she didn't feel as if she knew him.

Tristan's shoulders came forward, then he closed his eyes and pinched the bridge of his nose. "Would you pour me a drink, please?"

While she beat a path for the crystal decanter on its trolley beside his chess table, Tristan moved into the room and sank into the settee she'd crouched behind. When Ella handed him the drink, he thanked her and knocked back half.

Head back, he concentrated on the ceiling. "You know how you don't like your brother?"

Drago Scarpini? She nodded. "Yes."

"That was mine. How does the saying go? You can choose your friends, but you can't choose your relatives."

She knew Tristan had a younger brother, Josh. But he'd never mentioned anyone named Cade.

A shudder crept up her spine. She wanted to ask what had happened in that room, in their past, for the anger between them to be so strong.

Tristan answered her unspoken question. "Cade wants me to go back and work for the family business."

"Which business?"

He flicked her a curious glance. "Barkley Hotels."

"Your family owns that?"

He leaned forward, holding his Scotch glass between his knees. "I assumed you knew."

He'd never mentioned it, nor had any one of the numerous guests he'd had to the house. Neither had she read anything in the magazines she flipped through.

Looking down, he swirled the liquor in his glass. "I don't suppose you should have. It's been a while since I left the company, and everyone and his dog knows the subject is banned from my ears."

"Because of your brother?"

He eyed her as if she might be withholding some interesting secret. "Sit down, Ella. Here next to me. I need your advice."

She couldn't help it. She laughed. "*My* advice?"

He patted the cushion. "Sit."

She sat. But, even with an arm's length separating them, she felt it—the sexual charge arcing between them like a powerful magnet.

But Tristan seemed oblivious to the sparks and the pull. He was preoccupied with what had transpired in his study moments ago.

He took another sip and let the Scotch sit in his mouth before his Adam's apple bobbed and he swallowed. "My brother's getting married."

"Cade's getting married?"

"Not Cade. Josh. They're as different as day and night. Light and dark. Josh wants Cade and me to mend our fences so we can play happy families at his wedding."

"And that can't happen."

He looked at her as if she'd said something prophetic. "Exactly. I won't forgive and forget."

"Why do you need my opinion?"

"I'd like a woman's point of view. Josh wants both of us to stand beside him when he says I do. I don't want to hurt Josh. But whenever Cade and I are within a mile of each other, volcanoes erupt. If I don't agree, I'll let Josh down. If I do, I'm afraid I'll hurt him even more."

She saw his point. No one wanted a scene at a wedding. "Cade feels the same way?"

"Cade is the eldest. He sees it as his duty to keep the family together, which in his language translates into manipulating everyone to his agenda, including getting me back on board at Barkley Hotels." Tristan huffed over a jaded smile. "You know what beats all?" His eyes grew distant. "I wish things were different between Cade and me. I always have."

Instinctively she reached out and touched his arm. It was an eye-opener to see this vulnerable side to such a masterful man. But it only made her respect him more. He was human.

He loved, even when he thought it wiser not to.

Tristan blew out a weary breath. "It's been one hellova day."

When his gaze found hers, the distance in his eyes gradually crystallized into something here and now, and the kindling that seared down below whenever he was near leapt high. That blush spilled down her cheeks again and she began to push to her feet. She felt uncertain, so out of her depth.

"Ella, don't run away."

Pressing her quivering lips together, she lowered back down. "I thought you might want another drink. And the washing-up's still there—"

"I don't want a drink." The hot tips of his fingers urged her chin higher. "I want to ask you another question. But there's something I'd like to do first."

That was all the warning he gave before he leaned forward and kissed her.

As his slightly parted lips lingered on hers—moist, soft, agonizingly inviting—shock set in at the same time fireworks exploded through her veins. A staggering heartbeat later, instinct took over. A tiny whimper escaped her throat and she leaned in, too.

When his mouth gently left hers, in the shadowed light she saw his dark eyes gleam.

"That was nice," he murmured, their lips all but touching. "We should have done this sooner."

Cupping her nape, he brought her near again, and before she could wonder whether this was good, bad or simply necessary, she submitted fully, her mouth opening to welcome more of his caress, her mind shutting down to everything other than the crazy, magical sensation she'd always known this man's embrace would bring.

Her hand inched up from his bicep, over his shoulder. Uncompromising masculine power. What would the sculpted rock of his body feel like beneath his shirt? What would she give to have him naked now as she'd seen him that morning?

But she wouldn't run from him this time. This time she wanted him close, as close as two human beings could get.

Yet, as the kiss deepened and Tristan's heat and hardness moved in more, Ella saw a flash of Cade Barkley and the emotion changed.

Even a man in control of his world could have an Achilles heel. Clearly Tristan's was his family. He'd been knocked off balance tonight. She didn't want this intimacy to go further simply because he needed to expend some pent-up energy and frustration. She didn't want to surrender this part of herself to serve a purpose that had more to do with Tristan's imminent need to dominate his environment and so much less to do with romance.

Breathless, she dragged herself away and murmured, "I'm sorry."

She couldn't meet his gaze. As desperately as she wanted to, she didn't want to read whatever she might see shimmering in those hypnotic eyes.

His voice was low and rough. "No. I'm the one who should apologize. Like I said, it's been a long day." He pushed to his feet. "We can talk more tomorrow."

As he left the room, Ella's tummy fluttered.

Tristan might have apologized, but he didn't say he wouldn't do it again. And the hunger his kiss had awakened inside of her made her wish he would.

Five

The following evening, Tristan smiled to himself when heads turned as he escorted his date into the prestigious hotel's grand ballroom.

He slid a glance at Ella's profile, radiant in the subdued candelabra light. She wore her golden hair down in long, loose ringlets. The style complemented the serene quality of her bone structure—small straight nose, classic rosebud mouth, a complexion that confirmed good health.

Last night when they'd kissed—softly at first, then with growing passion—he'd lost himself in a moment that had felt so incredibly right. Although he'd pulled back when she'd asked, truth was, now that he'd had a taste, he couldn't wait to have her in his arms again.

After her positive response to his kiss, he was certain

Ella would pay attention to the proposition he had in mind. Sexual compatibility in a marriage was, of course, a necessity. The off-the-scale sizzle factor they seemed to share was a most welcome bonus.

They wove through the glitter and pomp of the highbrow crowd and reached their table. Tristan pulled out her chair, noticing six places at the round table were filled, but two, aside from their own, were still vacant. He took in the nearest place card, Herb Patterson, the man he'd wanted to speak with tonight. When introductions were made around the table, Tristan was told Herb wouldn't be attending.

Ella leaned close to whisper for his ears only, "That's bad luck."

Tristan pulled his chair in more. Perhaps, but he wasn't upset because now he could focus his undivided attention upon the gorgeous woman seated beside him. Remembering that kiss, it was difficult not to sit a little closer, or find some excuse to touch her smooth, tanned skin, or to tell her about the proposition he had in mind—a civilized, sensible arrangement that should suit them both.

Following small talk around the table, which Ella handled superbly, entrée was served.

Above the lilting dinner music, Mrs. Anderson asked, "So, Ella, what do you do for a living? Do you model?"

Ella stopped buttering her bread roll to blink over at Mrs. Anderson. "Me? Model?" She looked as if she might laugh.

"Ella's my housekeeper," Tristan piped up.

Mrs. Anderson coughed on a mouthful of soup. "I beg your pardon? Did you say *housekeeper?*"

Tristan rested his hand on the back of Ella's chair. "Her desserts are heaven on earth."

While Ella's smile said she was a little embarrassed by the attention, Tristan felt nothing but proud. From the expressions on the other men's faces, they wished their help's looks and charm compared. Housekeeper turned perfect special-occasion-partner. If things panned out, she'd become much more than that.

Ella and Mrs. Butler, who'd married a successful dot-com entrepreneur, struck up a conversation that lasted through mains. By dessert Ella was sharing recipes with the other women, who vowed to pass the secrets on to their own cooks and housekeepers. Betty Lipid suggested Ella put together her own celebrity cookbook.

Ella sipped her dessert wine. "I'm hardly a celebrity."

Betty raised a brow. "But our Tristan is." She directed her next words to him. "And might I say, you're looking uncommonly well. All that good living?" She grinned. "Food, I mean."

Tristan didn't take offence. Let Betty Lipid and the others think what they would. In fact, soon he hoped their speculation over himself and Ella being more than employee and employer wouldn't merely be gossip. The more he considered it, the more a proposal of marriage seemed to fit. She was attractive, poised, attentive, demure—he'd bet a bankroll Ella would make a great mother. He'd always envisioned himself with a big family of boys. He wanted to be the kind of dad his father had never been.

He took in Ella's unsuspecting profile and his smile faded.

Her conversation with Mr. Scarpini last night was another reason this idea was a good one. Unless Scarpini was as stupid as he was cowardly, he would quit hassling Ella once he discovered her bystander-employer would soon become her protective husband.

Ella pushed away her mousse and held her stomach. "Delicious, but I can't eat another bite."

Tristan set his napkin on the table. "I'm done, too."

When he stood and took her hand, a look of terror filled her eyes. "What are you doing?"

"They're playing our song."

He tugged and she reluctantly got to her feet. "We don't *have* a song."

"We do now."

A step behind, she followed him out onto the dance floor. When he wound his arm around her, she stiffened, but as they began to move, her rigidity dissolved bit by bit. Positioned against each other like this, his body pressed lightly against her supple curves, he knew she was thinking about their kiss. So was he. He couldn't wait to sample those honeyed lips a second, then a third time.

But he could wait…at least until he got her home.

"Have you spoken to your brother?" she asked.

Tristan frowned. If she'd wanted to temper his mood, it worked.

"No, we haven't spoken," he replied. "But I'll need to, I suppose. Josh is holding a get-together tomorrow with his fiancée and her family. Cade will be there."

Her grin was wry. "Good luck."

Tristan's palm traveled to the dip in her back. "Would you like to come?" he asked, swaying with her, enjoying the up close and personal contact more than she could know. With her alongside him, the family ordeal with Cade present wouldn't seem half as unpleasant, which was a bit of a revelation. He'd never felt so assured about a woman's company before.

"Are they needing someone to serve?" she asked innocently, and he laughed.

"No, Ella, I want you to accompany me."

She blinked and her sapphire eyes sparkled. "How will you explain me?"

He played with a frown. "How *should* I explain you?"

She trod on his toe and they both flinched. "How about as the woman who can't dance to save herself?"

"You have other talents. You don't need to dance well."

She huffed good-humouredly. "At least you're honest."

"Not insensitive?"

"I can't imagine you ever being that."

Her lashes lowered and he gathered her slightly closer, smiling at the same feeling he'd experienced when he'd hired her months ago. This—*she*—felt right. Last night when he'd gone to bed, he hadn't been able to shake the image of how good she'd looked in that pink bikini. Then the bikini had vanished and he'd imagined them together in his bed. The more he thought about it, the more he wanted it. Wanted her.

With his mouth resting against the shell of her ear, he murmured, "You look stunning in that gown."

After a moment, she replied in a thready voice, "Thank you."

"But you didn't wear your earrings."

He deliberately brushed his lips against her ear again and smiled as a tremor ran through her.

"I'm afraid they wouldn't pass the 'are they real or not' test."

He grinned. Yes, those sapphire drops he'd seen in the jewelry shop window would have looked perfect tonight. But perhaps Ella didn't like sapphires. Some women preferred emeralds, others wanted only diamonds. He'd known a few women like that. "Do you have a favorite stone?"

"A gem, you mean? I've never thought about it."

He heard the note of strain and uncertainty mixed with brewing arousal in her voice and realized how much pressure his palm had exerted on her lower back. He was aroused too, and Ella, as well as the area above her thighs, would no doubt have recognized the fact.

Not feeling nearly as contrite as he should, he said, "I'm making you uncomfortable." She accidentally trod on his foot again. Hiding a wince, he pulled back and cleared his throat. "Would you prefer to sit down?

Her face was pained. "I think *you* would."

He chuckled and admitted, "Next time I'll wear steel-toe boots."

"You're a sucker for punishment."

"It's no hardship, believe me."

No truer words had been spoken.

He wasn't quite conscious of the movement, but as he smiled into her eyes, his head bowed over hers until her spine arched slightly back. He felt her intake of air and saw in her eyes… She wondered if he would kiss her again, here in front of everyone. And, God above, he was tempted.

Instead he found the strength to show some mercy and release her. On their way back to their table, they bumped smack-dab into Mayor Rufus.

Hiding his surprise—he wasn't prepared for this meeting—Tristan squared his shoulders. "George. I didn't realize you'd be here."

They shook hands and the mayor nodded once. "Tristan. Nice to see you." But the mayor's tone wasn't convincing.

Tristan set his jaw. He'd invested not only large amounts of money, but also his heart and soul into his current resort project. This man could seal the deal with a nod on rezoning, and just as easily run a red pen through and obliterate twelve months of Tristan's working life—geological reports, feasibility studies, copious meetings with architects.

Did Rufus still blame Tristan for his daughter's death? If he knew the entire story, perhaps Rufus would understand. Although the temptation was there, Tristan couldn't consciously tarnish Bindy's memory or scandalize his own family name, though Cade hardly deserved his loyalty.

The mayor turned to Ella. "I don't believe I've had the pleasure."

Tristan made the introduction, knowing Rufus would be remembering a time when his daughter had been the woman on Tristan's arm. "George Rufus, this is Ella Jacob."

The mayor smiled. "Are you new to town, my dear? I don't believe I've seen you at similar events."

"Ella works for me," Tristan said. The mayor would have discovered as much when he arrived for dinner in two weeks' time.

The mayor nodded as if that made some sense. "Personal assistant?"

"Housekeeper," Ella admitted.

The mayor's brow creased before his face lit up. "So you're the young lady who bakes a caramel apple pie to die for?"

Ella lifted a modest shoulder. "I've received a few compliments on that recipe."

"I'm looking forward to adding to those compliments. I presume Tristan told you I invited myself over for dinner?"

She smiled. "I'm planning something extra special."

"But caramel apple pie for dessert?"

"With your choice of cream or warm brandy custard."

The mayor chuckled. "I'll look forward to it." His smile tightened. "I hope Mr. Barkley is taking good care of you." He redirected his attention to Tristan.

Tristan inwardly cringed. Ella didn't know the full implication behind the mayor's words. But if he decided to take this relationship to the next level, Tristan supposed he'd best tell Ella the whole sordid story. He hadn't pushed Bindy Rufus toward her untimely death. She'd chosen her own path, which included infidelity with the worst possible partner.

A photographer with rumpled hair and an ill-fitting suit interrupted them. "Mind if I get a shot for the celebrity page?"

Tristan acquiesced and after some minor staging, the flash went off. Seemed he, Ella and the mayor would share the limelight somewhere in tomorrow morning's print.

The mayor bid them good-night and, back at the table, Ella stifled a yawn.

Tristan studied her face. He should have noticed earlier the shadows under her eyes. "You're tired."

"No, I'm not," she replied too quickly.

She didn't want to spoil his night. Sweet, but it suited him to leave. Now that he'd made up his mind, he didn't want to delay moving forward.

He was serious about pursuing the marriage-of-convenience proposition. For Ella it would mean a stable husband with the resources and temperament to treat her well. He in turn would have a wife other men would envy—the veritable girl-next-door with no pretences or ulterior motives. No headaches. No heartache.

Tristan's good humor dipped as he swept his jacket off the back of his chair.

Ella's naiveté was all the more reason to keep an eye on Cade tomorrow. His older brother had white-anted him before. No reason to trust him now.

He collected Ella's purse from the table. "It's almost eleven," he said, handing the purse over. "Time to call it a night."

Her eyes unwittingly flashed with gratitude before she shrugged. "Well, if you're sure you're ready."

Tristan smiled at his beautiful companion. He was more than ready.

During the drive home, Ella was floating.

She'd never attended an event quite like tonight's. Those people were some of the wealthiest in the state—in the *country*—but despite having had next to no sleep last night, she hadn't made a social blunder. The reason was clear. Her companion.

She looked across at Tristan sitting relaxed behind the wheel, his expression intent as the night shadows flickered over his classic profile.

He'd been the perfect escort, making her feel not only beautiful but…*special,* even when she'd trodden on his foot, not once but twice.

Ella dropped her gaze to her hand holding her knotting stomach. The night wasn't over yet. More than instinct whispered to her what was in store. Tristan planned to kiss her again. She saw it in his eyes and the tilt of his mouth whenever he smiled at her.

He'd obviously thought more about last night's embrace and wanted to test those waters again. What else did he have planned? How much was she prepared to give? she wondered. What exactly did Tristan want from her?

Possibly a brief interlude with an employee who would be out of his life in two weeks. Fulfillment of a curiosity with no lingering ties. Surely nothing more than that.

As Tristan drove into the garage, Ella tried to divert her thoughts. The dinner she intended to prepare for the mayor seemed a good topic.

"Do you know of anything special other than pie the mayor would like served?"

"Actually he's a big fan of clam chowder. His wife served it whenever I shared a meal with the family."

As Tristan shut down the engine, Ella unsnapped her seat belt. "I didn't realize you two were that close."

"Not anymore." He opened his car door. "Some time ago, I dated Belinda Rufus."

Ella looked hard at him. No mistaking such a unique last name. "The mayor's daughter?"

He nodded, then got out of the car and rounded the vehicle to escort her inside.

"We'd been seeing each other for three months," he continued, thumbing on the kitchen lights. "She died in tragic circumstances—a car wreck."

Ella was taken aback. "I'm sorry, Tristan."

He nodded then added in a low voice, "The mayor blamed me."

"Were you driving?"

He shook his head and leaned on the back of a kitchen chair. "I'd invited Bindy to a friend's wedding. Not far into the reception party, it was clear she'd had far too much champagne. When I suggested we leave, she stumbled out onto the balcony. The fresh air only made her intoxication worse. She must have known I wasn't impressed, but she wouldn't stop. I thought she was talking nonsense at first, and then she told me—" His Adam's apple bobbed, then he cleared his throat and scrubbed his jaw. "She said she'd slept with Cade the week before."

Ella fell back against the bench. "But why?"

"She seemed to take relish in the fact that Cade was the wealthiest of the Barkley brothers."

"Oh, Tristan. No wonder…"

"Although she obviously expected me to, I didn't explode. Instead I had this perverse urge to laugh." He sneered. "Big brother Cade was at it again."

She couldn't imagine feeling so betrayed. Scarpini might be her half brother—if, in fact, that were true— but Tristan had known Cade all his life. They'd grown up in the same house, shared the same parents. How could brothers turn out so differently? She hadn't known Tristan long, but instinctively she knew he would never act so appallingly.

He shrugged and pushed off the chair. "Perhaps Bindy wanted a duel at dawn. But it only crystallized what I'd been feeling more and more. We weren't right for each other and that confirmed it." Deep into his thoughts, he moved toward her. "Bindy stumbled away. A minute later I saw my car speed off. She'd had my keys in her bag. I followed in a friend's car, but…"

Ella continued for him. "She crashed."

He blinked then nodded once. "She died instantly." He took a deep breath and rubbed his forehead. "The mayor blamed me. Said I didn't take care of his little girl. He thought I'd tried to dump her and had broken her heart." A corner of his mouth pulled down. "What a joke."

So that's what the mayor had meant by that comment, *I hope Mr. Barkley is taking good care of you.* She'd thought his tone, if not his words, had seemed off at the time.

"What did the mayor say when you told him the truth?"

Tristan rolled back one shoulder and lifted his chin. "I didn't say anything. Bindy was dead. Nothing would come from discrediting her name to her father or anyone else."

"And Cade? What did he say when you confronted him?"

His jaw flexed. "We didn't discuss it."

"Never?"

Tristan's right hand fisted by his side. "Cade knows

what he did. What he *always* does. He thinks about himself. I have no desire to rehash it."

"But if Bindy was drunk…" Ella shrugged. "Well, maybe she got confused."

His smile was a sneer. "She wasn't confused about Cade's appendix scar or the 'cute' tick at its lower end."

She guessed scenarios such as this played out in real life more than people would like to admit, and not only among the rich and famous. Money and sex had the potential to warp people. Sometimes destroy them.

"And now you have to face Cade at this get-together," she said.

"I'll do it, but only for Josh's sake. And I'll behave. Hopefully Cade will, too."

He looked at her then as if there might be a deeper meaning to his words and she wondered. Surely it wasn't mistrust of *her* clouding his eyes.

They weren't a couple, and even if they were, she would never cheat as Bindy had done. If things weren't working out between two people who weren't married it was better to sever the relationship than continue to hurt each other. She'd followed her own advice when she'd called off her relationship with Sean. Apparently he'd never thought her good enough in any case…

Ella pushed away the ghosts from her past. That was all so long ago. Like Tristan, she didn't enjoy revisiting the less memorable pages of her personal history. And, remarkably, Tristan's skeletons competed with hers. They'd both been accused of killing a person they cared about.

Tristan moved closer. "Ella…there's something

else I feel we need to discuss." His gaze probed hers. "It's about us."

Her insides tensed as a thread of panic wound through her. Tristan was going to bring up that kiss. But after the emotion of that conversation—his being with another woman and her untimely death—she wasn't ready to go there, even to discuss it.

Curling some hair behind her ear, she slid her foot back toward her bedroom door. "Do you mind if we talk in the morning?" She gave him a weak smile. "I'm more tired than I realized."

His earnest expression deepened before he nodded and said, "Of course."

She slid back her other foot and smiled. "Great. Well…good night. Thank you for tonight."

He seemed about to say something more, then only nodded again. "My pleasure. Sleep well."

But Ella didn't sleep well. Anything but.

After tossing and turning for what seemed like hours, she wandered out to the dark kitchen for a glass of water. With her hand on the refrigerator door, she heard a shuffling noise, then a rustle. Her stomach pitched and she went cold all over. A light was shining down from further in the house, possibly the library. Then she heard stealthy footsteps on the tiles.

When Tristan appeared, she released a tension-filled breath at the same time their eyes connected in the shadows. He stopped dead before a warm smile spread across his face and he moved toward her.

One part of her wanted to retreat to her bedroom— she was dressed in a negligee, without a wrap. But the room was filled with forgiving shadows, and the air surrounding them was suddenly heavy with curiosity.

When he stopped before her, silver moonlight shining in through the window highlighted his broad, bare chest. The masculine scent of his body filled her lungs. How she loved that smell.

"You can't sleep?" His voice was a deep rumble that resonated through to her bones.

"Not a wink," she admitted.

"Me, neither." He slanted his head on a teasing smile. "Maybe we shouldn't sleep together."

She looked into his eyes and knew what he was suggesting—the exact opposite. She couldn't deny that the idea of sleeping together was frighteningly appealing.

As the seconds ticked by, the space separating them seemed to compress and at the same time stretch an agonizingly forbidden mile. Did she want to breach that space? The stillness of his towering frame told her that Tristan only needed her nod.

She quivered inside.

Should she?

Shouldn't she?

She wet her dry lips. "Tristan?"

"Yes, Ella?"

Her throat convulsed and she swallowed. "You want to kiss me again, don't you?"

His smile changed. "Yes, I do." He moved closer until his body heat seemed to meld with hers. "And I think you want me to."

Quivering again, she stepped away from her safety net and nodded. "Very much."

Six

When Tristan drew her close and his mouth covered hers, Ella gave herself over to a tingling tidal wave of pure pleasure. After the anticipation of wondering these past twenty-four hours, Tristan's kiss tonight was even more than she remembered—better than heaven, as if that should be a surprise.

As the strong band of his arms urged her closer still and he expertly deepened the kiss, she could have passed out from the blistering sensual overload. So many times she'd contemplated enjoying the intimate attentions of this powerfully attractive man. People were naturally drawn to and admired his superior bearing. Why should she be any different? She was only human, even if tonight *he* felt like a god.

Tristan's palm spread and pressed low on her back

as his other hand cradled and almost imperceptibly turned and kneaded the back of her head. Trembling inside, Ella clung to his chest, reveling in the musky scent of pure male and feel of flesh-and-blood granite. Such a moment should last an eternity, but now that they'd started, Ella wanted more.

More of what she'd glimpsed that day in his bedroom.

When Tristan reluctantly broke the kiss, he scooped her up in his arms and Ella's breath left her lungs in a soft exclamation of surprise. His heavy-lidded eyes lingered on her lips as he began to move out of the kitchen, toward the stairs…

The stairs that led up to his bedroom.

At a jab of alarm, her eyes must have rounded because he stopped abruptly and blinked twice. "I'm moving too fast," he said.

There was little doubt what he would expect when they arrived upstairs. And she was certain that's where he was taking her. In truth, wasn't a night in each other's arms what she'd dreamed of experiencing, too? It'd been so long since a man had held her, and this wasn't just any man. If that was Tristan's intention— to make love to her without reservation—shouldn't she grab the opportunity, as well as the memories that would last a lifetime? This wasn't a case of Tristan merely needing to expend some energy. Regardless of what happened after tonight, right now he truly wanted her as a woman.

And she wanted him, too.

Her tummy fluttered as she looped her arms around his broad neck.

"I'm game," she murmured, "if you are."

His eyes widened as if he were almost taken aback by her reply, but then his expression softened. "I'm more than game." He began to walk again.

"If we're awake at midnight you can wish me happy birthday."

"It's your birthday tomorrow?"

"I'll be twenty-six."

He smiled that sexy smile. "Then I guess we have some celebrating to do."

She crossed her ankles and sucked in a decisive breath. "I could whip up a cake." She liked chocolate torte, but Black Forest with lots of cherries was his favorite.

Holding her tighter, he mounted the stairs two at a time. "I don't want you in the kitchen, Ella. I want you in my bed."

They crossed the threshold into his room. The butterflies in her stomach went berserk when he flicked on a lamplight and the tawny satin coverlet and ruby-colored cushions of his king-size bed materialized out of the dark. She'd smoothed his sheets hundreds of times and had wondered about stretching out on them just as often. Difficult to believe that tonight her fantasies would finally come true.

He set her on her feet and his warm, steady hands slid down the sides of her satiny nightgown.

"This is nice." His mouth lowered to sample the curve of her neck.

She angled her head, shivering as she gave him better access. *Nice?* Was he referring to their new situation or her negligee? she wondered.

"I bought it the same day I picked up my evening gown."

Her voice sounded thick as his teeth slowly danced down her throat, making her flesh tingle and nipples bead tight. When her fingers found his head and flexed longingly in his hair, she felt his smile on her skin.

"Do you always wear this kind of thing to bed?" he asked. "Or were you hoping we'd bump into each other tonight?"

"I usually wear button-up pajamas."

His raspy jaw grazed as he kissed an adoring line of fire up her throat. "Tonight it's difficult to imagine you in anything other than French silk."

Through the haze of building desire, a vague sense of self-consciousness sparked. She wasn't like the women with whom he usually kept company. She wasn't at all…refined. "I don't normally buy silk negligees or spend a lot on perfume or jewelry."

"Then maybe it's time someone did for you."

His sultry admission threw her. But before she could think more on it, he found the bow at her cleavage and tugged the ribbon loose. Then he cupped her shoulders and, with a sculpting movement, dragged down the thin straps of silk.

The negligee slipped into a soft puddle around her feet. She sucked in a breath at a kick of raw, physical need as he brought her close, his long, muscular legs creating a V either side of hers. His rumbling tones resonated through her as his hands massaged her upper arms, drawing her up and toward him. He tasted the slope of her shoulder as if she were a fine delicacy.

"Is this okay?" he murmured against her skin.

Dissolving into him, she sighed on a delicious shiver. "*Okay* isn't the word."

His slightly roughened hands combed down her arms, detouring over her rump to scoop her in and up. Her breath caught.

He was so hard.

He took a seductive, lingering kiss from the corner of her mouth. "You're perfect."

If he hadn't been holding her, Ella would have swayed. And she could barely breathe. Every bubble of oxygen had been consumed by the fire raging inside of her.

He kissed her again—thoroughly this time, until her head spun and limbs floated away. When he left her lips and looked into her eyes, his gaze was hot and purposeful.

"Ella, I want you."

Her body tensed as trapped air burned in her lungs and stars began to dance in her head. The reality of having Tristan Barkley kissing her, telling her he *wanted* her, was overwhelming, almost too much to absorb.

His knuckle nudged her chin up and he searched her eyes. "Remember, if I'm going too fast, we can take it slow—as slow as you want to go."

She tried to even her breathing, to grasp what was happening and accept it. "Tristan…I…I…"

He blinked several times then let out a breath and pressed a kiss to her brow. "It's okay. You don't have to say it. It's too soon." He smiled as his gaze roamed her face. "Let's get you dressed."

Dropping onto his haunches, he found her negligee

at her feet. She wanted to pull him back up, tell him he was mistaken and then lock her lips with his again. But she stilled when his hands slid up her legs as he towed the fabric along. Halfway up, when he reached her hips, his progress stopped.

His warm breath lingered on her thighs, high where her legs joined and a hypersensitive spot had picked up on the heat of his mouth and had begun to beat and glow. She was agonizingly aware of how damp her panties were—how desperately, shamelessly, she wanted him to touch her there. If he did, she just might explode.

Like a warm, soft breeze, his mouth brushed her navel and a whimper of longing escaped from her throat.

"I don't mind you being shy, Ella. But I want you to know you don't have to be. You're beautiful." His mouth brushed again and his hands slid higher to hold her hips. "Just…please, give me a moment," he groaned, "then, I promise, I'll let you go."

He didn't wait for permission this time. Instead he tasted long, moist kisses that led down from her belly to her panty line. The warm tip of his tongue trailed back and forth just below the elastic as his fingers dug gently in, angling her hips even more toward his skilled mouth.

Tipping back her head, Ella sighed as her hands drifted to his hair. Tristan thought she was beautiful. He'd asked if she wanted to make love. And with every word—every wondrous graze of his lips—she wanted him more and more.

She was about to surrender all when his mouth left

her burning flesh. Pushing to his feet, he towed the negligee up with him, replacing the straps over her shoulders.

Ella exhaled as a chunk of her sizzling tension fell away. But she wasn't ready to let that feeling go. She wanted that scorching, drugging heat to continue. She wanted his mouth on her again, but this time she wanted it *everywhere* and all at once.

She cupped his stubbled jaw in two hands and willed him to see the depth of the need in her eyes.

"Make love to me," she whispered.

His brows knitted then his expression changed in a way that made her feel all the more desired. A way that made her simmer then burn. He studied her for a long, super-charged moment.

And took her hand.

He led her to his bed, ripped back the covers then sat on the edge of the mattress she'd covered with fresh, fragrant sheets that morning. Standing before him, she dropped her negligee then he slipped her panties off her hips, down her thighs. When she stepped out of the scrap of silk and stood before him completely naked, she felt at once released, totally free and at the same time incredibly vulnerable.

His warm hands on her waist drew her toward him, twirling her as he brought her down onto the cool sheets so that she lay on her back, partly captured beneath him.

His smile flashed in the shadows. "We'll toast your birthday with French champagne at midnight."

A tantalizing thrill rippled through her. "I like the sound of that."

Two fingers wove up the inside of her thigh. "I like the *feel* of this."

He proceeded to show her how much.

He caressed her body from head to toe, and with so fine a skill she wondered whether she would ever descend from the clouds. When she was beyond ready, when her breasts were on fire and her core screamed for sexual release, he found a condom in his side drawer, then, dotting meaningful kisses on her brow, he gently nudged in.

The breach stole her breath away. Yes, it had been a long while, and she hadn't had many sexual partners, but this…

This sensation was beyond anything she'd ever dreamed.

As her lips parted to take in more air, she opened her eyes and looked up into his dark, appreciative gaze.

"Relax." His voice was low and husky. "I don't intend to rush."

With the deep, steady thrum of his words drifting through her, his knee edged hers out a little farther, then he began to move with such a beguiling, animalistic genius, soon she couldn't remember a time before this. Before *them*. Her fingers trailed over the damp rise of his broad back and some insane part of her wanted to hold on—past tonight, into tomorrow and right the way through to next week and next year.

A few delicious moments later, all thought vanished in a blast of steam as an inferno gripped her low and wonderfully deep inside. Holding on to his hips, she cried out and clamped down around intense, raw pleasure—bright, throbbing, exploding sparks. Radiating waves pulsed through her, drawing another gasp from her lips, making her soar far away from any worry or doubt she'd ever had. She'd never felt more alive.

As the divine waves slowly ebbed, every muscle in his body locked above her. Her hands wove up between them, her touch reveling in the brute strength of his chest and his neck. She welcomed his final thrusts—his deep groan of pleasure and release—at the same time a serene knowledge settled over her.

This was what it was like to know a real man's love.

She wanted to know it again.

The next morning, Ella awoke feeling as if she were still in a dream. Lying on her side in the darkened room, she opened her eyes to a sliver of daylight spearing through a crack in the blinds. The air was still, the mattress soft, and on her skin—in her hair—she smelled him.

As sensual remembrances cascaded through her mind, Ella touched her lips. Her mouth still burned from his penetrating kisses. Her body glowed from a night that had been the most wondrous of her life.

A ball of nerves bunched high in her stomach.

Now it was morning. Was she still Tristan Barkley's lover, or was she back to being the maid?

Bringing the sheet with her, she carefully rolled over. Sound asleep, Tristan lay on his back beside her. One hand cradled his head on the pillow; his other arm was sprawled out at a right angle to his side. She could testify that his abdomen was indeed as rock solid as it looked. So were his biceps and barreled chest, which rose and fell in the steady rhythm of his slumbered breathing. A bristled shadow darkened his square jaw. His full lower lip was relaxed and frighteningly tempting.

He looked totally at peace, and every cell in her body begged her to wake him with the touch she now knew he liked best.

She fought the urge. They'd been up past dawn. He needed sleep. Then he'd need breakfast. She'd start with hash browns.

She eased away from him, but before her toes met the soft carpet, a hot hand caught her wrist.

"Where do you think you're going?"

Her attention shot back around. At the same time she saw his smile flash, he pulled her down. Her respiratory rate doubled as his fingers funneled through her hair and he brought her mouth to his.

When he deigned to release her, flushed with fresh arousal, she relaxed upon the plateau of his hard chest.

His eyes twinkled into hers. "Happy birthday."

Fully in his thrall again, she sighed. It was the best birthday in the history of the world.

"Are you hungry?" she asked.

"What's on the menu?"

"Hash browns and eggs."

After pretending to consider it, he frowned. "I don't think so."

She sat up, taking with her some sheet as a cover. "How about pancakes?"

"With maple syrup?" She nodded, but he shook his head. "What else can you offer?"

"Anything you want."

His expression sobered. "I'll have you."

A swell of emotion brought moisture to her eyes.

After eight months of fawning and only one night of passion, this couldn't be love. The overwhelming need to know his heat and masculine power against her…to hear the hypnotic rumble of his voice…

No, this couldn't be love, but it was something pretty close to it.

When he moved to collect her in his arms again, his gaze hooked to the right…to the clock on the side table. He cursed, and when she saw the time she knew why.

"When is the family get-together today?" she asked.

He fell back onto the pillow and groaned. "Too soon for me."

She lay back down facing him. Her hands beneath her cheek on the pillow, she surveyed his grave profile—his straight nose, the proud, jutting chin.

"Maybe Cade won't show up."

"Not his style," he said. "From the time he could talk, he needed to be the center of attention. Kingpin. At football, at studies…"

At women?

Her next words were a whispered thought that slipped out. "You'd never be second best to me."

When he darted her a surprised then thoughtful look, she wanted to add that she'd never meant anything more in her life.

She sucked down a breath.

Time to move before she said something really incriminating.

She sat up again. "I'll fix breakfast."

"You like taking care of people, don't you?"

She stopped and gave a mental shrug. "I guess so."

"Your mother, even before she was ill?"

She looked hard into his knowing eyes. How could he have guessed? Had it been her comment about her mother not coping with cooking?

"My mother had a bad fall when I was quite young," she explained. "Her physical injuries healed, but her mind stayed slightly impaired. She didn't cope very well after my father died. I helped where I could."

Moments before he'd passed away, her dad had asked Ella to look after her mother. She'd have done it anyway. Roslyn Jacob had been a good mother, just…disorganized, which was kinder than the things some people had whispered behind their backs.

Tristan reached to curl some hair behind her ear. "It's time someone took care of you."

Ella blinked as emotion rose in her throat. If she wasn't looking after someone else's needs, at the very least she was looking after her own. The idea of being cared for, rather than caring for others, was a concept she couldn't fully form in her mind. It was too…*not her*.

And yet, how wonderful if it could be.

His lazy smile broke the moment. "Before we do anything else, let's have a soak."

Mmm, what a nice idea. "You want me to run the tub?" His bathroom was an imported marble paradise, the spa bath more a small pool.

"I'll let you pour in the bubbles," he promised, running a fingertip down her arm, "if I can scrub your back."

"Just my back?"

He mimicked her teasing grin. "Already you know me so well."

Then, to prove his point, rather than leaving the bed, he brought the sheets up way over their heads.

Seven

An hour later, fresh from the spa bath, she and Tristan were in his car and on their way to his brother's house. It wasn't far into the trip before Tristan announced he needed to make a quick detour.

After parking, he ratcheted on the handbrake and turned to Ella.

"I need to grab something." He snatched a kiss from her cheek and smiled. "Won't be long."

She inwardly sighed at the tingling effect his kiss left behind. "I'm fine. Take your time."

She didn't mind the time alone. In fact, she'd take every minute she could to get her mind around what had happened last night…and this morning. Had she really spent such an unbelievable night with Tristan Barkley, her boss? Every time she closed her eyes, she relived the euphoria of their lovemaking. What would tonight bring?

Settling into her seat, Ella let her eyes drift shut.

Tristan hadn't been gone a minute before her car door swung open. She sat up, expectant.

"Well, will you look who it is."

Ella's hand flying to her mouth didn't muffle the sound of her gasp. Her pounding heart felt in danger of leaping from her chest. "What are you doing here?"

Drago Scarpini laid a forearm over the door window and leaned in. "Catching up with my long-lost sister." His grin was a leer. "Long time no see, sis."

The scent of his cheap aftershave worked on her senses like salts and Ella's fright turned to sickened anger. "You followed us?"

He ran an eye over the luxurious interior of the Bugatti. "Wealth becomes you."

Her chin lifted. "I suggest you leave. My boss will be back any minute."

"Your boss. Yes. I've done some checking. You started work for Tristan Barkley when you disappeared off the face of the earth eight months ago. You're his housekeeper." He raised a thick black brow. "Although, from the look, you're a little more than that. House-keepers don't passenger with their employer on Sunday mornings." She didn't notice the newspaper until he bent back a page and held it under his chin. "And they don't wear evening gowns and rub elbows with mayors when they work." His menacing eyes gleamed. "You've gone and landed yourself a whale, haven't you, Eleanor?"

Her fingers dug into her lap but she kept her voice

low and amazingly calm. "You don't know what you're talking about."

He pulled up straight. "I'm talking about you saving us both a lot of agony and agreeing to share some of your good fortune." The twisted smile fell from his face. "My patience is running thin."

Five minutes after Tristan had entered the jewelry store tucked inside his building's lobby, he left with an unmarked packet in his hand and a ripple of anticipation coursing through his veins. He'd bought two birthday gifts for Ella—a gold pen set to autograph that bestselling cookbook when it came out and those earrings.

He'd thought about buying a diamond ring to present to her when he put forward his proposal. Last night and this morning had only validated what he'd already known. She'd make the perfect wife and hopefully he was something near what she had in mind for a husband. She couldn't deny now that the barriers were down, they communicated well, in and out of the bedroom.

With his mind made up, he didn't want to waste time. He didn't want to risk her pulling a disappearing act on him like she had her half brother. Not that Ella had any reason to flee. The way she'd clung to him last night in his bed he was certain she'd be more than open to his proposition. A union—a marriage—that would suit them both.

When he hit the sidewalk and his gaze landed on the car, his pace slowed then came to a dead stop. Near the passenger side window stood a man—medium height, swarthy complexion. Tristan had the feeling he wasn't asking directions.

All senses swinging to red alert, Tristan picked up his pace, but by the time he reached the car, the stranger had seen him and slid around the corner. Tristan ached to follow, but seeing Ella staring straight ahead, looking dazed, he jumped into the driver's side instead. He placed the bag containing the gifts in the door pocket, then frowning, reached for her hand. It was icy.

"Who was that?"

She looked blankly at him at first, then awareness broke through the daze. "It was him. Scarpini. He followed us."

Tristan belted his fist against the steering wheel and swore. He jammed his key into the ignition. "We're going to the police."

"No!"

The same trepidation he'd seen the other night when he'd mentioned the law widened her eyes now. He wanted to empathize: she didn't want to churn up bad memories of being questioned after her mother's death. But, dammit, he couldn't let this slide.

"Then *I'll* talk to him," Tristan offered. How dare that man phone his house, follow his car, harass the woman he planned to marry?

Ella's complexion dropped another shade. "There's no need for you to get involved."

"There's every reason."

She gripped his hand. "If I stick to my guns, he has to give up eventually."

Tristan growled and, after a tense, prolonged moment, reluctantly nodded. "But if that bastard bothers you again, I won't be thinking—I'll be acting."

Her lips trembled on a grateful smile, then she let

out a breath. "We should probably get going or we'll be more than fashionably late."

When they pulled up outside of Josh's two-story Mediterranean-style home a short time after, Tristan's insides jerked. The new silver Porsche in the drive was Cade's.

He exhaled heavily. And the day had started out so well.

They walked in together, Ella's arm linked securely through his. There were perhaps thirty people dotted around the perimeter of the architect-designed pool, which faced a spectacular view of colorful yachts drifting over the harbor below.

Head and shoulders above the rest of the guests stood Cade, mirror aviator glasses hiding his haunting yellow eyes—their father's eyes.

Tristan's free hand clenched at his side at the same time Josh appeared, partly breaking the tension.

"Hey, big bother." After the customary bear hug, Josh held out his hand to Ella. "I'm Josh Barkley."

Returning the smile, Ella accepted his hand. "Ella Jacob. We've spoken on the phone."

Josh's frown was amused. "We have?"

Before Tristan could explain, Josh's fiancée, Grace, left off speaking with a middle-aged couple—her parents, Tristan presumed from the resemblance—and flung her arms around him. Tristan chuckled. Petite, blond, from a respected, well-to-do family and always with the friendliest of smiles—she was perfect for Josh. He wished them nothing but happiness.

Grace pulled away. "Thank you so much for coming,

Tristan. It means so much to us both." She held out her hand to Ella. "I don't believe we've met."

After Ella introduced herself again, Grace linked her arm through Josh's and looked between the two of them. "So, have you been seeing each other long?"

Tristan grinned. Straight to the point. He liked that. "Ella works for me."

Josh beamed. "Oh, you're *that* Ella. I've heard all about your talents in the kitchen. I could kick myself for not getting around to inviting myself over and enjoying them myself." He gazed adoringly at Grace. "Been busy with other things."

Grace's matching smile drifted to Tristan. "I think it's easy to see that Ella's much more than Tristan's housekeeper now."

While Ella blushed, Tristan linked his arm around her waist. Grace was definitely on the right track. And if everything went according to his plan, his and Ella's engagement announcement would come next.

Grace snuggled into Josh's arm. "Josh and I have been dating for three months." She dropped her voice. "If my folks are a little frosty today it's because they'd like us to wait. But we both know it's forever."

Josh smiled. "When you know, you know."

Tristan was aware that Grace's family fortune was equal to the Barkley brothers' coffers. She wasn't after Josh for prestige or security—just as Ella wasn't after his. Tristan wasn't forgetting that Ella would marry a plumber as soon as a CEO, the defining factor being love.

He had no problem with love, per se. Love would grow, but only after the most important pieces of a relationship were in place—trust, respect, friendship. The kind of common-sense, solid love his parents had never shared.

Grace took Ella's hand. "These two boys don't see each other half as often as they should. Why don't we leave them to catch up while you meet my family?"

Ella asked Tristan, "Is that all right?"

When Tristan saw Cade sauntering over, he understood that Grace was clearing the path to get any initial brotherly discord out of the way.

He nodded. "Go ahead."

As Ella and Grace moved off, Cade reached the men and put out his hand. For Josh's sake, Tristan gritted his teeth and accepted the gesture.

Cade removed his sunglasses. "Pleasant day for it."

Rather than look at his eyes, Tristan inspected the clear blue sky. "Yep."

"Apologies for intruding on your privacy the other night," Cade added.

"Don't mention it."

"I hope it didn't take too long for you to cool down after I left."

"Please don't concern yourself."

Cade's wry smile said he saw through the sarcasm. He slanted his head. "Don't suppose you've thought anymore about my offer?"

When Tristan took a breath, Josh must have anticipated the shrapnel about to fly and interrupted. "Why don't you guys come over and meet the rest of the guests?"

Tristan held his hand up at Josh.

"I'd like to answer this first." He served Cade an ice-cold look. "Like I told you the other night, there's nothing to think about. Nothing to discuss—now, later, here or anywhere else."

Pushing his hands into his dark trouser pockets, Cade muttered, "Still as stubborn as ever."

A growl rumbled in Tristan's chest. "And you're still as big a pain in the—"

"Hey!" Josh stepped in to physically separate the rivals. "Fellas, keep it nice."

After a tense moment, Cade tipped his head while Tristan scrubbed his jaw and grudgingly nodded once, too.

Josh was so much like their mother—fair hair, striking blue eyes, the mediator—while Cade was the epitome of their father.

A self-serving bastard.

Bristling, Tristan spun on his heel. He needed some space before he did something he might regret. He'd meet Josh's guests later.

Josh followed him to a quiet lawn around the side of the house.

One hand on his hip, the other cradling his hot forehead, Tristan glared at the ground. "He makes me want to kick something. *Hard.*"

"You two haven't changed." Josh walked past Tristan to collect a baseball off a far ledge and roll it from hand to hand. "Always competing."

Josh threw the ball. Almost, but not quite, taken off guard, Tristan caught it and grinned. Josh knew pitching a baseball had always been Tristan's premium way to let off steam.

Tristan concentrated on his target then shot the ball back. "Competition's a good thing," he pointed out.

Rigging Barkley's board decisions and sleeping with your brother's girlfriend were not.

They tossed the ball to and fro a few times before Josh asked, "I know you get hives whenever it's mentioned but, seriously, why don't you consider going back to Barkley's? Think about it. If you two could get over your rift, our hotels could expand to be world leaders."

Tristan smirked. Nice try. "Why not you and Cade?"

"Uncompromising success takes two hundred percent commitment. I want a life."

"And I don't?"

"Hasn't been evident lately." Grinning, Josh tossed the ball back hard. "Although you might have turned a corner now you've hooked up with Ella."

About to throw again, Tristan heard Cade's laugh, followed by a woman's. Josh had to duck when the ball left Tristan's hand and the wild missile almost took off his head.

Not waiting for Josh—no time—Tristan charged away. Cade was talking with Ella—only Ella—in a foliaged corner near the pool.

Tristan stopped before them. "Funny joke?" he asked, with not a drop of humour in his voice.

Ella sized up his expression and immediately sobered. "Your brother was just telling me about—"

"What?" Tristan growled at Cade. "What were you telling her about?"

Cade looked perplexed. *What an actor.* "We were talking about you."

He could just imagine.

Ella touched Tristan's arm. "Would you like something to eat? There's a beautiful spread."

"I'm not hungry," he ground out. "In fact, we need to go."

Cade bringing up Barkley Hotels again, then Josh, now this. Coming here had been a mistake. And it could only get worse. For Tristan, happy families time was over.

Lobbing an apology Josh and Grace's way, Tristan took Ella's arm. He strode off, Ella half a step behind.

At the car, he thumbed the automatic release on his key control and opened her door. When he slid in the driver's side and, still overheated, wrung the steering wheel with both hands, Ella spoke up.

"I know today was difficult, but you don't need to be upset about Cade and me talking. I was telling him how happy I've been working for you."

He slid her a look. "And that's why you were both laughing?"

Her brow furrowed. "He was telling me if anyone needs a cook, it's you. He said when you were seven, you once made your ice cream with chunks of cooking chocolate, a liter of milk and a can of whipped cream. You were so proud he didn't have the heart to turn down seconds when you offered."

A sweet story. Might even tug some heartstrings, but Tristan held himself firm. "A lot of water's passed under the bridge since then."

And he wasn't about to forgive and forget. Cade could keep his filthy mitts off Ella. The SOB would take her just to prove he could.

Tristan fired the engine and shoved the stick in Reverse.

"Are we going home?" she asked.

He thought for a moment then he threw his arm over the passenger backrest and, looking behind, reversed the car in a swift but precise arc onto the road. He planted his foot and the car sped off.

"I'd like to take you to a place I think you'd be interested in seeing." Somewhere that would get his sights back on the bull's eye.

They barely spoke during the thirty-minute drive. Not because Tristan was trying to be difficult…he simply needed time to shake off the prickling sensation left from his older brother's poisonous presence. When they parked on a vast and magnificent stretch of land by the sea, Tristan had regained a measure of his composure.

They got out of the car and Tristan inhaled the fresh, briny air. The rolling emerald waves always revitalized him; this particular quiet corner of the world seemed to hold a special kind of magic.

In a pretty blue-cotton dress and white sandals, Ella held her hair, which waved in golden ribbons around her head in the stiff breeze. "Tristan, this is *amazing*."

They strolled toward the ocean. "All I need is the go-ahead from Rufus and people from all over the world can come here to enjoy five-star comfort and a mega-star view."

He'd double his fortune. Who the hell needed Barkley Hotels?

She sighed. "Imagine living here. It'd be like living in paradise."

"A couple of years from now, anyone with an obscene holiday budget can find out."

She let go her hair and hugged herself against the cool wind. "You really need to do it, don't you?"

His gaze quizzed hers. "Of course I need to do it. I've spent a bucket load of money, I can't count how many hours—"

"I mean, show your brother you can be more successful than he is."

His stomach kicked. He shoved his hands into his pockets and looked back at the sea. "That's part of it."

They both focused on the crashing waves for a long moment before she murmured, "I know what you told me about Cade…"

He examined her hesitant expression and frowned. "Please don't say you don't believe me."

Her face filled with sympathy. "It's just…after meeting him today it's hard to grasp…how he could do something so abhorrent as seduce his brother's girlfriend. I couldn't help thinking how much he reminds me of you."

Tristan's lip curled. "People aren't always what they seem."

Even brothers. She might be naive in a lot of ways, but shouldn't Ella know that wolves grin just before they bite? Hadn't her half brother charmed her mother while trying his best to have her change her will?

They turned back and when they reached the car, he asked, "Can you wait here a moment?"

Her brows fell together but she nodded. He rounded the hood and opened his door. When he returned to the front of the car, he presented her with the packet.

She looked inside, saw the packaging and her face lit up. "A birthday gift?"

"Hope you like it."

Carefully she unwrapped the paper and ribbon and

sighed when she saw the gift. "A gold pen. It's so shiny."

He scratched the top of his ear. "It's to autograph that bestselling book you're going to write."

Her gaze jumped up and now she truly was smiling. "My cookbook?"

He nodded.

Her cool hand touched his cheek as she kissed his lips lightly. "That's so thoughtful. Thank you."

Drawn by her sparkling blue eyes, he fought the urge to go fetch the earrings. But he'd already decided to delay presenting her with that more personal gift until after he'd received her response to his question. *The* question.

He held her hand and gave it a meaningful squeeze. "I had an incredible time last night."

Her eyes shone with heartfelt understanding. "I'd think it was all a dream if we weren't standing here now."

"Ella, you're different from any woman I've known."

She laughed. "You mean the supermodels or the society princesses?"

He gave a crooked grin. "My point exactly. You're wholesome and uncomplicated."

Her left eyebrow shot up at a wry angle. "You must have forgotten my half brother, the stalker."

A muscle in his jaw flexed. "I'm not forgetting him. In fact, your situation with that excuse of a man gives my proposition even more weight."

Her head slanted. "Your proposition?"

"We're compatible, you and I."

Her warm smile told him she was remembering last night and this morning. "You could say that."

"I respect you, Ella."

Her gaze grew more questioning. "I respect you, too."

"Aside from that," he grinned, "you do amazing things for my libido."

Her cheeks pinked up. "You'll swell my head."

"Enough to say yes?"

"Yes to what?"

He filled his lungs and searched her eyes. "Ella, I want to marry you."

Eight

The sound of waves crashing faded beneath the sudden rush of blood in Ella's ears. The world was spinning, setting her completely off balance. She had to focus on Tristan's smiling eyes or risk toppling over.

"I'm sorry?" she croaked out. "Did I hear you right?"

Curling her arm around his, he lifted and kissed her hand. "I want to marry you. I want you to be my bride."

Her words came out a hoarse, disbelieving whisper. "Now I know I'm dreaming."

"Think about it. We'd be perfect together. You're everything I want in a wife. When you're with me, it feels…" His shoulders rolled back. "The only word is *right*. That feeling's been knocking at the back of my brain these whole eight months. This last week—last night—simply put it into sharp focus."

She coughed out a laugh. "At the risk of sounding clichéd, this is all so sudden."

He chuckled. "It is, but I wanted to put this to you sooner rather than later. I didn't want any chance of you up and leaving before I'd told you how I felt."

Yesterday she'd believed it was too soon to think about love. Yet today—now—every overjoyed fiber of her being was shooting her closer to that conclusion. Her growing feelings for Tristan had been a wonderful work in progress. She wondered if Tristan was saying that he was falling in love with her, too.

She smiled into his eyes. "How *do* you feel, Tristan?"

"Certain," he declared. "Convinced that we'd make an ideal pair. You won't want for a thing. Of course, we'll need to hire another housekeeper, not a live-in this time." His thumb brushed the sensitive inside of her wrist. "We'll want our privacy."

Ideal pair? Not want for a thing? She waited, hopeful, knowing there must be more. "And?"

His brow pinched. "Well, I wouldn't expect you to cook all the time, only if you wanted to. You'll be accompanying me to business and social events. I don't mind if we have a big or a small wedding. I'm thinking with your temperament you'd go for small." He thought for a moment. "What else would you like to know?"

The air seeped from her lungs. With each word the foundation of what he was suggesting became clearer. She pressed the pen set against her stomach as her insides clutched. "You're talking about an *arrangement?*"

Relief at her understanding shone in his eyes. "Precisely. An arrangement that would suit us both."

So, this proposal was for a marriage of convenience. The term sounded archaic, so businesslike, and yet Ella knew in her heart that her assumption wasn't mistaken. After feeling elated, now she merely felt numb.

The happiness she saw in his eyes had nothing to do with love. He'd had a run of ambitious women who, he believed, had coveted him for his money as much as anything. Now he thought *she* would make the perfect accessory. Wholesome, uncomplaining, anything-else-I-can-get-for-you Ella.

This was so far from the kind of proposal she'd expected from the man of her dreams. Remarkably, it seemed she was the woman of Tristan's dreams—but in a practical rather than emotional sense.

A thought surfaced and lit a spark of hope.

If she accepted his proposal—if they did become man and wife—was it possible he might grow to love her? she wondered. Was that too much for a lowly housekeeper to hope for?

She bit the inside of her cheek to stem the emotion building at the back of her eyes. "Can I think it over?"

He flicked a glance back at the car but then smiled. "It's an important decision. You *should* think it over." He stepped closer and set their clasped hands against his hard, hot chest. "Here's something to help you make up your mind."

His mouth touched hers in the perfect persuasive kiss. Almost persuasive enough to make her forget that at this point he was after a collaboration, not a soulmate.

Two weeks later, Ella still hadn't given Tristan an answer. They'd continued to share a bed and she'd con-

tinued to be his housekeeper. Tristan was delighted
with the first arrangement and not so pleased by the
second, though he didn't openly object to her continu-
ing to dust and iron. He was giving her time to think
his proposition through without any pressure, just as
he'd said he would. And given she hadn't agreed to his
proposal of marriage yet, she couldn't very well give
up her duties.

However, news she'd received today had as good as
made up her mind. She'd been stunned at first, but as
the shock had worn off, she only hoped that Tristan
would be as thrilled as she was.

She was pregnant. Having Tristan's baby. Whenever
she imagined the precious seed growing inside her, she
could barely contain her awe and excitement.

Still, she needed to keep the startling fact that they
were going to be parents to herself a few hours longer.
Tonight Mayor Rufus was coming to dinner. She didn't
want Tristan distracted from what must be the most important business meeting of his career to date.

If Rufus gave the nod on the land rezoning, Tristan
could go ahead with construction of his dream project.
This deal wasn't about money, it was about self-worth.
He needed this so he could move forever from beneath
the shadow of big brother Cade.

Ella added the final seasoning to the chowder, remembering the scrumptious hours she'd spent in his
bed. Tristan could be a shoe salesman and it wouldn't
matter a fig to her.

When the kitchen extension rang, her heart leapt to
her throat as it had every time the phone had peeled
these past weeks. But she was overreacting. She hadn't

heard from Drago Scarpini since that day by Tristan's car. Perhaps knowing she and Tristan were more than employee and employer had given him pause for thought. One look at Tristan's determined bearing confirmed he wasn't a man to mess with.

Wiping her hand down her apron, she picked up the receiver. "Barkley residence."

"Eleanor. You sound as charming as ever."

As her legs lost strength, she sank into the seat behind her. "It's you."

Scarpini only laughed. Gulping down a breath, she regained her composure. "You're wasting your time."

"On the contrary. I've invested too much time in this to give up now."

She wanted to fling the phone at the wall. Instead she kept her voice steady. "Tristan and I will go to the police."

"Oooh, Tristan and I," he sing-songed. "This does sound serious. Should I expect a wedding invitation in the near future?"

"That is none of your business."

He laughed again, genuinely amused this time. "So you've struck gold! Congratulations. I'm sure your wealthy lover won't miss the little recompense you throw my way."

"You don't frighten me. Nothing you say or do will convince me to give you a penny more."

"I'd rethink that. Tristan Barkley's a mighty fine catch. You wouldn't want to risk losing him."

She thought of the police that night, their wary, almost accusing looks, but she swallowed her fear.

Her chin kicked up. "I have nothing to be ashamed of."

His voice lowered to a deadly growl. "If you want to push me, be warned, I'll only push harder." His voice lightened. "I see the Barkley property gates are open. Seems like an ideal time to pay your fiancé a visit."

When the phone disconnected in her ear, Ella let her head fall between her legs as nausea pushed up in her throat and perspiration broke on her brow. Scarpini was obviously within walking distance of the house. The last thing she'd wanted was to bother Tristan with anything tonight, but she had no choice. Scarpini sounded deranged enough to do as he threatened and knock on the front door. What he intended to say, she couldn't guess. But Tristan needed to be forewarned.

Two minutes later, standing in the doorway of his bedroom—their bedroom—Ella pressed down a shaky breath and uttered the words.

"I need to talk to you."

Looking scrumptious in dark trousers and a crisp white shirt, Tristan finished securing a gold cufflink, checked his wristwatch then moved away from his mirrored wardrobe toward her. "Does this have to do with tonight's dinner? Are you missing some ingredient?"

If only it were that simple.

She shook her head. "Everything's prepared."

Her face must have been white. He cupped her shoulders and his frown deepened. "My God, you're shaking."

She opened her mouth, ready to blurt it all out, but the doorbell rang and every muscle in her body tensed.

Tristan's attention shifted and his hands dropped to his sides. "The mayor's early."

"It's not the mayor," she shot out. "Scarpini phoned. He said he's paying us a visit."

Tristan's expression clouded over until it resembled a thunderstorm. "He *what?*"

"I have no idea what he expects to happen when he gets here."

Tristan threw back his shoulders and strode out of the room ahead of her. "I've had all I'm prepared to take from that—"

His curses trailed behind him as Ella followed. Downstairs, when Tristan swung open the front door, she straightened, ready to face whatever might come. But Scarpini didn't stand on their doorstep. It was Mayor Rufus after all.

"George." Tristan ran a hand through his hair, looked past the mayor's shoulder then offered his hand to his guest. "Good to see you."

Accepting the gesture, the mayor's smile grew when he saw Ella.

Ella swayed on her feet, giddy with relief. If she and Scarpini had to have a showdown, she hoped it wouldn't be tonight. This dinner was too important to Tristan.

Somehow she willed her rubbery mouth to work. "Hello, Mayor."

He presented a labeled bottle. "I've been looking forward to this evening."

She reflexively accepted the wine. "I hope you're not disappointed."

The mayor flicked Tristan a glance. "I'm sure it'll be a memorable occasion for everyone."

Tristan's gaze scanned the shadowed front lawn before he shut the door.

The mayor frowned. "Are you expecting another guest?"

"There'd been talk of it, but I'm sure that's all it was. Talk." He gestured the mayor inside. "Would you care for a drink before dinner?"

Looking a little uncertain, the mayor nodded. "A whisky sour, thank you."

"Ella, we'll continue our conversation later."

While Tristan showed the mayor to the dining room, Ella dragged her leaden feet to the kitchen. Barely aware of her actions, she garnished the clam chowder.

When she delivered the first course, the mayor inhaled and patted his chest. "That smells delicious." She set the plate before him and he chuckled. "How did you know chowder was my favorite?" He quizzed Tristan. "Did you tell her?"

Tristan nodded. "I thought you'd enjoy it."

The mayor explained to Ella, "My wife passed away not long before our daughter—" His lips pressed together and he lowered his eyes. "Well, thing is my wife was happiest when she was in the kitchen."

Ella joined the dots. The mayor's wife had died not long before Bindy.

For a moment Ella forget her own dilemma. It was terrible to lose someone close. It must have been horrible to lose two people you loved within a short span of time.

She wanted to say something supportive. "Sounds as if your wife took great care of you."

The mayor's eyes grew distant before he looked at her more closely and smiled. "Good women aren't so easy to find."

When the men returned to their conversation, Ella slipped back to the kitchen. With her mind flitting between Scarpini's antics and the baby growing inside of her, she garnished the main course. In the dining room again, she retrieved the empty bowls, pleased with the mayor's compliments. When she returned with their meals, he and Tristan were discussing the land rezoning.

The mayor sipped his wine. "I don't see a problem, Tristan, but with one condition." He set his glass down. "The council would like you to donate a portion of the land to develop a harbor for a marina. You won't need to worry about management issues. We'll have someone look after that. But you will need to work together on the development and coordinating ongoing logistics."

Tristan sat back and rapped his knuckles on the table. "I have very specific objectives, George. After dessert I'll take you into the study and show you the plans—"

"I've already gone through them with the town planner in great detail. They're innovative, well thought-out and bound to afford you a successful enterprise."

The mayor leaned forward as Ella moved around his chair to pepper Tristan's meal.

"I've thought long and hard about this compromise," the mayor continued. "I'm happy with the rezoning as long as you'll cooperate with this marina. It'll mean increased employment opportunities and prestige for the area. The voters are eager to advance the community."

Tristan rubbed the back of his neck, his smile apologetic. "I've thought this through carefully, too. My investors are expecting a certain return and what you propose will cut into that profit."

While Ella topped off the wine glasses, the mayor's face reddened. "Son, the marina *will* bring money in."

"Not enough to compensate for the added head-aches."

The mayor's hand fisted on the tablecloth. "What you're saying is you're not prepared to bring in anyone else. Not prepared to consider anybody else's…"

Ella left the room and that conversation behind. She could think only of her stomach—a churning mass of nerves.

Would Scarpini show up? How would Tristan react when he found out he was going to be a dad?

Her mind half on the job, she opened the oven door. As she pulled out the pie dish, the phone's ring pealed through the room. Startled out of her skin, she dropped the dish and the noise of smashing glass exploded like a bomb blast through the high ceilings. A lick of hot caramel splashed her bare legs. She cried out in pain, and then bit her lip against the tears about to spill. What on earth else could happen today? she wondered in panic.

"What's going on here?"

Her breathing ragged, she tried to focus through the moisture edging her eyes. Tristan stood at the kitchen entrance, his face dark, his body poised for action.

She scrubbed the shaky heel of her hand across her wet cheek. "I dropped the pie dish."

He moved forward and held her shoulders as he searched her eyes. "Was that him? Did Scarpini call again?"

She couldn't look at him. "I've ruined dessert."

His grip tightened as his voice dropped to an urgent growl. "Ella, tell me."

She peered into his stormy, expectant eyes—eyes that said, I'm here… I can help.

She swallowed against the swelling ache in her throat and told him.

"I'm having a baby."

Time stood still before his jaw unhinged. Then he dropped his hold as if he too had been burned.

Ella covered her mouth. That thought had been pushing at the forefront of her mind for hours, but how could she have blurted it out now, at the worst possible time?

After a strained moment, color returned to Tristan's face. He kept his voice low. "We've been sleeping together two weeks. Is it possible?"

She struggled to order her thoughts and explain. "I needed a script for my hypertension medication."

He followed her thread. "High blood pressure…it runs in your family."

She nodded. "Today, during the check-up, my doctor asked the usual questions. I mentioned I was a couple of days late. We did a test." She swallowed again. "They're very accurate these days."

Tristan's frame tilted. His hip hit the counter as he dragged a hand down his face. "We're…*pregnant?*"

The mayor's disapproving voice broke the moment. "Congratulations."

Tristan swung around.

The mayor lifted a gray-tuft eyebrow. "I came to see if I could help. It sounded as if someone was being attacked."

"Nothing that drastic," Tristan groaned. "But it might be best to cut our evening short. I'm sorry."

"By the sound of it, you shouldn't be apologizing to me." The mayor nodded at Ella. "Good luck, my dear." His tone said she'd need it. "I'll let myself out."

When the mayor had left, Tristan faced her again.

Ella's midsection twisted. "He didn't look too happy."

"Don't worry about George. I'll work that out later. Right now you and I have something more important to discuss."

She took heart that he thought her news was more important than his pet project, but then she flinched. "Are you upset?"

"I'm surprised." The line between his brows disappeared. "But, no, I'm not upset. And I think this situation answers the question I asked two weeks ago. We'll get married as soon as possible. If I'm going to be a father, I want to make certain the child bears my name. No mistake."

A wave of relief washed over her. Her own father had been a wonderful influence in her life. Ideally, Ella wanted this child to grow up in a traditional household, which included two parents. Already she could imagine her baby's smile. She hadn't planned to conceive, but now that she had, she well understood how powerful maternal instinct could be.

The phone rang again. Ella jumped but before she could speak, Tristan strode to the extension and snatched up the receiver.

"Who is this?" He nodded and growled. "This is the last time you contact anyone to do with this house, do you hear me? You try this kind of stunt again and I'll see you in jail."

He slammed the phone down and strode back to Ella.

"I'll have a police friend from the neighborhood station track Scarpini down and pay him a visit to explain the situation—back off or face charges. I was ready to break that jerk's jaw before your news tonight. No way in the world is he getting near you now."

She opened her mouth, but he held up a hand.

"No reprieves this time. After I speak with my friend, I'll organize the paperwork and we'll fly to New Zealand for the wedding."

"You want to get married overseas?"

"New Zealand requires only three working days' lead time for Intention to Marry applications."

He *was* in a hurry. "In Australia you only need a month."

She knew because at one point she'd considered marrying Sean. What a mistake.

"I want to marry you and I want to do it as soon as possible." He took and squeezed her hands so tightly his grip almost hurt. "Ella, is there anything else you need to tell me?"

"I'd have thought you'd heard enough."

He didn't smile at her joke. "So there's nothing?"

She shook her head, wanting to ask the same of him. Was there anything he'd like to tell her? Perhaps that he was starting to see their relationship as something more than a mutually beneficial contract. That, after the wondrous nights they'd spent together, his feelings for her had grown. If they did in fact marry, would she ever hear the words her father had said to her mother every morning and every night?

I love you.

But while his expression eased, the words she longed to hear didn't come.

"Then Monday you should shop for a wedding gown," he said instead. "This time next week, you'll be Mrs. Tristan Barkley."

Nine

"You may now kiss the bride."

Hearing the minister's request, Ella clung to her lily bouquet and tried to convince herself this wedding—*her* wedding—was really happening. Smiling into her eyes, Tristan trailed two fingers around her cheek and lifted her chin until his mouth met hers.

His kiss was lasting and meaningful, an embrace that released ripples of joy through her bloodstream and filled her with the promise of what the coming years would bring. This morning they'd flown to New Zealand. As of this minute they were man and wife.

But it would take more than a consummation of their marriage contract to cement a true bond. Full commitment would happen when the light that had shone in his eyes just now transformed into words. Words of love she ached to hear and offer in return.

Tristan relinquished his hold and gently broke away at the same time the delighted minister cast back his cloaked shoulders and closed his book. "Now we only need to get some papers signed."

Tristan kept his smiling eyes on Ella. "And then it's done."

After the newlyweds had signed, a lovely couple who were staying at the mountain resort where Tristan had booked the honeymoon suite witnessed the document. With the minister's good wishes, Ella and Tristan left the reception lounge through a set of expansive, floor-to-ceiling doors, which lured them out to appreciate the spectacular view.

On the chilly balcony, Tristan stood behind her, drawing her back against his solid warmth and circling her waist with his arms as they gazed out over the soaring mountain peaks spotted with snow. The clean air was filled with a blend of spring bouquets, as well as laughter from a group of tourists wandering up the chateau's shrub-lined path.

Sighing, she leaned her head back against his chest. "I've never seen anything more beautiful."

He kissed her crown. "I have."

He turned her around so they faced each other. His hands laced together low on her back, he touched his forehead to hers. "Are you disappointed we didn't have a traditional wedding?"

Once she'd envisaged her wedding with a church full of people, mountains of flowers, her mother patting away a tear, her father proud and standing beside her...

Setting aside any regret, she answered truthfully. "I wouldn't swap today for anything."

He kissed her and she melted against him as the delicious heat in her belly spread lower. She was nearly breathless when their lips parted.

Grinning, he nipped her bottom lip. "I've organized a private dinner. I think we should go and enjoy the view from our room."

Her skin flashed hot at the thought of being alone with Tristan—his sexy smile, his sexier body. Her fingers kneaded his shirt. "I think so, too."

They hadn't made love since she'd told him about the pregnancy. Oh, she'd slept in his bed, and he'd held her close each night. There'd been no mistaking his state of physical arousal, but he hadn't gone beyond kissing, although she'd ached for him to.

He hadn't explained why he'd refrained. Perhaps he was coming to terms with the idea of becoming a married man. Maybe he wanted to keep their wedding night special, as if it wouldn't be anyway. Whatever his reason, in the dark when he'd held her she'd sensed his mind ticking over.

As they traveled up in the lift, she gazed down at the gold wedding band on her finger and, next to it, the dazzling tear-shaped diamond that effused a rainbow of prisms.

He'd proposed on the basis that they were compatible, that a marriage arrangement would work well for them both. Did he hope that his love for her would follow? She couldn't believe that a passionate man like Tristan would purposely—coldly—preclude love from the marriage equation, particularly now that there would be a baby. She had only to think of their child, the newborn she would hold in her arms one day soon, and her heart overflowed. Surely Tristan felt the same way.

When they reached their door, he swiped the card then swept her up into his arms. As her feet left the ground, the air whooshed from her lungs in a delighted rush.

Grinning, he kicked the door open and crossed the threshold. He didn't set her down until they reached the center of the room, where a table was laden with an exquisite array of fruits, breads, savory dishes and a silver-plated ice bucket chilling a bottle of champagne.

The ice crunched as he retrieved the bottle. A moment later, the pop of its cork reverberated through the room and foam frothed over his hand.

She laughed and he dropped a cloth over the bottle to stem the flow.

"Glasses!" Laughing too, he waved his free hand at the flutes. "Hurry!"

She grabbed the glasses and he poured.

When he set down the bottle, he raised his glass. "To us."

Suddenly overwhelmed by the significance of the moment, she raised her glass too and murmured, "To us."

As they sipped, she noticed a fire lit and crackling behind them. Despite the dropping temperature outside, the room was toasty and threaded with the subtle scent of rising heat and glowing wood.

He slid his glass onto the table. "I have an idea." He crossed to the bed and swept the gold brocade quilt off the mattress and onto the carpet before the fire. "Let's have a picnic."

She drifted over. "Mmm, very romantic."

"But I'm not sure we're dressed for the occasion."

Stepping closer, she ran a fingertip down his blue silk tie. "Maybe we should go change."

His smile was wicked. "There's no need to go anywhere."

He looped his arms around her and, keeping his eyes on hers, slowly unzipped her dress. "I'll say it again. You look beautiful in this gown, but after almost a week without you, you'll look even more beautiful out of it."

The dress dropped. Her cheeks glowing, she stepped out of the ripples of exquisite imported white silk.

He let out a long, low whistle at her new lacy lingerie. "That's *perfect* attire for an indoor picnic," he said. "I think we should kick off our feast with strawberries." He tipped his chin. "They're there on the table."

Falling back into her housekeeper role, she immediately crossed to fetch the fruit. When she returned, his head was slanted, his gaze feeding on each step of her advance.

Shifting his weight to one leg, he crossed his arms and grinned. "Have I mentioned how much I like your lingerie?"

Grinning back, she lowered the plate onto the quilt and then set her hands on her hips. Not so long ago she would have died of embarrassment to stand before him like this. Now she felt proud of the way his eyes danced.

"Would you like me to get anything else?" she teased.

He ripped off his tie and dropped it. "Suddenly I'm not hungry."

Grabbing her wrist, he brought her near. With his hands cupping her waist, he dropped his head to savor the slope of her neck.

She shivered with undiluted longing. "You know, we didn't have much lunch," she teased again. "Maybe we should eat first."

He flicked open the strapless bra clasp at her back. "We'll eat *after.*"

As his mouth closed over hers, her hands drifted up, impatiently undoing his buttons then dragging the shirt-tails from his trousers. He maneuvered her bra from between them and groaned against her parted, desperate lips, "Lie down."

Happy to oblige, she sank onto the quilt. Her eyes remained glued on his actions as he speedily stripped off his clothes then stood before her gloriously naked—every muscle pumped, hard and gleaming in the flick-ering firelight.

He joined her, his powerful chest hovering near, his forearms resting near either side of her head. But instead of taking her mouth, his lips trailed her throat toward her cleavage. When the hot tip of his tongue traveled over and around one nipple, rhythmically flicking the bead, she could've gone up in flames. His erection ground against her as his teeth grazed, tugging the sensitive peak until, half out of her mind, she moaned for him to stop.

He did. But only to roll onto his back and swing her

above him. When she straddled his hips, he snatched her panties' crotch aside then maneuvered her forward and back until she felt him throb and slide inside.

Filled with him, her movements stilled.

In awe, she watched the shadows flicker over his face.

Then slowly she began to move above him, his hands on her hips guiding her strokes, increasing her rhythm until all her concentration compressed in on the sizzling hub pulsing inside of her. As his fingers fanned over her abdomen, the pad of his thumb angled down between her legs and there he gently rubbed.

A bone-melting moment later, an inferno imploded then flashed electrifying white heat through her system. As his body locked then shuddered beneath her, her contractions kept coming until finally the flurry of sparks began to shower back down.

She fell on top of him, exhausted, exhilarated.

And in the shimmering afterglow of their lovemaking, when he held her close but didn't say the words, she didn't despair. They had time enough. Time for his love to grow.

They ate strawberries, some bread and dip and then they made love again, with less urgency this time, knowing they had tomorrow—times ten thousand.

They ate more and later lay in bed, under the covers. Ella curled up around his hard body and traced circles through the crisp hair on his chest. Her fingertip slid up to the hot, beating hollow of his throat and higher, over his raspy chin, then across the soft contrast of his perfect lips.

She felt safer than she ever had. Not least of all because Tristan had kept his word.

Last Monday he'd filed a complaint with his police friend who had located and dropped in on Drago Scarpini. Surely that would be the end of it. Unfortunately, Tristan hadn't yet been able to rectify the damage done to his negotiations with the mayor. George Rufus had been officially unavailable since last Saturday night.

Remembering that Tristan had checked his messages earlier, she pushed up slightly and rested her chin on her stacked fist on his chest. "Did the mayor return your call yesterday?"

Tristan's jaw shifted. "No."

"What will you do next?"

"Sit on it for now."

In other words, try to find a way to have his resort without giving up on his vision of it. If she hadn't dropped that dish—if she'd served up that dessert instead of smashing it all over the floor and announcing her pregnancy—perhaps Tristan would have had time enough to talk the mayor around to his way of thinking.

"Do you think you'll need to give in to his request for land for a marina now?"

His chest inflated and he shifted to cradle the back of his head in his hands. "Where there's a will, there's a way. There's a solution to the problem." In the fire's dying shadows, she saw his eyes narrow. "I just need to find it." He frowned down his nose at her. "But why are we talking about Mayor Rufus?" He craned slightly to kiss her brow. "Let's talk about what comes next for us. Let's talk about you and me."

She rolled onto her side and propped her head in her hand as excitement spiraled through her. "I'm all ears."

He scooped hair behind her ear, the way he did whenever he was thinking deeply about her. "We're going to have a big family, you and I. Seven children. Four sons and three daughters."

She stopped to quiz his eyes. "Are you serious?"

"Josh and I used to say we each wanted enough for a baseball team." He winked at her. "Want to learn how to pitch?"

She laughed a little nervously. "But, Tristan, *seven?*"

"What? It's a lucky number."

She chewed her lip. "If you really mean it, there's got to be a better reason than lucky numbers and baseball teams."

His smile faded. A muscle in his jaw flexed before he stared up at the ceiling and explained, "Our father didn't have much time for us. In fact, we rarely saw him. Josh and I used to goof around on the baseball diamond in the park, pretending we were dads coaching and cheering on our kids. The idea grew from there and just stuck."

She took in his deeper rationale then asked quietly, "Cade didn't join in the discussion on families?"

Tristan's mouth thinned. "Cade's so self-absorbed, I doubt he'd have even one. Unless it was a mistake."

Her stomach dropped and she pushed up on her elbow. "Like ours was a mistake?"

He brought her back down so they lay on their sides, facing each other. "*This*, my darling, was meant to be, just as the minister said, from this day forward. In fact, I brought something along, a wedding gift I'd like you to wear on our tenth anniversary and on our *fiftieth*."

She smiled. Surely those weren't the words of a man who saw marriage merely as a convenience. But before she accepted his gift, she needed to settle their previous conversation.

She eased back into it. "You must see lots of grandchildren on our fiftieth."

"Hopefully," he grinned. "Sure." Then his brows tipped together. "Don't you want a big family? I thought you liked looking after home matters. You seemed so excited about the baby."

"I *am* excited. But there's a difference between being someone's housekeeper and running a household that includes seven little lives."

Ella's cousin had had four children before she was twenty-three. She was happy when she wasn't totally exhausted. But Ella had always envisaged having maybe a pigeon pair so she didn't feel as if anyone would miss out on her love and attention.

His concerned face dissolved beneath understanding. "I don't expect you to clean the house or look after nine lots of laundry. As soon as we get back I will hire someone to take over your former duties. And when the baby comes, we'll find the best nanny in town."

Ella inwardly cringed. A stranger looking after her baby? Perhaps it was the way of the rich and famous, but she'd come from more grounded stock. "There are lots of things I don't believe parents should leave to a nanny. Like homework and sport days and bath time."

She'd always imagined doing those chores herself, bonding with her children along the way, being involved in every facet of their lives…just not seven times over.

"I can help with those things," he offered. "I want to."

That was sweet, she thought. "But you don't get home until late most nights. Young children need their sleep."

His brow lowered and he blinked twice. "What are you saying?"

"Only that producing our own baseball team sounds a little over the top."

His eyes narrowed almost imperceptibly. "How many children do you want? Surely not just one?"

He kept staring at her and the nerves in her stomach pulled tight. "We should have discussed this before…"

"Call me stupid but I assumed…" He frowned. "Seems I assumed wrong."

A light rap on the door broke the moment. Exhaling audibly, Tristan slipped out of bed. "Must be room service to finally collect the trolley."

After pulling on a robe, Tristan answered the door. An exuberant bellboy presented a gift basket. "Flowers and champagne, sir. From Mr. Joshua Barkley."

Tristan tipped the boy and brought the basket inside.

Ella pulled the untucked top sheet off the bed and around her then wandered over to inspect the arrangement. Lilies, orchids, roses… "They're gorgeous."

Tristan read the message. "This is more than a congratulatory card. Josh and Grace have organized a reception for us this weekend."

Ella read the card. It was short notice, but so thoughtful. That was a woman's touch—something she would like to do for a sister if she'd had one. She and Grace were destined to become fast friends.

Scowling, Tristan flapped the card against his thigh. "I won't be happy if Cade dares to show his face."

She threaded one arm around his neck and willed him to see the trust and, yes, love shining from her eyes. Was Cade the outright villain Tristan believed him to be? She simply couldn't believe it. Now that she was his wife, was it her place to say? she wondered.

She came up with a piece of less pointed advice.

"Try not to give anyone that power over you. It'll be our day. Let's just enjoy it regardless of who's there."

"Hell, maybe we should invite Cade over to share a toast."

He was smiling but his eyes were hard as flint.

A little hurt, she let her arm drop. "Maybe we should…if sharing a drink with Cade would help to get you two talking rather than arguing."

A pile of demons haunted Tristan…ghosts who whispered to him about childhood, Barkley Hotels and Bindy Rufus.

With an air of inevitability, he returned the card to its plastic slot in the arrangement. "I think it's time for a little family history to clarify things."

She tilted her head. "If you like."

A pulse beat in his jaw as he stared blankly at the flowers. "Josh was only nine when my mother died, too young to understand what had gone on. But I was thirteen, Cade fifteen. Our mother was an angel and yet our father couldn't resist sleeping with his best friend's wife." His chin tipped up. "She didn't leave a note, but I have no doubt my father's betrayal was the reason she took her life."

Feeling winded, Ella sank down onto the couch

behind her. After a moment, she got her thoughts together. "What does this have to do with Cade?"

His brows shot up. "Isn't it obvious? Like father, like son."

"He was your father, too."

"A man can also make choices."

"And part of those choices include what we choose to believe." He pressed his lips together, annoyed, but she wasn't finished. "Do you truly believe Cade is capable of such a thing?"

A moment of doubt flickered in his eyes before they hardened again. "You don't know my brother."

"Isn't it possible there's another explanation?"

"Sure. Bindy was in the operating theatre and stitched up the wound when Cade had his appendix out?" He set his hands low on his hips. "Why are you so eager to defend him?"

"It's not about defending Cade. It's about finding the truth and giving you peace of mind. You're ready to believe the very worst, but do you have any proof he slept with Bindy other than her word?"

Ella tried to remember what Tristan had said the other week. That Bindy's admission of infidelity had only crystallized what he'd felt more and more—they weren't right for each other. If Bindy had been aware of Tristan distancing himself before that night, she might have said anything to gain his attention. People could say and do some foolish things when they were smashed. Ella had only to remember Sean's behavior to be certain of that. The things he'd said that last night had turned her blood cold. Things like she was too plain and stupid for anyone to love.

"Ella, no one purposely sets out to despise his or her brother. You know that. He brought it on himself."

Or was it more that Cade's guilt made it easier for Tristan to walk away from the pressure of constantly needing to compete with someone who saw him, not as an equal, but rather as a younger brother.

But even if her intuition was right, Tristan wasn't ready to listen.

Rubbing the back of his neck, he turned toward the bathroom. "I'm going to shower."

Ella leaned back against the couch, her mind consumed by thoughts of today's ceremony and the conversation just now, as well as their future. Tristan didn't like to compromise. He liked to win. And he'd won her with so little effort…

She gazed down at her enormous diamond ring, which was a little too big for her finger, then laid that hand on her tummy.

She wondered if Tristan truly saw her as his wife. Or was she merely an employee who'd won a star promotion and the opportunity to produce his heirs?

Ten

Two days later they were back in Sydney. As Tristan stood among friends at the garden-party reception Josh and Grace had organized, he ordered himself to take a deep breath and chill out.

Over the previous two hours, a hundred or so guests had enjoyed a fine selection of finger food, gold label wines and a billion-dollar view, courtesy of the restaurant's vantage point overlooking the harbor, with the giant arch of Sydney Harbour Bridge glittering in the far background.

He'd caught up with friends from business and university. Grace had located some of Ella's friends, too. She was talking and laughing with one now. He sighed looking at his bride. She had no idea how beautiful she was, how she stood out in that simple yet exquisite red dress.

On their wedding day, he'd felt closer to her than ever before. When he'd made love to Ella, knowing his rings had glittered on her finger, he'd found himself considering their union beyond the parameters he'd initially laid out. For the first time since he'd hit on the idea, he'd glimpsed the possibility of their union being something more than simply practical.

But, although a romantic at heart, Ella had gone into the arrangement on the same basis as he had—compatibility, convenience and lastly the fact that they'd conceived. Those were the reasons this marriage made such good sense. And when their talk had turned to family size and later to Cade, any more traditional ideas—ideas concerning deeper feelings—had taken a turn, and not for the better.

They hadn't seen eye-to-eye on the size of a family. Just as troubling, she'd as good as sided with Cade on the Bindy Rufus disaster. He'd been a little on edge ever since.

"Your bride is a charming young lady."

Brought back from his thoughts, Tristan turned from the small group of his university friends to a colleague, Don Schluter.

Despite his recent niggling misgivings, Tristan had to agree. "Yes, she is."

"She's a lucky woman, going from her position to marrying one of the most eligible bachelors in the country."

Tristan conceded, "It doesn't happen every day that the housekeeper marries her boss."

Don's brows fell together. "Not her position as a housekeeper."

Tristan wondered aloud. "Then you knew about her caring for her ill mother?"

"Well…no."

"Working in a doctor's surgery?"

"I mean *dating* a prominent doctor for a short time then having it all fall apart. My wife was a patient at the practice and got all the gossip. Today she recognized Ella straight off." Don shook his head. "Horrible business when he came to strife, losing it all over some scandal or another. Of course she had the good sense to get rid of him before that was finalized." Don's banter and smile dissolved. "Surely you knew."

Tristan blinked several times then remembered to breathe. "She mentioned…something."

Don shrank into his collar. "Perhaps I shouldn't have said anything."

Tristan glanced over. Ella was no longer talking with her friend.

A depraved idea struck, his stomach wrenched and he jerked a look around. But Cade hadn't shown his face here today.

For Pete's sake, what was he thinking? He trusted Ella. He couldn't be wrong about her character. So she'd had an affair with a doctor and left him when his career had stalled. That didn't make her a gold digger. And, no, perhaps she wasn't certain at this time about the size of a family. That didn't mean she'd lain in wait for months, seizing the right opportunity to introduce a miraculous makeover and, soon after that, a surprise pregnancy.

She wasn't that kind of woman.

A waiter interrupted his thoughts. "Excuse, Mr. Barkley. A gentleman asked if I could give you this. He wasn't able to stay."

Setting his glass in the crook of his arm, Tristan accepted an envelope and, preoccupied, tore open the seal then pulled out a black-and-white photograph. He took a double take at the revealing picture. Ella hugging tight a man of medium height and swarthy complexion. A man Tristan recognized.

Drago Scarpini.

Tristan gripped and bent the photo as his surroundings warped and creaked around him. Ella hated Scarpini. All this time he'd been trying to extort her. So why was he embracing her in this photo?

He stuffed the photo back into the envelope as his body began to burn.

He needed an explanation and he needed it now.

Tristan lodged his glass on a passing waiter's tray, then, in search of her, strode around the corner. Astounded, he stopped dead.

Cut off from the other guests, Ella stood at the end of a far garden, surrounded by scarlet creeping roses. Tristan had been just in time to witness Ella's half brother grab her face and kiss her—with more aggression than affection, but a kiss nonetheless.

Josh's voice broke into Tristan's consciousness, which was framed by a building red haze.

"Hey, there you are!"

Tristan swung around and put up his hand. "One minute, Josh—"

But when he wheeled back, both Scarpini and Ella had disappeared. He looked closer then took a few steps forward. What was this? A magician's trick!

Grace was with Josh. "Tristan…" she asked hesitantly. "Have you lost something?"

Dazed, Tristan ran a hand through his hair. "I'm… not sure."

"Some guests are getting ready to leave," Josh told him, "but before we head off, Grace and I wanted to ask what you'd like for a wedding gift. She says a honeymoon in Fiji, I say a home theatre. I know you have one, but with the latest technology the audio is amazing." Tristan felt Josh's hand on his arm. "Mate, is something wrong?" Josh asked in a lowered voice. "Did Cade show up after all?"

Tristan shook his head. "For once Cade had the good sense to do the right thing and stay away."

Grace stepped in. "Is Ella okay?"

Dumbfounded, Tristan huffed. "I really don't know anymore." When they both simply stared at him, Tristan rubbed his forehead and backtracked. He didn't want to alarm anyone. "Sorry. It's been a big week."

But even as he spoke, his mind wound back and forth over the possibilities.

If Ella was afraid of Scarpini, why was she talking to him—here of all places? Why were his arms around her in this photo? He remembered how reluctant she'd been to bring in the law. Could it be? Was it possible they were in on this extortion scheme together? Some warped plan to filter out his money. Perhaps Ella had wanted to shake Scarpini now that she was married, and this photograph was Scarpini's ammunition to bring a double-crosser down or bring her back into line.

Or was Ella once again merely an unwitting victim in this? But that didn't explain this photo. That embrace.

He, Josh and Grace moved back to the main area and Ella was there, saying goodbye to a friend. Tristan held tight the envelope, watching her movements through different eyes. He wouldn't condemn her—everyone deserved a fair trial.

Ella was wound up tighter than a spring by the time they arrived home that afternoon. Striding into what was now their bedroom, Tristan seemed just as uneasy.

His face a mask, he threw his jacket on the bed then peeled off his black jersey shirt. Without looking at her, he walked to the bedside table and emptied his pockets. Steadying herself, she leaned on a wall and slipped off her red high-heel shoes.

Tristan had been a little reserved since their wedding night when they'd discussed the size of families and, later, Cade and Bindy. But his mood now was something else again, and the reason was clear.

He must have seen her with Scarpini at the reception. Perhaps he'd even seen Scarpini take the most shocking of liberties. When she'd told him to go to hell, he'd forced a repugnant kiss on her mouth. The last time he'd tried a similar stunt, he'd also taken her off guard, but given those circumstances she hadn't made a scene. Today, however, she'd shoved him and darted away as fast as she could.

Now she crossed the room, sat beside Tristan on the edge of the bed and took a deep breath. He was upset that Scarpini had found out about today's celebration and had dared to show up. So was she.

"You saw Scarpini there today," she murmured.

Nodding, Tristan kept his eyes on his feet. "I saw you with him."

"He stayed only a minute, just long enough to laugh about your police friend's warning. He said nothing would stop him getting that money. He said now I have plenty to spare."

She shuddered remembering his blazing eyes, his cheap cologne and the way his mouth had quivered when he'd demanded that she listen.

She hugged herself against a sudden chill. "He seems so...*desperate.*" Scarpini had grabbed her arm so hard she knew she'd have a bruise tomorrow. After showing up so brazenly today, she couldn't guess what he was capable of.

"Tristan," she murmured, "he frightens me."

Tristan stood and measured her with his eyes. He didn't seem half as upset as she thought he would be. Rather, he looked wooden.

"You can lay charges," he said simply.

She supposed now there was no choice. "He said that the men he owes want more money. I didn't think I'd ever say this, everything tells me it's wrong, but... Maybe we should give him something more, just enough to get him out of the trouble he's in. Maybe then he'll leave us alone."

Wincing, she dropped her head in her hands and groaned. That wasn't the solution. She'd thought the same thing a hundred times over, and giving in to Scarpini's threats—even if he turned out to truly be her half brother—wasn't what needed to be done.

Tristan moved to the mirrored wardrobe and slid the door back. "I was thinking today about your position here as housekeeper." He pulled out a button-down she'd ironed that morning. "You never said who told you about this job."

Ella's brow pinched. Why was he changing the subject? "It was my mother. She mentioned it the day before she died."

"How did she find out about it?"

Ella remembered back. "She said a friend saw the position advertised in the classifieds. Her daughter was planning to apply."

"The agency didn't print my name," he said without emotion.

She tried to see past his mask. "I'm sorry, but they must have."

Buttoning his shirt, he sauntered back over. "Your mother must have been disappointed when your relationship with the doctor didn't pan out."

A twist of sick apprehension curled in her stomach. She didn't like his dead tone or the steely look that hardened his eyes.

"I went out with a doctor for a time," she freely admitted. "Where is all this going?"

"I spoke with a colleague today who knew him. Or rather, knew of your affair. He said the doctor lost everything."

Ella blinked several times, unable to absorb where this conversation was headed. "Sean was sued for malpractice. He drank. It caught up with him."

"So you decided to cut him loose?"

She bristled. "He drank more after the suit was filed. He blamed everyone but himself for his misfortune, including me."

"You seem to get yourself caught up with less than scrupulous characters."

"I misjudged him."

"And Scarpini?"

"I never wanted to have anything to do with him."
Growing more indignant by the second, she lifted her
chin. "Now do I get to hear about every affair you've
ever had? I have a few hours."

Her fingers dug into the mattress either side of her.
She hadn't meant to say that. But she didn't like his
questioning, as if she hadn't deserved any kind of
romantic life before he'd come along.

"How did Scarpini know to find you here?"

She shot to her feet. "Is this an inquisition?"

His eyes were cool. "Should it be?"

She crossed her arms. Fine. She'd answer his questions. "He said he got the name from the lawyer's receptionist. He told her he wanted to get in touch with
his sister to thank her."

Tristan put his hands low on his hips. "I doubt any
solicitor's employee is that stupid."

A withering feeling fell through her middle. "Tristan, what are you accusing me of?"

His eyes narrowed almost imperceptibly then he
crossed to his jacket and pulled an envelope from the
pocket. The photograph he slid out and displayed made
Ella's stomach roil.

"Can you explain this?"

Her gaze lifted from the photo to the muscle
jumping in his jaw. "Someone must have taken it at
my mother's funeral."

"The funeral. Doesn't look as if you're running too
hard from him here. In fact…" He studied the photo.
"This is quite an embrace."

Her throat thickened. It wasn't how it looked. "I'd

just put my mother in the ground. Lots of people came up to console me. I could barely see through my tears."

He merely looked at her as if he was trying to see beneath the surface to something that just wasn't there—guilt.

"He sent this to you to cause trouble," she went on.

He huffed. "Yeah, well, it worked."

"He wants me to pay him off so he'll leave us alone."

Scarpini had told her not to push or he'd push back harder, and he'd been true to his word.

Expressionless, Tristan crushed the photo in his hand.

Her throat convulsed. "Tristan, don't you believe me? What other explanation is there?"

His narrowed eyes dimmed and then lowered. His hand with the photo dropped to his side. "Doesn't matter what I believe. I simply want this situation fixed. You're my wife. You're pregnant with my child."

She held her forehead, trying to fit the jumbled pieces together. "What you mean is you acted impulsively by marrying me and now you're paying for it."

"Don't put words in my mouth."

"Can you deny that's what you're thinking?"

He turned away from her. "We'll talk tomorrow when we have cooler heads."

Tears burned in her throat. She wanted to talk now. "I have a past, Tristan, and it's not squeaky clean. Neither is yours."

"I'm an open book. I don't hide behind anything."

"Then why haven't you come out and spoken to Cade about his sleeping with your ex?"

As he slowly turned back to her, his chin dropped along with his voice. "I don't need to lower myself."

"You said it…a man has choices, and you'd rather sooth your conscience by refusing to see the truth."

His nostrils flared. "Be careful with your next words, Ella."

She faltered, but she couldn't back down now.

"You haven't spoken to Cade because it suits you to blame him for Bindy's death. You have an excuse for your decision to abandon Barkley Hotels and go off to prove that you're bigger and better." She crossed her arms. "I don't believe Cade slept with Bindy and, deep down, I'd bet neither do you. You said she knew about his appendix scar. Could there be another explanation? Is it possible she'd ever seen Cade in a swimsuit?"

When he looked at her hard, frowned then blinked rapidly, she knew he'd remembered something connected.

Her shoulders went back. "I can't be sure why Bindy would've made up that affair. But I can guess. You'd begun to freeze her out like you're freezing me out now and she wanted to hurt you."

He scowled. "Don't twist things."

"If Cade is the villain you want to convince yourself he is, wouldn't he take pleasure in admitting the affair?"

"Not while he wants me to work for him."

"And that's the bottom line, isn't it? You're not prepared to work with him. It's your way or no way."

His jaw tightened. "I thought you understood the type of man I am."

"Seems we've been working at cross-purposes, then. You're the man who can't make a mistake so you wanted to believe I was perfect. I had this idea that I was only good enough to serve, so I put you on a pedestal like you were some kind of god—"

He threw up his hands and turned away again. "You're not talking sense."

She talked over him. "But the truth is we're both human."

They both deserved to be loved for who they were.

She stopped to think that through and suddenly the understanding and decision seemed clear. Resolved, she headed for the door.

His voice followed her. "Ella, we're not finished."

Her throat aching, she turned at the door to face him. "I think we are."

He took a step closer. "What's that supposed to mean?"

"Tristan…" Her nose stung as her eyes welled up. "I thought I could, but I can't…I can't live like this."

She wasn't a chattel, or an automaton. She had emotions. She needed to belong and to be loved and believed. She knew now that Tristan would never acknowledge that.

His eyes flashed before turning to cool black stone. "If you're planning on doing something rash…if you're thinking for one moment of divorce…" His throat bobbed then his jaw clenched. "I'm the father of that baby. I'll do what I have to."

"I know you will." She walked away before he could see the tears. "So will I."

Eleven

Early the next morning, Ella emerged from her downstairs bedroom to the sound of oil hissing in a pan and the smell of warm toast.

Tristan stood at the hot plates, naked from the waist up, a towel wrapped around his hips, a spatula in his hand. Sunshine streaming through the window lit his body from behind, leaving a silver halo around his bronzed, masculine frame. She almost sighed.

He glanced up from the pan and smiled hesitantly. "Good morning."

She frowned and, head down, moved forward. "You're cooking?"

"Eggs and mushrooms."

She inspected the pan as she passed. Nothing

burned. But she didn't offer to take over. Instead she crossed to the fridge and found the pitcher of juice.

Tristan returned to his work. "Would you like some?"

"No thanks."

He turned on the charm with a crooked grin. "I can vouch they'll at least be edible."

"I'm not hungry."

The pan hissed more. While he flipped eggs, she retrieved a glass, refusing to give in and ogle at the way his muscles worked down and across the broad expanse of his back. His hair was mussed. A lock bobbed on his forehead and his biceps flexed as he scraped to ease the egg from the pan.

He'd never looked more handsome.

"Did you sleep last night?" he asked.

Snapping back to reality, she averted her gaze and poured the juice. "I don't want to do this right now."

"You don't want to talk?"

"I can't pretend that what happened yesterday didn't."

Juice in hand she started back toward her former bedroom. She had a busy day ahead. She needed to get dressed.

His deep voice followed her. "I've had a chance to think things through."

Her stomach lurched and she gripped the glass tighter. "Let me guess. You've decided that you can live with your mistake if it means keeping your child."

"I've decided I may have jumped to conclusions."

At her door, she turned to face him. "And suddenly everything is better."

"I'm trying to mend things." Oil splattered in the pan. Growling, he jumped back, rubbing his six-pack where it must have hit and burned.

He looked like such a wonderful contradiction, for once out of his depth yet still master of his environment.

"Want to know something?" she murmured, almost without thinking.

He grabbed a tea towel and rubbed himself again. "I'm hopeless in the kitchen?"

"I love you."

His gaze shot up to find hers.

"I hadn't told you before," she went on, "because like a schoolgirl I was waiting for you to say it first. Marrying you was like a fantastic dream come true for me. But last night told me one important and very sad thing. For whatever reason, you feel trapped. As much as I'd like to pretend and tell myself you'll grow to love me, too—"

Her heart squeezed, but she found a resigned smile and shrugged. "I don't believe it anymore. And I can't live like that…not for all the money in the world."

"Ella—"

He started forward, but she stepped back.

"Please respect me enough not to patronize me and say you love me now. I deserve more. From this point on I'm going to put myself and my baby's needs first." She took a moment to be sure of her words. "And I'm not certain bringing up a child in this environment is best."

His brows fell together. "You don't know what you're saying."

"My father only ever treated my mother with respect, even after the accident. When she came out of her coma, she was still kind and loving but...different. Slower. But it didn't matter to my father. That's love. I won't settle for less."

His gaze lowered as he thought it over and he nodded, although she didn't believe he'd accepted her decision. When Tristan Barkley wanted something, he didn't give in easily.

Leaving him, she closed her bedroom door and headed for her wardrobe. Now she had to deal with Scarpini and knew exactly what to do. Go to the police. She should have done it a long time ago.

She heard the bedroom door thrust open. She spun around and Tristan was standing in the doorway, proud, tall, fire glinting his eyes.

His voice was low and rough with determination. "I can't let this end."

She stood her ground while her heart thudded madly in her chest. "This time you don't get to choose."

"You need to listen to me."

Two long strides and he caught her upper arms. Her body betrayed her, reacting to his touch, begging her to lean into him and believe he was the husband she wanted him to be—trusting and wholly in love with his wife.

Finding the strength, she put her palms against his chest. "A marriage can't be a business arrangement. Not my marriage, anyway. I can't live in the same house knowing that I'm not the convenience you wanted to find."

He focused on her lips. "Ella, you know how I feel about you."

Yes, she knew. She was supposed to have been everything he'd wanted in a wife. She'd fit the bill. But
now he'd found out that she was a woman with a past
and regrets like everyone else. And she hated him for
wanting her to be more than human. Yet when his grip
tightened on her arms and his mouth grazed her brow,
that knowledge seemed to evaporate as she trembled
with traitorous desire.

She meant to push against his bare chest, but instead
her fingers kneaded hot, tensed muscle. "This won't
change my mind. I already know we're compatible in
the bedroom."

"This isn't compatible. It's *combustible*." His mouth
trailed her temple, as his hand, moving to her behind,
urged her body firmly against his. "Tell me you don't
want me," he murmured against her cheek, against her
lips, "Tell me and I'll go."

She wanted to, so desperately, but the words
wouldn't form in her mind. Her thoughts were
consumed by images and sensations that left her
speechless. When his hands slid up to ease the robe
from her shoulders, she felt too weak to do anything
but sway.

"Tristan…"

"We're man and wife. You belong to me as much as
I belong to you. That's what you're feeling now. What
you can't resist."

She felt his towel drop from around his hips to their
feet then sighed when his mouth covered and claimed
hers.

Kissing her deeply, he walked her back toward the
bed. She wanted to tell him to leave and yet a voice in

her head whispered that this was the last time. The last time she kissed him, held him, made love to the man she would love forever.

"Well, this is a surprise."

Sitting in the stands of a vacant baseball field, Tristan glanced up at his visitor. An hour had passed since he'd followed Ella into her bedroom, since they'd made love with an energy and desperation he'd never experienced before. He'd believed he could talk her around. Convince her to stay. Instead, afterward she'd dressed and coolly asked him to leave.

Her face had been so set, he'd known it wasn't the time to push further. But he'd have gone crazy waiting for the chance to speak with and touch her again. So he'd made a phone call and had come here.

Now Tristan nodded at his brother, who had made it in record time.

"Thanks for coming, Cade."

In jeans and a black T-shirt, Cade took a seat beside him. "As if I wouldn't. What's up?"

Tristan leaned back, resting his elbows on the slats behind. The words came remarkably easily. "Josh is right. This feud needs to end."

Tristan heard Cade's sharp intake of air. After a protracted pause, Cade exhaled on a broad smile. "I can't tell you how glad I am to hear that."

Tristan forced himself to look into his brother's eyes—eyes he'd thought he'd grown to hate but now realized he'd only envied.

"If you want to know the truth…all these years I resented your success."

Cade scoffed. "My success? Sorry, but is this the class captain five years running talking? And if I recall you currently own one of the most successful property development businesses in the country." Arching a brow, Cade leaned back, too. "I think we're at least even in the success stakes."

"But you've never had to try." Tristan lowered his gaze. "I can't take my eye off the ball for a minute."

Cade laced his hands between his thighs. "I'll tell you a secret, one you already know. Inheriting money is one thing, but no one hands success to you on a platter. You have to work damn hard for it, make the right decisions—" his knuckles turned white as he clasped his hands tighter "—and sometimes be prepared to know you've made the wrong decision and still move forward."

Tristan exhaled. He'd known this was coming and he was prepared to concede. "You're talking about my wanting to refurbish."

Cade nodded. "I owe you an apology."

Tristan's mouth dropped open. *"What?"*

"You were right. We should have refurbished those hotels. It could have got us back on track much sooner. But I was scared witless we'd get ourselves in too much debt. I chickened out and the board is always ready to agree to the safe option."

Tristan tried to absorb the admission and apology. He'd lain awake some nights anticipating this kind of turnaround, but he'd never truly believed this day would come.

Cade continued. "I was tough on you, Tristan. Too tough. I only had the best interests of the company at heart, but I didn't blame you when you walked."

Tristan gave in to a grin and, leaning sideways, knocked his shoulder against Cade's like he used to when they'd been young. "Well, thanks for that. It means a lot."

"I should have said it sooner."

"Except I wouldn't let you anywhere near me."

Cade chuckled. "There was that." His expression sobered. "But a lot of things have changed. The biggest being Josh shares the chair now. If you came back on board, decisions could be made based on unanimous vote or best out of three. We wouldn't need to arm-wrestle every play."

Tristan went through the last two decades in his mind—their youth, the tumultuous time working together, what he'd achieved on his own.

He cocked his head. "Let me think about it."

Cade stuck out his hand. "That's all I ask. You'd be a fantastic asset to our company."

Tristan doubled back. "*Our* company?"

"The three of us," Cade confirmed. "You, me and Josh. That'll never change."

As Tristan studied his brother, his insides looped. Should he ask Cade about Bindy? he wondered.

But he didn't need to. Cade was big enough to admit that he'd been wrong about the refurbishment issue, and Tristan was big enough to admit that Ella had been right about so many things.

Cade might be ruthless in the business world, and he might look like their old man, but no way was he like him—not as far as cheating was concerned. When Ella had kept digging, he'd remembered that Bindy had seen Cade by the pool once briefly, but obviously she'd taken notes. Her wild accusation of Cade's seduction had been just that—a story he'd been all too willing to believe.

But that supposed betrayal had ratified Tristan's decision to break out into business on his own—to prove himself without feeling as if he were crawling out from beneath big brother's shadow and deserting the family business. He needed to acknowledge that now.

"Cade, there's something else I need to say." Lord, how to start? "I let myself believe someone's lies and it colored my view about you even more."

Cade clasped Tristan's hand and smiled. "Enough said. Let's just let bygones be bygones."

Perhaps Cade had somehow found out about Bindy's accusation, or maybe he was simply happier to let go of the bad feelings without more explanation. Either way, if Cade didn't want him to push, Tristan wouldn't.

Cade sat back again, squinting into the noonday mirages simmering over the baseball diamond. "We should drop by Josh's and tell him the news."

Tristan shook his head. "Not today. I have some major groveling to do."

"Don't tell me…your first marital spat?"

"It's a doozy."

Cade sucked air in between his teeth. "Can't help there. I'm a confirmed bachelor. But one piece of advice might fit. If you want something, work hard enough and you'll get it."

Tristan gazed at the empty baseball field. He didn't want complications. He wanted predictability, smooth sailing, an easy life. But he also wanted to protect and care for Ella, and be a real father to their baby.

Predictability.

Ella.

One cancelled out the other. So how the hell could he have both?

Twelve

Ella eased out a relieved sigh and smiled as she spoke into the phone receiver.

"Thank you, Mrs. Shelby. You've been a great help."

As Ella disconnected, a terrific wave of vindication rolled through her.

After Tristan had left, she'd pulled herself together enough to make a couple of phone calls. Just now she'd contacted her mother's friend. She hadn't seen an advertisement. Seemed her daughter had known the housekeeper Tristan had just let go and heard about the job that week.

Ella had also contacted the lawyer's office to inquire whether the receptionist had indeed given Scarpini her phone number. The new receptionist promptly transferred her to a junior partner who explained they'd needed to let the previous receptionist go; was there any matter she wished to discuss?

Ella declined. A complaint now would accomplish nothing. The junior partner's inference was good enough for her. If the receptionist had been less than competent, she could very well have erroneously given out personal details. While that settled the issue in Ella's mind—Scarpini had told the truth about how he'd obtained her phone number—she couldn't make up Tristan's mind for him.

Neither could she forget the look in his eyes when he'd shown her the photo of Scarpini stealing an embrace at Roslyn's funeral. When he'd rushed into his proposal, Tristan had envisaged a worry-free married life. Instead he'd got her. How he must curse the day he'd ever assumed that they'd make a "good pair."

The intercom buzzed and, shaken from her thoughts, Ella crossed to the communication panel on the wall. Her stomach muscles tensed as she reached for the button.

Oh, but she was tired of Scarpini's sinister cloud hanging over her. If he was brazen enough to show up at the gate, dammit, he could bring on his worst. Her next phone call was going to be to the police, anyway.

She depressed a button and her greeting was harsh. "What do you want?"

The intercom snapped back. "Ella, it's Grace. Can I come through?"

Ella slumped and opened the gates.

A moment later, Grace was at the front door, her pretty face pale with worry. "I hope you don't mind me dropping in like this."

"Of course not." In truth, Ella was glad of the company. "Can I get you anything?"

Grace laid her light jacket on the sideboard. "How about a zip for my mouth?"

Ella linked her arm through Grace's and led her down the hall. "What's happened?"

"Josh and I had our first quarrel."

"About the wedding arrangements?"

Big weddings were known to cause all kinds of differences. Who to invite, what cars to hire, whether the in-laws would cause any heartache—not that Ella had had to worry about those things when Tristan had sped her off to New Zealand. She'd chosen a gown, he'd organized the paperwork, they'd said their vows and that had been that. Done and dusted.

Grace lifted a coy gaze. "We argued about you and Tristan."

Ella frowned. "I don't understand."

As they entered the kitchen, Grace rushed it out. "We sensed the vibes at the end of the day yesterday. Things between the two of you were obviously strained. I wondered if it was something to do with the reception. If anything had upset you, I wanted to know. But Josh said to butt out. He doesn't understand that sometimes women need to talk things through."

Ella poured two coffees. "Men are different."

They were "doers," always ready for action, whereas females were more likely to rely on language. She wished she'd spoken more to Tristan about his proposal. But he'd seemed so certain, and she'd felt so strongly about him for so long. Then, when she'd found out about her pregnancy…

Her stomach knotted and she looked down at her tummy.

Her innocent baby was stuck in the middle.

They sat at a wrought iron table, the warm sun on their skin easing the strain. After Grace got a few grumbles off her chest, she came to the conclusion that Josh had been a little short with her because he believed Tristan would come to him if he needed to talk.

Then Ella confessed that she and Tristan were going through a rough patch because of a man from her past, but she didn't go into detail. She didn't want Grace to know how serious the situation had become. It would only worry her more.

An hour later, they were at the door, hugging and saying goodbye. As Ella wandered back inside, she smiled, knowing she was lucky to have Grace as a sister-in-law. No matter what happened between herself and Tristan, Josh and Grace would always be her baby's uncle and aunt. No matter what came, she wouldn't deprive anyone of seeing their family.

Wincing, she caught her forehead in her palm.

Oh God, she didn't want to think about divorce. But she simply couldn't go through life living with a man who valued her cooking over her heart.

Another knock on the door brought her back. Her gaze landed on Grace's jacket, still on the sideboard.

Understanding, she grabbed the jacket and called out, "Coming."

But when she opened the door, the garment slipped from her hand as dread drained through her like a poison.

Drago Scarpini didn't bother with pleasantries. He elbowed the door open and pushed his way inside.

"I'm leaving the country," he announced, looking around the pristine interior of the vestibule with a deep scowl on his face.

Willing her breathing and her racing heart to calm, Ella folded her arms. "Good."

"And you're going to give me a parting gift."

He named a price and Ella recoiled. "That's my entire inheritance."

He grabbed her arm. "Don't forget, as compensation for getting rid of me, you receive a hassle-free lifetime with Richie Rich."

She wrenched her arm free. "You can't intimidate me."

Contempt blazed in his eyes. "Miss high and mighty. You think you're so much better because you grew up with the nice family. You had my father while I had to listen to my grandparents refer to their only grandson as *the bastard.*"

Ella cringed.

"I got by," he explained as his spicy cologne assaulted her senses. "But I won't be satisfied until that man repays just a little of what he took from me when he left. And you're going to help me."

"You can't blame my father for not knowing he had a son."

Scarpini's hateful mouth turned down. "Jump in my shoes and maybe you can." He yanked her arm again. "So let's sort this matter out once and for all."

He dragged her down the hall, shuffled her into the kitchen and came across her handbag.

"Is this where you keep you checkbook, or is it in a drawer somewhere?" He wildly spun around. "Your bedroom maybe."

"No!" She tugged back. She didn't want any other man near there, particularly Scarpini. Beaten for the moment, feeling his hold tighten mercilessly on her arm, she ground out, "The checkbook's in my bag."

Grabbing the underside of the bag, he shook it and dumped everything out. Her brush clattered to the tiles, a lipstick twirled across the counter. Desperation drawing down his face, Scarpini trawled through the jumble and found his treasure.

A lewd grin crept over his face before he flicked the checkbook at her over the counter. "Write it to cash. And so you can't make any nasty phone calls, you're coming down to the bank with me."

She clenched her jaw in a bid to stop the shaking. "I won't do it."

"Sign. The." He slammed his fist on the counter. *"Check!"*

Jumping, she took in his crimson face, the dark warning simmering in his eyes. She closed her own eyes and prayed.

"No."

She yelped when he yanked her through the back doors and outside. With the checkbook scrunched in his hand, he forced her to kneel. As the gravel bit into her knees, he whipped out a gun from his coat pocket and held it to her forehead. Ella almost blacked out as a wave of light-headedness swept over her.

The cold metal nudged her brow. "You have a choice to make, *bella*. Make it the right one."

Fighting the nausea pushing up the back of her throat, Ella opened her mouth to speak. The growl of an engine rolling up the drive stemmed the words. She could have laughed out loud with relief.

Then she remembered the gun and her surroundings receded as the possibilities narrowed down to one.

Reading her expression, Scarpini grinned and repositioned his gun, aiming its shiny barrel at the back doors.

"Sign your name now, let me cash the check and I won't put a bullet through his head. And before you think of doing anything foolish—like trying to warn him—please know my solemn vow. If I don't succeed now, if you do anything to stop me from getting that money, I'll come back and finish the job."

Tristan parked his car in the garage, his thoughts crowded with his discussion with Cade, but more with how he should approach this crucial time with Ella.

She'd been right. In a way he had felt trapped, but it was a cage of his own making, built on pride and stubbornness.

How could he make this work? How could he make *them* work?

As he entered the kitchen, his step faltered and his frown grew. Her handbag was on the counter…dumped upside down as it had been once before. Fine-tuning every sense, he slowly eased around, his gut wrenching tighter as he completed a full circle.

He'd nearly panicked the first time he'd come across a similar scene. He'd been wrong about the situation, like he'd been wrong about so many things. But this time—today—felt different.

His nose lifted on a scent. Perfume?

The hair on the back of his neck prickled.

No, cologne. Something cheap.

He pricked up his ears… No sound. He crept to the living room and saw nothing untoward. But this intuition—the deep-seated sensation that something was very wrong—wasn't his imagination. He moved quietly to the side window and painstakingly pulled back a blade of the blind to get an angled view of the back lawn.

His heart jumped then crashed madly against his ribs. He had to bite his lip to stifle a growl of blind fury. Ella was on her knees and that lowlife, Scarpini, had a gun. Not aimed at her, but at the back door, anticipating *his* movements.

Tristan's hand curled into a deadly fist.

She'd said Scarpini was desperate and he'd dismissed it. Now he was paying the ultimate price. But this battle was far from over. That mongrel not only had his wife, he was holding Tristan's unborn child hostage.

As he watched, Ella scribbled something, and Tristan honed his vision. A checkbook? But how did Scarpini think he would get away with this? Or maybe that didn't matter anymore. Maybe Scarpini wanted this to end and he didn't care how.

Tristan slid away from the window and gathered his intelligence. But he didn't have time to sift through every scenario. He had to act quickly or that gun might go off and Ella was the closest target.

He threw a glance toward the kitchen door.

He'd left the garage door open. Grabbing an orange from the fruit bowl, he focused to calm his voice, pretending to suspect nothing so as to put Scarpini off his game.

"Hey, Ella! You here?"

No reply, of course, although he might have expected Scarpini to have her answer to lure him outside—a sitting duck for target practice.

Tristan crept out of the kitchen, through the garage. Counting each heartbeat, he stalked along the side of the house until he edged his nose around the corner. Ella's head was down, resigned but also courageous.

The woman he loved.

The woman Tristan knew in that moment he would always love and be willing to die for.

Scarpini had his back to Tristan. With the check in one hand, the gun in the other, Scarpini held his gaze on the back door and began to reverse—one step, then two—no doubt hoping to escape. Tristan stepped out into the open, took aim then filled his lungs to capacity and called out.

"Scarpini!"

The other man whirled around. Tristan had barely enough time to register the shock on his face before he pitched the orange. At the same time the orange hit Scarpini's hand, the gun went off. Leaping into action, Ella scrambled and dived on the gun. With shaking hands, she leveled it at Scarpini.

She chanced a glance to her right and quivered out a thankful smile. "You've got quite an arm there."

Rushing over, Tristan took the gun from her, his eyes on Scarpini the whole time. "Thanks," he replied, and then unclipped the cell phone from his belt. "Call the police."

She brushed her knees and took the phone. "With pleasure."

Tristan spoke to a sneering Scarpini, who had grudgingly raised his hands in the air. "And you…don't twitch a muscle. At this range I can't miss." Tristan grinned. "And, believe me, I don't want to."

Thirteen

Later that day, Ella stood at the front door beside Tristan as he bid his police friend, Detective Sergeant William Peters, goodbye.

Tristan shook the sergeant's hand. "Thanks, Bill. I appreciate you taking care of this."

"It'll give me the greatest pleasure to make sure every document and shred of evidence is locked in. This creep won't get out of a hefty prison term." His chin came down. "I'll see you both down at the station tomorrow morning for your statements."

Tristan nodded. "Bright and early."

The sergeant spoke to Ella. "Afternoon, Mrs. Barkley." He tipped his head. "You're a gutsy lady."

As Tristan closed the door, Ella tried to fathom what would come next. Today had been a tumult of emotion and activity. It was difficult to believe the long, tragic episode with Scarpini was finally over.

But there was another problem to solve—her marriage to Tristan. She was sick to her stomach for it, but she couldn't see any solution. If she couldn't be any more to Tristan than a glorified housekeeper, her conscience, her heart, her very soul told her she had to say goodbye.

He faced her, so tall and invincible…her every primal urge cried out for the strength of those arms to enfold her. She'd never forget that he'd saved her today. Unfortunately, his act of bravery wasn't enough to save their marriage.

As if reading her thoughts, he slid his hands into his pockets. "You must be exhausted."

She exhaled some of the tension. "You'd think so. Must be adrenaline, but I feel as if I could climb a mountain."

"Are you up to a drive?"

She hurried to shake her head. "I don't think that would be a good idea."

"Let's try it and see."

She thought of refusing again, but his eyes held a certain emotion she hadn't seen before. And he had come to her rescue in the most swashbuckling way.

She let out a sigh.

Oh hell, after that harrowing ordeal she could admit she'd still like Tristan close for just a little longer.

When they were in his car, Tristan cruised out onto the open street. After a few minutes of uneasy silence, Tristan admitted, "I saw Cade today."

Her head snapped toward him. "He called you?"

"Other way around. Ella, I might not have wanted to hear it, but you made me face a lot of things I'd tried to ignore in the past."

He sounded completely humbled, entirely sincere. Different from the defensive man who'd refused to listen yesterday, or the persuasive force she'd succumbed to this morning.

"You were right," he said. "I wanted to believe the worst so I could justify my self-righteous departure from Barkley Hotels. I told Cade as much today."

A smile eased across her face. If nothing else, this episode had got two brothers, who deep down cared greatly about each other, talking again.

"Are you going back to work for Barkley's?"

His jaw shifted. "I haven't decided yet. It's not totally out of the question."

"Do you really believe you could work together? You've been on your own for a while."

"You mean if I'm not prepared to budge on the marina to feather my own nest, it's unlikely I'll go for a three-way split of power between me, Josh and Cade?"

Familiar tension gripped between her shoulders. "I shouldn't have asked."

He kept his eyes on the road. "Let's try to enjoy the drive."

Her stomach churning, Ella looked blankly out the window. If Tristan didn't want to talk, she wouldn't push. Rather, she would try to enjoy his company, albeit pensive. She'd need to face reality, and their separation, soon enough.

She wasn't surprised when they turned into the road

that led to Tristan's prize parcel of land. He pulled up close to where the parkland met the white sand and glistening blue sea.

When they alighted, the breeze was mild and warm, the setting sun throwing back a smoky rose-gold glow over the endless horizon.

"Still think this is paradise?" he asked.

"Who wouldn't?" she replied. "You'll make a lot of money when it's developed."

"I'd rather have you."

She swung her glance from the rolling waves to his profile. She knew he wanted her. But wanting and loving weren't the same thing. And she couldn't stay in a relationship where only one person loved the other. It was a formula for heartache. In Tristan's mother's case, it had been a recipe for disaster.

"You said once you wanted to live here." His gaze found hers. "I'm giving it to you."

Did he think that this was the answer to keeping her, keeping their child? It wasn't.

"What about your deal and Mayor Rufus? You were near desperate to get that rezoning."

"After I left Cade today, I phoned the mayor. I let him know I was happy to give him the land he needs to develop the marina, but I didn't need the rezoning on the portion that we would retain. I want to build our family home here."

Pain struck her chest like an arrow. She had to look down, away from his searching eyes. "Tristan, please, don't…"

"I'm sorry, Ella," he said in a low, steady voice. "I'm sorry for not appreciating you for everything you are. I'm sorry for doubting you. This trouble between us isn't your fault. It's mine."

"Because you normally only bet on sure things," she finished flatly.

Tristan's face said he didn't agree. "I trusted you from the moment we met. I've told you…you felt right in every way, like no other woman or person I've ever known. I should never have doubted that instinct. I should've simply let myself go and believe." He faced her fully, taking her hands in his much larger ones. "I can't blame you if you can't forgive me, but I'm asking you to give me another chance. For us. For our child."

His words were heartfelt. His warm hands holding hers filled her with tingling want and need. But no matter how wonderful all he'd said might sound, he still hadn't fully committed to her, and there could be only one reason why.

He couldn't say the magic words because if he did, she'd see the lie in his eyes.

"There's something else." He pulled a small, wrapped box from his trouser pocket. She shook her head—this wasn't the time for gifts. But he placed the box in her hand. "Please. Open it."

Feeling drained, she gave in, unwrapped the box, opened the lid and was struck nearly speechless. The stones were dazzling.

"Tristan, they're beautiful." Sapphires.

She remembered his words on their wedding day.

Was this the gift he'd wanted her to wear on their fiftieth anniversary? she wondered.

Mesmerized, she slipped one earring from its velvet

bed and twirled the jewel in the last of the sunlight. "They're the color of the ocean shallows at noon."

"They're the color of your eyes. I love your eyes." He brought her close. "Ella, I love you."

Her vision misted over as her throat swelled with emotion. She couldn't bear to look into his face for fear of what she might see.

He tilted up her chin. His eyes were clear and true. "Look into your heart—trust your instincts."

A hot tear slid down her cheek and around her jaw. Her heart was beating so madly, she could barely catch her breath. "You do?" You *really* do?

His thumb grazed her parted lips. "So much, it hurts."

A happy sob escaped. He couldn't have made that up, because she felt the exact same way.

Bouncing up on tiptoe, she wove her arms around his neck. Holding on tight, she murmured against his ear, "I love you, too."

And when he kissed her, it felt as if she always had.

But a thought struck and she pulled away quickly. "Tristan, do you still want seven children?" She wasn't prepared to hold back anything. Not ever again.

"Weren't you listening?" His smile was easy. "I want *you*."

"You're not just saying that now?" Perhaps he would change his mind and regret it later.

His brow pinched slightly. "I had this perfect illusion going on in my head—me with an old-fashioned gal taking care of several polite, well-behaved kids. I would come home at the end of every working day and pat each on the head before tucking them in bed." He shrugged. "I much prefer what we'll have together."

"What's that?"

"A family who understands about commitment and patience, openness and love, no matter how many members we end up with."

She breathed in, absorbing the fresh, salty air and as much of this magical moment as she could. "And you'd give up this land—a fortune—if it made me happy?"

"Without losing a wink of sleep." His mouth dropped over hers again. This time his kiss lifted her beyond any heights she could have imagined.

When he gently broke away, he peered into her eyes. "Ella, be mine. Be mine forever."

Her palm slid from around his neck to cup his jaw. "Only forever?"

His eyes crinkled at the corners before his warm lips brushed hers again. "That'll do for starters."

Epilogue

Ahead of the newlywed couple, Ella moved with the rest of the bridal party out onto the church steps. With the jubilant guests streaming out behind, Josh stopped to kiss his bride, theatrically tipping Grace back until her leg kicked up, sending her white tulle hem flying in a ruffling wave.

Standing apart from the applauding crowd, an orchid bouquet clasped to her chest, Ella first laughed then let out a sigh. A memorable ending to a moving ceremony. What could top two people declaring before friends and family their love for each other forever?

From behind, a deep voice near Ella's ear chased delicious tingles over her skin.

"Mmm, that looks good," he murmured, referring to the kiss. "Wanna try it?"

Ella smiled as Tristan turned her in the loving circle of his arms. Gathering her close, he kissed her with the right amount of passion mingled with the perfect balance of restraint. Not that there was a dire need for decorum. All eyes were on the beautiful bride and her enamored groom, who were smiling for an avalanche of photographs.

Ella ignored the flashes. At this moment, amid streaming jets of confetti bubbles, all she wanted to know—all she needed to feel—was the blissful security of her husband's arms. Whenever he was near, her world was complete.

Softly Tristan broke the kiss, looked deeply into her eyes then toyed with one of her sapphire eardrops.

Still floating from the effects of his embrace, she arched a teasing brow. "You like?"

"Yeah, I like." He touched her nose with his and smiled. "The earrings are okay, too." His fingertip trailed her throat. "I think I'm in love."

She melted more. "You'll never know how good that sounds."

The happy couple appeared at their side and Josh extended his hand to his brother. "Well, that went off well, don't you think?"

Tristan shook Josh's hand and brushed a kiss against Grace's cheek. "As a matter of fact, we're so impressed, we're planning on having a big day of our own."

Ella pulled a wry face. "Tristan, we're already married."

"But we didn't do it like this." Tristan squeezed her hand. "I was in such a hurry to make you my wife I deprived you of a day like today. We should do it again, this time with all the bells and whistles."

Ella couldn't speak. Their ceremony and been special but very private. Enjoying a wedding day with all the trimmings would be better than wonderful.

Bursting with excitement at the news, Grace leaned forward to kiss Tristan's cheek. "You are so thoughtful." Grace kissed Ella next. "Now I can return the favor and be your maid of honor."

"When you've sorted out the date," Josh said, leading his bride away, "join us for photographs. We're heading off in ten."

"Oh, and Ella," Grace got in. "You know the magazine I work for? The editor wants to talk to you about contacts."

Ella shrugged. "Contacts?"

"For publishing that cookbook when you've finished."

Grace gave a wink then disappeared back into the crowd with Josh, emerging at the other side where the stretch limousine waited.

All the more excited, Ella began to move off, too, but Tristan held her back.

His warm lips nuzzled her temple. "I just have to let you know…you're driving me wild in that dress. What say we leave early from the reception?"

She shivered as familiar heat unfurled through her bloodstream.

"We can't do that. You're best man."

"Cade can take over my duties." He slid a speculative look to his left. "Although big brother does seem a little preoccupied."

Ella glanced over. Near the limousine, Cade was deep in conversation with his partnered bridesmaid, a

A sneaky peek at next month...

By Request

RELIVE THE ROMANCE WITH THE BEST OF THE BEST

My wish list for next month's titles...

In stores from 18th July 2014:

☐ Seduced by the Rebel – Susan Stephens, Anne Oliver & Lindsay Armstrong

☐ Tempting the Millionaire – Maureen Child, Jackie Braun & Cassie Miles

In stores from 1st August 2014:

3 stories in each book - only £5.99!

☐ Royal Seductions: Secrets – Michelle Celmer

☐ Propositioned by the Playboy – Cara Colter, Fiona Lowe & Brenda Harlen

Available at WHSmith, Tesco, Asda, Eason, Amazon and Apple

Just can't wait?

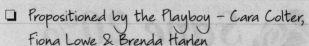

Visit us Online

You can buy our books online a month before they hit the shops! **www.millsandboon.co.uk**

0714/05

"You won't need to try. You're a natural. I've never been more certain of anything in my life."

"Then maybe we should think about having another one."

His eyes widened. "Another baby?"

She hitched up a shoulder. "It would be good to have another close to our first."

Ella had given it lots of thought. She would've loved a little sister or brother growing up. She wouldn't let her episode with Scarpini change her mind about what a family should be.

He cupped her cheek, the pad of his thumb grazing the slight cleft in her chin. "Count me in on all baby-making practice, but as far as extending our family—that's only *if* and *when* you're ready. I've learned to be thankful for what I hold most dear. I'll never risk losing either of you again."

Grateful tears sprang to her eyes as she placed her palm on his chest. "I love you, Tristan…so very much."

His dark eyes glistened. "Not nearly as much as I love you."

Feeling as light as the bubbles dancing around their heads, Ella surrendered to her husband's kiss, knowing fairy tales could and *did* come true.

* * * * *

brunette with flashing blue eyes and curves few men could resist.

Tristan chuckled. "Seems bachelor boy is smitten. Perhaps we'll see their wedding day next."

"Imagine…all three brothers hitched."

Although he maintained his own business concerns, Tristan was a consultant for Barkley Hotels, and the brothers knew they were there for each other whenever and wherever needed.

How different Tristan's sibling situation was from her own. It was still difficult to believe she and Scarpini were related. After his arrest, he'd refused to consent to a DNA test, so she'd hired a private investigator, who confirmed through his inquiry that her father had indeed sired Drago Scarpini.

Sensing her train of thought, Tristan's brows nudged together. "If you are agonizing over Scarpini, don't. He's in jail and will be for a long time to come. He won't hurt you again."

She pressed her lips together. "I know. I just wish things had been different."

"You're not responsible for him, Ella. He had choices, like the rest of us. And speaking of choices…" His frown eased. "I'll never stop thanking God you chose me." He fanned his palm over her second-trimester tummy. "How long now?"

She couldn't help but laugh. "Same as when you asked this morning. Four months to go."

"You're going to make the best mother."

Her heart grew at the note of raw pride in his voice. "I'll try my best."

Join our *EXCLUSIVE* eBook club

FROM JUST £1.99 A MONTH!

Never miss a book again with our hassle-free eBook subscription.

★ Pick how many titles you want from each series with our flexible subscription

★ Your titles are delivered to your device on the first of every month

★ Zero risk, zero obligation!

There really is nothing standing in the way of you and your favourite books!

Start your eBook subscription today at www.millsandboon.co.uk/subscribe

The World of Mills & Boon

There's a Mills & Boon® series that's perfect for you. There are ten different series to choose from and new titles every month, so whether you're looking for glamorous seduction, Regency rakes, homespun heroes or sizzling erotica, we'll give you plenty of inspiration for your next read.

By Request
Relive the romance with the best of the best
12 stories every month

Cherish™
Experience the ultimate rush of falling in love.
12 new stories every month

INTRIGUE...
A seductive combination of danger and desire...
7 new stories every month

Desire™
Passionate and dramatic love stories
6 new stories every month

n o c t u r n e™
An exhilarating underworld of dark desires
3 new stories every month

For exclusive member offers go to
millsandboon.co.uk/subscribe

Discover more romance at

www.millsandboon.co.uk

- ❤ WIN great prizes in our exclusive competitions

- ❤ BUY new titles before they hit the shops

- ❤ BROWSE new books and REVIEW your favourites

- ❤ SAVE on new books with the Mills & Boon® Bookclub™

- ❤ DISCOVER new authors

PLUS, to chat about your favourite reads, get the latest news and find special offers:

- Find us on facebook.com/millsandboon
- Follow us on twitter.com/millsandboonuk
- ❤ Sign up to our newsletter at millsandboon.co.uk